HIGH WATER

HIGH WATER

Peter Tonkin

HEADLINE

First published in 2000
by HEADLINE BOOK PUBLISHING

A HEADLINE FEATURE hardback

10 9 8 7 6 5 4 3 2 1

British Library Cataloguing in Publication Data

Tonkin, Peter, 1950–
High water
I. Title
823.9'14 [F]

ISBN 0 7472 7480 0

Typeset by Palimpsest Book Production Limited,
Polmont, Stirlingshire

Printed and bound in Great Britain by
Mackays of Chatham plc, Chatham, Kent

For Cham, Guy and Mark

And in memory of John Wright,
1950–2000; good friend, wise
adviser, unvarying inspiration

MAP TO SHOW THE MAIN ACTION OF
High Water

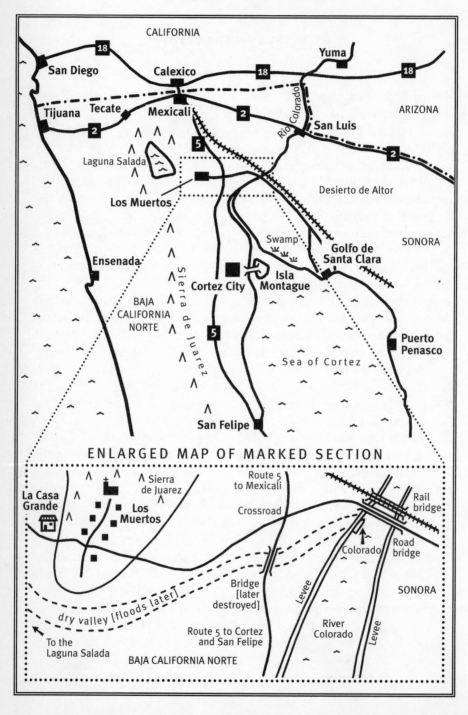

CALIFORNIA

San Diego

Calexico

Yuma

Tijuana Tecate Mexicali

ARIZONA

Rio Colorado

San Luis

Laguna Salada

Los Muertos

Desierto de Altor

Swamp

Golfo de
Santa Clara

SONORA

Ensenada

Sierra de Juarez

Cortez City

Isla
Montague

BAJA
CALIFORNIA
NORTE

Puerto
Penasco

Sea of Cortez

San Felipe

ENLARGED MAP OF MARKED SECTION

La Casa
Grande

Sierra
de Juarez

Los
Muertos

Route 5
to Mexicali

Crossroad

Rail
bridge

Colorado

Road
bridge

Bridge
[later
destroyed]

Levee

SONORA

dry valley [floods later]

River
Colorado

Levee

To the
Laguna Salada

Route 5 to Cortez
and San Felipe

BAJA CALIFORNIA NORTE

Chapter One

Richard Mariner eased himself in the saddle, his long frame still stiff from yesterday's hard ride down here, his muscles and joints not much relaxed by the soft beds at Phantom Ranch. He looked back at Robin fleetingly but her grey eyes were lost in the wonder of the Grand Canyon towering around and above them in the early light. He glanced over at Harry Magnum, riding point on their straggling expedition, but the narrow eyes beneath Harry's stetson were on the disgruntled tourists from LA who had never sat a horse before and were out of their depth, occasionally actually at risk. Richard pulled his rein to the right, guided his mount a few careful steps down off the beaten track and onto a little shoulder of bay where he could sit for a moment silently looking down.

Right before the hooves of Richard's patient burro, it seemed, the mighty Colorado burst from sweeping, red-flanked, serpentine power into a thundering welter of foam, rising into a series of static breakers seemingly tall enough to have threatened even the largest of the many tankers Richard had commanded in a long, distinguished career at sea. Further downstream, he knew, lay still more big rapids, the closest being Granite Rapid, then Hermit Rapid: white water often measuring VI on a scale of I – VI. And it looked as though the rapid in front of him was the better part of a VI here and now.

A silent stirring at his side told him that Robin had joined him. He turned to look at her, and their eyes met for a fleeting, intimate instant which went far beyond the words denied them by the mighty river's roaring, then his bright blue gaze moved past her and away up the twisting, fast-moving waterway. Round a red-walled bend hurled a big rubber-sided vessel, larger than the sixteen-seater Zodiacs Richard was used to. Tightly packed with more hard-hatted and life-belted figures than he could readily count, the big inflatable whipped past at an incredible speed, seeming to leap of its own volition into the first great standing wave of the rapids.

As the inflatable shot past the silent witnesses and away down the river, a lone figure took flight out of the back of it. Black against the

1

white water, the flying form was etched with more than natural clarity like a Victorian chiaroscuro. It was possible to see every finger, each thumb, on the thick-gloved hands reaching for the slowly spinning paddle. It was possible to see the profile of a long, bearded face beneath the hard hat, calling to the others still aboard for aid. It was possible to see the whip-thin snake of the safety line tighten and snap like thread.

Richard was out of the saddle, decorative lariat in hand, clearly hoping that the woven leather of the old-fashioned lasso was stronger than whatever the safety line was made of. Robin turned in her saddle, swinging her leg up for the dismount as though still at dressage lessons long ago and far away during a peculiarly English education. Her eyes sought help, as though the power of her mind could go where her voice so clearly could not. And perhaps it could. Harry Magnum turned and looked back.

Down on the shoreline, Richard was unlooping his lasso with the speed of a sailor familiar with cordage of all sorts. His bright blue eyes were fixed, not on his dextrous fingers but on the next stage of the tragedy unfolding before him. Another figure in the inflatable turned, just as the man overboard's lifeline whipped past. A quick-thinking pair of hands grabbed the black rope – but it answered the good deed by whipping into a mare's nest tangle around the would-be rescuer's wrists. The weight of the man overboard came fully onto the rescuer then, just as the power of the rapids took the inflatable and sucked it unstoppably forward. The rescuer cartwheeled out of the inflatable and seemed to hang in the air for an instant, suspended above the churning madness of the foam. Then the second safety parted and the two figures were bobbing in the last of the still water before the first white-backed surge of the rapids which gulped their friends and vessel away.

Here, the floor of the river course rose into a series of shallows and hazards, but the great red rock walls of the canyon closed together also. Rising for hundreds of metres sheer and only falling back at their distant upper slopes, these walls of timeless rock were at once awe-inspiring and overwhelmingly threatening. They seemed to grind together like jaws chewing on the exploding welter of the river. But at their base on this side of the river, some flaw of stratification, some extra surge of riverine power in more recent geological time had carved a series of overhangs. These were so low as to stand little more than a centimetre above the smooth surface of the water, though it was possible that further in, the roofs might rise. Under the first of these, the river slid

2

relatively quietly, though with dark and seemingly sinister purpose.

It was one of the effects of the strange physics unleashed by the force of the rapids that the back of the great waterway seemed to rise up at this point. This presented the two in the water with a downhill slope towards the sinister overhangs. The first victim might have floundered across to safety with little or no help, but the weight of his would-be rescuer pulled him away downstream even as he tried to power his way towards the shore with all the strength at his command.

Richard was in the rushing stream up to mid-thigh when he hurled the lariat. It fell into the water with unerring accuracy, right in front of the first figure. As the slack was gulped down by the river's power, sweeping the loop towards its target, Richard was able to step back and pull against the strain. And it was well he did so, for the jerk with which the line tightened came near to tugging him into the river as well. But then the big, solid figure of Harry Magnum was at his side and they shared the strain, two sets of narrowed eyes watching the figure at the far end of it surf helplessly across the relentless pressure of the roaring water and vanish beneath the red rock overhang. Side by side the two men stepped back. In concert, like a well-trained tug-of-war team, they heaved. They were both massive men, fit and in their prime. Harry Magnum was a tad over six foot two and had the solidity of shoulder and thigh that tells of a life on horseback; Richard was taller, his chest deeper, his back longer and stronger, his thighs every bit as solid, his thews just as whip-strong despite the steel pins holding his knees together, which had set off the security alarms at Gatwick and Houston airports on the long flight west to be here. But it was clear to both of them that they were no match for the great river. With the sensitivity of fingertip only the most experienced fishermen enjoy, Richard felt the braided leather of the lasso strain to spring apart, and he eased the pressure slightly.

'It's going to snap, Harry,' he called at the top of his lungs. 'We'll need another line out if we're going to pull them both in. Maybe two lines.'

Although he was using his 'foretop' voice, designed to carry down the length of his command in the heart of a storm, his words only just reached Harry. The big guide nodded, and looked around for help. And there it was coming right up behind him.

Robin Mariner had not been standing idly by while her husband and Harry took the strain. She had stepped down from her horse and run up the slope to the others in the Grand Canyon tourist party.

Everyone was willing to help, but most of the other tourists, like the group from LA, were out of their depth here. Harry's associates, several of them family, were another matter, however. It had taken only moments for her to join their quick-thinking team. A radio call had alerted the Phantom Ranch where they had spent the night. A four-by-four would be here soon. But it would be too late to help unless they could find a way of strengthening that one slim lariat lifeline. And from the look of things the pair in the water would be drowned soon in any case, trapped as they now were below the sinister thrust of the blood-red overhangs which seemed to touch the surface of the water.

It was this thought which prompted the men – old-fashioned, courteous and, it seemed to Robin, naturally protective of the weaker sex – nevertheless to countenance her plan. She would have to be the one to go into the water, she reasoned tersely and swiftly. She was light, but strong for her weight. She was a trained ship's officer, used to emergencies, and she held medical certificates up to accident and emergency standard. And she was not going to be taking any unnecessary or ill-considered risks, for this was no haphazard expedition. It was well-equipped and prepared for every emergency that two long days climbing down the canyon sides and then back up again might bring. There was braided nylon climbing rope. There were strong metal hooks, anchors and pitons, should anyone slip over the precipitous sides. There was an oxygen bottle and sturdy face-mask should anyone find the experience of moving from temperate through tropical to desert conditions within thirty-six hours too much to take. There were heavy gloves and life preservers. There were hard hats. There were extremely robust, waterproof flashlights. There were more big men – though none to match the pair holding the lariat.

Robin Mariner, helmeted, gloved, masked, with the oxygen bottle secured to her chest beneath the red polystyrene-filled life preserver and the full upper-body harness, strode past Richard and Harry and waded into the river as three of Harry's closest relatives took the strain on the Kevlar-coated climbing rope. Pausing with the red water foaming around her thighs, Robin stooped and clipped herself to the lariat with a big metal climbing clip, then she eased herself into the icy clutch of the rushing water, careful to ensure that her clip was running freely down the braided leather.

Then the time for care – and indeed for much clarity of thought – was gone. The force of the river overwhelmed her and all her concentration focused on holding the tightly secured face-mask in place, for there were icy claws of water trying to tear it away and drown her. It was instantly clear to her that she had underestimated the sheer power of the element she was dealing with here. Underestimated, indeed, the simple numbing, incapacitating force of the buffeting cold of the current. Unless things were very much calmer under the overhang, the two people she had set out to rescue would have been far beyond her help long ago.

As her body followed the iron-hard line of the lariat, so the power of the current did, in fact, begin to ease. Vision began to widen. Existence began to expand beyond a wild, mindless tumble for survival. The vital breaths of oxygen cleared her mind to an icy clarity which sat well with what was going on around her. She distinguished up from down, light from dark. She understood that she was near the rushing mirror of the surface and, with very little struggle, she broke through and saw the red rock precipices and the distant, achingly beautiful sky. There was the roaring of a bow wave foaming around her head and shoulders, pounding on her hard hat like rocks thrown from far above, numbing the whole of her upper body. There was movement she could measure and begin to understand – careful movement downstream as the men on the shore paid out the rope which kept her safe. There was movement across the water as she followed the black line of the lariat and the great red cliff of the south wall closed down on her like the end of the world.

Had there been time for rational thought, Robin might have wondered what Richard was going to say about this adventure when they got a chance to discuss things alone. In the old days, they had fallen into more scrapes than she could readily count and it had all been part of life's rich pattern to them; but then children had come along; increasing responsibilities; maturity. She had begun to worry about Richard and the danger he got into on his voyages all over the world. And he was equally protective of her these days.

The overhang swung into place above Robin like the closing of a massive door. The rock face hit her with considerable force and would have broken her nose had she been unprotected. Instead it scored the face-mask and punched her under the water. She gasped without thinking and was fortunate indeed that the oxygen system stayed in place. Fighting to stay calm, still facing upwards, she reached up without thinking – and so discovered that her arms were not quite as numb as she had supposed. The fingers within her gloves were sensitive enough to feel the rough roof close above her but the gloves themselves were so heavy that she could not tell whether the rock roof was above or below the river's rushing surface. And there was not enough light in here for her eyes to help her. She began to grope for the torch, abruptly aware, also, that she needed most urgently to see how much lariat was left or she would be kicking the subject of all these heroics hard in the face with her massive Cat Colorado hiking boots.

The beam of the flashlight when it came was surprisingly feeble, as though Robin were swimming in liquid brown bottle glass, not water. But it was bright enough to show her the sturdy line of the lariat and the amber glimmer of the surface. She pushed her head up into the low-roofed little cavern and saw the first victim just an instant before the river swept her down upon him. He was lying on a silty little red-mud shore just above the reach of the writhing water. At first Robin could not work out why he was lying in such a strange position, then she realised he was racked – literally, as though being torn limb from limb – between the taut lines of the lariat looped round his wrists and the tangle of line stretching on downstream behind him. As the light fell upon the waxy whiteness of his face, his eyes stirred behind dark, thick-veined lids. His body convulsed in a tearing breath. Robin eased herself alongside him, tugged her safety line to signal for more slack to the men on the other end, and pulled free some extra cordage she had brought. Expertly – even in her thick gloves – she knotted the line to the lariat and then to his harness so that the terrible pressure on his wrists was relieved. He stirred at once and groaned – though Robin could hear no sound but the rushing water. Clearly circulation returning to his hands was uncomfortable. But he was alive at least – and likely to stay that way, she reckoned grimly. She flashed her light around the little cavern, looking for the straight black line which would lead to the second victim.

Something stirred. A furtive scurry of movement caught her eye, vanishing inward and upward. Could there be black cats in here? she wondered. She flashed her light onto the cave's low roof and looked up without thinking. And screamed.

The roof of the cavern immediately above her – so close that her helmet must have been brushing up against it as she worked – was alive with huge spiders. They looked like tarantulas to her, but her daughter Mary had wanted one for a pet once and so Robin knew the huge arachnids did not like the wet at all. Certainly, they were about the same size as tarantulas, and, in the torchlight, their massive bodies glittered black and sand and red as they scuttled for the shadows. Or all of them did except one, the largest of them all dropped straight onto her face. As she lay there, rigid with shock; frozen in the water, its fat black body sat squarely on the thick plastic of the oxygen face-mask, as cold and weighty as a hairy toad, and it looked her squarely in the eye with eight or so of its own. She jerked her head down into the welcoming grasp of the river and let the mighty Colorado wash the thing away, all too well aware that she would have to edit this part of the adventure if she ever told it to Mary.

Only when it was long gone and enough time had passed for all the rest to have hidden too – and for her heart rate to have slowed – did Robin pull herself back onto the shore and complete the delicate operation of transferring her climbing clip from the lariat to the safety line joining this body to the next. Then she signalled with a tug on the rope and it began to slacken once again.

Down the last few metres she went, bumping along the underside of the water-smoothed cavern, with all the weight of the hundreds of metres of rock above seeming to bear down on her. She let the torch hang on its safety line, pulled by the river to point the way ahead as she used her hands on the slick, slippery surface above to guide herself, thankful of the thick gloves, her mind still full of the images of the huge spiders.

The second victim also had washed onto a kind of shore. Perhaps there was some sort of inevitability to it, Robin thought wearily, some balance between the downward rush of the river and the outward swing of the human-weighted pendulum of the lariat and the line. She flashed the torch around the low-roofed little cavern. There were no spiders to be seen. Battered, frozen, numbed, almost invaded by the rushing river, she pulled herself up onto the slick, silty shore until she could reach the figure lying prone on the red flank of the mud.

As she crawled forward, Robin found her tired thoughts side-tracked by the patterns the water had left on the mud beneath her, revealed by the low cross-light of her torch beam. They were sinuous, writhing, weirdly beautiful. They reminded her of something, but she couldn't quite bring it to mind. It hardly seemed important in any case. The second victim seemed in far worse shape than the first. Arms reached upwards, almost imploringly, into the tangle of safety line. Again, it looked as though thick gloves had averted severe damage to the wrists and hands. The body lay face down on the red mud and when Robin eased the white face to the side, a little river water vomited out of the slack mouth – and then it was stirred by the faintest breath. That was enough for Robin. She had no time – or inclination – for first aid here. She checked the rest of the body

7

perfunctorily and then fastened the climbing clip to the safety harness so that her own body would protect this one from further damage. She briefly considered giving her comatose patient a draught of oxygen but decided against it. Instead, she took the flaccid shoulders and rolled the weighty body back towards the water, over those sinuous markings in the mud. And as she did so, her errant memory slipped them into place. They were exactly the same as the marks made by the bodies of big snakes climbing sand-dunes in the desert.

And the instant that the realisation hit her, so did the snakes.

What sort of snakes they were, or how they had got here, she had no idea. But they were long – longer than she was herself – and they had been lying beneath her patient. When she moved the still body, the pair of serpents appeared as though by a terrible magic and struck across the barricade of stiff flesh between. Without thinking, Robin hit back. A backhand perfected through many hours with a tennis-mad son allowed the torch to bat one swift head away as Robin threw herself wildly backwards, bouncing off the ceiling, dragging her burden along with her. The second snake, however, struck straight and true. As Robin was gulped back into the hungry heart of the Colorado, it sank its long, reticulated fangs into the point exactly above her heart.

Chapter Two

All four men holding the lines felt Robin's convulsive action as vividly as if she has been a trout or a marlin. They gave a sort of unified shout and began to pull in as quickly as they could, hand over hand, throwing their weight into the work with such urgency that not even the winch on the front of the big old four-by-four which turned up then could have snatched the three bodies from the clutches of the river any faster. The next shout came when they saw the first body break water and come surfing up against the current, swinging out into the quieter outwash of the bay before managing to jerk a waxy white face up, all dark eye sockets with white-rimmed eyes and black gape of gasping mouth.

Richard gave this first body only the scantest of glances. Then he was fastening his keen blue gaze on the rushing water where Robin's safety line continued to jerk and whip from side to side as though there were massive fish fighting on the end of it. The sight of it filled him with foreboding. The manner in which it cut into the crystal river – and seemed to hum like a musical string tuned to a lost chord while chopping out a bloody foam of bubbles where it entered the writhing water – told him something was badly amiss with his intrepid wife at the furthest end of it.

But none of his foreboding prepared Richard for what he actually saw when Robin and her still companion broke through into the daylight together. Robin was wrestling the snake which was wrapped round her, flailing wildly, its great head striking down at her face and chest even though she held it in her thick-gloved hands as though trying to strangle the life out of it.

'What is that?' yelled Richard to Harry.

'Danged if I know,' came the faint reply over the rushing water. 'Looks pretty nasty to me, though. Sure is a huge son of a . . .'

Richard handed the lariat over to Harry and ran down the shore to where the others were pulling Robin in. His mind was racing. Most men, faced with such a situation, would freeze, panic. Richard had only survived for as long as he had because he never froze. He met each situation head on and never faltered until he had bent it to his will – if such a thing was possible. Of all the people he had shared his adventures with over the years, only Robin had this ability in equal measure. And she was exercising it now to the utmost.

'Bring the truck down here!' yelled Richard. That his voice carried was miracle enough – no one who heard the command could fail to obey. But even as the great tyres marked the flank of red river sand, Robin rolled face down into the water and when she flipped back over, the monstrous thing was gone.

'Jump leads,' Richard yelled, and threw the bonnet of the vehicle open. His gaze fastened on the big old battery. A 12-volt job by the looks of things. 'Where are the jump leads?' he bellowed.

As he spoke, the first survivor swept onto the bank at Harry Magnum's feet. He was hauled half erect and passed, choking, back to the tender mercies of the tourists and the staff from the ranch who had come down with the truck, all except the bemused young man who was helping Richard connect the jump leads to the battery. 'Get back in and get ready to start her up!'

Richard was in the water again, wading out along the line towards the two soggy bundles of humanity at the end. He caught Robin up and threw himself shorewards with her in his arms. 'Where did it bite you?' he bellowed as he went.

'It didn't,' she gasped.

'I saw it. We all—'

'I'm fine, Richard. But this one's been bitten, I'm pretty sure . . .'

No more discussion ensued. Richard put his wife down and they both turned to the second victim. They followed the stiff body as it was hauled up the slick mud bank, noting a swollen strike mark in a much inflamed cheek. Then, wordlessly co-ordinating as a team like well-trained doctors, they went to work. Robin eased clothing, checking pulses and vital signs.

'Faint and fading,' she yelled, her fingers on a cold curve of throat.

Richard nodded once, his hands busy ripping wide the red life jacket and the olive shirt beneath. Then he tore away the T-shirt and the bra beneath that. He caught up the jump leads and jabbed them astride a pale left breast. 'Start her up!' he yelled and the four-by-four obligingly sprang to life. Even through his thick riding gloves, Richard felt the power of the shock. The woman beneath him jerked. 'Again!' he bellowed. The motor turned. The body twitched. The breast heaved and the eyes flickered. Robin was up and off, busily about some further mission of her own.

10

'Nice work,' came a broken whisper apparently from very far away.

Richard looked up into the sallow bearded face and long dark eyes of the other survivor. Richard nodded tersely, gave a deprecating half-grin. 'We have to get her to hospital pretty quickly, though,' he said.

'Air ambulance full of paramedics on its way,' said the survivor distantly.

Robin was back. She had borrowed a nasty-looking Bowie knife from Harry Magnum. As she moved forward, she slid the point of the blade into her breast where the snake had struck. She cut deftly four times, then pulled free a flap of red life jacket and a thick section of solid polystyrene foam from beneath it. 'Give them this,' she said. 'It's full of venom from whatever sort of snake that was. Freely donated, several times.'

In the event, Robin gave the paramedics the venom sample herself. Harry insisted that she went for a check-up with the other two, and Richard tagged along with her. 'Pity to miss the second half of the ride, though,' he said with mock sorrow as they waved down at the crowd of their trail companions getting smaller below them.

'You'll survive,' she said. 'And anyway I know you'd rather have done it by chopper than burro in any case.'

'Maybe,' he temporised. Then he slipped his camera out of the saddlebags Harry had slung in at their feet – all the luggage they had been allowed on this particular trip – and took a couple of pictures as the chopper climbed up through the geological millennia towards the Canyon rim. Abruptly, a square, black-haired hand was thrust across his view. He looked up, and there, sitting up on one of the stretchers and smiling wryly, was the man they had rescued.

'I just want to say thanks,' he said.

Without his hard hat he looked younger. A shock of black hair framed a thin face which managed to be both lined and youthful-looking. His eyes were long and the irises were a dark but vibrant brown. The eyes were extended over high, sharp cheekbones by clutches of crows' feet stretching back to his hairline. A neat moustache curved round into a short-clipped beard. His colour was back, giving a rich darkness to his skin which matched his eyes and emphasised the gleam of his teeth. Without the life jacket his uniform shirt was revealed, battered and creased but unmistakably military, with his badges of rank and qualification.

'You're very welcome, Major,' said Robin, to whom the proffered

11

hand, like the smile of thanks, had been offered. She shook his hand and returned his smile. 'Always pleased to be of service to the army.'

'Tell me,' said Richard, 'what do those badges mean? Are you a medic or an engineer?'

The long brown eyes switched to Richard's face at once, a faint frown of surprise came and went. The grin broadened. 'You're well informed, sir, for a . . .'

'For a limey tourist, yes.'

'For someone outside of the army, sir. I'm an officer in the Medical Corps on secondment to the Corps of Engineers.'

'On some kind of exercise, Major?' asked Robin.

'Well, no, ma'am. Not exactly. It's something much bigger than that.' His focus faltered for a moment, then snapped back, his priorities reassembled. 'I have to report in. Tell them about me and Captain Allday there. Excuse me, sir, ma'am. I just have to talk to the pilot for one . . .'

And he was gone.

In his absence the senior paramedic glanced across at them. 'That was pretty smart work with the electrical shock, sir,' she growled. 'The captain here would have been a gonner but for that. Quick thinking about collecting the venom specimen too, ma'am. You've been making our job pretty easy here. You two must've been about quite a bit to pick up tricks like that.'

'You wouldn't believe the half of it if we told you,' said Robin with grim cheeriness.

'It'll be one of life's little disappointments that I'll never get the chance,' said the paramedic. 'But the captain's cool for the moment. Now, ma'am, can we check you over, please?'

Modesty was never one of Robin's strong points, and of all the priorities built into an air ambulance, private examining facilities are the lowest. When he returned from the cockpit, the young major found that he hardly knew where to look, – what with Captain Allday's lopsided and slightly singed bust being carefully packed away while his nubile rescuer got hers out on display. And then, having swiftly established that not the faintest venomous scratch had come through the life jacket to sully their perfection, she pro- ceeded to unveil lesions and abrasions in ever more intimate locations.

'We haven't been introduced,' said Richard smoothly, capturing and holding the young medic's gaze. 'My name is Richard Mariner and your rescuer is Robin, my wife. You'll have guessed from the

12

accent that we're English. From what little I've heard of your accent I'd say you're from California.'

'Mexico, originally, sir, but you have a good ear. San Francisco for more than thirty years. My name is Miguel Vargas, but my friends all call me Mickey. As I hope you and Señora – Oh! Excuse me!'

'Think nothing of it, Major. But I would have thought any experienced doctor would be familiar with the feminine gluteus maximus, especially when bruised and battered to the extent that my poor one has been.'

'Call me Mickey, please.'

'Under the circumstances it seems the least we can call you,' said Robin cheerfully as she adjusted her clothing and covered her bruised buttocks.

The air ambulance brought them into a quiet backwater of McCarran International, and here the four of them split up – Captain Allday to the nearest emergency facility, Major Vargas to report in more detail and receive further orders, Richard and Robin to their hotel.

They were staying at the Luxor, the great pyramid-shaped hotel which seemed to dwarf even the real pyramids in size and opulence. It was like living in something larger than the Great Pyramid at El Gîza where every room was Tutankhamen's tomb. Robin gained piquant amusement from watching Richard in the overwhelming comfort and busy, dazzling extravagance of the place. Her beloved husband had been booked here by business associates eager to impress, and it was not his sort of place at all. He looked a little like Lot in Gomorrah in this Hollywood–Biblical opulence. Robin, too, derived little real pleasure from the frenetic 24-hour-a-day bustle of Las Vegas where everything seemed to be available for a buck or on a bet.

While she soaked in a large foam-filled tub in the sumptuous comfort of their suite, Richard checked on his voice-mail, his e-mail and his faxes. His position as CEO of a large international shipping company meant that there were a good number of all of these in spite of the fact that he and Robin had only been away for thirty-six hours of a proposed forty-eight-hour excursion, a break from what were becoming increasingly bruising business negotiations here in Las Vegas.

'There's one from Aldo Cagliari here,' Richard called through. 'If we're back in time are we up for dinner tonight?'

Aldo Cagliari was emerging as the man Richard needed to do business with – the leader of the opposition. Robin didn't like him, but she knew well enough that Richard needed to work with him.

13

'If we can eat here, and early,' she said. 'I don't want to go trailing up and down the Strip and end up with a cold steak at midnight somewhere full of girls in rhinestone g-strings.'

'OK. We'll say eight at Isis if we can get a table. And if we can't I'm sure Aldo will know someone who can. I think I want to pick up the tab though; I don't want to owe Aldo any favours if I can help it. Actually, that will allow us to kill two birds with one stone. Major Vargas wants to buy us a drink downstairs at seven.'

'Things should be quiet then, apart from the pre-ballet crowd gearing up for *Swan Lake*.' The one thing which had swung Robin's acquiescence to all this was the Bolshoi's return season at the Luxor's prestigious theatre. They had seen the ballet on the night before their excursion to the Grand Canyon.

Robin pulled herself out of the bath and towelled herself off gingerly in front of the mirror. Her body was covered in scrapes and bruises from this morning, some getting really colourful now, particularly those across her buttocks. These dictated her clothing: thicker pants than usual; heavier trousers and a sensible top which revealed none of her battle scars.

Richard as ever looked effortlessly stylish in a cream cotton travelling suit with a starched shirt and a sand-coloured tie.

Mickey Vargas was waiting in one of the quiet little bars downstairs at seven, resplendent in full uniform and fizzing with news. 'It's all OK. We still go as planned, even after the accident! We meet at the foot of the Hoover at oh nine hundred tomorrow for the publicity guys. Off at ten or so. I'm still on the team but Captain Allday's not going to be about for a while so there's a place going if you're interested. Either of you done any white-water work?'

Realising that they would have to tease some background information out of the major if they were going to make any real sense of this, they led him to a quiet corner and introduced him to a bottle of tequila. Then they listened.

Since the mid-nineties the hydrology section of the Corps of Engineers had been working on several major waterways in the heartlands of the USA. Part of the work had been of local interest – opening the mouth of the Texan River Colorado behind Galveston harbour, for example. Part of the work had been of national importance and undertaken at the instigation of the President himself – resurrecting the water flow of the over-controlled Missouri River was an example of that. But the greatest of all the projects had been the one Mickey was associated with, and which the raft ride was

14

designed to celebrate. It was the one truly international project on the North American subcontinent, the Millennium Project (although it had run a couple of years behind schedule), agreed between the US President, the President of Mexico and a whole slew of international governments and agencies: the rebirth of the River Colorado and the re-establishment of regular flow along the entire historic watercourse from Wyoming to the Sea of Cortez.

'Having completed the work and attended the official opening, a bunch of us got permission to raise the profile a bit and raise some cash money for good causes by doing a sponsored raft ride down the entire length of the thing,' he concluded nearly an hour later. 'We split into teams, and we're the third. Our team hadn't really started off for real. Team Two did the Canyons, we were just getting our hand in for lower down. But we officially kick off from the foot of the Hoover Dam at ten tomorrow. We'll carry the inflatable and the kit round the dams downstream – and any rapids worse than strength IV. And there's a place going for anyone with a week to spare. So I asked the CO if I could put it to you guys first. I mean, you can handle yourselves; we've all seen that. I'd want you at my side if the going got tough. So if you've ever done any white-water work and I have a week or so to spare, then there you go. Listen, here's my number. Think about it. Give me a call.'

Richard caught Robin's eye, and a slight frown flitted across his face. He knew she wasn't all that happy here in the Luxor's luxurious confines. And she did know her way round white water very well indeed – though they hadn't done any serious rafting since the kids had come along. And, as luck would have it, they both needed to be on the Sea of Cortez in a week's time, to say goodbye to an old friend. Richard was here on Heritage Mariner Shipping business. Robin was here to represent her father Sir William Heritage and his late friend Sir Justin Bulwer-Lytton at the decommissioning ceremony of the Mexican Navy's oldest coastal protection vessel, a venerable D60-class destroyer, commissioned into action by the US Navy as a FRAM 1 in 1944 – just in time to save a couple of young Royal Naval officers whose own vessel had been torpedoed, and who would never otherwise have grown up to be knights of the British realm. The vessel had served in many theatres since, from Korea and Vietnam to the assault on Grenada, before being purchased by the Spanish and then the Mexican Navy, and had saved many lives in the interim, so Robin and Richard were not likely to be the only strangers at the ceremony in a week when the USS *Colorado*'s career came to an end. But they were going to be there on the battered old foredeck – no matter how they travelled down.

Just then a bear of a man arrived at their table – a bear with two svelte golden minks in tow. 'Richard! Robin! Here you are!' boomed Aldo Cagliari. 'The kids and I have been searching! Time's awasting and we're running late. And they don't hold your table for long in Isis. Hey, I didn't know you knew anyone local. And a military man at that. Why not bring him along?' It was typical of the man to bring guests of his own to someone else's party, then invite more into the bargain. Richard shrugged and shot Robin a rueful grin.

As the six of them made their way along the caryatid colonnade towards the restaurant's great glass doors, Aldo threw the names of his young associates into the conversation – Jo and Jody – but their relationship with him and their reason for being here was never touched on. Richard allowed himself to be swept into Aldo's ambit just as Robin had allowed herself to be taken by the Colorado this morning. She watched him, amused at his courteous quiescence, though he was not likely to need Harry Magnum with a lariat to pull him back when he wanted out again. She herself wanted to talk to Mickey about the wild ride south along the Colorado, but Jo and Jody attached themselves with pleasant persistence. As similar as their names, the youngsters were blond, tanned, brown-eyed, white-toothed, fragrant and slim. Jo's torso looked perfectly sculpted beneath his white cotton jacket and skin-tight T-shirt. The cutaway skirts of the loosely buttoned jacket, however, showed that the hips below were as strong – perhaps as well endowed – as a donkey's and the thighs were those of a well-fed leopard. She looked up and found he was watching her examining him. He gave an open smile of simple pride. He was a damn near perfect specimen and he clearly appreciated her appreciating the fact. To cover her embarrassment, Robin looked over at Jody, just in time to see Mickey completing a similar examination to her own. But his hot eyes had clearly not stopped at the white cotton surface.

'So,' said Robin conversationally to Jo as she wondered how on earth breasts that full could sit so high without obvious support and how a waist that thin could actually exist, let alone swoop into hips and buttocks that curvaceous before plunging into thighs that long. 'What do you do, Jo?'

Jo was a TV actor and, as the great gold-winged glass doors swung shut, was still giving Robin his résumé, not letting the fact that she had seen none of his work upset him at all. Rather cynically, she suspected that Jo had had lots of practice in not letting that upset him. At the table, Robin sat between Jo and Mickey, with Jody between him and Richard, while Aldo sat opposite and a little aloof. Jo and Jody eschewed alcohol, drank Perrier and ate seared tuna with alfalfa salad. Mickey tore his eyes away from Jody's golden cleavage for long enough to glance around, a little over-awed. Clearly he would have been more at home in the Luxor's steakhouse rather than in the gourmet restaurant. Robin's sudden urge for major sustenance with a little moral support led to her demand for a New York steak, salad and fries. Mickey followed her lead with no little relief and the pair of them ordered Budweiser to accompany the feast. Richard and Aldo were wrapped in an impenetrable discussion about finances, production guarantees and the whole paraphernalia of sailing Richard's SuperCats, the fastest commercial vessels afloat, out of the newly revitalised Galveston and all over the Caribbean, and out of San Francisco up and down the coast. They simply accepted what the waiter recommended. Then they ploughed their way thoughtlessly through the courses in a manner which would have reduced the chef to tears.

Still, thought Robin, it was an amusing evening. The steaks were superb, the beer was great, and the slivers of gourmet heaven she snaffled from Richard's plate were perfectly complemented by the sips of nectar she stole from the glasses left untended in brimming succession beside his Perrier. Jo was an amusing, attentive companion, surprisingly witty, acquainted with an astonishing range of stars and superstars, and possessed of a dry, wry wit supported by waspishly merciless observation. He kept her gurgling with quiet amusement all through the meal.

Even had this not been the case, Robin would have derived much quiet amusement from the enthralment – almost the enslavement – of Mickey by Jody. She was a dancer and their talk was of the kind of popular music icons which either of Robin's children would have known more about than she did. But the body language said much more than the words. Every pout of her lips, each flash of an eye and toss of a curl pulled him deeper. When she leaned towards him he all but dived into her chest. When she leaned back, he was almost in her lap. Robin had a wide circle of acquaintances, many among the hot-blooded races, but she had forgotten how ardent a young man full of that peculiarly Spanish macho can be.

At midnight, however, she had had enough. 'That's it, darling, it's been a long day,' she said firmly.

Richard looked up, his eyes distant, mind still in the middle of some abstruse calculation. She knew he would talk the deal over with her later but she was simply too tired to stay up any longer now. 'You don't need to see me up. I'll be fine,' she concluded, pulling herself erect a little stiffly.

'Allow me,' offered Jo gallantly, rising at the same time as the punctilious Mickey.

'I must be off too,' said the major. 'Early start. Thank you again, Captain Mariner, Mr Cagliari.'

'Think nothing of it, kid. Happy to show the military a good time,' said Aldo expensively.

In the lift, Jo finished off a particularly scurrilous anecdote about some long-dead Hollywood star and followed Robin down the hall. Outside her door she turned to bid him goodnight, holding out her hand to shake his. His response was to pull her swiftly into a clinch, wrapping an arm round her waist and pressing his mint-flavoured lips to hers. She just had time to realise what an excellent kisser he was before outrage began to well. She pushed him away, and his torso moved back but his hands remained, sliding across the bare flesh beneath her blouse above her trouser waist.

'No!' she said firmly. 'Thank you but goodnight!'

Incredibly, he did not bat an eyelid. Smirking, full of self-confidence and certain of his irresistibility, he slid his hand down her trousers, beneath her panties and over her buttocks. He felt there the results of this morning's adventures and misread the sign. 'Hey,' he said with pleased surprise. 'Spanking games! Well, we can do that!' He pressed her against the carefully cut front of his trousers, leaving her in no doubt at all of what he was ready, willing and able to do.

The impact of her hand on his cheek sounded like a shot and the force of it landed like a shell. She had been a full ship's captain in her day and had always packed a mean punch to support her authority. He was blasted back, not just shocked but stunned. His hands, free now, went to his cheek where the marks of her fingers had raised red welts. Feeling these, he automatically turned, horror-struck, to find a mirror and assess the damage.

Robin slammed the door and double-locked it – though she was certain that, sleazy though this was, Aldo Cagliari's associates would never step further out of line. Sure enough, when she looked out of the security spyhole an instant later, the corridor was clear.

Fifteen minutes later, after she had showered and scrubbed herself pink, she was standing by the telephone listening to it ring in Mickey Vargas's room. She suspected strongly that he would be exercising his potency on the fair Jody and she really hoped the unexpected call would not spoil things for him, but she had had more than enough of this particular business trip. Clear air, good companions and the great outdoors for a week would be just what the doctor ordered. And it would give Richard something other than business to talk about when he finally came to bed, and ensure that he didn't ask any questions about Mr Cagliari's young friends.

Chapter Three

'Look out,' yelled Mickey Vargas, his eyes wide beneath his hard hat and his beard glittering with spittle and spray, 'here comes another one!'

Robin looked back up the river course and saw that he was right. Another surge of water was bearing down on them like a big sea, the swell of its leading surface webbed with foam and armed with an assortment of debris. The wave itself should do them little enough harm, she calculated, steadying her aft starboard corner section with a careful paddle, it would simply gather under the transom and toss the big inflatable high. But some of those long, sharp branches would make all too effective spears. Neither her back nor the back of the big vessel would take too kindly to being run through.

The surprisingly low-key fanfare of the send-off seemed a long way away already, as distant as Richard's understanding farewell. Both the press and he, it seemed, had higher priorities for the time being.

'What do they think they're doing?' snarled Kramer, the engineer in charge of the expedition. 'They shouldn't be letting water into the sluices like this!' The bundle of his life vest made him look bigger than he was but the tightness of his hard hat emphasised the size of his cranium. He was built like a matchstick but seemed possessed of a restless physicality to match his intellectual decisiveness and strength. He was a little overpowering, but Robin found she liked him a lot.

It had been Kramer who had put her through her paces, clearly only grudgingly willing to take Mickey Vargas's say-so on her abilities, in spite of the rescue. And his care had built up Robin's own confidence in the project, confidence which had been extended by the thoroughness and professionalism of his briefings. There had been two briefings. One for the perfunctory, preoccupied team from the local press and one for the crew. Robin found she needed confidence now because someone upriver of them seemed to have opened the floodgates at the foot of the Hoover Dam, sending a wall of water down the river after them.

The wave slid under the inflatable and Robin fended off the nearest branch, feeling her paddle crack and her shoulders pop.

'You know how it is,' called Mickey with forced cheerfulness. 'Some little thing upriver gets passed on down. They haven't much choice – the dams are all up to capacity this year with no reservoir space left. Someone pisses in Lake Mead and it's going to come on down to us.'

'That's it, is it?' bellowed Kramer. 'Don't blame us, blame El Niño!'

'Come on, Kramer,' called one of the others. 'You know that's what it was about all along. Shit, if the greenhouse effect hadn't pushed up the precipitation from Mexicali to Montana we'd never have got the Colorado project off the ground. Everywhere from the orange groves of LA to the fountains of Phoenix it's no longer drought they're scared of, it's flooding. They don't want another Imperial Valley. They can't afford another Salton Sea.'

This assessment sounded cynical enough to convince Robin, though she understood almost none of the references. She filed a series of questions away with which to enliven conversation around the camp fire beneath the Arizona stars tonight.

Precisely how long they got around the camp fire – indeed, how much sleep they got at all – would depend on the speed of their descent. As Kramer's briefing to the crew had pointed out, they had the better part of 500 kilometres to go. That meant 65 kilometres a day, no matter what. Oddly enough, in spite of the dangers of a following sea, the outwash from the Hoover Dam was helping them nicely along. The hard work would come when they had to paddle across the placid waters of Lake Mojave and portage down round the Davis Dam; then paddle across Lake Havasy and portage round the Parker Dam and so on round the Headgate Rock Dam, the Palo Verde, the Imperial, the Morelos and the Yuma – though then, apparently, according to the briefing, the steady flow between the old tracks of the newly strengthened levees astride the newly dredged channel should sweep them easily enough across the last one hundred kilometres or so from the Mexican border to the Sea of Cortez.

Seven days, 65 kilometres a day, five dams with associated lakes and canal systems. And that didn't begin to count the complexities presented by the inwash of a couple of lively tributaries along the way. They might make the confluence of the Bill Williams River tonight. They would be at the Gila five days after that. Both had been threatening to flood recently, by all accounts – like the San

22

Juan, the Little Colorado and the Virgin had within the last few weeks, apparently. Hell, maybe no one had peed into Lake Mead at all; maybe this was just the guys up on the NASA-style computers at the Hoover Dam's main control room giving them a bit of a push-off for luck!

But no, thought Robin more soberly, seeing white water come tumbling into the steep-sided river course behind them. This was more serious than that.

'Here we go again,' she and Mickey chorused together.

They made it to the Bill Williams River and swung wearily into their planned bivouac in the Wildlife Refuge a little before sunset. Kramer called a series of orders and they unloaded their supplies then pulled the big inflatable up onto the shore and tethered it to a solid-looking cottonwood tree. Two of them went off upstream with fishing poles hoping to supplement their supper with something fresh while the rest of them set up camp. Robin was well enough acquainted with the general requirements of camping, but the way the bivouac went up was clearly a well-practised team effort with no immediate place for her, so she contented herself with collecting cottonwood and driftwood for the fire they would obviously need later. Kramer called to her to take care. She raised one well-gloved hand to him and he nodded.

By the time the fishermen returned with what looked to Robin like a couple of huge bream, the camp was up and the fire alight. A latrine had been dug down by the river for the men and another up on the edge of a cattail reed bed for the women – for Robin was by no means the only one aboard. As Kramer had pointed out at the press briefing, the Corps of Engineers was proud to be represented by so many female officers on this particular project. Robin had been introduced to them all, and had exchanged quite a few words with those among them who had liked and respected Captain Allday, but she hadn't really got to know any of them yet. To an outsider, they seemed to make quite a tight, exclusive group, focused as they were on an agenda she did not fully understand. Even so, Robin was reserving judgement for the time being. And anyway, Kramer and Mickey Vargas were social enough for the time being.

After her experiences in Las Vegas it was more than enough for her to sit with a plate of roasted fish and beans, a fragrant cup of coffee at her side, and watch the last of the sunset settle beyond the big old cottonwood while some sort of cuckoo sang in its branches and flycatchers whipped over the surface of the murmuring river, screaming in apparent ecstasy.

'Explain to me about the stuff from this morning,' Robin said to Kramer and Mickey when they had finished supper. 'About the dams all being full and the Imperial Valley and the Salton Sea. You all seem to take it so much for granted but I have no idea at all and I want to understand.'

Mickey shrugged. 'History and background's your bag, Kramer. Enlighten the lady.'

'Yeah,' added the cynical voice from earlier, deep and timbrous but clearly feminine; the voice which had talked of the greenhouse effect and the fears of the people of Phoenix. 'Tell the lady what she's mixed up in here, why don't you?'

'Long story,' said Kramer.

'I'm a good listener.'

'Even so, I'll simple it down and cut to the chase whenever I can.' Kramer leaned forward into the light of the dying camp fire like a cowboy telling a ghost story. The red light made his face look almost mystically Native American, deepening the lines and hiding his eyes, all except for the faintest glimmer.

'The Colorado's a dangerous waterway, but folks've always been trying to tame it. It brings so much water through so much desert that it's an obvious temptation. You can see that. Native Americans tried it first – Hohokam, Anasazi and Mogollan. They all made successful irrigation systems and lived in villages beside them more'n three thousand years ago. But the Colorado, she's a big old girl and it don't take much to make her flood – or the Salt or the Gila or the others that feed her. Like this one, like the Bill Williams, for example. The Spanish found her – named her the Colorado – but they didn't know what to do with her. They came up her from the sea looking for the Seven Cities of Gold, the Fountain of Youth or whatever. Killed the tribes. Died out themselves. End of story for a few more centuries. White folks like us didn't start serious exploration till after the Civil War but even as our predecessors, the military expeditions, were saying she was useless, could never be tamed or populated, gold fever was pulling folks into the flood plain while migrants going on west needed water. That brings us to the Imperial Valley and the turn of the last century. You take it for a while, Mickey. You're from California.' He gave Robin a wide grin. 'Two thousand nine hundred years in less than five minutes. Now that's what I call cutting to the chase.'

Mickey took up the tale. 'In nineteen hundred a couple of guys called Chaffey and Rockwood got the rights on this place outside of San Diego called the Valley of the Dead. The *Valle de Los Muertos*. They renamed it Imperial Valley and proceeded to irrigate it and sell farming lots. They built a dam on the Colorado called the Imperial Dam and dug a big canal. Their system worked sweet as you like for nearly five years, then the Colorado flooded. It smashed their dam all to kindling and actually switched its flow straight down the canal, right through Imperial Valley at, what, five hundred cubic metres per second? It took more than two years before our predecessors, with the help of the Southern Pacific, closed it all off again, by which time nearly forty cubic kilometres – about the entire contents of Lake Mead itself – had poured straight onto the sorry suckers.'

'It cost more than three million dollars to put things right,' Kramer took up the tale again. 'And that was a tidy sum in nineteen hundred and seven. You could fight a good few Desert Storms on the equivalent today; bomb a good many Bosnias. The water's still there, too, what's left after a century of evaporation. It's called the Salton Sea. But the fact was that they couldn't let it rest at that. The river obviously meant money. Folks were coming west. Someone needed to control the river properly, sell all that water to the farmers for irrigation, sell all that power to the cities. So they built the Hoover Dam. Simple as that. Said it was to control the flow, keep the river safe, but in order to do that, Lake Mead would have to stay low – soak up floods and such. But it cost so much, they wanted it to pay its way, so it sells hydroelectricity, and in order to do that, Lake Mead has to stay full. Limited capacity for soaking up floods; river's not quite so safe after all. But money wins every time. Money and politics. After the Depression, the New Deal all but used the Hoover Dam as its symbol of success. The guys who built it, the federal government's Bureau of Reclamation, got the kind of Washington funding which would have put NASA on Pluto by now. Just on the Colorado alone they built eleven more dams, sharing out the water, the irrigation, the power, the political clout. Couple of presidents at the very least got to the White House from dam projects.'

'But,' said the cynical voice from out among the shadows, 'the problem always stays the same. The dams went up to control the flow, pass out the water for irrigation and such. So the lakes should stay low and carefully controlled. But the immediate payback comes from hydro-power – hell, the pumps that pump the water into the irrigation systems are all powered by hydroelectricity. And that can only be generated if the dams are full. Which sure as hell screws the river management aspect.'

'And just one of those systems, the Central Arizona Project, pumps water nearly four hundred kilometres from Lake Havasu to Phoenix and Tucson – most of it uphill,' added Kramer gloomily.

Robin sat silently for a while. 'Look,' she said at last, 'a couple of things have got me confused here. Firstly, I've been hanging around Americans all my life. It's unusual to hear so much negativity about American icons, projects and history from Americans. What's so different this time?'

'I guess,' said Kramer, 'it's 'cause you're talking to some worried people here. We're associated with this project. It's got our names on it. If anything goes wrong with it, then right here is where the buck stops.'

'I can see that,' said Robin, thinking of the collective guilt which hung around Los Alamos about the success of the Manhattan Project. 'But what can go wrong? You've re-established a major waterway. You've scored one for conservation like no one in history yet.'

'Too little, too late, that's the danger,' came the voice from the shadows. There was an abrupt movement and a tall woman strode into the firelight. In the shadows it seemed to Robin that her uniform was different to the others, but that was only a fleeting impression, for it was her face and her voice which claimed attention. 'What we have here is one of the most over-managed river systems in the world caught in a rapidly changing situation. Between the mid-twenties and the mid-nineties the flow in the Colorado fell. Folks budgeted on twenty cubic kilometres of water a year and got thirteen or less in some years. There was a heck of a lot of wrangling, lawsuits and whatnot. The Bureau of Reclamation did what they could and the lawyers and politicians got fat. The Colorado River ran dry south of Yuma on a regular basis but south of Yuma there was only desert in any case and Mexican desert at that. And the Mexican government managed to get the Mexicali Valley irrigated pretty well most years so what did it matter if the river managed to trickle down to the Sea of Cortez or not? I mean who really gave a—'

In the distance, there came a coughing snarl – a hunting cougar, maybe – which rumbled away into a quietness, the sound extended almost magically at a level only just audible, only just this side of imagination, by the merest whisper of thunder.

'But the greenhouse effect has turned all that on its head now. Weather's going all to hell. Historical extremes which seem to peak around the turns of centuries are threatening to climb up off the scale.

We've got El Niño activity almost every year now. Storm systems spinning out of the Caribbean ever deeper into the heartlands, ever higher over the Rockies. Suddenly there are people – serious scientists, not just cranks and doom merchants – telling the Bureau of Reclamation they can maybe expect twenty-five cubic kilometres of flow this year. Maybe thirty. They all know what to do with too little flow – they've been practising for more than seventy years. But what are they going to do with too much flow? How are they going to handle an extra ten cubic kilometres when all the reservoirs are full?'

'They seem to have made a good start with you people,' said Robin. 'Making sure any extra flow can at least get down to the ocean if and when it comes. Surely that has to be a good start.'

'Well, if the extra flow comes in tens of cubic kilometres at a time then you have a problem, lady. Have you any idea what even one little cubic kilometre is, when it comes in the form of a flood? A kilometre long, a kilometre wide and a kilometre high – can you even imagine what that looks like? What it weighs? What power it unleashes if it starts to move? What damage it'll do if they lose control of it at any point or at any time on a watercourse like this one?'

A little silence ensued. The speaker stepped back into the shadows and sat. Her voice grew quieter. 'But, yeah, you're right at that. It is a good start, only I think it's come at the wrong time. Like our history books tell us, you know? It was probably a good time to start a war with the Japanese in the nineteen forties. But waiting till after Pearl Harbor still looks like a big mistake to me!'

The hands on Robin's body were so big they could only belong to Richard. Richard had the biggest, gentlest hands in the world and they could play every thrilling nerve in her like Rachmaninov played pianos. She heaved languorously as the knowing fingers trailed the most delicate whisper of fingernail across her skin from the undercurve of her breasts across the corrugations of her ribs. Their loveplay often began like this, in the dark, silently and sensuously. His hands would flutter inward and downward in a moment, then he would pull her over towards him, moving her with that massive, contained strength of his as though she were weightless.

Given how she worried about her figure since the twins had come along, she found the feeling of being weightless almost the most erotic thing of all.

His hands were on her tummy now, sending out thrilling shivers like great spiders broadcasting ecstasy through their webs.

27

Not spiders, perhaps. Not after . . .

He touched her again, stilling the errant thought. She felt her swollen lips part and gasped as the weight of him swung on top of her. She opened her eyes and met the bright blue dazzle of his gaze. So bright, it seemed, that his eyes flashed in the dark, driving the shadows back. He was speaking to her – no, calling to her, but she could not make out his words above the thunder of her ecstatic heart. Abruptly his look of tender joy was snatched away and replaced by a mask of sorrow.

He began to cry. Robin felt the impact of his hot tears on her face and it was this which jerked her awake. She had never seen Richard cry.

She jerked awake and sat up just as Kramer's hand closed on her shoulder and the second bolt of lightning came, its brightness defining every drop of the rainstorm pouring down on her.

'We got trouble,' said Kramer. He was not a man who wasted words, but this was a redundant observation if ever there was one. The torch beams of the others cut the atmosphere like light sabres as they fought to pack away everything that might be damaged by the deluge then ship their own stuff as swiftly as possible. It was clearly going to be a fine call as to whether they would be safer up here on the high bank well clear of the already rushing Bill Williams River or whether they should get down into the water and away as fast as possible. A born leader who made decisions like this without a second thought, Robin was nevertheless glad that she did not have to make the call. Kramer did.

'Get it in the water,' he bellowed. 'We'll be safer back on the Colorado.'

Working beside Robin, Mickey gave a terse explanation. 'Weather's way east of here. If anything floods, it'll be the Williams. The dams may not soak up much extra water if the Colorado floods, but the Colorado herself will soak up anything the Williams can throw at her without even varying her flow all that much. Maybe get a little more *colorado* in places but that's about all.' The way he said the Spanish word brought out his Mexican accent for a fleeting moment and Robin realised that the woman who had explained about the cubic kilometres of extra flow had spoken with a Mexican accent too.

As they worked swiftly, packing the last of the soaking bivouac into the inflatable down on the restless water, Robin asked Mickey about her. 'Yes, she's Mexican. Hydrological engineer. Liaison officer. Seconded into their army for the project, I guess. She's a major

28

like me.' *Major*: again the Mexican-Spanish inflection. 'But she's probably the least military person I have ever come across. Don't get the wrong idea, though, I haven't had much to do with her myself. None of us has. She's pretty stand-offish, you know? Her name's Conception Lopez but the guys all call her Conception NNO.'

Robin dumped the last of her stuff over the fat, slick side of the inflatable and opened her mouth to ask what he meant, when thunder suddenly exploded without warning, and very close. The ground beneath Robin's feet heaved and shook. Automatically she glanced upstream, expecting to see a wall of floodwater come bursting out of the darkness. But even as she did so, a column of lightning struck down onto the watercourse a couple of miles away. The river was in full spate, but the instantaneous flash of illumination revealed no great wall of water. The thunder was something else, therefore.

Robin looked for Kramer, but he was in the inflatable, looking downstream towards the Colorado whither they were bound. She looked at Mickey but he was scrambling over the inflated side and yelling at her to get aboard. Robin hated to act mindlessly, however, and there was something here she did not understand. The real thunder from the lightning flash faded and the thunder upstream was nearer, louder. The sound wasn't coming from the thunderstorm and it wasn't rushing water. Robin looked back at the wall of waving reeds.

She looked up the precipitous bank and saw one last figure standing there.

Mickey was wildly trying to push off, but Robin grabbed his shoulder and stopped him. She took his flashlight and shone its beam up the bank, straight into the face of Conception Lopez. As the beam struck her, so a look of disorientation and confusion cleared and she was in action. Following the beam, Conception came floundering down the bank towards them. And not a moment too soon.

The wall of reeds was smashed away and a herd of big game came stampeding down the river bank. In the darkness, with nothing more than torch beams, none of them was sure what the creatures were. They were big. They had sharp horns. They were in full stampede. That was all any of them needed to know.

Conception hurled herself across the bank and threw herself past Robin who held the inflatable for her. Then Mickey and Kramer both jerked Robin in and the wild rush of the Bill Williams in full spate snatched them out from under the hooves of the stampede and whirled them away towards the temporary safety of the Colorado.

Chapter Four

Richard's fingers traced the outer curves of the cool, full breasts, pausing to flick his broad thumbs gently across rising nipples, exploring with the delicacy of a blind man learning a face. He curled his fingers slightly so that the pads of his fingertips gave way to the gentlest claws and these he drew down her sides as she rose beneath him, curving her spine and offering the distinct ridges of her ribs, caught between ecstatic gasps and helpless laughter.

Lower and lower the fingers explored, moving off the rib ridges into the hollow of her tummy. From the tip of her breastbone down past the cup of her navel she had the most tempting little valley and his fingertips traced this, as light as spring rain. There were, he knew – though he did not open his eyes to look, not yet – tiny golden hairs here which would swirl into patterns beneath his tongue and which gathered into fuller fleecier abundance the lower he went, his hands exploring the forbidden, hotter, lower regions like Jason come to Colchis in search of the Golden Fleece.

'Robin,' he breathed.

But when he opened his eyes he saw the golden glory of Jody spread like a centrefold before him.

Richard jerked awake and found himself sitting erect. The sheets were gathered around him and the room was cool and dark. He breathed deeply and pulled himself out of bed. He reached down to switch on the bedside light and checked the time on his old steel Rolex – too venerable a timepiece to be luminous. Coming up to 4 a.m. He crossed to the bathroom and ran a cold shower, hoping that the cold water – as his masters at boarding school so long ago had promised – would wash the errant thoughts out of his head. Instead, the icy blast merely served to wake him up and within ten minutes he was back, wrapped in his white towelling robe, mind wide awake.

He opened his laptop and slid the connecting lead into the cunningly disguised port in the base of an apparently ancient lamp. He connected to the Net, accessed his favourite engine and called up Heritage-Mariner in London. As the H-M website came up, he checked the time again. It would be coming up for 10.30 a.m. in London. Would the man he needed to contact be in his office yet?

On top of the familiar logo, a series of pictures and titles came up. His own picture was there, and so was Robin's, but the words giving name, title and responsibility were in amber, signalling to those who knew the system that access was limited and would be in the first place with private secretaries.

Immediately below them, Bill Heritage and Helen DuFour's pictures stood above red writing. The chairman of the board and his wife were not available. Actually, Bill was in a little private hospital just outside Cheltenham having some work done on his hip and Helen was with him. Richard had the phone numbers if he needed to call. But then, even as he watched, Helen's details went amber – she had sent her secretary in, just in case.

At the bottom of the first page stood the rest of the senior managers, the people with day-to-day responsibilities, and, alone above these, stood the picture of Charles Lee. When Richard and Robin were away, it was Charles who ran the company. His calm, Hong-Kong Chinese face looked out at Richard and their eyes met as though they were already in communication. The name and title below were green. Richard clicked on them. Then he entered a series of codes and bypassed several security cut-outs. Two minutes later, Charles's face filled the screen. 'You're up early,' said Charles.

'I'm a bit restless.'

'They say Vegas has that effect on people,' said Charles.

'This is something more. But that's not why I called. Things are moving here but not quite in the way we had anticipated.'

Charles leaned forward, his interest engaged. His long black eyes dominated the screen. 'Ah?' he said, with a curiously Eastern inflection. 'In what way?'

'There seems no doubt that we would be able to run the SuperCats under the auspices of our existing American subsidiary Heritage Mariner New York . . .'

'You want to bring C.J. in on this then? Shall I arrange a party line?'

Richard thought of C.J. Martyr, their American chief executive. No spring chicken, he would be up and about – it must be coming up for seven in the Big Apple – but he wouldn't be in the office yet and in any case he was really only shooting the breeze here, as the Americans called it.

'No. Maybe later. I just want to chew the fat. Running things won't be the problem, or getting licences and suchlike. We'll have

32

to duplicate some of the federal work in the individual states, maybe, but that all seems fine. I just can't quite work out where this man Aldo Cagliari fits in. I've been to Houston and Galveston and the Texan end seems OK for the Gulf, the Keys, the West Indies and so forth. I've been to Los Angeles and everything's fine, then they said to talk to the people in San Diego and suddenly, here I am out in Vegas, talking to Aldo Cagliari and all I know for certain is that he has a counter-proposal. He has money – from where I don't know. He seems to have JetCats, though I haven't seen any of them or any specifications so I don't know if they'll stand up to our SuperCats. He keeps waltzing around vague propositions. Maybe we can both run the best routes and do a deal – limited competition, like the old airlines. Maybe we could go halves on some routes, full partners, whatever. Maybe he will simply queer our pitch if we don't play ball with him . . .'

'Richard, is this man Cagliari saying all this to you?'

'Not in so many words, no.'

'Sounds like an opportunist to me. I'll have him checked out, though. Unless you want to. You're in the ballpark there.'

'I'd rather you did it, Charles. I'm too close to the game here. And I have a sneaking suspicion that some of my options are being limited behind my back.'

'Dirty tricks?'

'It's been known.'

'Leave it with me. Anything else?'

Weariness suddenly washed over Richard. He looked at his watch. Well after five. Perhaps he could snatch a couple of hours before his breakfast meeting. 'No, thanks, Charles.'

'Take care. Love to Robin.'

The mention of Robin brought the unwelcome but graphic picture of Jody back into Richard's mind. He closed the laptop and threw himself back on the large bed. At the foot of the great, white-sheeted plain stood the biggest television he had ever seen. Thoughtlessly, wanting to do nothing other than clear his mind as he dozed off, Richard caught up the remote and punched some buttons. There were many channels available, but he could find nothing to engage his interest. Even CNN had nothing of immediacy to report. But simply channel-hopping was enough to send him off to sleep.

Richard was awoken by the chambermaid some hours later. He assumed she had knocked and, gaining no reply, had let herself in to tidy and make the bed. The first thing he knew about her, however, was the sight of a Mexican-American face shocked into frozen immobility above a snowy mesa of towels. Blinking owlishly, he followed her gaze. She was looking at his television.

On the big screen one of the sport channels seemed to be playing, varying their usual seasonal baseball coverage with a wrestling match. But then Richard realised with a *frisson* of genuine shock that this was no wrestling match. The garishly oiled bodies writhing between each other's arms and legs were exclusively and graphically female.

Richard reached for the remote control and rose with an apology, but the lady was withdrawing from the room and, long before he could explain, she had gone. With a sigh and a shake of his head, Richard turned, levelling the remote at the offending adult channel and frowned, incongruously whirled back into the grip of the vision which had started this. For there, spread on the screen exactly as she had been in his dream, apparently, was the fair, full frontal, naturally blonde and obviously available Jody.

The breakfast meeting got off to a stormy start. 'Just what was the idea, Mr Cagliari, of bringing prostitues to dinner with my wife and myself?'

Cagliari raised a shaggy eyebrow and glanced around the table, clearly calculating his response. All the faces there were masculine, many of them young and most of them those of bachelors alone in the big sexy city until the deal was done. He grinned briefly and shrugged. 'Show people, Captain Mariner. I thought you might find them amusing. This is Vegas, after all. What do they say? "When in Rome . . ."?' He looked round the table again. Swung an open, insouciant face back to the frowning Richard.

'Well, I'm afraid that sort of thing is not at all to our taste, thank you very much.'

'No, I guess it isn't.' Cagliari let it hang in the air infinitesimally. Was there some kind of double meaning in the words? Then he threw his great paws wide and showed his teeth. 'I apologise, Captain. No harm done, I hope. The incident is closed as far as I'm concerned and won't be repeated, sir. Can we carry on from here, please? We both have a lot to lose if we come to a falling-out now.' He glanced around the table. 'I believe we all do,' he concluded quietly.

Richard's eyes narrowed. He was within a hair's breadth of walking away from this but he simply could not see a way of walking away from Cagliari without walking away from the Texan, Californian and federal authorities or their representatives gathered around the table here, with whom Cagliari was so pally; of walking away from the whole deal, in short. That remained an option, but it was not one that he wished to take quite yet. He wasn't due aboard the good ship *Colorado* for another five days though he would have to start making his way south in four. Charles Lee would give him some information on Cagliari tonight or tomorrow morning, and if need be he could bring in teams of executives from London and teams of lawyers from New York then.

So on balance Richard decided to let it ride a while. It was some time since he had gone head to head with anyone who punched his weight. A stirring of excitement came not just at the prospect of the deal but of sparring with Cagliari for the next few days as he fought to pull it off. And the fact was, Robin's trip down the Colorado was quite liberating to him. While the others, it seemed – and his own subconscious perhaps – might enjoy using that freedom to wrestle with Jody and her like, Richard intended to do some real, hard-nosed, down-in-the-gutter business in a way that he hadn't since building up the China Queens Company in the deadly alleys of Hong Kong before handover. The prospect of a good scrap excited him. Perhaps there was more testosterone, more macho, in him than he had realised.

Richard was too old a hand not to suspect that Cagliari would be playing with as many dirty aces up his sleeve as he could stash there – but that promised to be part of the fun. Particularly if there were any more like the nubile Jody. On the other hand, he realised, even in the opium dens of Tsim Sha Tsui and the gambling hells of Macau there had been men whose job it was to watch his back, but he was all alone on the mean streets here. And that, of course, only made it all so much more exciting.

Richard placed his hands flat on the white linen of the tablecloth and leaned forward over the coffee, cinnamon toast, blueberry bagels and doughnuts with which his plate had been loaded. He fastened his gaze not on Aldo Cagliari but on the man sitting next to him, the slight, grey, bespectacled federal representative, incongruously called Killigan. 'Right,' he said, fixing the federal attorney's watery gaze with his steeliest look. 'Let's play hardball.'

Things got a lot more exciting that evening, though not in the way Richard was expecting. The breakfast meeting made definite progress, perhaps because of his new, more confrontational approach, though it went against the grain to pick on someone as apparently defenceless as Killigan. The rest of the day passed largely with faxes and e-mails flying between all the associated headquarters as notional routes and schedules were agreed at first stage. The afternoon extended into the area of maintenance facilities and the questions of building, buying or leasing terminal space. If they were planning to build passenger and maintenance terminals in all the centres to and from which they would be operating, where to look for planning permission; if buying, where to look for affordable property; and if leasing, from whom, for how long and under what terms. And, beyond the facilities themselves, there would be the question of staffing them, particularly the maintenance areas, for the only people currently trained to maintain the SuperCats were all English and French. Not a green card amongst them.

Then Aldo Cagliari invited Richard across to his suite at the Sands. It was late afternoon and Richard was beginning to feel more like a shower and a snack than a ride across town but Aldo had the perfect bait. 'I want you to look at the plans of my JetCats,' he said. 'My people should have faxed them over today and the people at Sands reception say I've had a couple of faxes the right size from the right source. Whaddya say?'

The prospect of poring over marine plans of a rival to his own SuperCats tempted Richard more than Jody could have, dipped in honey and served on toast.

Sure enough, the plans were there, and with them a range of detailed specifications which made Richard's mouth water. 'I'll have to show these to my technical people,' he said at last. 'These Cagliari Mark 1s—'

'That's the Cagliari MACH 1.'

'Oh yes. Mach 1, I see that now. Well, they look bigger than my SuperCats and even faster too. It's amazing, as though you had taken Concorde, made her the size of a jumbo jet and still got her to travel faster than the speed of sound. This looks an amazing thing altogether.' Then the significance of the name sank in. 'Are you telling me these things go faster than the speed of sound? Mach 1?'

Cagliari shrugged. 'Nah. It's just a name. Tag line for advertising, more than anything. They're pretty nippy, though.'

'How fast, exactly?' The SuperCats he was associated with could approach 100 knots and they were the fastest things afloat he had ever heard of. Now here was this man talking of moving vessels ten times the size fast enough to have named his prototype after the speed of sound.

'They're fast,' said Aldo. And that was that.

'When are you expecting delivery, then? When will you be proceeding into commercial arenas with these things?' asked Richard, switching to another tack.

'Pretty soon,' said Aldo, taking back the designs and rolling them carefully away. 'You'll see. I've maybe got a little surprise lined up for you tomorrow.' He winked conspiratorially. Then he looked up at the clock on the big TV cabinet masquerading as a chest of drawers. 'Hey, it's later than I thought. What say we slip out for a drink and a show? My treat? I owe you after dinner at Isis. No work and nothing special. Just two guys out on the town.'

Richard looked at the clock. It was after eight. He narrowed his eyes like Hawkeye checking for a Huron ambush. He did not say, no more stunts like Jody, though. He said, 'Yes. I suppose so. Why not?'

Of course it was nothing at all like an innocent boys' night out. It was like a chess match without board or pieces. It was like a federal agent debriefing a supergrass he did not trust over a case he could not afford to let go. Richard's motives were clear, as clear as the risks he was willing to run to get his questions answered. He needed to know more about his opponent. More about him as a man to begin with – Charles Lee would fill in the business details later. Waiting for him on the laptop when he got back to the Luxor would be everything from articles in *Business Week* to gossip from the gutters of Wall Street, if Richard knew Charles Lee. In the meantime, he needed to know more personal things. Was Cagliari married? He wore no ring; had called no wife on his cellphone, had boasted of no kids. Where did he hail from? Richard couldn't place his accent. Where had he been educated? What were his hobbies, if he had any beyond big business and bigger JetCats? What made Aldo tick? It was all a closed book to Richard at the moment and if he was engaged in a chess game here, he seemed to be playing against an opponent who was armed with invisible pieces. Maybe Aldo would open up a little tonight away from the dealing and the negotiating, on the boys' night out.

Even in the cool of the air-conditioned cab, Richard's mind was coldly at work, chewing over the fundamentals, balancing the odds, assessing and evaluating the risks he might well be running, putting himself so completely in his opponent's power. What sort of a man was Cagliari? Desperate enough for kidnapping? Blackmail? Murder? So far out of his own yard and so far away from immediate help, the questions flashed into Richard's tired mind. But they were filed and dismissed. Richard only had first impressions to go on, and they were by no means enough for business matters, but they affirmed that Aldo certainly meant what he was saying at the moment. He had on his mind dinner, not murder.

Richard sighed and settled back, watching the lights of the restless city flash past his window like constellations of falling stars. It was certainly time for a little fishing expedition. And Richard knew too well that you only caught the big fish by going down to the water – no matter how deep or murky it was.

They went first to a place just off the Strip; a simple little steak and beer hall. Richard didn't think much of it at first, but he had had enough gourmet food to last him quite a while. Aldo recommended the beer and shook his head when the teetotal Richard demurred. Richard had second thoughts when the meal arrived, for if the drink was a match for the food, it was worth his attention. He was served with a sixteen-ounce New York steak broiled on an open barbecue out back. It was served with Idaho's finest potatoes baked to fluffy perfection and topped with sour cream. It was lucky the food was served on a platter slightly smaller than a trough otherwise there would have been no room for the coleslaw, the green salad or the condiments. And if Richard, presented with English Worcestershire and A1 Chop sauces, felt an instant of regret over the lack of a piquant Dijon mustard, it lasted only until his first mouthful of the steak affirmed that here was a juicy lily which needed no gilding whatsoever.

They ate in silence, which allowed Richard to continue his examination. It said something about Aldo's character that while he had been happy to negotiate and renegotiate through the finest gourmet dinner in one of the finest restaurants in the States, he treated the perfection of the beef farmer's, meat butcher's and barbecue cook's arts with almost sacred awe. Richard reckoned Aldo would have been restless in *Swan Lake* but riveted by the Red Sox – or whoever. And yet he did not want to jump to any conclusions about the man across the table.

Aldo Cagliari's eyes twinkled a cheerful Father Christmassy dark brown between their sleepy, slightly baggy lids. But they betrayed nothing. There was no intelligence – no calculation, even – obvious in them. And that disturbed Richard, for this had to be a highly intelligent man. So why did he keep his eyes masked? He had an abundance of black, curly hair. Though no longer in the first flush of youth – his face was well lined and the effect of this was opposite to the lines on Mickey Vargas's youthful countenance – his hair and eyebrows gleamed a bright, well-oiled black. So did his sideburns, Richard noted, which reached unfashionably far down his jaw in front of his big, untidy ears. His nose was flat at the bridge like a prizefighter's, but the nostrils were fine above full, well-sculpted lips which turned up at the ends into a permanent slight smile. The chin, grey now – as grey as Richard's own since neither had showered or shaved before coming here – was a great lantern spade of a thing, hung with the beginnings of a pair of jowls.

From the chin, the next natural focus of Richard's character divination was the hands, which were passing up neat, well-trimmed forkfuls of food. They were big, square, powerful, forested with black hair on their backs. The fingers were square and the nails thick, the object of some manicurist's attention recently but unused to such ministrations. And, thought Richard, with a little jump of revelation, that was true of the body too. It was massive, bear-like, infinitely more powerful than the decorative perfection of Jo's the night before last. And it had received the attention of a decent tailor only recently. Nothing quite fitted. The shirt collar was at once too tight across the throat and yet loose enough to allow a thicket of black chest hair to curl over the tie knot, apparently knocking it askew. The jacket strained at every seam, buttoned or loose, and as the steakhouse was by no means as well air-conditioned as the cab had been, dark stains were beginning to gather beneath the arms. The trouser waist was wrinkled within the solid belt, but from memory the seat and thighs strained like the jacket did. As with the nails, there was a roughness shining through the patina. Partly in ready sympathy, partly as a simple experiment, Richard eased the almost weightless silk-lined linen jacket of his Gieves and Hawkes bespoke travelling suit onto the back of his chair. 'Do you mind?' he asked politely.

Aldo grinned briefly, nodded once and copied him with every sign of relief. It might have been the first sign of a relationship – perhaps of an armed truce – if the brief smile had got past the crow's feet and into the eyes themselves.

The removal of the jackets, closely followed by the removal of the empty steak platters, was a signal for a new phase, however; an escalation, perhaps. Richard introduced the subject of families by saying he had agreed to call Robin at ten. She was due to be encamped on the shores of Lake Havasu then. Richard then described his offspring and their current whereabouts before asking the obvious follow-up question. Aldo shrugged and sipped a beer. There was impatience, perhaps a little boredom in his eyes. No family then. A loner, by the looks of things: business focused.

Richard asked about the designs he had seen earlier. A flash of enthusiasm came into Aldo's eyes but it was immediately tempered, like a candle under a snuffer. The Cagliari Mach 1 became a subject for more animated debate but, as with the actual business propositions at the table here, the more Richard went after detail, the vaguer things seemed to become. Once again, he was tempted to walk away and perhaps the flat brown eyes across the table saw this in his open azure gaze. For the subject suddenly changed again.

'Hey,' said Aldo, rising. 'I promised you a show . . .'

There was a phrase which popped into Richard's head from the last time he had visited New York 'off-off Broadway . . .' It came back to him now as the cab pulled up outside a tawdry-looking little joint and Aldo piled enthusiastically out. Richard paused on the pavement and looked up and down the street. There was glitter and there was bustle not too far away. There seemed to be a cab rank on the corner of the next block. The street was well lit. There were a couple of cars and a small van parked nearby, though this didn't look much like a domestic neighbourhood. There were no sinister shadows and he was a big boy. And if he didn't have a gun then neither did Aldo – unless it was tucked in his sock. Aldo still looked like the opposition here.

Then Richard remembered a bar in the Wanchai district of Hong Kong where naked girls had swum with fish, performing an erotic cabaret in a huge tank behind the bar, and priceless, occasionally lethal information had been for sale in the seemingly submarine shadows of the place. He crossed the pavement then paused again, torn between the conflicting desires to check the place out as much as possible on the way in and to keep up with Aldo who was through the door into the darkness like a ferret down a rabbit hole.

Inside, it was not so different to the bar in the Wanchai, though there was no great fish tank behind the bar. Instead there was a mirror which reflected the action on a little stage, round which tables were grouped, most of them full, all of the full ones full of men. Aldo was at the bar, talking quietly to the bartender. When Richard joined him he turned with a grin and ushered him to an apparently discreet table in the corner.

'Just negotiating things,' said Aldo quietly. 'Seeing as how you don't drink alcohol, we have to pay French rates for fizzy water – like paying import rates for domestic champagne.'

Richard looked across at Aldo who shrugged and grinned. 'It's all they serve,' he said.

'Very high-class,' said Richard dryly. He did not have a good feeling about this but there were no alarm bells ringing at the moment. He looked around; everybody was focused on the stage. The cabaret was always going to be graphic, perhaps a little shocking to his English sensibilities. But he had been a tanker captain on enough Gulf runs to have stumbled across a sufficiently wide range of perversions on tape at least. If this was how Aldo got his pleasure,

40

then he would note it for later use. And in the meantime, when the hair came down, the tongue got loose, particularly when fuelled by domestic champagne – though Richard suspected it would be little stronger than his soda unless Aldo really did have a close relationship with the barman.

On the stage stood a statuesque African-American woman of Amazonian proportions, dressed in a dazzling array of black and red leather. Each skin-tight leather section was secured by silver buckles. And, moving busily around her, largely on her knees, a white girl dressed in nothing at all was removing the leather, piece by piece, using only her teeth, tongue and lips. There was music accompanying the performance, but it was by no means enough to drown out the appreciative applause as each new item dropped onto the mounting pile on the stage beneath the spike-heeled boots. Manfully refusing to speculate as to how the Amazon's thigh-length, spike-heeled boots were going to be removed, Richard turned to Aldo, and was mildly surprised to find that Aldo was watching him – and closely, too.

A sense of incongruity, a feeling that he was being taken for a ride here, being set up for something, made Richard decide to cut to the chase.

'If we want to move forward as partners, Aldo,' he said, just loudly enough to be heard above the brassy throb of the music, 'Heritage Mariner would be in for sixteen million all told. Pounds, not dollars. We have two SuperCats ready to run from each location as soon as we can find and fit out the facilities. If need be we have ten ready to go next week. We have people in New York as well as every major oil-shipping port in the States. For this project we would move them around as necessary. Whatever the market demanded. We will have a training programme for our maintenance people and a shipping programme for our spares in place before we move. If you want in, then you'll have to match some good solid part of that with money, personnel or equipment. If you can't stump up . . .' Richard stopped, surprised and a little disquieted by how angry he had become so quickly. He had been about to say, 'If you can't stump up, sod off.' Aldo had probably got the message without having it spelt out. Richard fleetingly hoped he hadn't just declared war, then wondered whether he really cared all that much.

The music stopped and applause began. Richard glanced up to see the Amazon revealed in almost all her glory, with only the golden curls of her kneeling valet preserving what little was left of her modesty. No, he thought, irrelevantly. Valet wasn't the right word at all. He would have to ask Robin . . .

41

His personal phone began to ring, its distinctive chime the first few bars of Sir Edward Elgar's *Four Sea Songs*. Without thinking, he reached for it and answered. It was Robin, reporting in from the shores of Lake Havasu. Sun-dried, windblown, and apparently content for the moment to be alone as the others set up the bivouac, she reported uneventful progress down the Colorado since last night's upset, updated him on Mickey Vargas and on a couple of new friends – Kramer and Conception Lopez. 'Only fancy, darling, they call her Conception NNO because when she's introduced to anyone, she always says – get this, it's a scream – she always says she's called, "Conception – that's a name not an offer".'

'Really, darling? That's very funny.' Richard was surprised by how concerned and protective he suddenly felt. It was as though he was talking to Mary, his eleven-year-old daughter, and not his extremely competent wife. 'And how are you coping?'

The conversation carried quietly on through the departure of the last act and preparation for the next. Richard actually closed his eyes, the better to concentrate on Robin and what she was telling him. When at last he broke connection and came back into the reality of his sordid surroundings, it was with a shock of surprise.

Aldo's eyes were on him, unnervingly bright after all the hooded secrecy so far.

'My wife,' said Richard. 'Camping on Lake Havasu . . .'

'That's pretty far away,' said Aldo, shifting his gaze.

Richard raised an eyebrow, then turned to follow Aldo's eyes. On the stage an old-fashioned blackboard and a couple of desks had appeared. Beside the blackboard stood the Amazon from the last act, dressed in a teacher's robe and wearing a mortar board. Before her at the desks sat the girl who had removed her bits and pieces, and another, who looked disturbingly like Jody. Fleetingly, Richard thought that either he was becoming fixated or the svelte blonde must be very much a typical type out here. He wondered whether having to sit through whatever was to follow was worth what he was apparently learning about the big, bear-like man opposite and his strange predilections.

The girls at the desks were wearing school uniforms with tight tops and short skirts – and were taking no care at all of their modesty. To have done so would clearly have been redundant in any case, for as the teacher called out questions and her students failed to answer correctly, each incorrect response resulted in the removal of some item of increasingly intimate clothing. There was a simple sexual drama here, independent of the striptease and the beautiful

42

bodies it was relentlessly revealing. The audience became partisan, cheering for one girl or the other and booing the teacher. Until at last one of the students sat clad only in her short white socks and her sandals. The tension in the club reached fever pitch, intense enough to engage Richard's full attention for the moment. The next question was rapped out and the naked girl's hand went up with enough enthusiasm to animate her extremely unscholastic chest.

'Yes?' snapped the teacher.

'Forty-two?' replied the student, suddenly less than confident.

'Wrong!' snarled the teacher. 'Get your ass up here, girl!'

Amid a kind of collective sigh, the girl did as she was told while the teacher sat upon a stool and disposed her robes to show that they were all she wore. She patted her ample lap and over this the student bent as the dark, tutorial hand reached for an old-fashioned crook-handled cane.

'What is this filth?' demanded Richard, explosively, well beyond his adult limit. Heaving the table to one side – with a good deal of disturbance to the well-watered domestic champagne and the water-filled bucket it was sitting in, he stalked out of the place, even as the audience chorused, 'One!'

Outside on the pavement, Richard paused, looking towards the taxi rank. Suddenly it seemed a good deal further off than he had calculated. He had taken only a couple of steps towards it when Aldo erupted out of the door behind him.

'Hey! Richard . . .'

Richard lost his temper. It didn't often happen, for he was a big, powerful man and all too well aware of the damage he could do, but it happened now. He rounded on Aldo Cagliari, shouting, 'What the hell was that all about?'

'Jeez,' panted the American, apparently wrong-footed by the Englishman's rage. 'I thought you'd like it, you know? I mean he said you were into that kind of thing.'

'What? Who said?' Richard strode up to Aldo and for all the latter's bear-like solidity, he stepped back, almost babbling.

'Jo. Couple of nights ago. Remember? Jo and Jody? I bought them in for you but the Mexican took the girl and Jo told me your wife wasn't interested in him 'cause he wouldn't whup her ass . . .'

Through the red mist in front of Richard's eyes there was a glimmer of understanding about Robin's damaged bottom, the Colorado and the way in which the scratches and welts might be misinterpreted by someone leaping to sexual explanations. He took Aldo by his tie and swung him sideways against the wall. Aldo's wide shoulders shook the shatterproof plastic over the poster boasting 'MISTRESS AMAZON AND HER SPANKABLE SLAVES'. Richard's right fist swung back to its fullest stretch—

'Hands up, asshole, get your fucking hands up,' bellowed a voice.

Richard swung round, caught in mid-blow, to find himself confronted by a white man in his early twenties carrying a big and very dangerous-looking gun. He froze. He let Aldo go without seeming to move his fingers at all. He put up his hands as ordered. Aldo leaned back against the poster and did the same.

A couple of minutes later they were both without their wallets, standing shaken in the suddenly empty streets. Both had cellphones tucked away. Both reached for them at once – Richard primarily to alert Sentinel to cancel his company gold card at once. Before they could even get a dial tone, a police cruiser screamed up. They were surrounded by uniforms and bundled into the back before either had a chance to say a word.

Chapter Five

Dan Killigan sat in the back room of the police station at the southern end of the Strip watching through two windows made of one-way glass into two interview rooms. Every now and then he would get up and walk across to one or the other for a closer look, though the words being said in each were broadcast through here clearly enough. And, like so much else, were being taped in any case, for current record and future use.

It was safe to assume that both men realised that the mirrors in the interview rooms were really windows to somewhere else, yet they were both sitting there like lambs answering questions about a mugging, good as gold. Neither had requested counsel. Now how unusual was that? And how suspicious? The slight, grey man posing as assistant to the federal negotiator slipped off his glasses and massaged his forehead, eyes and nose. Killigan did need spectacles but usually wore contacts, the same as everyone else. Lenses like the bottoms of shot glasses were a pretty good disguise, giving no mean psychological advantage, but they played havoc with his sight and his sinuses.

Killigan picked up a stalk microphone from the Formica-topped desk at his side and spoke into it quietly. 'I need a little more time,' he said. 'Move them to interview room four then send in the girls after five.'

Richard was ushered out of the first interview room and into a second, slightly larger, with a big partners' desk and half a dozen chairs. He had only just taken the opportunity to sit, catch his breath and start to work out why the LVPD had so many questions to ask a man who had only had his wallet lifted, when a door in the far side opened and Aldo Cagliari was ushered courteously in to join him. Richard looked across at the rumpled American for a moment, then he let his tired eyes drift closed. 'That's another fine mess you got us into, Aldo,' he said quietly.

He sensed Aldo coming to sit on the chair next to him. 'You going to try and punch my lights out?' demanded the American resentfully.

'Hell, no, Aldo. This is a police station. And you know very well that even if they don't have great big one-way mirrors all over the place, there'll be something somewhere letting them watch us and listen to us.'

'I guess,' said Aldo.

'Oh, come on, Aldo, give me a break here. Are you trying to tell me this is the first time your trouser seat has polished a munici-pal chair?'

'Guess not.'

'OK. Then let's just sit still and see what pokes up next.'

Unexpectedly, the American gave a choke of laughter.

'What?' asked Richard at his most icily English.

'Considering where we just come from, that was a singularly badly chosen phrase.'

'Ha bloody ha,' said Richard, slitting his eyes and looking around the room for the hidden cameras currently filming them.

'He's cool enough,' said Killigan, looking down at the computer-enhanced close-up of the Englishman's face. 'He's checking the place out. Any of the monitors reading anything on him?'

The technician sitting by his side shook her head. 'Everything baseline normal,' she said. 'He could be sitting in his front room watching CNN.'

'Naw,' said Killigan. 'That'd have his pulse rate up at least. And his pupils dilated, given the right report. Or the right newsreader, come to that. Send in the girls.'

There came the distant sound of a door opening and closing and the second technician, the one watching Aldo's vital signs, sang out, 'I have pupil dilation. I have enhanced pulse rate.'

'He isn't dead, then,' said Killigan dryly.

Richard rose courteously as the two police officers entered. It was this movement, perhaps, which stopped his vitals from registering like Aldo's. The pair of officers would have been individually striking enough. Together they were simply stunning. During the next twenty minutes, under the gently courteous influence of low, feminine tone, flattered perhaps by the batting of long dark lashes curled over hazel eyes and green, certainly put at ease by the carefully calculated show, the two men – relaxed, confident, confiding – talked to the cheerfully understanding beauties. But what they said amounted to little more than they had told their less attractive colleagues earlier on. Time slipped by unnoticed, even if no more confidences slipped out.

As far as Killigan was concerned, it was the time which was the most important. About fifteen minutes into the lazy interview, the door behind him opened and one of the men who had sat in a parked car opposite the front of the strip club slid a CD recorder onto the table. 'It's not perfect by any means, sir,' he said, 'but it's the best we could arrange under the circumstances.'

Killigan pressed PLAY and a rumbling hiss filled the room. Clapping came. A leathery swishing sound and a silvery tinkle.

'. . . If we want to move forward as partners . . .' came the English voice suddenly, only to be drowned by heavy breathing. '. . . sixteen million all told . . . Pounds, not dollars . . . Ten ready to go next week . . .'

At the words 'next week' Killigan's eyes snapped up to meet the gaze of the nearest operative. Her eyebrows rose. Significant or coincidental? Killigan wondered.

'. . . people in New York . . .' the English voice persisted. 'Move them around as necessary . . . Whatever the market demands . . . If you want in, you'll have to match . . .'

'What was that?' asked Killigan. 'Match me?'

'Sounded like that to me, sir,' said the operative with quiet assurance.

'OK, that's it,' said Killigan decisively. 'I'm taking this upstairs. In the meantime, proceed as we discussed. After half an hour or so pull the girls out and let them go.'

'Take them home, sir?'

'Give them a ride home, sir?' asked the second operative.

Killigan paused for a moment then he said, 'Sure. It's what the LVPD would do. I mean, we have a couple of poor tourists here just been held up and mugged. Sure. Give them a ride home. But warn us that they're coming in, will ya? We may not quite be finished in their rooms.'

In Richard's room, even as Killigan spoke, the lights came on. His laptop still lay on the desk, connected to the Internet by the cable into the ancient-seeming lamp and the search engine. A set of strong dark fingers flipped up the screen. The NetScape page was up, with the search box blank. The fingers tapped the cursor into the box and typed HOT SEX.

The machine immediately switched to the adult channels, with all the warnings about limited access for children, all the promises about unlimited action within. It took the dark fingers only an instant to move the cursor onto the raunchiest alternatives and to open them.

A box came up at once demanding a credit card number and expiry date. After only the most fleeting hesitation, the fingers typed a number and date into the requisite boxes. The channel opened. The fingers tapped a few more buttons and suddenly what was happening on the little laptop screen made the action on the TV this morning look like a vicarage tea party. The fingers pushed the top back down, but did not quite close it. They picked up a snowy mesa of folded towels. A silent flick of a uniform skirt. A moment later the light went out, but the not quite closed laptop screen winked like the brightness in a dozing demon's eye.

The squad car took them to the Sands first. In the face of Richard's icy silence in the back, Aldo apparently decided it was time for a gesture at least, so he asked the officers to wait a second while he sped up to his room and came back with the plans for the Cagliari Mach 1. These he pressed into Richard's hands. 'Take a good look at them,' he said. 'Fax them to your people in England. Whatever. But don't walk away from this. I'll call you in the morning.'

Richard still said nothing. Walking away was his preferred option right now. The negotiations seemed to be going nowhere and he know as little as ever about Aldo, except that the man had some curious ideas about what sort of hospitality he would enjoy. The whole situation made him very uneasy and he was strongly tempted to throw in the chips now and see if there was a way to meet Robin down at the Parker Dam tomorrow. But as the squad car pulled away from the Sands, heading for the Luxor, he opened the folded designs and almost against his will began to re-read the familiar words.

Richard knew at once that someone had been through his room. He put the plans down carefully and looked around. Nothing seemed to have been moved or disturbed, and yet everything felt as though it was in a different place to where he had left it. His first reaction was to call the concierge for the floor. She assured him that only the cleaners and the chambermaid had been through the suite since he went out. Perhaps that was it, he thought. But his hackles were still erect.

He put the plans on the top of the television and took a quick shower. Then, wrapped in his big white towelling robe, with the feeling that someone was watching him tugging obscurely at the back of his mind, he sat at his desk. It was after midnight here. In London it would be 6 a.m. or so. Charles Lee would not be in his office but he would have left his information, encoded, in Richard's private,

48

limited-access in-tray. Richard flicked up the screen. He blinked at what he saw. The offensive strip show was a children's puppet show by comparison. He pushed the cursor up to the big BACK button. Back and back he went, searching for the blessed relief of his NetScape page from where he could access his records and his company mail. But instead, he seemed to be caught in nightmare circles of obscene screen after obscene screen. He hadn't even got to the stage of wondering why it was there; he simply wanted out of the deluge of filth that seemed to be filling up the whole of his laptop's memory, wiping out everything decent and normal there. He switched off the machine and pulled the lead out of the antique lamp to break contact. But as soon as he started the machine up again, every attempt to communicate with the office and pick up Charles Lee's report on Cagliari and his business simply slipped back into more and more uncontrollable floods of pornography. At last, feeling obscurely as though he was drowning in the tidal wave of sexual sewage, he switched off the computer again, flung himself onto the bed and slept.

The Drug Enforcement Administration had flown a special agent in from Phoenix to talk to Killigan. Side by side they sat in a rarely used office in the bowels of city hall and they watched the picture of the sleeping man on the little monitor.

'So,' said the special agent. 'Tell me about this Richard Mariner.'

Killigan shrugged, frowning. 'He comes over as straight as a die,' he said. 'Ordinary English businessman. Nice wife. Good deal. Trying to do his best.'

'Then why is he so pally with someone like Cagliari?'

'Don't think he is. I think Cagliari's trying to muscle in on his deal. Cagliari's pretty desperate.'

'That's where we want him,' said the special agent. 'Like De Lorean. He can be a great magnet for the real scum and we can clean up. And anyway, the English aren't always so squeaky-clean. What about that big guy in Belize? Became money-man for the English Labour party couple of years ago.'

'That's like saying all Englishmen should have humps because Richard the Third was English. Or they should all like carving up tarts because of Jack the Ripper. Except the Ripper was American, of course. Doctor from New York, if memory serves . . .'

'Yeah, maybe,' temporised the special agent, 'but it still makes a disturbing pattern. Especially now that the squeaky-clean little English wife seems to double as Superwoman and is off downriver.'

'There is that,' agreed Killigan. 'That's a worrying thing, even though—'

'Three worrying things,' interrupted the special agent. 'What's the old saying? There's only three levels of coincidence: happenstance, circumstance and enemy action?'

'That's James Bond, sir,' said Killigan. 'I do not believe the DEA should be using the thoughts of a fictional English spy to guide our operations.' He paused. 'But still,' he admitted warily at last, 'it's a worrying combination. Aldo Cagliari, the Colorado and the *Colorado*.'

'When are they due aboard her?'

'Five days, same as everyone else. For the decommissioning ceremony, when she moves out of one service and into another one entirely.'

The special agent looked at the sleeping man tossing restlessly on the monitor. 'I'd give a lot to know what's going on in that head,' he said quietly. Then he remembered the pictures from the laptop he had seen coming and going over the white towelling shoulder. Maybe not, he added silently. His eyes flicked across to the picture of Aldo Cagliari on the monitor beside it. Cagliari was hunched with his back to the camera but both men knew that he was snorting a line of coke from the little mirror he always carried for the purpose, though neither could see that he had cut it and straightened it with the edge of Richard's stolen credit card.

As is sometimes the case with over-reliance on technology, in fact, there were several things the special agents were blissfully unaware of. Because they had their secret camera in place, they had failed to watch the door to Aldo's room – though, as the woman who had slipped the Gold Card and an accompanying message beneath it worked both at the Luxor and the Sands, she might well have gone unnoticed. The note, spread by the cocaine-sprinkled mirror, detailed the way this woman had been able to pick up the card as agreed after the fake mugging, and to use it as she was hired to do, to cripple Richard Mariner's laptop – and his records, communications and immediate back-up.

The camera was a fine instrument for observation, therefore – almost as effective as the long-range microphone in the restaurant had been – but it simply did not allow the agents the insight into Aldo's desperate plans which they supposed it did. Nor could it allow them to see the way in which the microphone's cryptic eavesdropping had led them to suppose there might be an association between Richard and Aldo when there was only the wild attempt of a desperate man

50

to muscle in on a legitimate business deal. At the very least, Aldo was hoping he might pull a little bribery or blackmail; get a payoff to desist maybe if he could isolate Richard from his people and panic him. On the other hand, with his more legitimate approaches, perhaps Aldo might even be able to interest Richard, as a market leader, in a couple of little products he had been trying to get into production. But his position, like his allegiances and his finances, were so twisted and knotted at the moment that he could hardly see a clear way forward himself. So if the camera had been able to see inside his mind as clearly as it could see the back of his head slumped sleeping on his desk, the sleepy agents would have been little wiser themselves.

Chapter Six

Captain Jesus Miguel de Hidalgo y Vega stood on the bridge of his venerable D60 destroyer *Colorado* and brought her into the harbour of Topolobampo at slow ahead. Those long, dark, narrow eyes beneath that perfectly tilted captain's cap knew every bay, inlet, rock and shoal on both sides of the Sea of Cortez better than any pilot – better than most of the tuna fishermen scurrying to get their boats from beneath his majestic bow; better than anyone aboard the ferry from La Paz huffing impatiently astern; better even than the great sea lions which had given the place its name and which were also floundering out of his way.

'Reduce power,' Vega ordered quietly as the long, low shape of the ocean-going warship crept beneath the shadow of the huge tuna cannery and into the little bay of the inner harbour, almost, but not quite, losing steerage way. 'Steady as she goes.' The long eyes flicked across the familiar landmarks as though taking no account of the much more scientific detail of the electronic ship-handling systems all around. First Officer Hernan Gutierrez almost stepped forward to order the helm over, but his captain quietly prevented him: 'Helm over. All stop.'

As *Colorado* came quietly into the unaccustomed berth at the industrial end of the burgeoning harbour, Jesus Vega looked up at the cranes hanging like metal gibbets above his command. The thin set of the aristocratic lips between the clipped moustache and the razored shovel of his chin twisted bitterly. It was not enough that *Colorado* would be decommissioned within the week, she would be going to the ceremony stripped and bare. Fifteen kilometres up the railway line from this busy port stood the town of Los Mochis, a blossoming export centre crying out for metals, equipment, anything that could be hooked up or melted down to aid the greater glory of the new economic revolution. Like wisdom teeth, the trusty old 127mm L/38 cannons in their twin mountings would be pulled before the end of the day. His men, those few of the skeleton crew left him after today, were to cover the wounds in the decks with canvas and

53

boarding – and make sure none of the honoured guests fell in them at the decommissioning ceremony.

Already waiting on the dockside as the harbour lines went out, Vega could see the electricians who would rip out the Lockheed SPS-40 and the Raytheon/Sylvania radar systems, the Western Electric gun-control systems – redundant anyway now that the guns were going – the sonar, the great mass of the communications, the weather prediction and the navigating equipment. At least they would leave the Babcock and Wilcox boilers and the Westinghouse turbines they powered until everything else was over and done, though Captain Vega would not have been much surprised to learn that he was expected to paddle *Colorado* to her own funeral service as though she was a canoe.

'Take over,' he snapped at his first officer as he turned on his heel. 'I will talk to the men before I allow those cannibals aboard my command!'

Lieutenant Hernan Gutierrez watched the tall figure of his captain stalk off the bridge with a tiny smile of sympathetic understanding. In the two years they had served together, Hernan had come to respect the captain; had come to admire and perhaps even understand him a little. But he had not really come to like him. Captain Vega was a man out of his time, who made no allowance for the twentieth century and its attitudes, let alone for the twenty-first century in which he was now stranded. He wore the old-fashioned high-collared white uniform which had gone out of fashion more than twenty years ago – and Hernan had never seen the tight collar unloosed, even on the rare occasions when he had been called upon to visit the captain in his quarters. The captain's cap was always worn at an exact angle, with the peak as low over those long dark eyes as it would go, allowing the back to sit high above the thick waves of steel-grey hair which fell to the collar and curled there, unfashionably long. The white cotton of the jacket and the trousers was always as well pressed and as well presented as though it had just come out of the tailor's beside the Portales de los Mercaderes in Mexico City. The white deck shoes were always immaculate.

Hernan could not help but wonder how the old man was going to keep up appearances now that his personal steward was being transferred off, along with everyone except the skeleton crew designated to take the stripped hulk up to the decommissioning ceremony at the point of her greatest exploit, just off the Punta San Felipe. Then she was due to be torn apart right at the north end of the Sea of Cortez she had protected for so long, in the new facilities built as part of

54

the Mexican/American Millennium Project giving rebirth to the great river for which the ship had been named. What was left her, so it was whispered, would be transferred north across the border and sold to the land of her birth for scrap. Long before that final indignity, Hernan Gutierrez would take a little shore leave and then go on to another posting. Captain Vega, by the look of things, was on the scrapheap, like his command.

Hernan's thoughts were interrupted by the chimes of the ship's address system, and the young officer had no trouble picturing his respected commander sitting at the desk in his day room, the old-fashioned stalk microphone close to his lips, as he spoke to his crew for the last time, collar tight and cap low on his eyes.

'My friends. This is the last time I will have the opportunity to speak to all of you together. I have chosen to say farewell in this way rather than to have you all assemble on the main deck as we are under the eyes of the men who are waiting to tear our ship apart. Those of you who have duties still to perform, whether you are staying aboard until Friday when the ceremony will be held or are assisting with the dismantling of your equipment, I know I can rely on you to preserve the reputation that you and your predecessors aboard the *Colorado* have worked so hard to earn. Those of you paid off and ready to depart when the gangplanks go down, make certain you have with you everything you wish to take and leave quietly. If you find a cantina or a bar this evening, drink to the memory of a fine ship and a fine crew. But remember, drunk or sober you will not be allowed back aboard. From the moment work begins on her, the ship is a secure zone. Anyone coming or going without authorisation will be arrested and may be shot. *A Dios.*'

How typical, thought Hernan wryly, slipping off his cap and running his fingers through the great mop of midnight hair which made it fit so badly, that the old man should leave that last thought with them, and then make two clear words out of the farewell. Not many of them, he suspected, were actually going to God.

The bridge phone buzzed and he picked it up as officer of the watch, settling back his cap the best he could. 'Gangplanks away,' came Captain Vega's voice. 'Let the vultures aboard.'

The chief engineer's name was Juan Ortiz but everyone just called him El Jefe, the Chief. He was the closest thing Jesus Vega had to a friend aboard, as is sometimes the case, the two posts being equal in rank on many ships. But the friendship, such as it was, rested on an attraction of opposites. The captain was tall, slim, aristocratic,

55

neat and courteous, while El Jefe was short, square, ape-like, almost always covered in oil and blessed with an unvaryingly scurrilous mode of address.

'Now just what the fuck is all this mess on my deck?' he was bellowing right now. At his feet lay a small sea of oily fluid from the hydraulic control lines designed to move the forward gun mounting. Before him two of his engineers stood sheepishly beside a huge dock worker holding an axe.

The surly dock worker sent in to remove the mounting shrugged. What did a bit of oil matter? he demanded. The ship would be scrap in a week. It was easier to chop lines than search around for cut-off points. They had to have the assignment completed by knock-off and the boss had promised no overtime on this job.

'Can you not see?' bellowed the apoplectic Jefe. 'Can you cretins not see that it runs through these ventilation shafts here and drips down into the magazine below? There are enough 127mm shells down there to blow your stupid ass to heaven. And that's the only way you're likely to get there! If you close this valve you can detach the line with no loss of fluid. No mess.'

Again the shrug.

'Right!' snarled El Jefe to the engineers. 'You two, get this mess cleared up or you'll find yourselves in the magazine below polishing up every fucking round! You may take as long as you want about it but there will be no overtime for you either. That's an order. Get on with it.' He turned away, then turned back. 'And you can spend the rest of the day following this big ape and his cretinous companions around my engineering decks making sure they leave not one drop of oil, not one dirty fingermark behind!'

As the door slammed shut behind him, the dock worker swung his axe again, severing another offending line. 'You service guys may have to put up with shit like that,' he growled. 'I sure as hell don't. I'm a union man. That nasty little goblin had better keep his hairy head clear of me and *el grande* here or there'll be a nasty accident.' The last few words he said were barely audible as the big gun mounting above him was lifted straight up and out through the deck and into the air, where it hung for a moment, turning slowly on the end of the crane's lifting chain, spraying hydraulic fluid and oil like a head being raised beside a guillotine. The big man looked up at it, wiping his forehead with the back of the hand holding the axe, smearing it with oil like war paint. Then he looked down at his feet and his bright little eyes followed the way the oil slipped out of sight into the magazine below.

*   *   *

56

If El Jefe's rage at the sight of some hydraulic fluid on his engineering deck had been hot, the captain's was incandescent. Never
in his wildest dreams had Jesus Vega imagined that he would be
forced to witness the brutal dismemberment of a ship still under his
command. But he discovered all too soon that if he was all-powerful
at sea, he was utterly helpless here. His calls to the manager of
the dock work crews went unanswered. His call to his super-
iors in Ensenada could not be connected. And even his emergency radio message to the Admiralty in Mexico City was broken
off before the minister could be called from his meeting – and
then the big radio had to go, leaving him with equipment just
about powerful enough to contact Chihuahua, or maybe Durango
at a push.

By the time the stifling day settled into a humid, restless, thunder-
threatening night, the guns, the majority of the electrical equipment,
and all of the senior officers' patience were gone. The crew members
detailed to help and advise the teams from the docks had been
disregarded or dismissed. Most of them had quietly collected their
belongings and departed, including the two young engineers who had
been told to clean up the mess beneath the forward mounting. At least
three decks were a mess and the weather deck was awash with a range
of liquids which had El Jefe, at least, worried about the fire risk.
But the mess was the least of it. Along with the equipment officially
detailed to go, a range of other stuff had vanished too. There would
be no easing of the stifling atmosphere aboard – the air-conditioning
system had been ravaged. There would be little enough light to work
by since most of the bulbs had vanished. There would be no hot food
because someone had managed to pirate the stove right out from
under the galley crew's noses. There would not even be enough cool
drinks to go round, for two out of the ship's three big refrigerators
had vanished, along with one fully stocked freezer.

Far into the night, Captain Vega, the chief and Lieutenant
Gutierrez, as the three most senior officers aboard, went through the
ravaged skeleton of their command, armed with torches, cataloguing
the desecration and preparing a report. The report would have been
memorable, perhaps even historical, but events overtook them at
midnight.

The big dock worker with the axe named *el grande* was called Cuzco.
Nobody knew precisely why this was so; it certainly was not the name
on his ID. He was not really a union man either, more like a petty
mafioso with his gang of half-organised thugs. They stood up against

the unreasonable demands of their employers and they took a little payment from everyone else for doing so, whether they wanted to pay or not. But Cuzco and his men weren't about their union business tonight. They had seen what a treasure trove the hulk of the *Colorado* represented – and they had only penetrated four decks into her. What else might be down there of a saleable nature, behind a very thin ring of sleepy security guards and protected by only a token crew? Why, the harbour watch had even left the gangplanks down so that if they could get past the security wire and into the shadows between the dim dock lights, they would have no trouble sneaking aboard. No trouble at all.

In order to facilitate the first part of this project, Cuzco had brought, not *el grande* but a massive pair of bolt cutters. As the others crouched in excited silence behind him, the big man cut quickly up through the security fence. When the gash was coming up for two metres high he pushed it wide into a rough A shape and whispered, *'Rapido!'*

There were eight big men in all. Half a dozen had been enough to take the fully laden galley freezer, so there was little they could not hope for if they could work for a while without being discovered. In case discovery looked likely, Cuzco had also brought an old Smith and Wesson .38 Police Positive, each of its chambers filled with a hollow-pointed load.

Across the shadowy dockside they went until they could crouch, gasping and sweating, in the shadow of the forward gangplank. What lighting there was cast long shadows on the rakish bow beyond the gaping pit where the forward gun mounting had been. The sides of the gangplank were solid and high and, as a result, the walkway itself held shadow like a dark stream within it. One by one, Cuzco and his men whirled round the landward end of the gangplank and disappeared into the shadows in a tiny flicker of movement. The inboard end of the gangplank sat in the shadow beneath the bridge wings and the men had no trouble following their leader as he dashed through more shadow to the dull gape of the open forward bulkhead door.

Cuzco and his men were not here on a pilfering expedition. This was not petty pickpocketing but grand larceny if they could pull it off. So they left the crew's quarters alone for the moment. They also eschewed the command bridge, for although there was likely to be expensive equipment on it, there would also be watch officers able to raise the alarm at the very least. Down they went, therefore. Down the forward companionways, pausing at each deck level to watch and listen for threatening movement or sound, though it was all but impossible to hear anything above the restless wind, the stirring waters, the throbbing of the ship's alternators, the cries of sleepy gulls and the shrilling of shoreside cicadas echoing down the black hole, three decks deep, where the forward gun housing had been. Reaching up through the lower decks were the vast engine rooms. Like the bridge, the engine rooms were manned.

Between the gun hole and the engine rooms was a kind of no-man's land. Here lay the stores, the armoury and magazines. Cuzco and his men would have been interested in ASROC missiles and Mk 44 torpedoes if they could have imagined how to move and market them, although the systems for targeting, firing, launching and controlling them were all gone. They would have carried away 127mm shells by the truckload if they had known a fence for military materiel. But they were not of the right class to deal with any of the hardware still resting here. And in any case, the captain, punctilious in this as in all things, had left an armed guard outside the main magazine doors.

Cuzco still had a dazzling shopping list in his head, however. There would be no one in the galley at this time of night. There were two more big ranges, a couple of ovens, a freezer and several fridges to be liberated. There was the rest of the air-conditioning system. There would be extra supplies to keep all these systems well maintained. Somewhere aboard there would be a stash of small communications devices – handheld radios and the like. And, finally, if the major armament was beyond their commercial capability, the ship's crew's armaments were certainly not. This was a coastal protection vessel, designed to pursue and arrest everything from illegal immigrants and fishermen out of place or season to the well-armed drug smugglers plying their trade between here and the USA on either side of the Baja California. Of course there had to be flare guns, pistols, rifles, ammunition. Equally, there had to be fully stocked lifeboats. The ones on the sea side might be easy to lower and steal complete. If the worst came to the worst, there was a well-maintained, probably armed, powerful-looking inflatable hanging over the bow.

Cuzco pushed on. The others followed him. Above them, to the sounds of the cicadas and the seabirds was added the thudding patter of a gathering downpour and, away out over the sea, well to this side of La Paz, the first great bolt of lightning pounced down.

Cuzco found the small-arms magazine just before midnight. It was on engineering deck three, no great distance from the point where he had first crossed swords with El Jefe. The guard at the door was asleep at his post so Cuzco did not even have to produce his Smith

59

and Wesson. Instead he walked forward, his footsteps covered by a snarl of thunder seemingly from right overhead. He picked up the guard's rifle and poked him in the stomach with it. 'Up!' he ordered. 'And open the door.'

The shocked sailor pulled himself to his feet at once. 'I can't,' he said. 'Only the captain has the keys. He and the first officer have the keys to everything.'

Cuzco saw the logic of this and was filled with a sudden blaze of rage that he had not thought things through better, and that the lapse should be shown up here and now in front of his most faithful followers. Blind with rage, he swung the rifle up, ready to use it as a club. As he did so, a bolt of lightning hit *Colorado*'s radio mast high above. The surge of power and brightness burned right through the ship, bursting many of the remaining light bulbs. The one nearest Cuzco exploded like a grenade. The shock and the surprise made him pull the rifle's trigger and a stream of bullets hosed down the corridor, trailing sparks like fireflies. Someone screamed shrilly. Whether it was the lightning or one of the bullets which ignited the oil in the puddle Cuzco and *el grande* had made, no one would ever know, but within instants of that first strike, and the first shot, engineering deck three was alight immediately beneath the great hole where the forward gun had been, and there were no longer any automatic fire-fighting systems in place to contain it. But the fire alarm was still in place and working well. It went off at once, warning not just the ship but the whole harbour of the danger.

Cuzco was simply stunned by what was happening around him. He swung the rifle down, but the guard had disappeared into the shadows – and would be back again soon enough, well armed and with help. Cuzco whirled round – but retreat was closed off by the flickering brightness whose gathering strength and burgeoning rumble warned all too clearly of deadly danger that way. The would-be pirate looked at his men and found they were all looking to him for decisive leadership. All except the man who had screamed – part of his face blown away by a ricochet. He was floundering blindly towards the fire, whimpering. He staggered round the flame-edged corner and gave another scream. He did not come back and none of his brave companions went to check on him.

Cuzco took to his heels, running wildly down the corridor after the fleeing sailor who had been guarding the door so badly. But here, too, escape seemed blocked for, with military and well-rehearsed precision, a squad of men was moving forward, filling the corridor, carrying with them what looked like a cannon and at their head the bearded dwarf El Jefe whom Cuzco had threatened to kill. As the men came face to face down the length of a corridor, El Jefe bellowed, 'Fire!'

Cuzco hurled himself sideways into a companionway. One side led up, the other led down. Lost and deeply panicked now, Cuzco plunged wildly downwards. His men, given one fleeting instant to discover that it was only fire-fighting foam being fired, all had the presence of mind to run up three twisting flights of companionway, out onto the deck and over the side into the sea in a twinkling. Cuzco was on his own.

Captain Vega stood erect and silent on the bridge, looking down at his forecastle head. Had Gutierrez been there instead of below relieving El Jefe on the chemical hose, he would have derived some small satisfaction in seeing his captain bare-headed, long grey hair sweeping uncovered down to the high, tight collar. The instant the engine-room telegraph rang, Vega was beside it. 'I would like to leave the harbour, Jefe, preferably before we blow the whole of the port to smithereens. How soon can you give me slow astern?'

'I left the alternators running. The boilers are still hot. Fifteen minutes. Perhaps. With the grace of God.'

'I believe it was God who started this. Let's not rely on His grace.' Vega depressed the loudhailer. 'Deck crew, prepare to cast off all lines. Do not ship the gangways; we will retrieve them on our return.' He crossed to what was left of the radio equipment and picked up a phone. At least the shore line had survived the lightning strike. '*Señor*,' he said courteously to the harbourmaster, 'this is *Colorado*. I am informing you of my intention to quit the harbour with all possible despatch. If you have any vessels at all inbound, I most strongly urge you to request they stand off.'

'Of course, *Colorado*. *Vaya con Dios*.'

'*Gracias, y hasta la vista*.'

Vega crossed to the helmsman's side, rested his left hand on the engine-room telegraph and his right hand on the boy's shoulder. His eyes flickered up towards the brass-bound chronometer on the wall above the tilted clearview, and down into the volcano in the centre of his forward deck. His sculpted lips thinned and the flare of his aristocratic nostrils narrowed; but his hands on the telegraph and the young steersman's shoulder remained reassuringly relaxed.

In spite of the trembling that the fire created in the whole hull, Vega's feet told him when he had power. He patted the helmsman's shoulder and rang down for slow astern. *Colorado* eased herself out of the berth and Vega was glad to see that she left none of her fire behind on the dock. He stepped out onto the port bridge wing and looked down at the dockside slipping away beside him. Then he turned and looked out past the brightness of the factory on night shift. He had no room to turn in the little inner harbour, and no time either. At any speed he could summon within the next few minutes, *Colorado* would run as fast astem as she would ahead. Only in the open sea with a good run-up could she still deliver the 35 knots for which she had been famous.

But there were more problems to solve before she could attain the open sea. There was a bar across the harbour between the inner and outer bays and the tide was down. How much room had he beneath his keel? Five metres at most, and *Colorado*'s 120-metre hull drew six. Vega could picture the great double screws of his command go chewing into the topmost metre of the rock-hearted bar. He could see his command swing, helpless, under the cliff below the factory. He saw the armaments exploding then, their force riding straight up under the overhang and sending the factory and everyone within it up towards the thundery clouds. Vega wavered, indecisive for an instant before he went back in. He breathed in deeply, his eyes on the gathering inferno of the forward deck. But then his face cleared. The thin lips curled into something very like a weary, ironic smile.

He took the telegraph. 'Keep on that,' he said to the young helmsman. 'Exactly. Do not deviate by a degree. Or Topolobamo will become famous for barbecued tuna.' Then he rang down for full astem.

Hernan Gutierrez later swore that it was the absent guns that saved them. If they had still been in place, the ship would have grounded under the tuna factory, but the removal of all that equipment took more than a metre off *Colorado*'s draft. And so they were able to get out of the harbour safely.

Out at sea in the heart of the downpour, the massive hole left by the forward gun contained the fire while the rain and spray carried it downwards rather than outwards – and that turned out to be lucky too, for the automatic fire-fighting systems in the 127mm shell magazine worked flawlessly and very quickly, releasing a smothering combination of inert gas and chemical foam. What little oil was left was either extinguished by the first officer's fire-fighting team or washed further down still into the recesses of the empty servicing rooms below, all with their safety-first drainage system.

So it was that, with the morning tide, and to a wave of cheers that began at the canning factory and then swept into the harbour before her, *Colorado* returned to the innermost berth. And today, every man who worked aboard her did so with the care, courtesy and respect which stood due to a great lady. But then, of course, Cuzco and his team were not working on her today.

Cuzco had no idea where he was. He simply knew he was lost and hurting – and that he had probably broken his leg. Sometime during the wild hell that had been last night he had slipped and fallen. The rifle was gone. He still had his Smith and Wesson wedged in his belt but was too disorientated to think of it. He was up to his waist in filthy, stinking water in any case, and the fumes were making him light-headed.

In fact Cuzco had managed to get himself trapped between the servicing rooms and the chain locker, in a maze-like series of drainage bays and bilges. The water in which he was half immersed was a potent mixture of oil, hydraulic fluid and chemical fire-fighting agent. Choking, disorientating waves of the foulness came and went. The space was designed to be pumped out while the ship was at sea, but after her little foray to ensure the safety of the harbour, she had settled back again and the engines and the pumps had been switched off.

Slipping in and out of consciousness, Cuzco passed the day as the heat built terribly and then eased. Like the Ancient Mariner, he found that the most terrible part of his hell was that he was burning with thirst and up to his waist in water that was absolutely impossible to drink.

At last, just before sunset, he saw a glimmer of light. Pulling himself wildly towards it he sloshed through the thick, oily ooze, calling at the top of his lungs. But all that came out was the merest wheeze, certainly nowhere near loud enough for anyone to hear above the clanking pounding of the dockside work. And the light which promised so much proved illusory too, for when he reached it he found that it was a little opening scarcely larger than a trap door where the floor of the magazine had been lifted away, with all the lethal shells within it. But still he made it to the light, and stood shouting in his broken whisper up at the men conferring so seriously up above his head. They looked around. They frowned. They nodded. Who were these men working in his harbour whom he did not know? wondered Cuzco, light-headed and indignant.

But then his worries came to an end. The trap door was blocked for an instant and something heavy, square, and securely wrapped fell into the bilge. The wash of effluent its splash-down made sent

Cuzco staggering back. He crashed into a nearby wall and the way he landed trapped the pistol between his belt and his hip painfully enough to remind him it was there. Wheezing with panic, he fought to get safe purchase in the slimy, restless ooze as more and more packages rained down into the bilge around him. *'Hola!'* he was screaming.

Then the rain of packages stopped and, fighting his way forward, the stunned man discovered that there was a mountain of them, reaching upwards from the water in front of him almost to the trap door. But even as he understood this, the trap door began to close. 'Stop!' he yelled at the top of his voice but no one on the deck could hear. He scrabbled wildly up the slippery slope of packages. Only at the last instant, when there was little more than a glimmer left above him, did he think to pull the trigger. But the gun misfired. Shaking it wildly and howling brokenly, he pulled the trigger again and again until at last it went off.

The gun fired just as it was pointing exactly at one of the well-wrapped parcels. The barrel was so close to its side that the gun was effectively silenced by it. None of the men on the deck above him heard a thing. And it would have made no difference to Cuzco in any case, for the hollow-pointed bullet made a section of the wounded package explode into his face. He gasped with shock and filled every mucous membrane from his scalp to his stomach with grains of pure cocaine. The shock of it killed him at once.

Chapter Seven

Robin was an expert at working out group dynamics. More times than she could readily remember, as junior navigating officer, as senior officer, even as captain, she had found herself arriving aboard ships, taking up duties, learning about her mess mates and fitting in, all within a round of watches. The ships were often sick, the crews stunned, victims of some unforeseen tragedy. Before she became involved with her husband's company, Crewfinders, and became a specialist in replacing officers killed or injured mid-voyage, she had risen through the ranks from cadet to third lieutenant in the tanker arm of her father's shipping line, Heritage Shipping, coming up the hard way, without grace and favour, the way she liked it.

Weighing up the motley bunch aboard the big inflatable was no great task, therefore. Robin discovered at the foot of the Hoover Dam that they had christened the inflatable *Pequod* after Ahab's ship in Herman Melville's *Moby Dick*; though, from the way she handled, Robin thought they should have named her after the whale itself. By the time they made their first camp on the Bill Williams River, she had sorted out the pecking order, if not quite all of the names yet. Kramer thought he was in charge, and when it came to paddling, steering, loading, unloading and practical things like that, he was, because he knew most about rivers in general and the Colorado in particular, its foibles, strengths, weaknesses and dangers – especially the dangers. So the others listened to him and obeyed him, for the most part.

For the rest, Conception Lopez was in charge. It was not that she had more expertise or wisdom than any of the others; it was certainly not that she carried any more weight or clout, a lone Mexican among a bunch of American army engineers. It certainly wasn't because she outranked them – although she did – because she never threw her rank around. It was simply that she was one of those extraordinary people who dominate any setting that they happen to find themselves in.

Conception Lopez was breathtakingly striking. Her looks went beyond beauty into another realm altogether. Her face was long, at first glance all eyes and cheekbones. The eyes dominated, shaped like cat's eyes with long, abundant lashes, and irises like the darkest of chocolate edged with the thinnest charcoal line. Beside these, the whites looked like driven snow. Her eyelids were sultry as though weighted by the lashes, and the brows above were heavy, even for a woman of Latin blood, sweeping up and away like sculpted eagle's wings across the high planes of her forehead. All the force of her character seemed concentrated in those eyes, making them flash, flame or smoulder according to her mood. But to concentrate upon her eyes was to do less than justice to the rest of her face – to her long, straight, perfectly chiselled nose; to the thrust of her mouth, so full that even Robin mentally characterised it as pouting; to the intransigence of her square jaw and solid chin. All of this set beneath thick raven hair and perched on a long neck which sat with unconscious queenliness on a deep-chested, slim-waisted body with hips, bottom and legs that Robin would personally have sold her soul to possess.

Robin was not alone. It was clear that Mickey Vargas would have sold all his bodily organs except two to possess Conception Lopez. Wherever she was, his youthful, ardent, bearded face was close by, frowning with fearsome concentration. When he was not immediately beside her, his long eyes were forever seeking her out, lost in those long wrinkles, surveying her like the eyes of an old-time cowboy, watching the way west. But Conception was toying, not so much with Mickey as with the idea of the relationship. To Robin, the Mexican woman looked like an 'all or nothing' girl; and when she gave her 'all', the results were likely to be considerable, possibly more than the ardent Mickey anticipated or was quite prepared for.

But because Conception was thinking about Mickey and keeping him at arm's length as she did so, the rest of the *Pequod*'s complement kept him isolated too. Only simple, square, rock-like Kramer stood by him having, apparently, a liking for the young man which sat well with the leader's unwillingness to be seen to be influenced by a lesser member of the team. And Robin stood by him, feeling that faint sense of responsibility which is said to come when you save someone's life. Mickey himself could not have been more cheerfully grateful to Robin, and had she drifted into Conception's orbit, he would certainly have found a way to follow her there.

But in all of her thoughts about the men and women aboard *Pequod* as she followed the Colorado five hundred kilometres down to the Sea of Cortez, she did not at any time in those early days think of them as a crew. 'Crew' was the obvious word to apply to a bunch of people, even army people, occupying the same vessel. But the group around Robin was simply not a crew. The word had in her mind associations of unity which she could not see here. There was a unity of purpose, to get *Pequod* down to the Sea, but that was all. Within that there was a series of individual agendas and private motives which broke up the homogeneity of what should have been a crew. What needed, in fact, to be a crew, as the near death of two of their members during their trial run had shown all too clearly, as had the fact that they had nearly left one of their number to be trampled beneath the hooves of stampeding antelope on the banks of the Bill Williams. But at least the second night's bivouac, on the shores of Lake Havasu, proved well-organised, quiet and restful enough.

The third day of the run took them along the rest of Lake Havasu and down to the complexity of the Parker Dam which fed two of the greatest manmade water systems in the world. From the northern outflow, it filled the All American Canal leading away across the Californian deserts towards Los Angeles where it would join with the Los Angeles Aqueduct served by Owen Lake and with the Californian Aqueduct reaching right up towards San Francisco nearly a thousand kilometres away to the north-west. From the southern outflow, it filled the waterway of the Central Arizona Project, carrying water nearly five hundred kilometres south-east past Phoenix down to Tucson. Here they were lucky enough to hitch a ride. Instead of being forced to portage round the dam and down the canyon walls in front of it, they were lifted in a couple of hops by a friendly chopper pilot. The first ride took *Pequod*, with all her equipment still aboard, Kramer, Robin and Mickey down. The second brought the others. As Robin and Kramer held the plump vessel bucking under the down draught of the returning helicopter, Robin saw Mickey sprinting over towards the landing site. A moment later he was helping Conception out of the side and following her back down here, his attention focused firmly on the seat of her pants.

'We're going to have to do something about that boy,' said Kramer quietly, catching Robin's eye and speaking like a man who owned a stallion ripe for gelding.

'If he keeps that up, Conception'll probably save us the trouble,' said Robin cheerfully.

'One way or another,' rumbled Kramer. 'We ain't seen nothing yet.'

By lunchtime they were under way again, along the river course heading almost due south towards the Imperial. The river here was by no means running as fast or as deep as it did between the Glen

67

Canyon and Hoover Dams, but it still sat well below the level of the desert plateau and threw rapids, chutes, little waterfalls, boulders and all sorts of other hazards at them. And, as an old rafter's saying that Kramer liked stated all too clearly, if there's a rock, you'll hit it, if there's an eddy, it'll take you. They still had their work cut out.

The sides of the canyon down which they were paddling stood high enough to bring darkness early that third night. Kramer consulted the maps he had brought – state of the art overlays of satellite photographs and detailed army surveys, all digitised and fed into his GPS system's memory. For their camp site he chose the long, low bank formed by the inwash of another, much smaller river. As they set up on the sandy tongue, the simple routine of the nights before was repeated. Kramer reported in and began to fill in his records. Mickey and Robin saw to the safe disposition of the trusty *Pequod*. Conception and her little team erected the bivouac. A couple of more practised campers busied themselves with locating and digging the latrines, then saw to the creation of a fire, while a couple of sporting types went off to catch or kill something worth cooking on it.

Unlike the evening on the Bill Williams where they had fished close by and pulled a tasty dinner out of the water pretty quickly, here they vanished up the little river and were away for quite a while. Kramer finished his report. Robin did some reporting of her own – over the phone to Richard's answering service at the Luxor. The rest of them talked, mostly about the heat. It had been a hot day and the high-sided canyon seemed to have trapped the sultry evening air as well as heavy, vaporous shadows. Humidity and heat made an enervating combination. With a wordless sound, almost a cough, Conception rose, unlaced her uniform boots and kicked them towards her sleeping bag. Then she stripped down the fatigue trousers which matched the ones the others all wore as though on official military manoeuvres. Her shirt tails made an acceptable enough skirt – or would have done had she stopped there. But the shirt also came off to reveal an olive vest, deep-scooped at front and back, falling just past the waist of a pair of regulation green shorts, long-legged to upper thigh, button front, double-stitched in the seat. With a belt, she would have looked like a bather from a 1930s advertisement. But her extremely feminine shape was wearing a masculine bathing costume and even in the thirties the effect would have been outrageous. It raised one or two eyebrows now, and activated a range of glands, many salivary. When Robin looked across to talk to him, Mickey's mouth was certainly watering.

Most of the others followed Conception's lead and soon only

68

Robin and Kramer were fully dressed. Mickey had removed his shirt, revealing the torso of a man who took care of himself and worked out regularly; but, like bits of Robin, bits of Mickey were bruised and abraded. The quick eyes of his solicitous saviour were swift to note also some marks she had failed to notice in the air ambulance. Especially what looked suspiciously like a pair of bullet wounds, entry just beneath his right shoulder blade, exit between his six-pack and his right short ribs. Conception noticed too, and one of them would have asked him about it had the fishermen not returned then, laden with fish and information.

A kilometre or so upstream, they said, the little river fell over a series of upper galleries into a pattern of pools and waterfalls. There were cool swimming ponds, lush vegetation, mysterious caverns, many with streamlets chuckling along their floor and with strange rock paintings on their walls. There was an immediate movement, led by Conception, to run up and explore. But Kramer put his foot down. Cook, eat and clear away, he ordered. There would be no chance to explore in the time left before lights out either. They all had duties to perform, maintenance tasks to complete and records to write. This was a military expedition, not a holiday excursion. Their prime directive was to get down the river by next Thursday, not to explore along the way.

They saw the logic and so they obeyed, but they clearly didn't like it. The fish tasted excellent, however, and the good food lightened the atmosphere considerably. With a series of grudging but increasingly genuine jokes about booking back here for their first furlough, they settled down. Tonight there was little discussion about the state of the waterway or anything else. They had had a hard day and there was another one in prospect tomorrow when they would have to paddle as fast as they were able through a long series of level IV rapids down towards the Imperial Dam. The whole company found it wearing, and they had all been training for this. Robin was sore all over. From her battered thighs, past her bruised bottom, up the pulled length of her back to the stiff square of her shoulders and the disjointed weights of her arms, she was bone weary. She slipped into her sleeping bag and zipped the net head section closed against mosquitoes. She didn't call Richard again and switched off her phone so that he would not disturb her or her companions later in the night. She didn't even have time to consider how perfect a bed was made by the firm river sand and the stiffly inflated base of the all-in-one lilo and bag. She was asleep.

★　　★　　★

69

Robin woke at moonrise, jumping from deep sleep to absolute wakefulness. There was someone standing over her looking away up the valley. The white light caught his face.

'Kramer?' she said.

There was an instant's pause, then he answered her, just as though he had woken her on purpose.

'Mickey's gone,' he breathed. 'I reckon Conception NNO's gone off and he's gone chasing after.'

'You want me to follow along?' asked Robin.

Kramer hesitated again then moved abruptly – strangely. It was as though he was putting something in his right hand, something like a knife.

'You're the best bet,' he whispered. 'If he's trying anything foolish, the others'd likely as not string him up – if Conception left enough to make it worthwhile.'

'I think she likes him,' said Robin, unzipping as quietly as she could and trying to force her rigid muscles to the dictates of her iron will.

'I guess. I keep telling him if he wants her to follow, then he's just got to walk away.' Kramer gestured. Both his hands seemed empty now. Just a trick of the light, thought Robin.

'Might work,' she said, reaching for her boots, tipping them up and tapping them to move any visitors along. 'He might just get a long and lonely walk, though.'

'You're a woman. You should know.' His voice was a little louder, a little cheerier now.

'With Conception? You're joking. My guess is as good as any-one else's.'

As Robin stood up, Kramer said, 'You want to take something.' It was an order, not a question. 'Flashlight. Gun. They got cats in some of the wild places here, if I remember my briefing right.'

'Torch, yes. Gun, no. What do you mean by cats?' Robin was easing life and suppleness into her shoulders, back and thighs, thinking of pussycats, house pets.

'Cougars and suchlike. Aren't many. Mostly steer clear of folks, but you never know. And, there's snakes and scorpions out there.'

'Got anything with a red dot?'

'Laser sight? Big Smith and Wesson automatic comes with a laser sight. Also comes with magnum load. Hit what you aim at and do not hit anything else.' He turned away as he talked, rummaging in the shadows. A zipper opened and closed. He straightened, turned back.

'I know. What I hit comes off or comes to pieces. Arms. Legs. Heads . . .'

70

'That's right.' He handed her the big square gun. Where had he kept it? she wondered. It was warm. 'Who told you that?' he asked.

'Man called Edgar Tan. Detective in Singapore.' She flicked on the sight and the red dot shone briefly on the ground between her feet.

In the moonlight she caught the glint of interest in his eyes when she looked up. 'Long story,' she said. 'Maybe some other time. Is there a shell up the spout in this?' She waved the automatic at him.

'What?'

'Is there a bullet in the chamber?'

'Yup.'

'I'll try not to stumble and shoot myself,' she said.

'Try not to shoot anyone at all, please,' Kramer said, quietly but forcefully.

Robin followed the beam of the torch up along the steepening bank of the cheerfully gurgling little river. Such was the sensual intensity of the night that it overwhelmed all of her mind, closing down even her thought processes for a time. She hardly needed the torch, for there was a low, full desert moon seemingly pressing itself amorously against the upper lips of the canyon. The whole place was flooded with a still blue light which added to the natural beauty and created a breathtaking effect. As Robin moved, she cudgelled her tired mind, trying to calculate whether it would be better to arrive unannounced and try and deal with what she discovered, or to make such a commotion in her arrival that she guaranteed there would be nothing untoward to deal with when she did arrive. It was the old conundrum of a parent approaching the door of a teenage son entertaining his first girl in private at the far end of a long corridor.

In fact, Robin realised, the noisy warning approach was impossible. The boisterous river, alive with frogs and cicadas, not to mention bats, combined to make a din that would have covered the charge of the Light Brigade. And the moonlight ensured her torch would be hardly visible. The higher up the valley she got, the noisier the river became and soon she entered a mistily fragrant area full of almost tropical greenery where a series of tall, thin waterfalls threw themselves like molten silver off the edge of a high plateau. Here Robin discovered Conception like a nymph in a lingering bath. One glimpse was enough to turn Robin's heart within her bosom and bring a tinge of envious green to the normal equanimity of her gentle grey eyes. Beneath the fall of water, Conception's perfect body became a thing of nature and almost ethereal beauty. Robin had only

71

seen a figure like that in her son's Tomb Raider games; it had never occurred to her that a body like Lara Croft's could actually be real.

'I hate that woman,' Robin told a passing scorpion, and the little creature, hearing the tone of her voice, very sensibly scuttled away to hide.

But it was not Conception she was looking for. As quickly as she could, she began to quarter the jungle thickets looking for Mickey Vargas, hoping she would not find him lurking like a peeping tom behind any of the nearby bushes.

It was with something akin to relief that Robin saw the glint of his torch beam further back along the valley and a good deal higher up. But then she frowned. Even down here among the trees, her torch beam remained pallid and almost invisible in the moonlight. Mickey must be in a cave to make his torch look quite so bright. She began to climb a gentle slope of scree.

There were not many caves on this side, and none of them, apparently, still had streams meandering across their dusty floors. But as Robin entered the low portal of the one she had seen the light in, her boots warned her of something liquid, and as her nose told her that this was where the bats came in the day. Bats. Suddenly and very poignantly she found herself hoping that these were not the notorious vampire bats of the far south-west. It was this thought more than anything else which made her flash her torch beam around. Only after she had established that there were no bats still in here did she realise that nothing else seemed to be either. Nothing and no one. Out she came, and crossed to the next cave.

The second cave was much bigger and very much deeper. She stepped over the threshold without having to stoop and was pleased to discover that there was nothing semi-liquid on the floor beneath her feet. And yet there was a strong, distinctive smell in here. Something which reminded her quite forcefully of childhood visits to zoos. There came a strange, hissing, stirring sound from deep within the cave and Robin, adrenaline flooding her system, pointed her torch straight in there. A section of the rear wall seemed to be sliding down, a pile of sandy shale slipping down onto the floor, with something almost as big as a bear behind it. Robin focused her torch on the threatening movement and brought the Smith and Wesson up as well, putting the red dot exactly in the centre of her torch beam as though the circle of light was a target. The wall settled into a great pile of dust and the threatening loom behind it pushed forward with terrible purpose towards her. She tightened her finger on the trigger.

The cat came with a terrible roar from the left, from somewhere even deeper in the cave. Such was the power and unexpected ferocity of its charge that Robin whipped the gun and torch beam towards it, both moving exactly together as she had been taught. Her finger closed on the trigger and three swift shots spat in and down, making fountains of sparks like fireworks across the floor. The sound and the light turned the cat and, instead of throwing itself at her, it raced straight past her and out of the cavern mouth as though it, too, was terrified of the great bear-like thing still smashing its way outwards from the back of the cave. Robin swung back but was too late. The monster from the back of the cavern hit her in a kind of rugby tackle, wrapping long arms round her waist and thrusting its head with bruising force straight into the pit of her stomach. The light went one way and the gun went another. All too human arms tightened with back-breaking force round her as she fell. The flare of agony as her battered bottom hit the unforgiving rock cleared her mind and she changed the gasp of discomfort into a bellow. 'Mickey!'

His weight came upon her. One of his arms tore loose and swung back, catching the moonlight. Automatically she reached up for it and caught it as it swung down in a wild haymaker towards her head. 'Mickey! Stop! It's me! Robin Mariner!'

The power seemed to go out of the blow then and she flipped her hips, throwing him over and rolling her own lithe weight onto his chest, holding him down until he could see her in the moonlight.

'It is you,' he gasped. 'I couldn't see. Flashlight in my eyes. Who had the laser sight?'

'I've got it now,' came a deep, throaty growl from just outside the cave mouth. 'So why don't you both just sit still until I work out what is going on here.'

A torch beam shone down past Robin onto Mickey's dusty face. Robin looked up and saw Conception standing on the scree a little way below. She was wearing her boots. That was all. She carried the Smith and Wesson as though modelling it for an Armani ad. God, thought Robin. I hate this woman.

Moving very slowly, she climbed off Mickey's chest and let him begin to pick himself up.

'Why, Captain Mariner,' cooed Conception. 'I thought you were married. And Major Vargas!' Was there a hint of genuine regret in her voice? Just a tincture of hurt? 'I thought you were *my* beau!'

Mickey made a gasping sound and, remembering Kramer's wise words about walking away if you want to be followed, Robin got ready to elbow him in the ribs if he said anything too slavishly adoring and undermined the very positive effect the adventure seemed to be having on Conception. But she needn't have worried. The sight of Conception standing naked in the moonlight like that apparently left him far beyond the power of coherent speech.

All in all, Robin the matchmaker was so satisfied with the way things had gone that she did not even deign to offer a defence of her own position – and honour. Side by side with the hypnotised Mickey, she followed Conception back down to the pool to pick up the Mexican woman's clothes. Then the three of them went back to camp. Robin's mind was so full of the events and relationships immediately around her that she handed the gun back to Kramer without a second thought and never really speculated about why he had asked her to go after Mickey when he, Kramer, had appeared on the point of going himself.

Much later, well after moon-set, the bobcat Robin and Mickey had disturbed crept carefully back into her nest in the cave. She was heavy with kittens and would not willingly give up such a snug, safe hideaway. Her mate, out hunting the desert rim above, would be back with the dawn to feed and groom her. In the meantime, she sniffed at the new pile of rubble lying at the mouth of a newly opened if ancient tunnel joining the back of her cave with the one that the bats used. She wrinkled her nose and snarled quietly at the stench flowing along it. Then she tidied up the area she had taken for her own, being especially careful with the bed she was planning to have her litter on. It was a bed made from old rags of ancient-looking cloth, mixed in with clear plastic sheeting, much more recent in origin. And in the seams of the sheeting lay one or two bright crystals, almost like salt, thankfully inaccessible to the bobcat's tongue or the tongues of the kittens she would have in a few days' time, just as the good ship *Colorado* was due to be decommissioned more than five hundred kilometres to the south of here.

Chapter Eight

Richard finally lost patience. In all his work, as ship's officer, captain, businessman, UN representative and CEO, he had unvaryingly found that loss of patience, any loss of control, was a weakness. Anger and panic were close bedfellows in his book, and only drunkenness on duty stood higher on his list of cardinal sins.

When Richard rose, it was with every intention of getting a firm grip on things and sorting them out one way or another. As he shaved he reviewed his situation, and laid his plans. He still had not heard from Charles Lee. But then, his laptop was not working properly. Under normal circumstances he would have simply given it to the hotel's people to fix but there was a lot of sensitive stuff on the hard drive, and what was wrong with it still had the power to raise a blush on his lean cheeks. Buying a new one solved little either, for he needed a series of programmes installed on it so that he could use it properly at once, but he did not know exactly what those programmes were. An old-fashioned phone call to Charles Lee had raised only his answering service but the last thing on the message Richard had left was an order for a replacement machine to be programmed and couriered out to him as quickly as possible. Federal Express would get it to him overnight, he knew, but he had no idea how long it would take to get it programmed. In the meantime he was on his own and playing it by ear.

Aldo Cagliari had said he had something important to show him today. Either it was a blinding success or his foot was coming down hard. As far as Richard was concerned, if the Americans wanted to deal with him, fine. If they were going to be swayed by Cagliari, then he was picking up his ball and playing in another park. There were many routes worldwide which would beg him to bring his SuperCats.

Having come to this point in his deliberations, Richard towelled his face dry and went to his wardrobe. He had no idea what he and Aldo would be up to today and so he chose a lightweight but robust set of khaki drills which Gieves and Hawkes – perhaps alone in this new-fangled age – were willing to produce to his specifications. Those specifications were almost identical to the specifications his grandfather had given them on his way to serve on the North-West Frontier soon after the end of the First World War.

Shaved and dressed, looking faintly military and strikingly old-fashioned, as though just about to settle a solar topi on his head and explore dark regions of central Africa, Richard checked with the desk. No messages, faxes or voice-mail. His lips thinned. He shook his head. He glanced around the room and went down to his breakfast meeting.

Richard's breakfast meeting today was with Aldo Cagliari alone. Aldo was waiting for him almost dancing with excitement, dressed in a kind of bush jacket, open-necked shirt, jeans and boots. Whatever was planned did not include a formal business meeting, then, thought Richard. He rather hoped it was going to include a long look round the Cagliari Mach 1.

They ate quickly and left the hotel, Aldo almost aglow, clearly bursting to show him something but childishly unwilling to reveal his surprise too early. When the parking attendant brought a comfortable limousine, Richard assumed that they must be driving over to see something within or just outside the city bounds, but Aldo swung the big car due east and out onto the interstate heading for the Hoover Dam and Lake Mead, nearly fifty kilometres away.

'Couldn't we have taken a helicopter?' asked Richard. It would take them the better part of an hour each way at this rate. That threatened to be a waste of time, unless they could do some serious work in the interim.

'The mugger took my gold card too,' said Aldo blithely. 'You may be able to fall back on big bucks with your company cards gone astray, but I don't have that luxury. Anyway, it's a nice ride out and we'll have lots to talk about on the way back, I'm sure.'

Richard sat back, his lips thin, and watched the magnificent desert unfurl. It brought back memories of his years in the Middle East, but even the greatest of the deserts round the Gulf did not have the sheer scale of this place. And, he thought, relaxing a little, not many of the cars had air-conditioning this efficient either.

'This had better be good, Aldo,' he said, almost without thinking; certainly without calculation. 'I'm strapped for time here and you're slowing things down. I need to get these schedules and outline plans agreed and you're screwing the process up. We either climb into bed together by the end of the day, everything cut and dried and plans in place between us, lawyers briefed, or I'm walking. Walking on you for certain, and warning the federal and state people that I'm leaving their table as well if you're still seated there at breakfast tomorrow.'

There was a little silence then Aldo said, 'That's fair enough. But what I got to show you today should just blow your socks off!'

'As long as it isn't Jody in a swimsuit.'

'Hey! Legitimate business ploy, Richard. Creature comforts and all. And, if you're still in the game, your socks aren't the only thing old Jody'll bl—'

'Thanks, Aldo, I get the picture. But I came here to do business, not to get laid.'

'There's a difference? What else is power for? The best aphrodisiac bar none, the biggest rush after coke and the best pull after cash money.'

'Aldo,' said Richard, 'you should run for President.'

'Too much responsibility. Flatten that country. Assassinate that dictator. Balance that budget. Hell, I couldn't even be happy running a family – all that negotiating, arguing, settling for second best. 'Sides, no woman ever looked at me just the way I liked. 'Cept maybe for cash. Naw. President of my own little company's enough for me.'

'As long as the company's successful. Nobody gets their jollies from being the captain of the *Titanic*.'

'I don't know, Richard. I bet that old boy got his rocks off every second of every day until she went belly up under him. I'll bet the ride was so good, it was almost worth what happened in the end. Hell, once he'd been there at the captain's table with the Rothschilds and the Vanderbilts or whoever, what did he have to look forward to anyway? Cottage in Cornwall?'

Richard thought about it. 'I'm not sure about the logic of that. You can't judge everything by the ride rather than the outcome. Otherwise it would have been good to be Adolf Hitler . . .'

'From thirty-five up until forty-five, probably the best thing in the world. Go anywhere, do anything. No limits. No barriers. Come on, Richard, be honest here. Isn't there a little of that in you too? OK, maybe not old Adolf, but Captain Morgan, maybe, perhaps even Captain Kidd? Long John Silver, then. Wouldn't you just love to go off pirating sometimes? No ties, no responsibilities? No board of directors to answer to? No shareholders tying your hands behind your back? No petty-minded bureaucrats with their pettifogging bits of red tape all over? Don't you just burn to cut loose sometimes and go off? Do your own thing? Be your own man? No limits? No laws? No one to answer to? Even I can remember when business could be like that.

Twenty-four-hour-a-day hard-on. You wanted it, you went out and fought for it. Took it – or made something that would take it for you. Nowhere you couldn't go; no place you couldn't conquer. Like I imagine big-game hunting must have been before the guilt set in. For those guys like Hemingway, you know? When catching something or hunting something and shooting something wasn't just desecrating the environment but the measure of what sort of a man you were, what sort of respect you held for the things you killed in order to show how much of a man you were! I remember when business was like that even for me. God, it used to be so good!'

'I was wrong, Aldo. You shouldn't be a president, you should be a Caesar. Caligula by the sound of it. Or Nero.'

'When you're right, you're right, Richard. The old Italian blood shows up every time. Caligula Cagliari. Got a hell of a ring to it.'

Richard gave a bark of laughter. 'That it has. But watch out for the Praetorian Guard.'

As Richard spoke, a big Mac truck pulled off a small road and settled in behind them. They topped a low rise and Lake Mead lay shimmering like blue silk in front of them. Aldo swung the limo off the major blacktop and onto a small local road which followed the rim of the lake round to the north. The truck followed them. After another fifteen minutes or so the road they were taking began to settle, swooping down a series of slopes as the cliff edges fell back, until Aldo pulled to a stop at the back of a shallow bay. The big truck parked in a cloud of dust just beside them.

Both vehicles had swung round at the last moment so that their backs were to the water. This made no real difference to the limo, but was important to its companion, as Richard discovered when he climbed out into the fearsome desert heat.

The back of the big truck had swung open and a ramp was sliding down apparently of its own volition into the restless shallows. Two men in white overalls moved about in the gloom of the truck's interior and Aldo worked alongside them. When Richard tensed himself to climb up and lend a hand, however, Aldo called down excitedly, 'No, Richard, just you wait there a while. I want you to see this little beauty in all her glory all at once. Maximum impact!'

With the most ridiculous feeling that Aldo was still going to produce Jody, stark naked on some kind of platter, Richard stepped back. In reality, of course, he was expecting some kind of working model of the Cagliari Mach 1. The Mac truck was big, but Richard's reading of the specifications Aldo had shown him made it clear that not even a half-size mock-up would have fitted in the big container at the back.

At least Aldo didn't make Richard close his eyes. Instead, the big Italian and two mechanics rolled out, not the Cagliari Mach 1 but the neatest and prettiest little two-man vessel Richard had ever seen. She sat low and demure on a small platform, skirts spread out and black rubberised sections flat, surrounded by tanks of gas and pressurised air. She was not much longer than a Volkswagen Beetle but she was open, with a lengthways motorcycle seat down the middle, controls and windscreen in front, bulk of power plant behind. Her skirts, sections and interior were gleaming, leathery black; her body was a bright cherry red and shone like a showroom automobile. Or, more precisely, like a brand new Harley Davidson waiting to be sold.

'My God, Aldo, what is this little beauty?'

'She is something, isn't she?' beamed Aldo, rolling her down the ramp until she was held by a catch just clear of the water. 'She's called the AC2 at the moment, but I'll tell you what, she's so pretty I'll name her after the prettiest little lady in your life . . .'

'The *Robin*?' said Richard, his mind simply dazed by her.

'Well, I was thinking of the *Jody*,' said Aldo, his grin fading a little. 'But I guess the *Robin* fits her pretty good. Can't get one over on you old married men, eh? You want to hazard a guess what she is, Richard?'

Richard sucked in a long breath of hot desert air, little cooled by the rapidly evaporating lake beside him. 'I've heard of them, but I've never seen one this small.' He walked judiciously round her, noting the black-throated nozzles protruding from the back at shoulder height with a down-pointing one running into a duct like a spinal column in between. He could not remember seeing one powered quite like this before, but he could only think of one vehicle which needed forward and upward thrust both at the same time. 'I'm more used to hovercraft being designed to seat forty – four hundred, even. This sits two?'

'Two and some cargo. Nine cubic metres of cargo. And she's more than a hovercraft. Look.' Aldo attached a nozzle from one of the tanks of pressurised gas on the platform and inflated the black rubber sections until she sat up neatly like the little sister of the inflatable that Robin had gone downstream in. Then Aldo attached the other gas tanks to the after section, beside the power plant. Immediately there came a low, controlled *whoosh* of power and sound. *Robin* sat up higher still, as eager to be off as a bird dog. Only the lines attaching her to the little platform held her in place.

Aldo raised his voice to carry over the sound of the engine. 'Most of these use turbines. I use modified jets. More lift. More power. We

79

can stand here looking at equipment and talking about specifications all day, but there's really only one way to get to know a machine like this, Richard. And you know that as well as I do.' He paused for one beat. 'Want to take her out for a ride?'

The pair of them stripped down to boxer shorts then kitted up in wet suits, life jackets and hard hats. The windscreen was low and raked so they needed goggles as well; but that, apparently, was all. As soon as they were ready, they climbed in, Aldo in front and Richard a very comfortable pillion. They strapped themselves in securely – though Richard noticed the quick-release discs and what looked like an automatic trip as well. Clearly no one was going down with this little ship if anything went wrong. Aldo raised his hand and the lines were slipped. Exactly like the motorcycle she so strongly resembled, *Robin* roared off across the little bay.

Richard craned round Aldo to see his hands on a pair of crossbars which seemed to control everything, though he noticed Aldo's feet were busy too. At their junction, just where it would have been placed on a bike, stood the speedo. Aldo pushed the throttle up by rolling his right hand forward. Richard saw the red hand on the speedo leap upwards, then he was crouching back into Aldo's wind shadow as the still air over Lake Mead tried to tear him off the little vessel and chuck him back into her wake.

Robin was steady as a rock, and she needed to be, for they were roaring across the water at a good speed. Aldo turned the handlebars and the bright little craft swept round to her starboard in a tight loop. She did the same to port, skimming at breathtaking speed across the water. After twenty minutes or so of hot-dogging, Aldo swung her back into the bay and let her roar up off the water onto the slope of the beach. The mechanics saw him coming and took shelter from the cloud of river sand in the cabin of their truck as Aldo guided *Robin* across the shoreline and beyond. The road at the back of the bay was the one they had followed in and it sloped up across the cliff face at more than thirty degrees from the horizontal. Aldo beefed up the revs some more and the game little craft skipped upwards with no trouble at all. At the crest of the rise, Aldo turned her and let her slide back down again. As she gathered speed, a combination of gravity and momentum adding to her frictionless air ride, Aldo hit a button Richard could not quite make out, and the jets immediately behind his head whined with a different note as *Robin* settled to a demure glide safely down to the lakeside and onto the little platform.

Richard was breathless. Aldo held up his hand. 'Demo part one,' he said loudly, still half deafened from the wind thunder and jet noise of their ride. 'You get to do part two yourself.'

After a short crash course in the major controls, Richard took the front seat and spent the next half-hour tooling about Lake Mead. He could not remember simple excitement like it since he took his first command. Or, reaching further back but coming closer, he suspected, since he drove his first E-type Jaguar.

His mind, sidetracked from the business which had brought him here, was full of plans to make Aldo an offer he couldn't refuse, to get these amazing little leisure craft on the Heritage Mariner books alongside the amazingly successful *Katapult* series of multihulls. But Aldo suddenly lost the open enthusiasm of his look and went all dark and cunning on Richard. 'Demo part three,' he said. 'And this is maybe where we should have called her *Jody* after all. 'Cause if this doesn't blow you away, nothing will.'

Out across the lake they sped again, with Richard back in the pillion seat. This time there was no hot-dogging. Aldo steered *Robin* with care and clear purpose. Out of the secluded little bay she came and down the gorge between the steepening cliff faces towards the dam. Just when Richard was beginning to imagine that they were going to sail right up to the great curve of the edifice itself, they swung hard right. 'Almost missed the sucker,' Aldo sang out. There in the canyon wall ahead of them stood a gate – clearly a tunnel mouth. The water lapped at its lower edge. As they approached it, Richard looked down and saw the curving walled sides of a sluice rising up through the clear water to meet the foot of the doorway. Above the sunken sluice, knocking at the bottom of the door, sat a mess of flotsam – mostly long wooden poles, as though a couple of trees had been washed into the river and broken up by the current further upstream. The perky little vessel skimmed across them as easily as she sailed over everything else, and so Aldo brought her right up to the door. What was unusual about the doorway, other than that it was set in a red sandstone cliff like something out of a fairytale, was that it was open. No bars. No doors or watergates. Nothing.

Aldo cut speed and *Robin*'s skirts deflated. Settling on her fat rubberised air bags, she drifted. 'Part of the reclamation project,' Aldo bellowed. 'Bottoms of the lakes are silting up. Some of the sluices are at risk. Increased danger of flooding because of the change in weather patterns. This is the answer. There's an emergency chute on either side of every dam. Computer controlled, but the computers are down at the moment. Big tunnels, angled at about forty degrees, designed to take big flows of water out of the lakes at the back here and put them straight into the rivers down below without putting added pressure on the dams themselves. There's a set like this in place on every system between here and the Sea of Cortez.'

Richard was about to say 'So what?' when Aldo gunned the jets and they were up and away once more. Over the doorsill they went, into a huge concrete room floored with water. *Robin* skimmed across it into the gloom of its recesses. Here the tunnel Aldo had described opened out. Before Richard could even ask what on earth he thought he was up to, Aldo drove *Robin* across a second sill and they were off down the black waterslide. Aldo hit a button as they fell and a bright headlight beam cut the featureless darkness in front of them. It showed a falling slope, a little wider than *Robin* herself, walled with concrete but floored again with the merest skim of black water down which they rode as though it was oil or black ice. The whole situation reminded Richard ridiculously of looking down an immensely long escalator tunnel – as though there was some new line on the London Underground constructed just a level or two above Hell.

The timbre of the jets behind Richard's head changed again and, as they had down the road in from the desert, they rode demurely to the bottom. Such was the visual boredom of watching the featureless walls that Richard found himself counting the dark emergency light fittings in the ceiling, and noting the way they were reflected by lateral cracks and fissures in the floor, as though the tunnel below that lively skim of water was made of flagstones. He counted nearly one hundred flagstones before they reached the bottom. Here again there was a huge room. Aldo slowed their progress and switched off the light. With a great deal more care coming out down here than he had exercised going in up in Lake Mead, Aldo slipped the trusty little vessel out onto the roaring current of the Colorado, just upstream from the point the first big wave from the sluicegates had hit Robin and her companions nearly three days earlier. At first it did not register with the stunned Richard how the little red vessel took no note at all of the river's bustling downward surge but skimmed across it with the easy grace of a swallow come down to drink.

'What on earth was the point of that, Aldo?' Richard bellowed, more confused than angry.

'That's only the first part of the ride,' called Aldo in reply. 'Let's take her home, shall we?'

The implication of what Aldo was saying hit Richard then. He opened his mouth to speak but the roar of the jets drowned his words. *Robin* whipped across the river's red flood and dived into the massive sluice room once again. Aldo hit the light and the throttle at the same time and the game little vessel screamed inwards then whirled and soared upwards. For Richard, at least, this was a very different proposition from the downward journey. That had been unique, but by all the laws which he served as a mariner, this was simply impossible. Here was a vessel which he automatically categorised as a water-borne vessel, sailing uphill. Not just up the front of a wave like a yacht with the wind under her skirts or a vessel at full ahead. This little boat was sailing up a more than thirty-degree incline against a river of running water coming counter to her. A shallow river, perhaps, but a river nevertheless. No locks needed, no control of the flow, no gates, no nothing. Open the throttle and off you go, up any watercourse of any steepness up to the limit, he assumed, of an actual waterfall. He remembered the big hovercraft he had heard of exploring the upper reaches of the Amazon. He remembered those he had used to move up and down the River Mau in Africa. They would never have been able to handle anything like this. This was in another league altogether.

A trembling in the air brought Richard out of his reverie. It was too deep and powerful to be called a sound – they were like mice caught in the bass pipe of an organ. Then the wind all around them was in sudden, rushing motion and *Robin*'s steady upward progress began to falter a little. Aldo gave her more throttle with a confidence which assured Richard that he must have a good deal more power to spare, and the black seat kicked Richard in the butt as she leaped on upwards. But the trembling continued to gather and attained the status of sound. It was a roaring, tearing, gushing sound and both men knew what it meant. The open sluice was performing the function for which it had been designed and there was a flood of water coming down out of the dark towards them. Richard remembered the wood flotsam immediately outside the doorway and he frowned. He saw Aldo's head twitching from side to side and followed the logic of his thoughts with ready empathy. There was no room to turn. To slam the jets into reverse might pull them back down in time – or it might not. In any case they would be caught by the wave and held by it either here or down on the river. That could only be disastrous.

On the other hand, if they faced a slope of water, not an outright wall, then *Robin* might be cajoled into riding up it, and, as her queenly disregard of the Colorado's current below had demonstrated, once she had level water under her she would skim on upwards as happily as ever. Then it would just be the light fitments on their hard hats they would have to worry about.

They had less than a second for anything like thought or calculation from the time the wave came into the headlight beam and the time it hit *Robin*. Both men acted by instinct and it was providential that their instincts worked in tandem. Aldo gave her all the power at his command and crouched low, like a biker over the handlebars. Richard, his eyes taking in the sharp wooden spears stabbing outwards from the great white wave bearing down on them, crouched upwards, hands ready to knock what he could aside and away.

When the wave hit, *Robin* staggered backwards helplessly and, in spite of the screaming jets which were trying to power her upwards, she began to surf back down. The jets held her just a little, however, so that the wild wash of water came under her, then up from sides and front and very nearly over her. Debris hit Richard in the head, arms and torso – fortunately none of it too sharp. Most powerfully, a long solid staff of wood came low over Aldo's head and slammed across Richard's short ribs. More by reaction than instinct he caught it. Some deep-buried part of his subconscious recognised what he held and suggested a use for it. Never would he remember reasoning or even thinking. He whirled, taking the stout staff over his head, scraping the skin from his knuckles against the concrete roof, and he spun the staff like an ancient steering board down over the back of the slipping vessel. It was many a long year since he had gone punting on the River Cam but the old skills had not deserted him. The pole, held upright in his iron grip, slammed down between the pairs of jets and settled against the power plant's solid spine. He felt the foot of the pole grating along the tunnel floor and thought that they were lost. Then he felt it bed in one of the lateral fissures he had been counting on the way down here, and wedge between two slabs. He held on like grim death, feeling his shoulders begin to tear and his safety harness start to rip asunder. But *Robin* stopped her backward slide. Her head slammed round and bounced against the wall on the right. But there was nowhere else for the game little vessel to go. She was trapped. Held. And, when the first great surge was past, there was even a slope along its foaming back down which she could be launched again.

As battered, shaken but unbowed as their vessel, the two men arrived back at the beach by the big Mac truck. The beach was suddenly very much smaller. The truck had been moved well forward and as the two mechanics pulled *Robin* out of the water onto the little platform, Richard noticed that the rear tyres of the limousine were now mere centimetres shy of the new tide line. Stripping off the battered wet suit, he looked away up Lake Mead and found himself frowning.

84

The blue-silk sheen he had noticed this morning was gone. It was as though the sky had turned unexpectedly stormy; he looked up automatically as he began to pull his clothes on, but the cerulean blue remained untroubled. There was something in the water, then. Something the new water which had tried to kill them had brought. Richard remembered a time when he had stood in the heart of an African jungle looking across the water in a dam. Those waters, too, had been dark, seemingly out of place in their lush, colourful surroundings. And that darkness had prefigured a great deal of death and destruction. Lacing up his suede-topped desert boots with the crepe soles, he found himself hoping fervently that these strange new waters prefigured nothing more sinister than a storm in the Upper Basin.

Robin had been packed away. Aldo Cagliari, still in his wet suit, was standing looking up at the taciturn mechanic in the truck's passenger seat. 'Mr Alighieri's not going to like this,' the man was saying quietly. 'Good as new, you said.'

'It was an accident. I couldn't help it. She'll be fine. Tell him I'll come by.'

'OK,' said the mechanic. 'But he ain't going to be pleased is all I'm saying.'

The truck fired up. Pulled away.

'What was all that about?' Richard asked as Aldo stripped off the wet suit.

'We scratched her up a bit. The guy who lent her to me'll not be pleased.'

'Lent her to you? I thought she was yours.'

'She is mine. I conceived her, designed her and built her. I wanted to show her to someone like you so we could discuss production. She's the prototype but she'd be easy to duplicate. Cheap to manufacture . . .'

'But you no longer own her.'

'Got in debt. Had to sell her.'

Richard crossed to the limo and leaned against it, looking away across the lake. From the northernmost end of the water, a series of charcoal loops were slowly widening across the slate-grey surface. 'We'll talk in the limo, Aldo; we have a lot of talking to do. But those are big waves and they're coming our way. If we don't move now, you'll lose your hire car on top of everything else.'

Chapter Nine

Richard settled back in the passenger seat of the limo in a cool pretence of ease as the darkening red of the afternoon desert unfurled, and took the bull by the horns. 'Aldo,' he said. 'Stop me if I go wrong, and if I insult you then I apologise. I'm just talking through impressions and following a line of thought here. What you have in *Robin*, or rather the AC2 since it's not yours to name, is a first-rate little pleasure craft. Salt-water or fresh; sea, lake or river. A beauty. All you're really interested in, however, is that she can carry nine cubic metres of cargo up a thirty-degree incline along unguarded drainage channels past every dam on the Colorado. Nine cubic metres is not a lot, so you have to be thinking contraband. Past the dams in secret means that you are interested in following the river, so your real interest in the prettiest little pleasure craft in ages is that she can smuggle stuff up from Mexico. That's like fathering an angel and trying to make her a whore. Only someone desperate would do that. You've sold her, so you're desperate for cash. You're an able inventor if you're telling the truth – and the AC2 and the Cagliari Mach 1 are your own work. You should be rich – at least independent. But you're not. You're in so much trouble that you're having to sell people your prototypes in spite of the fact that they're the only real chance you have of raising serious money and getting back into the game. So you're a gifted inventor but not a gifted businessman. That brings us to *us*, so to speak. I assume the Cagliari Mach 1 is either in prototype, pawned, or still on the drawing board seeking backers. I assume the former, because you have well-established contacts at federal and state level where I am working so you've been down these roads before, and you could only have got this far with a genuine product, tested and approved by the authorities. So what you're looking for is some way to use me to scare up the finance you need to get you back on track.'

'That pretty much covers it, I guess,' said Aldo quietly. Clever guy, this Englishman, he thought, and so 'jolly decent' – probably too jolly decent to imagine how desperate things are and how much

I'm willing to risk in order to get back up on my feet, let alone on top. He probably has no idea, that the mugging was a set-up, that the hotel maid is in my pocket; that this could become a very dirty game indeed.

Aldo's face gave nothing away, and neither did Richard's as he drew his conclusions. Unless Aldo or his contacts had found a source of small but incredibly valuable artefacts or jewels, he was thinking of smuggling drugs. And that fact made him and his associates very dangerous.

'Do you have any family, Aldo?' he asked. 'Is there anyone beyond yourself that you're doing all of this for?'

'Nah. I wasn't shooting you a line this morning. There's never been anyone for me. No wife or kids. Prefer it that way.'

'Parents?'

'Dead and gone ten years and more.'

'Brothers and sisters?'

'Only child. Like I said. Might as well be doing it for Jody. Not that I could afford her for long. She is one expensive item. Came in a good deal with Jo, though. They like working together.'

'This is a very strange conversation, Aldo.'

'Not really. Just two guys shooting the breeze, you know? I know where you stand. You know where I stand, pretty much. We work well together in tight corners, seems to me, but we sure as hell aren't going to do business now, are we?'

'No, we're not.'

'We'll just have to see how it goes with the rest of the boys around the breakfast table then. But I know pretty well what they'll say, don't I? On the one hand they've got some straight up and down limey business guy with millions behind him. Pounds sterling. Business standing from here to Honolulu—'

'Hong Kong.'

'Hong Kong then. On the other hand they're got a flat broke down-and-out from some lakeside ghost town west of Chicago no one ever heard of, with more debts than brain cells and a couple of busted dreams. Go on, Mr Sherlock Holmes. Give it your best shot! Which one d'you think they're going to choose?'

'You brought us head to head over this, Aldo, not me. And we're only head to head over the breakfast table, as you said. You leave me the plans of the Cagliari Mach 1 and a business card, I'll get my people to look at it. You give me any part of the AC2 and my lawyers will be onto your lawyers before sunset, and my financial people will be in touch with yours tomorrow.'

'Tomorrow'll be too late,' said Aldo, apparently coming to a decision. He lifted his foot off the gas and the big limousine began to slow. 'And your lawyers need to speak to Mr Alighieri's lawyers anyway. Not, I suspect, that they would.'

'I know some pretty dirty lawyers,' said Richard.

'Even the dirtiest of your people would be worried about the mess on their pinstripes after they tangled with Mr Alighieri. As for me, I'm in so deep not even the sweet little ass of the AC2 can pull me out again.'

The car was at a stop now on the sandy gravel beside the freeway. There was nothing but desert as far as the eye could see. Aldo leaned forward and popped the glove compartment. Richard got a flash of a gun in the depths of it but he never knew which one of them Aldo was thinking of using it on. He tensed himself to slam the compartment door on Aldo's hand if he reached for the weapon, but at that moment a helicopter dropped out of the sky onto the sand immediately in front of them. A wash of red grit swept up over the limo's bonnet and broke against the windscreen like a wave. Richard punched the door and was out, striding through the sandstorm. A tall figure stooped below ghostly rotors and approached him, straightening as he came. When he straightened, even Richard found himself looking up.

'Hell, Richard,' said C.J. Martyr. 'You're a hard, hard man to find.'

Richard took his old friend forcefully by the elbow and turned him. 'There's been a lot going on,' he said. 'Let's talk about it in the chopper, though. I don't feel too safe out here.'

He did not, in fact, lose that strange itching sensation between his shoulder blades until he was safely strapped in and they were a couple of hundred metres in the air.

'Why are you here, C.J.?' asked Richard as they settled into level flight over the red desert. 'Not that I'm not glad to see you, but . . .'

'But you just don't need babysitting, right? I know it's a long time since you needed anyone to wipe your nose for you, Richard, but to tell the truth, Charles Lee in London was getting a mite worried about the way things seemed to be shaping up out here. At least this is my turf. I know the form.'

'Fair enough, but I still think . . .'

'And this guy Aldo Cagliari may be a good deal worse than he seems to be on the surface. His companies are in debt way beyond any legal hope of recovery. He's done time for corporate fraud. He's in personal hock to the local loan sharks and all that seems to be keeping him alive is that he's also in tight with the Mafia and even you do not want an army of goodfellas and wiseguys coming after you.'

'I can see that. And I reckon he's only after me because I represent either the last hope of investment in one or two of his most promising projects or – failing that – because I looked like a good mark for bribery or blackmail to him. I've as good as told him so, though, so I'll be surprised if we see him again.'

'You told him all this?' C.J. swung round to observe his friend with something akin to awe. 'My God, Richard. We were lucky to find you alive!'

'You were lucky to find me at all,' said Richard suddenly struck. 'How did you pull that little miracle off, C.J.?'

'Not me. It was the car-hire people and a little good fortune. Cagliari paid with a cheque – something about his cards being stolen – but in this age of electrical cash, the people at Alamo found that a little strange and checked up on him. The cheque was all set to bounce, apparently, so they'd activated their tracker on the car in case it was being stolen and were on the point of alerting the local law when I lucked into the situation. I settled the account in return for the car's location then I grabbed a chopper and came out after you.'

'OK. Thanks. My next meeting is scheduled for the morning and I want to go in with all guns blazing so I can blow Aldo out of the water if he's still around. We take no prisoners from here on in, least of all Aldo. Did you bring any back-up of your own?'

'Only the smartest corporate lawyer on Wall Street.'

'That'll do nicely. Now, let's get our game plan straight . . .'

'As Wyatt Earp said, on his way to the OK Corral.'

At eight o'clock precisely the next morning, Richard put his bulging briefcase on the table gently so as not to slop the coffee over the doughnuts and the bagels. 'This is my American representative Mr C.J. Martyr, CEO of Heritage New York. With him is Ms Conway of Marshall, Cooper, Conway of Wall Street, our lawyers.'

'We are all familiar with Mr Martyr and Ms Conway, by reputation at least,' said Killigan accommodatingly.

'I do not see Mr Cagliari. We are here to tell you that either he is out or we are out.'

'He is out, Captain Mariner. Would you all please take a seat. You will see that there are sufficient chairs.'

'And enough doughnuts. How thoughtful,' said Ms Conway, slipping her svelte, designer-attired person into the nearest empty chair.

'Before we begin,' said Killigan with quiet authority, 'is there any air that needs clearing here? After Mr Cagliari's departure?'

'I have no complaints to bring before this forum,' said Richard, 'though I have been advised of the business and legal necessity of referring certain matters to certain authorities in due course.' Both C.J. and Cathy Conway nodded. Richard continued smoothly, like a medieval monarch passing on the judgement of his court, 'But that is, I am further advised, between those authorities, Mr Cagliari and myself.' He leaned forward and grinned wolfishly, his eyes sparkling with excitement. 'We came here to do a deal, gentlemen. OK. Let's do a deal.'

Aldo Cagliari had gone to Mr Alighieri's. He had nowhere else to go. The hired limo sat in the broad sweep of drive before Alighieri's ranch-style Vegas home, discreetly tucked well away from the road which was itself behind high security gates and private. Mr Alighieri was a man who, like Aldo, tended to see power as something which was there primarily to bring him the pleasures of the flesh, but he was also a man of immense self-discipline; unlike his younger associate, he balanced indulgence with strict self-control. His body, heading for seventy more swiftly than he cared to calculate, would have flattered a fifty-year-old. His muscles were firm, his step springy. He did not look foolishly out of place in tennis whites and trainers. His tan, beneath the thick white hair, made him look like a movie star.

Mr Alighieri led the quiescent, deflated Aldo through the airy brightness of his home, past the foot of a curling staircase at whose head stood his latest mistress, a rising pop star scarcely out of her teens. Through the servants' quarters they went, where his English butler was overseeing the polishing of the Mappin and Webb silver tea service. They descended into his cellar where his stillsman stood, considering whether there was enough Château Lafitte '69 to accompany tonight's repast. They passed the kitchen where Chef could not quite make up his mind between the quail and the guinea fowl and stood stroking the breasts of each – not unlike the master's last encounter with the pop star upstairs. Then they exited through the back and went out to the garage.

In the centre of the garage stood the two mechanics, one on each side of the battered AC2 which Mr Alighieri called *Beatrice* after his wife in New York. Her naming was a temporary affair, however, for he had further plans for the little red plaything. Plans that Aldo had put at risk.

On *Beatrice*'s full front skirt there was a long, pale scratch. To the right there was a square of abrasion. On the metal of her body's prow was a sizeable dent. Along both red sides there were long scratches and down the back, between the jets, there was a long indentation where the pole in Richard's hands had held her firm. 'As good as new you said,' purred Mr Alighieri. 'You'd show her off to this milch cow, scare up some money, and bring her back without a scratch.'

'I'll fix her up for you, Mr Alighieri. No one'll know. I swear,' promised Aldo, moved to some animation by physical fear.

'I've got Mutt and Jeff here to fix her up,' spat Alighieri. 'But it's *her* birthday tomorrow and this is what she wants.' On the word 'her', he glanced back at the house. 'It's what she wants and you scratched it. I warned you and you didn't listen, so I've been looking for some way to make my message clear to you. If you had a wife or a daughter I'd do this to her. But you don't. If you had any feeling for yourself I'd do it to you, but the speed you shovel nose candy into your stupid head shows you got no sense and no respect for yourself either. So I looked around. And this is what I found.' Mr Alighieri gestured as he spoke and two men moved forward out of the shadows. Between them, like an engine part, with her toes only just touching the concrete flooring, hung Jody.

'Mr Alighieri, she doesn't mean anything to me. She's just a tart I picked up to help me with some business. Hell, I haven't even had her to myself—'

'See, Aldo, the way I got it figured is this. These bits that stick out in front here, they got such an obvious parallel. See this where it's sort of cut here? What would that look like should it happen to a person? And that big graze there to the right . . .'

The next ten minutes were the longest of Aldo Cagliari's life. They made him wish that he had used the pistol on himself after Richard Mariner left the car. They were worse than cold turkey and he had not believed that to be possible. He was crying almost as wildly as the girl when at last they let him take her down and hold her, fainting, in his arms. She was a stranger to him, little more than an idle fantasy, and yet he felt he was solely to blame for her injuries. The knowledge did something to him. Something which made him lower, weaker than he had been before. Which was exactly what Alighieri had calculated. For when the lesson was over and the sobs began to die, he said, 'I'm pleased we came to this understanding here, because I've more I want to say.

'My men here, Giaccommo and Cesare, they'll look after your little friend for me. Tend her wounds and make her feel better. Not just for me but for you as well. Because I got this little job I want you to do for me, Aldo, and I want you to do it right. So every time you think of screwing up, you think of Jody here and what any dent in my schemes might do to her. Ten times worse than the scratches on *Beatrice* here.'

'I get the message, Mr Alighieri,' gabbled Aldo breathlessly. 'I get it loud and clear. What is it you want me to do for you?'

'I got a sweet little deal going down in Mexico, Aldo,' said Mr Alighieri, sweeping Aldo back into his orbit by throwing out his arm and hugging Aldo's shaking shoulders, man to man, as equals. 'I want you to go down and babysit it for me.'

'Of course, Mr Alighieri. Certainly, whatever you say. But why me?'

'You're already involved, Aldo. You already got contacts, reasons, *motivation*.'

Aldo looked over his shoulder automatically, to where the two goons were lifting up the pale but battered form of Jody.

'No!' said Mr Alighieri indulgently, like a schoolteacher addressing a promising student who had made a minor error. 'You got more motivation than your little fallen angel there. The milch cow you couldn't milk. The guy who screwed your plans, this Richard Mariner. He's somehow got himself mixed up in my little deal and, innocent though he is, word is he might be the kind of guy who could maybe do some damage. So I want you to take some cash and a list of contacts, both of which I will supply, and I want you to use that brilliant mind of yours to think up some excuse to follow him south of the border. He's heading onto a ship down there called *Colorado*, and I want you on board her to keep an eye on him for me. I'll give you some details of what's afoot, as they say, but let me tell you now that there's a little more coke aboard than the engines might need for *fuel*, catch my drift? And if it looks to you like Mariner's going to screw it up, I want you to kill the limey son of a bitch whether he's an innocent bystander or not. *Capisco*, Aldo?'

Aldo hesitated. Something within him revolted briefly. The bland assumption of this callous, self-indulgent, self-important little blood-sucker that a mixture of sadistic thuggery, helplessness and weakness would force him to follow Alighieri's whim simply sickened him. The Mafia don mistook simple sickness for calculation; for greed. He had used the stick. He tried a little carrot.

'Look,' he said reasonably. 'The ship represents a big investment to me and my people. We've paid *through the nose* for the extra cargo. You understand me? You can cut yourself in for enough of the product to blow your mind for life. Or you can go through to old age with the screams of this little tramp echoing through your nightmares. Not that you or she will *get* to old age. Now do you understand?'

In the silence which followed the question, Jody sobbed brokenly, the sound becoming distant as they carried her away. 'Yes, Mr Alighieri,' said Aldo. 'I certainly understand.'

Chapter Ten

The dark water Richard had seen in Lake Mead caught Robin and the *Pequod* on the run down to the Imperial Dam. They were weary and unprepared, having portaged over the Headgate Rock that morning and made it to the Palo Verde by the afternoon. Neither dam was a particularly enormous construction, but the effort of unpacking the *Pequod*, carrying their assigned loads and their designated section of the hull on narrow trails along the valley side, was an unwelcome alternative to paddling.

'I'd like to meet the guys who surveyed this route and said it'd be fine for an inflatable this size,' Mickey grunted bitterly on the way down round the Palo Verde. A hot wind rumbled up the valley into their faces. *Pequod* tried to take flight. Only the weight of their backpacks, it seemed, held them on the ground, and they stretched like guy ropes holding down a big top in a storm.

'It's do-able,' said Robin bracingly. 'I suppose they didn't say it would be easy.'

Mickey gave a bark of laughter. 'It takes a lot to slow you down, lady. You on Prozac all the time or something?'

Robin didn't dignify that with an answer.

Mickey's grim mood lightened somewhat when Conception changed her portage place and worked just in front of him. Her backpack was of a slightly different design to the others, sitting high on her shoulders and hips, with no low roll over her bottom. So every time the wind lifted the inflatable and Conception stretched elastically up with the rest, her uniform moulded itself enticingly to the fullness of her buttocks.

'Hey, Conception!' called Mickey, but there was no reply.

Robin smiled and shook her head. He was undoing all the good work they had performed rolling about in the bobcat's cave last night, she thought. Many more calls like that and Conception would return to her usual work area, confident that he was back in her thrall.

They came to a widening in the trail and Kramer called a halt. 'Hey, Mickey,' said Robin. 'Swap places with me.'

'Well . . .' he clearly meant 'Over my dead body' but was too much of a gentleman to say so.

'Oh, go on. You'll still be able to see the view. And I'll be able to look out across the valley too.'

Mickey gave in and Robin smiled to see Conception's fleeting frown. No more calling her name, though a certain amount more watching her ass, as the Americans said in another context entirely. And for Robin, there was the bonus of an uninterrupted view of the river below and the farmland spreading out from it in carefully irrigated sections beneath the shadow of the concrete-reinforced banks. It was near here, perhaps a day on down below the Imperial Dam, she thought, that the levees had broken in 1902 and the whole river had swung west along the Imperial Valley into the Salton Sea. From here it was possible to imagine how it had happened, and to see what work had gone into ensuring that it did not happen again. To her admittedly untutored eye, the Colorado looked as well-contained as the River Thames at the Embankment in her beloved London. Though she knew well how illusory that containment had been until the Thames Barrier was completed. She saw now as never before the practical implication of those long-ago geography lessons about alluvial flood plains and the way in which rivers heavy with silt laid down beds for themselves which slowly rose higher than the surrounding countryside. And if this was true here, where the mighty river was contained in concrete and controlled by dams, how much more would it be the case in three days' time when they would be paddling along the rushing river's surface high above the Mexican desert within sight of the Sea of Cortez?

It was strange to stand on the concrete of the Palo Verde Dam's sluices and lower the *Pequod* into a concrete-sided channel which led the river down into another concrete-sided channel running away downstream as far as the eye could see. They were at the furthest outreach of the sluice channel, nearly a kilometre downstream from the foot of the dam. As he always did before they got under way, Kramer was briefing them on the next section. 'This built-up section won't last too long,' he bellowed. 'Then, when we get back to the natural valley, we have to watch out for some rapids. We're on the right-hand side of the flow here and we'll have to padde for the centre of the stream as soon as we hit the water. As we found out upriver, and as we've got to bear in mind very forcefully downstream, there are major outflows with strong currents we do not want to get caught up in. The next is a couple of kliks downstream. That's kilometres to you, Captain Mariner. It's the major irrigation channel to the Palo

Verde Valley and it opens to our right, so let's get to mid-stream, people, and, if we can, keep left. OK?'

Everyone bellowed 'OK!' as they always did and the *Pequod* hit the water. An engineer at the head and an engineer at the stern – Mickey, in this instance, as Robin was considered too slight for the job – held the bucking inflatable in place while the first team climbed aboard and disposed their backpacks down the centre, securing them firmly in place. Then the second team went in. With all packs safely stowed, and everyone at their assigned paddling positions, armed with a paddle and clipped safely in place, the two holding the land lines nimbly leaped aboard and they were off, pushing with their paddles against the red-and-green slimed concrete, swinging *Pequod*'s square stern out into the foaming force of the water.

The manmade valley looked the better part of half a kilometre wide at this point and, as Robin looked down, she realised it must already be pretty deep as well. Even so, the river seemed ill-contained, almost forming a hill mid-stream as it thundered along. They were clearly going to have their work cut out to get up over the top of that within the next few minutes. Ever hopeful and never daunted, Robin dug her paddle in and strained in unison with the others to pull the *Pequod* left across the power of the stream.

The thunder of the water was a low, constant thing, unvarying enough almost to become background noise, a kind of Muzak from nature. Within it were a range of sub-tones bespeaking different pressures, different flows. It was just possible to yell a conversation, but only at risk of a torn throat. It was not possible to hear the songs of the local birds, thought Robin regretfully. Or, the thought popped into her mind from nowhere, the lost-soul sirens of the great westbound locomotives whose long lines strode across the country north of here. But . . .

What *was* that sound?

'I hear a siren,' she yelled at Mickey. 'Think it's a warning of some kind?'

'What?' Mickey shook his head, foam glinting on his hair and beard.

Robin leaned forward as close as she could to Conception's straining shoulder. 'I hear a siren,' she bellowed. 'Can you hear it, Conception?'

The Mexican woman turned her head, never varying the rhythm of her stroke. Then she nodded once, decisively, and leaned forward herself.

The sound Robin had heard was gone again by then, and it took

97

her an instant to realise that this was because the noise of the river was gathering in intensity. Without pausing in her own relentless pulling to get them across the stream, over the hill and safely into the left-hand flow, she glanced back over her shoulder. And so she saw what was bearing down upon them.

It was dark, almost slate-grey, with charcoal edges. It reversed the flow of the red river on which they were riding, for it foamed out towards the concrete sides as though trying to overcome them, and the centre of the flow was low, like a shallow valley. The speed of it was breathtaking, even to a woman who had faced all sorts of waters all over the world. 'Look out!' she bellowed in her loudest quarterdeck voice, and both Mickey and Conception looked round. Neither of them said anything, but both were suddenly paddling with the same desperate concentration that was tearing at Robin's shoulders as she strove to lift the frail vessel up onto the illusory safety of the central hill of water ahead of her.

But then it was too late. The black wave engulfed them. Had they been further out to the side it would have tumbled them down, but they had at least lifted themselves above the worst of the shore-side foam. They were caught instead at a strange overwhelming conflu-ence of slick black water and surging red. Two hillsides seemed to flow into each other in a strange quick valley beneath their keel. They were too well trained – too well aware of the terrible danger – to hesitate in their paddling, but they knew they were battling against forces far beyond their control. Though they still paddled uphill, the black tide snatched them sideways and slipped them down towards the white wall of foam which spread along the concrete bank like a disease. Down they swooped, as though all their arm-wrenching work was an utter waste of time; they were sucked out into the rushing maelstrom, like an old-fashioned lifeboat launched down a beach into a big surf. But this big surf was not only breaking inwards and shorewards, it was rushing along parallel to the coast at almost fifty kph.

Pequod was plucked out of the grasp of solid water and tossed high by the whirling foam. Robin refused to freeze. It was an immense effort of will, but it was hugely important – and not just to her. There would probably be debris in this raging foam. There was certainly a solid concrete embankment hidden somewhere at its back. Either debris or embankment could do fatal damage to the frail, inflated sides. *Pequod* was constructed in sections, and if too many of these were damaged, the whole vessel would be lost. In waters like these, any damage at all was likely to be fatal.

A wall of concrete leaped at them; it was the embankment's solid side. Robin recognised it and pushed against it with all her strength. The paddle was torn out of her grip but the inflatable bounced away from the concrete. Then Robin's right wrist, to which the paddle was secured, jerked sideways with such force that she nearly followed it overboard. Her safety harness stretched and groaned. Two firm hands took hold of her, one from the side and one from in front. She hadn't really though about it, but apparently she had become Conception's friend as well as Mickey's

'Thanks!' she bellowed and got a face full of foam which nearly drowned her. Coughing and choking, her thighs aflame as though she was riding the friskiest of stallions, she gripped her seat as hard as she could and began to pull the paddle in, hand over hand as though it was a marlin. And a marlin was what it felt like, kicking, jerking and jumping away in the grip of the wild water.

It was Conception's hand on her harness that warned Robin of the next section of the wild ride. At least, she assumed it was Conception's for it seemed to come from in front of her. Though by that stage 'in front' only meant 'in the opposite direction from the pull of the paddle' which she assumed was somewhere behind. The paddle could actually have been at any quarter. The raft could have been facing in any direction. Robin's world had shrunk to a raging, choking, howling little area slightly larger than her head. All of her body except for her arms was numb – though she felt that hand on the straps by her thigh with a shock of vitality. She could see only the vaguest shapes, slightly darker than the white water all around her – a couple of charcoal sketches, hardly more. The only thing she could hear apart from the strange screaming of the water was the relentless triphammer thumping of her own heart as it threatened to leap out of her heaving breast and flash away into the huge river like a salmon. She had no idea what the hand holding her was trying to tell her, no real understanding of how on earth Conception could see far enough ahead to warn anyone of anything.

But so it was. With the unnerving suddenness of the wildest fairground ride, *Pequod* was snatched right. It was not just an unnerving movement, it was one which Robin simply could not believe at first. As though God himself had designed a gun to shoot round corners, the bullet of the inflatable which had been moving one way at speeds far in excess of her design specifications – or those of her battered complement – was suddenly hurling sideways every bit as quickly.

And that was very bad, thought Robin, with flash of revelation. It was dangerous enough to be speeding out of control down a river course which at least they had studied and prepared for. But here they were proceeding, at the same speed, with the same lack of control, into uncharted waters. And, she suddenly realised with a poignant sinking in the pit of her stomach, they were sliding extremely rapidly downhill.

But then the raft struck hard – not bank or obstruction, but bottom. She bottomed again with explosive force and bounced up into the air, spinning majestically on her tail like a breaching whale. If Robin had thought it was like being a fisherman tied to a marlin as she pulled her paddle in, now, suddenly, she was like Captain Ahab's dead Parsee harpooner, forever secured to the side of the white whale. The instant her safety harness gave, her safety line jerked tight. She whipped out and slammed back again, indissolubly linked to the wildly cavorting vessel. She hit the water herself then and was jerked forwards before she could go too deep. Even so, like the *Pequod*, she bottomed pretty hard. She felt like a rugby ball converted at Twickenham. She actually had a ridiculous vision of herself aloft between the uprights, sailing over the top of the goal. Over and over she went, though she was beginning to lose the distinction now between what was real and what was fantasy. She hit water and concrete again and the lights went out.

'Welcome to the lovely Palo Verde Valley,' grated Kramer an hour later. 'To the Palo Verde irrigation system at least.'

Pequod lay on the slope of a concrete irrigation ditch, steaming in the sun. The crew lay around her, exhausted, battered and bleeding. Also steaming. Their kit lay in a messy pile, waiting to be sorted and re-stowed. It was too wet to be steaming; it was sopping, water running darkly out from under it to trickle down the concrete and away into the farmland Robin had admired from on high. Before them lay kilometre upon kilometre of channels watering everything from orchards to paddy fields. There must be some livestock nearby as well, thought Robin grimly, as the largest horsefly she had ever seen settled on her thigh and tried to share her blood.

Robin looked up from the mashed remains of the fly. Kramer was still talking. 'The irrigation return channel feeds back into the Colorado twenty-five kliks downstream or so. That's where we have to head if we're going to get back in the saddle, I guess. And that leaves us three main alternatives that I can see. We could call for back-up. We can have some chopper support if the going gets too tough—'

'Ain't going to get much tougher than this,' said Mickey.

'You hope!' growled Conception.

'Or we can try for some local aid. I mean this is fertile farmland. There'll be someone nearby who can give us a ride on a trailer or something. Or we can do it ourselves. Re-pack the *Pequod* and paddle her through the system by the shortest route we can find until we meet the drainage return channel further downstream. Anyone got any ideas? Opinions?'

Robin and Conception put up their hands together.

'Captain Mariner?'

'Is there anyone badly hurt?'

A series of negatives was answer enough.

'Then I vote we try it ourselves. We can do it without help so I think we should try. If your GPS system is still up and running, Kramer, you can guide us. The *Pequod* has almost no draft – maybe thirty centimetres – so we shouldn't run out of water as long as the drainage channels stay a couple of metres wide. And if we do run out of water or width, then we'll be in the middle of someone's farm. We can ask for a lift on a trailer then, I guess.'

'OK. Thanks, Captain. Major Lopez. You had a thought?'

'I agree with Robin. There is no reason to ask for help. We check our kit, load up and look for the drainage return channel. Nice easy paddle. Get us ready for the rapids before the Imperial tonight.'

So they checked and packed their kit. They repaired two damaged sections and reinflated them. They paddled for an hour. Then they met a kid driving a big John Deere tractor who was so amused by the sight of a small army floating along the channel at the foot of his father's melon patch that he hitched them up and towed them the twenty kilometres down to the return channel.

On the way down to the Imperial Dam, the nature of the river changed. The boisterous red water gave place to a darker, more sinister flow. The very properties of the water seemed different, and Kramer, as battered and exhausted as any of them, frowned with the added burden of leadership as he tried to calculate what this new flow would mean for them.

They came down upon the first series of rapids soon after rejoining the river. The manmade banks fell away after the irrigation return channel, to be replaced by gathering cliffs of rock. Wild sides closed in or fell back with a disturbing lack of control after the regularity of the concrete sluices, levees and drainage channels. The river bed rose and fell in waves. It became littered with rocks and boulders. Kramer had expected all this – it was recorded on his charts and

101

in his experience. But the water was behaving differently to what he was used to. Currents and eddies broke away in new ways, forever pulling *Pequod*'s head unexpectedly to right or left. Perhaps the surge which had swept them into the irrigation system had been enough to move the round boulders about. Certainly the rapids seemed more dangerous and subtly more unfamiliar than he had calculated.

At last they reached a section of beach on the back of a wide bend. It was further upriver than the place Kramer had planned to camp, but the strain was telling on them all. He himself had a thumping headache, threatening to gather into one of his rare migraines. The camp site was by no means ideal. Other than the river itself, there was no source of fresh water, and there was no obvious way out of the place should the river rise unexpectedly again. There was driftwood for the fire, however, though much of it was wet, having obviously been washed here by the dark water earlier in the day. He wondered what sort of food that sinister rush of the river would offer the fishermen, if any. But it would have to do. The next landing place was seven kilometres further on, after a series of class V rapids which he really did not want to explore at the moment. And this wasn't a Boy Scout camp-out; they were soldiers, well supplied for at least one uncomfortable bivouac.

Everyone worked in the slow motion of extreme exhaustion. *Pequod* was unloaded, then carried up the slope of muddy red sand to the high point of the bank. The basic bivouac went up. The latrines were dug in an inevitably exposed position as far down the bank as possible. Surprisingly swiftly, the fishermen caught four big, sluggish fish, strange looking and oddly marked. All through the preparing and cooking they argued irritably about what sort of fish they were. They tasted good, though, if a little smoky from the damp fire.

The smoke served another good function beyond adding flavour to supper. At the beginning of the evening, at least, it kept away the huge black mosquitoes which swarmed here in limitless numbers, all of them ravening for human blood. After dinner, they dispiritedly smeared their faces with insect repellent and climbed into their sleeping bags, still in their damp clothes – not that they noticed particularly; most of the sleeping bags were damp as well.

Round about midnight, a gentle, penetrating rain began to fall.

Robin was not really asleep. She was more uncomfortable than she had been since Richard had the bright idea of taking the twins on an Easter camp in the New Forest. She was at that particular point, half wakeful, half dozing, where the mind makes bright, clear, precise associations, often from utterly unrelated things. If she was thinking of anything, other than of her thankfully distant children and her suspiciously silent husband and camping, it was how her safety line had held her so surely to the side of the spinning *Pequod*. She saw herself, not as a rugby football but as a black figure soaring through the filigree of raging foam, the black line snaking away below her, like an umbilical cord attaching her to the fragile safety of the inflatable.

That imagined picture became overlaid with another which was real, from her memory. It was the picture of Mickey Vargas flying out of *Pequod*'s stern – from the very seat he had occupied this morning when the black water came. And of Captain Allday throwing herself back to save him, then cartwheeling into the water herself.

But Robin's line had been all but unbreakable today. She had felt as though the water could have shredded her out of her harness long before the Kevlar, carbon filament and nylon climbing rope could have frayed or snapped.

Frayed or snapped, she thought dreamily. Frayed . . .

Her eyes jerked wide, for there, just at the doorway to a dream, had stood the picture of Captain Allday's hands tangled in the mare's nest of Mickey's line as she had seen it just before the snake struck. And the end of it wasn't frayed at all. It was cut.

Chapter Eleven

As the arrival of that strange water had darkened the river, so the realisation that Mickey's safety line had been cut darkened the journey for Robin. It made her reassess what was going on and the people all around her. It made her less relaxed, more watchful. She remained just as inquisitive and involved in the lives of her chance companions, but more wary. With the realisation that Mickey might be at risk came the realisation that others might be. That she herself might be.

Robin's reassessment of the people around her, their characters and motivations, went on through a largely sleepless night. The first thought was whether the cut line could have been some kind of misplaced joke. As a ship's captain Robin had seen the kind of situations which could beget such dangerous 'fragging' and knew the tragic outcomes which could result. But it had always been her experience that the victims of such dangerous japes were hated authority figures – officers or petty officers who held their authority without ability, or who wielded it badly. Mickey seemed too gentle to be the victim of such horseplay. And it couldn't just have been Mickey, she suspected. The captain who so bravely tried to rescue him must have had her line cut as well, for Robin could not imagine two lines failing like that otherwise.

But if she could see nothing about Mickey to attract the attention of a vicious prankster, had she misread the man? Could there be hidden depths behind those deceptive wrinkles on the open, youthful face? Were there secrets behind those long dark eyes? Could there be something hidden behind the well-clipped mask of that beard? There could well be, she decided. There was at least a bullet wound – though that wasn't on his face of course. So, was the infatuation with Conception also a cover for something else? If so, it was effective enough, for it had neatly explained what he was up to last night. But if you were looking for a girl taking a bath or a shower, why search in the back of a bat cave?

OK, say there were hidden depths to Mickey Vargas, who else

knew about them? Conception? Possibly. Their relationship might well stand a bit of careful re-interpretation. Kramer? Yes. Had to be. He was the captain – in fact, if not by title. There could be nothing happening here he did not know about. And yet he could not know the full story, whatever that story was, or he would have had someone else aboard he could have relied on to go in search of Mickey last night. He only sent her, Robin reasoned, because she wasn't involved; couldn't possibly be involved. It seemed logical to assume, therefore, that he knew something was afoot but he didn't know precisely who was involved. But some niggling doubt about him remained in Robin's mind, some half-buried impression of the way he had behaved when she woke last night and found him standing over her. What was it he'd had in his hand? Why was the gun he'd passed to her warm? And what could anyone aboard actually be involved in? Attempted murder? Surely not. With all that equipment, even a cut safety line in the Grand Canyon rapids was more likely to lead to incapacity than death. The snake bite to Captain Allday's face was something no one could have calculated. On the other hand, that was a long and complex set of rapids. Level IV, level V in places. Perhaps the assumption had been that the pair would be washed along in the *Pequod*'s wake and get smashed to death.

It seemed to Robin that she should consider the following possibilities. Mickey, and maybe Conception, were up to more than met the eye. Mickey and the unfortunate Captain Allday may well have been up to more than met the eye. Someone aboard suspected they were up to something, had tried to incapacitate them both, perhaps kill them – might well try to incapacitate Mickey again and might well do the same to her if she got in the way. Whoever this person was, it did not seem likely to be Kramer as he did not act like a man who knew exactly what was going on. But then, of course, thought Robin, her experience based on the complete series of Agatha Christie's *Miss Marple* mysteries, looking as though you haven't a clue is exactly the best way to look when you are in fact pulling all the strings.

It was with thoughts of her favourite girlhood detective filling her mind that Robin at last dozed off. She did not see, in the dead of that drizzling, mosquito-haunted night, the single hooded beam of a torch examining the cliff at the back of the beach for caves, caverns, secret hiding places.

In a chill, grey, dispiriting dawn, they relaunched *Pequod* and got under way. Robin sat in her accustomed position, her mind a turmoil. Her restless night had raised questions and aroused suspicions but had delivered no answers at all. And, though it had seemed amusing enough to compare herself with Miss Marple, this was not a decorous vicarage of 1930s England. Events had shown that they would be lucky to get down the river alive if they were all on the same side and pulling together. If they were actually trying to kill each other off then they stood almost no chance at all. No wonder, thought Robin feelingly, poor old Kramer looked so careworn at times. This morning he seemed to have got himself pretty badly bitten too, and was clearly in no mood to answer any of the questions she would have liked to put to him.

At least yesterday's strange water had washed away downstream and the boisterous red companion of earlier days was back. The rapids between here and the Imperial Dam were not as bad as Kramer had expected and, with an early start in their rush to get away from the mosquito-riddled bank, they made good time. The early afternoon saw them safely to the Imperial and there Kramer made the decision that, instead of trying to sort out the flows between the river proper, the All American Canal diverting almost half its flow away to Imperial Valley, and the smaller outflow of the Gila Valley reservoir, they would wait until the morning and spend tonight in Yuma.

C.J. Martyr had known the Mariners for nearly twenty years. As well as being CEO of their New York subsidiary, he was a close personal friend. He had watched their backs – individually or collectively – more times than he could readily remember. Richard had been hesitant to tell him what was on the old laptop, not least because C.J.'s daughter Chrissie had been a porn star, once, in her desperate drug-haunted youth. But Richard was not a man to let an attack go unassessed, and whoever had filled his laptop's files, memory banks and hard drives with pornography from the Internet had been moving directly against him. It looked as though they had used his credit card to do it as well – after it had been stolen. Richard himself thought Aldo Cagliari was top of the list of suspects and he hoped the computer might furnish a clue, or perhaps something more solid, to confirm his suspicions. The police had asked him to leave his credit card active. Issued in England, it had an unusual code number for the States and the FBI's new cyberfraud computer would note its use anywhere in the country and alert the local police force within five minutes – hopefully in time to pick up the culprit still in mid-transaction. Richard agreed without a second thought. It never occurred to him that, as this was the card to his company account, Robin had another, identical to it.

While Richard and Ms Conway were locked in some tight negotiation over the fine print of a federal contract, C.J. was perched on a table behind the shoulder of a plump, hairy nerd called Honeywell, watching a woman taking off her clothes in a series of jerky stills. It was not a striptease show, simply the grainy image of a girl getting ready to take a shower, filmed from up near the ceiling of her poky little flat.

'Camera in the corner,' Honeywell was saying. 'Some girls use it for a little extra income. Install it, put it on-line, forget it's there. A guy I knew split up with his girl, then put one in her bedroom before he gave the key back. In the first six months after the end of their relationship, everything she did went out live on the Net. Embarrassing or what?'

The camera was so high that it showed very little of the girl's nakedness except the pale jut of her breasts. She stepped out of some almost invisible panties and proceeded in a series of ghostly jumps into the bathroom. She sat on the toilet, half in, half out of shot. The screen went blank.

'That's it for this file,' said Honeywell. 'That's the "Corporate Projections to 2010" file. These pictures sure soak up the memory, though.'

'Just wipe and go,' said C.J., easing his long frame and stretching his arms. 'I want the machine back ready to re-boot the original files.'

'Sure. Next file. Hey. More pictures. Better quality at least.' Two impossibly beautiful girls, incredibly well formed and unbelievably deeply tanned, soaped each other lazily in the shower. Again, the pictures moved as a sequence of jerky stills, the soap-filled screen jumping down foam-laced breasts to tummies and on down, four hands lazily busy.

'Simple girlie stuff,' said Honeywell. 'Just used to fill up the drives – wipe the memory. Nothing too bad yet, even counting the way these two are playing "hide the soap". There's nothing here that would have embarrassed Mr Mariner. He pretty straitlaced?'

'Not enormously,' grated C.J., running a great square hand, knuckles thick and scarred, through the sand and salt of his crew cut. 'You're wiping as you go?'

'Yup. And recording what I can of source, broadcast time, reception time.' He called up a digital clock from the machine's automatic memory, incongruously over a foam-filled delta of sandy curls.

'And another one bites the dust. Hey. Now this is a little different. This is one of those English magazines. Naughty schoolgirl, strict teacher stuff. This might embarrass someone a little more, I guess. Pictures again. Use up a hell of a lot of memory. Next in time sequence.' This time the date and time of reception appeared across the bottom of a schoolgirl who looked about five sizes too big for her uniform and a good fifteen years too old to be wearing it. 'Now if these had been real schoolgirls,' Honeywell said, but C.J. had left the room.

Away from the muck on the screen the big American could think clearly. Like Richard, he had Aldo Cagliari at the top of his list and, since he had passed on the files from Charles Lee in London, which lay somewhere beneath the garish rubbish Honeywell was sorting through, they both knew what a dangerous and desperate man Aldo Cagliari might be. The two great inventions of his life, the Cagliari Mach 1 and the AC2, had both formed the basis of failed business empires. Aldo had been to prison for fraud. In England, even under the new laws governing business, Aldo would have been a registered bankrupt, forbidden from ever holding corporate power. He was thought to have Mafia connections: drug connections, either as part of the Mafia set-up or directly with some very nasty Mexicans and Colombians. He certainly had a major habit. But he was being treated. He was on the way to rehabilitation. He was up for a second chance. And he was connected. Someone, somewhere, wanted Aldo Cagliari up and running. But who and why? And where? Who wanted Aldo running? Did they want him up for all business deals or only the ones Richard was doing? Certainly the Mach 1 might prove a competitor, or even a partner, for the routes Richard was discussing. But Richard had cash on the table, hardware ready to go, while Aldo was all pie in the sky and maybe we can swing it. No. He was only in this game because someone wanted him there. Someone wanting to queer Richard's pitch or someone with another agenda?

Wrapped in these thoughts which were really no further along than Richard's own reasoning, C.J. Martyr walked back into Honeywell's little office.

Honeywell was still chatting away to himself. 'This *is* embarrassing. This is American and way beyond the naughty English schoolgirls. Part of a sequence which is simply getting harder and harder the deeper it gets past the corporate stuff into the personal and communications areas. See how it's left the file name untouched but filled up the file memory? This is shocking enough, and it's just in his personal e-mail address. God alone knows what's in the secret, secure stuff deeper in. I'm not sure I want to find out.'

The tone of Honeywell's voice made C.J. very sure that he did in fact want to find out. The big American's wise eyes scanned the cluttered room. He was sure Honeywell was recording this for his own use, he just couldn't work out how.

But then C.J.'s personal phone started shrilling and Honeywell shouted, as though given an electric shock, 'Hey! I got incoming! Someone's trying to talk to this file!'

As Honeywell's fingers danced across the keyboard, trying to trace the incoming call, C.J. pressed the phone to his ear.

'Mr Martyr?' came an official-sounding voice.

'Speaking.'

'We have a trace on the missing card, sir. It is in use at the moment. Local law enforcement have been advised.'

'I half expected Yuma to be a one-horse town. Saloon, town jail, John Wayne with a Winchester somewhere,' yelled Robin over the sound of the coach's engine.

Mickey shrugged and grinned, scratching a mosquito bite under his stubbly chin.

'Hasn't been like that for a century and more,' bellowed Conception. 'Nowhere has. Haven't you seen *The Wild Bunch*?'

Robin shrugged and slitted her eyes against the afternoon sun as it struck in from the west across the city centre, all corporate high-rises, elevated motorways, white marble and black glass. Typical of the buoyant new American economy; businesses everywhere gathering in strength, old-fashioned heavy industry giving way to the new companies – all service and Internet access. Cyberbusiness. Even from here she could imagine what a magnificent website the city must have.

Kramer clapped the coach driver on the shoulder and they swung off the main road onto a municipal feeder into the suburbs where he had booked their motel, a short ride from the city centre. Robin for one had had enough of fish and field rations. She hoped the local restaurants at least were old-fashioned low tech and something John Wayne or any of his screen personas would have recognised. She wanted a large part of a steer. Preferably seared and smoking on each side and bleeding in the middle. Preferably, but not necessarily, dead.

Robin and Conception were sharing a room. There was a huge shower room *en suite* to the twin double-bedded chamber they got and they raced for it like schoolgirls in a boarding school. Robin had actually been to a boarding school so she won. Conception, kicking herself for the simple tactical error of taking off her panties by her bed and reaching for the towel while Robin hit the shower door in bikini briefs and stripped while the water ran, sat on the end of the bed and waited with good grace. She studied herself in the mirror above the distressed wood of the chest of drawers without a glimmer of self-satisfaction, her long black eyes far removed from the creamy chocolate perfection of her figure.

'Are we all going to eat together?' called Robin from the shower stall.

'That's the plan. Kramer knows a place.'

'Hope it isn't vegetarian.'

'Wouldn't think so. They all look like meat eaters to me.'

'You a vegetarian, Conception?'

'Hell, no. Mexican beef's the best in the world. Well, next after Argentinian maybe.'

'If the food's Tex-Mex, will you guide me a bit? I don't want to get mixed up between my quesadillas and my refried beans.'

'Go for the steak, girl.'

'That's what I want,' said Robin. 'It's nice to have someone I can count on for advice. You want me to leave this running?'

'Only if it's scalding hot. Scalding's what I want tonight.'

Two hours later, Robin was in heaven. The steak sitting on the plate in front of her must have weighed nearly a pound. It was as she had prayed it would be, black on the outside and red within. When its juices ran down into the mound of mashed potato, they were clear. The flavour of the first few mouthfuls had made her jaws ache; nature's way, her mother used to tell her, of ensuring one doesn't bolt one's favourite food.

Conception's steak was even larger, but that may merely have been because it was rare, Most of the others had settled for the simple perfection of big bits of meat exquisitely butchered, aged and cooked. Conversation was at a minimum. 'Pass the beer jug' more or less covered it for most of them. Hardly surprisingly, thought Robin, looking round the table; everyone looked shattered. But the steak was giving her energy, and she was a tourist here. She was going for a look around the town before she went back to the motel – an easy walk down a straight, unmissable road from here.

'You want to look round lively, downtown Yuma?' she asked Conception quietly.

111

'We're hardly dressed for a party,' said Conception, glancing down at herself then around the room. The group in army fatigues had cleared this section of what was clearly a popular eating house.

But Robin was not to be put off. With Conception almost reluctantly in tow, the energetic Englishwoman set off. Along one bland street after another they went, looking in plate-glass store fronts which could have been on Bond Street or Fifth Avenue. The feminine fripperies on show sat strangely on the military reflections of the women looking at them, but Robin at least gained a glimpse of the breathtaking creature her quiet companion might become, dressed by Armani or even Tommy Hilfiger.

At last, beginning to become concerned that they might lose their way after all, they turned to go back to the motel. After ten minutes or so, they came to a bustling little establishment they had missed on the way out. It was a Cyber Cafe called Netscape. Glancing in through the doorway, Robin saw a screen sitting idly at the back and turned in on a whim. There were all sorts of people there, men and women of all ages, but by far the majority of the clientele were men in their early twenties. They were locked into a range of locations in cyberspace which seemed to consume them completely. That being said, the arrival of two such striking women dressed in fatigues turned a few heads. Robin ordered a coffee for herself and Conception and sat at the empty screen. She glanced up and gave a grunt of laughter. It was screen number thirteen.

'What's the plan?'

'Domestic, I'm afraid. I haven't spoken to my husband in nearly four days now. I know nothing's up with him or the kids. His answering service told my answering service. But I just want to see him and have a chat, face to face.'

'I'll wait till you call him up then take a look around. You take some quality time.'

Robin's fingers were busy on the keyboard. As soon as the server came up, she swiped her company gold card through the strip reader, clicked OK against the number which came up, and dialled Richard's personal area on the laptop he always carried with him.

Robin expected to see Richard's picture at the very least – his corporate portrait with 'Richard Mariner can be reached at the following site . . .' written across it, the same as always.

Instead there flashed onto Robin's screen a picture of three women. There were two white girls dressed in black leather straps which were clearly designed to frame and enhance the more intimate parts of their bodies. Both wore masks across the lower parts of their faces, but

112

one of them had pushed an exceptionally long tongue through the zip-fastener mouth of hers. The masks wrapped round their cheeks and allowed long, golden ponytails of hair to stand erect from the tops of their heads. Apart from this golden profusion, neither girl seemed to have any body hair at all. The lack of natural adornment in this area had been more than compensated for by the application of a range of earrings and studs, though they could hardly have been called *ear* rings any more.

The two girls crouched like puppies at the feet of a tall black woman. She held leashes attached to the white girls' clothing. Her own clothing seemed largely to consist of red leather thigh boots, against the top of which the one girl was pressing her tongue.

Robin's fingers flew to clear the screen, but the image proved stubborn and would not fade to black. Robin, scarlet, glanced across to Conception and saw, behind the Mexican girl's stunned expression, a very much less attractive masculine one.

'Hey now,' drawled a deep voice, speaking for a sudden crowd of extremely interested bystanders, 'if you ladies like to play unusual games here, I think I can find a range of friends just itching to accommodate you.'

A heavy hand reached over to rest on Conception's shoulder, only to be snatched away and twisted into an incapacitating defensive hold. Conception towered above the rigid man and looked the rest of them straight in the face.

'My friend called up the wrong website,' she said. 'Nothing for you gentlemen to get excited about.'

Robin was up at her side. The face of the rigid man was twisting with humiliation and pain. He did not look like a man who was going to let things rest. Her calm grey eyes raked the cafe for an understanding gaze. But the women were all to the back, well clear of the situation. The man behind the bar hit a switch. The picture on Robin's screen died. But once he had done that he stayed still; kept clear.

'Simple mistake,' she said, echoing Conception. 'I'm sorry to have interrupted your evening. If you would just step clear of the door, we'll join our friends and get out of your lives for good.'

There was a tiny pause, then someone at the back of the crowd said, 'I don't see no friends, lady.'

That's it, thought Robin. We're dead.

The door burst open. Mickey Vargas stood there and his shoulders seemed to fill the frame. 'The ladies are with me, gentlemen,' he said quietly. But his voice carried.

113

The roomful of men swung round and looked at him, narrow-eyed. Undaunted, he stepped in and let the door swing to behind him. Once in motion, he kept going, walking round the outside of the crowd, talking quietly, with practised authority, as though this kind of stand-off was nothing new to him. 'We aren't looking for any trouble here. We're just part of a big military contingent passing through your fair city. The ladies will be leaving with me in a moment or two, after you all step away from the door and Major Lopez here releases the man who assaulted her. I'm sure she won't be pressing charges, sir, if you'll just straighten up and stand back . . .'

This last was said to the man who had touched Conception, as she gently released her grip on the cowboy's hand. Then the three of them stood together. There was an instant's more silence, then the cowboy working his damaged hand said, 'Emilio, you see any more of these military types outside?'

'No, Cal,' said Emilio. 'But I didn't see that sucker there either.'

'Well, I can figure one guy hiding in the shadows, maybe. Never a whole brigade. These guys are all there is up this end of town.'

The man called Cal swung back to face them and suddenly, there in his hands, was a six-shooter. An honest to God Samuel Colt Peacemaker .38 calibre. The gun that won the West. 'Now what do you think of that?' he said quietly.

'That what you call a gun down here?' said Mickey in the gentlest, most calming and unthreatening voice imaginable. 'That's not what I call a gun.' He did something too quick for Robin to see. 'Now *this* is what I call a gun,' he said, and the weapon was in his hand, pointing at Cal. 'Forces issue. Smith and Wesson. Extra load – take twenty shots. Forty-four magnum, hollow-pointed. Autofire. One at a time, three in a series, or the whole shebang in a second. Red-dot sight. Bullets go where the red dot points.' He swung the gun and not one man there failed to feel the red dot reflecting off the back of his eyeball where the hollow-pointed 44s would go. They all flinched back. Their leader's antique drooped weakly, until it pointed to the floor. 'Well, Cal, what did the man say? Are you feeling lucky?'

Cal's gun clattered to the floor. Mickey's followed it and his hands went up as two of Yuma's finest stepped in off the street, guns out and at the ready. They did not pick up on the tension. They did not at first see the guns on the ground. They had other fish to fry.

'The guy on screen thirteen,' said the first one in a loud, clear, polite voice. 'Show us your hands and step this way, please. I got the FBI telling me you've been using a stolen credit card.'

114

Chapter Twelve

'Where is that bloody man?'

C.J. Martyr had heard Robin refer to her husband as 'that bloody man' a couple of times before. It was a considerable danger sign.

'He's in a crucial meeting. Can I get him to call you back?'

'No. Tell him I want him on the end of this phone line now!'

'OK, Robin, but I may do some damage to the deal here.'

'Tell him to worry less about the deal and more about his marriage. In about five seconds from now he'll have to choose one or the other.'

C.J. had never heard Robin sound so angry. 'Of course. Where are you calling from?' he asked as something of an afterthought.

'From what I believe is called Yuma City Jail where I am being held under arrest for importing pornography into a public place via the Internet and for using a stolen credit card. Apparently the FBI have been looking for his company card without knowing my card is an identical twin. Now get the bloody man to the phone.'

Richard was there within moments and spent an intensely uncomfortable hour sorting everything out with the Yuma Sheriff's Department and with the FBI's stolen credit card people. And, most difficult of all, explaining things as best he could to his extremely irate wife.

Ultimately, though Richard did not know it at the time, it was only the fact that Robin was holding back from him certain information she did not want him to know yet – her suspicions about the cut safety line and her several close scrapes with death and injury – that allowed her to forgive him his failure to alert her to his own situation, though he did not go into any detail about Aldo's acrimonious departure or about the suspicions Charles Lee and C.J. had raised.

The end of the hour brought Robin's release; a promise from him that he would bring Audrey, his secretary, and a team of back-watchers to even the slightest business negotiation in future; grudging understanding and, if not forgiveness, then a kind of armed truce which Richard blithely believed would be easy enough to sort out when he saw Robin in a couple of days' time aboard *Colorado*.

But when he got back into the negotiating chamber, he discovered that, in spite of the best attempts of C.J. and the redoubtable Ms Conway, things had gone back several important steps in his absence, and it was suddenly not very likely that he would make the decommissioning ceremony in the Sea of Cortez on Friday after all.

After the strain of getting through Yuma, Robin found that Mexico was a pleasant surprise. They had slipped without great trouble past the Morelos and Yuma Dams and found themselves approaching the border along a wide, smooth, beautifully leveed waterway full of an almost blood-coloured, gentle flow. The force of the water – what relatively little remained of it after the last two dams and the Alamo Canal – was deceptive, however. They did not have to paddle very hard to find themselves sweeping along at quite a pace. But paddle they did, suddenly aware that they were on the homeward stretch. In fact, it took them some time to leave the States permanently, for the river itself was the border between the southern outskirts of Yuma and the town of San Luis Rio Colorado. South along this sweep of border they went, out of Yuma through Winterhaven and Crane. To the east of the flow they would be in Arizona still, to the west they would be in Baja Norte, Mexico. Here, in orderly sequence through the west side of the levee, little irrigation streams exited, carrying renewed flow away to the farmlands around Meridia, Ciudad Morelos, and Tabasco. They slipped almost unnoticed through Gadsden, then in the distance they saw the black line of the road bridge carrying Highway 2 from Mexicali to Sonayata and away south. Where the highway crossed the river was San Luis Rio Colorado. From side to side they swung, like children at play under the wide blue sky and the golden warmth of the sun.

They arrived at the border post at San Luis Rio Colorado before ten. Robin, tired after two sleepless nights, still shocked after her experiences in Yuma and angry after her talk with Richard, looked gloomily on the prospect of crossing the border, but as things turned out it was a debate as to which was shorter, the skirt of the official who glanced at their papers or the time she spent on formalities. And it was hard to say which was wider, the smile of welcome in that young official's face or the breadth of the blue Mexican sky which framed it. Then they passed under the brief shadow of the bridge and they were truly south of the border.

Things were different over the border. Just crossing the line out of Arizona into Sonora with Baja California Norte to the west seemed to

116

raise the temperature a good ten degrees, and everyone's spirits along with it. For the first time now, fatigue shirts were pulled off and even Robin and Conception paddled in the skin-tight cling of their white T-shirts. This particular type of dress not only showed Conception's eminently feminine torso to best advantage, it also emphasised the manly muscularity of Mickey's.

Since the incident in the cyber cafe, both Robin and Conception had looked on Mickey very much more positively. The wisdom of hindsight told them that he had not really saved them from gang rape and worse, for the police were on their way in any case, but none of them had known that at the time and the young man had confronted an ugly mob for them without a second thought; and perhaps even laid his life on the line. He deserved the smiles they gave him – and a good deal more, perhaps.

Robin found, however, that she could not help wondering where the gun had come from. And she found it a little disturbing, too, to realise that Mickey must also be harbouring dark suspicions about the accident in the Grand Canyon. Beyond that, the fact that he was now so well-armed bespoke considerable contacts: just how did army doctors on secondment to the Corps of Engineers come by state-of-the-art hardware? And the fact that Kramer was equally well-armed and clearly willing to let the situation stand had disturbing implications about the true relationship between the bluff leader and the love-struck major, and about who was actually in charge of this apparently innocent little money- and publicity-raising adventure. What were they all *really* up to here?

They were now riding high between raised concrete levees. Such was the care that had gone into the construction of the revitalised river course that the top few metres of these levees was all they could see. Through one or two of the openings they glimpsed stretches of low-lying desert dotted with areas of irrigated green, but for the most part, their work through the first few hours in Mexico was hot, hard and boring. Occasionally, away west, the peaks of the Sierra de Juarez were visible through the glimmering heat haze, but they seemed infinitely distant, like a glimpse of the daytime moon.

The bridges changed all that.

There were two bridges, side by side, in the middle of nowhere. The first was a rail bridge, striding across the river from the Desierto de Altor to the east into the foothills of the mountains westward which were, in fact, quite close. But it was the second bridge, the road bridge carrying a spur of Route 5 from Golfo de Santa Clara into the mountains of the National Park, which made all the difference, for suddenly, incongruously, in the middle of the baking day, in the middle of the desert with no more to mark the place than just a couple of bridges, they found themselves in the middle of a fiesta.

As they drew near the rail bridge, a westbound locomotive pulled out of the Desierto de Altor, its whistle hooting eerily, to clatter like thunder over their heads, showering them with sand and termite dust, distracting them just as the second bridge came fully into view. And what a sight it was, all gaily decorated and hung with bright bunting. Flags, streamers, effigies of animals and birds – real and from popular cartoons – hung everywhere, even from the beams beneath. As soon as they were spotted emerging from the shadow of the rail bridge, a crowd of cheerful, cheering Mexican faces yelled down at them to come ashore. Scores of pale-palmed, calloused working hands gestured irresistibly to the concrete shore where the footing of the bridge made a safe slipway for the inflatable and where men and women waited, temptingly waving bottles of tequila and beer.

It seemed to Robin at first to be an amazing coincidence that they should blunder in such timely fashion into a party inexplicably being held at a crossing in the middle of nowhere, but when they had pulled the *Pequod* up onto the levee and settled it safely in the shadow between the two bridges, she realised that this was not just any party, it was a party for them. And then Robin noticed who the centre of attention was. And the penny dropped. The fiesta was for Conception.

They left the *Pequod* under the watchful eyes of a couple of urchins and a powerful-looking teenager. Then, carried shoulder high, they were all borne down to a line of open trucks parked at the side of the road. Robin was placed in the first of these, beside the delighted Conception. They were handed glasses of golden liquid but Conception had no chance to sip her drink for as she stood there laughing she was enfolded in embrace after embrace and showered with kiss after kiss after kiss. The first man who kissed her, a heavy-set, beaming individual in a pair of khaki shorts and a Planet Hollywood T-shirt, climbed into the driver's seat and fired up the motor. The whole column did likewise.

'What gives, Conception?' bellowed Kramer distantly from the one behind.

'We are invited to my village for a fiesta,' answered Conception, but Robin had to relay the words in her quarterdeck voice before the others got the message.

They roared merrily off through the desert. At the left-hand side of the road ran an empty valley containing a dry river bed. Conception soon wrestled herself free of the jubilant party-goers and stood beside Robin. 'This valley is the old Colorado,' she said. 'One of the old river courses it used to follow. It leads away west to the Laguna Salada. The Colorado is a river with a mind of her own. All through the years she has sometimes come this way, sometimes that way.'

'You think you've tamed her now?' Robin looked back along the snaking, riverine roadway, surprised that she could still see, up on the eastern horizon behind them, the black line of the big levees. They had been coming downhill quite sharply since they left the river itself, she realised. Looking to the north she was quite shocked to see how far above their heads the westbound tracks of the railway had contrived to rise, maintaining a slight gradient for the Mexicali-bound locomotives by laying the rails on a considerable viaduct across the low-lying desert floor.

'I hope so, or a lot of these good people will find themselves in big trouble,' said Conception grimly.

The roadway began to climb westwards towards another raised horizon. Here, the spur road they were on crossed the southbound line of Route 5, just to the north of a great bridge which spanned the empty river valley, seemingly far too big for such a simple task. And from the ridge of Route 5, Robin found herself suddenly confronted with the mountains. The clarity of the still, unpolluted desert air brought them breathtakingly close. As the road swooped down again, the dizzy reach of the mountains seemed to rear like a great wave breaking. Robin found the effect awesome and she realised that she was clutching Conception's arm. The Mexican woman glanced down at her, face alive with pleasure and pride. 'This is my home,' she shouted, gesturing. And there, by the side of the road, a clear metal sign announced Los Muertos Sierra de Juarez.

The town of Los Muertos was, like the river that passed it, something of a ghost. It lay on the spur of a hill, dominated by a fine old adobe church. The church stood high on the shoulder of the hillside, with a village square in front of it. From the square, streets led away and down on three sides, two steeply, directly towards the valley bottom, and a third more slowly, out along the spur. Like the church, this road, lined with houses, looked across the valley to the low shoulder of the next hill to the south, one of a chain reaching down towards the Sea of Cortez. From the top of the church tower, Conception explained proudly to Robin as they disembarked in the little square ten minutes later, it was possible to see beyond Highway 5, along the railway track to the levees of the new river course twenty kilometres to the east. To the south, it was possible to see the new buildings and the dark haze of Cortez, the city which was being constructed beside the new mouth of the Colorado. Once it had been possible to see the Sea of Cortez itself, but Conception was proud of the new city which concealed it; the levee-tamed river and the town were the future, as was Conception herself. Beyond the range of hills to the south-west lay the National Park, with its carefully preserved environment of local flora and fauna: everything from the rich rainforest which had once clothed the high peaks here to the rattlesnakes, scorpions and gila monsters which now populated the desert wilderness this part of the country had become.

Due west lay wasteland which had once been the great *rancho* hereabouts. The *rancho* had been a cattle farm and the village was originally founded to service it. Many of its original inhabitants had been brought from the east – some, like Conception's own distant ancestors, from Spain itself – to mix and intermingle with the local Indian peoples. Beyond the ghost ranch, up at the head of the great dry valley which had once contained the errant Colorado, lay Laguna Salada, Mexico's own Salton Sea.

Time for further explanation was cut short by the arrival of the other trucks and the official welcoming committee. Robin found herself overwhelmed by the flood of cheerful Spanish, but Mickey soon found his way to her side and she was so relieved to have a translator that it took her a while to notice that the normally cheerful young man was withdrawn, even frowning a little. Assuming that he was just unwilling to share Conception with so much limelight and so many others, she took no notice but joined in the irresistible festivities with a will. The fact that she had managed to down three big glasses of tequila on the truck ride in gave some extra fuel to her *joi de vivre* and added a patina of extra brightness to everything going on around her.

Robin was treated as the most honoured guest after Conception and, because he was acting as interpreter, Mickey was soon included, but Robin was quick to notice that, like the one on the young man's face, there were frowns on one or two of the older faces around her. Conception seemed blissfully unaware of any of this; she led Robin through the village, from one family group to another, insisting that her guest sample all the carefully prepared and beautifully presented food and drink as the Englishwoman was introduced to the populace, most of whom seemed to be related to her. After introducing Robin, she would add, almost as an afterthought. 'And this is Mickey Vargas, from San Francisco.' That got rid of many of the frowns, if not quite all.

The man in the Planet Hollywood T-shirt was Conception's brother, and he had arranged the fiesta with the help of her father, the town's *alcalde* or mayor. He and one or two of the other municipal leaders held posts as rangers in the National Park and soon after news of Conception's arrival at San Luis Rio Colorado had been phoned through, so had a summons to find some lost gringos. But Robin met Conception's mother, a tall woman every bit as queenly as her daughter, breathtaking even in middle age. Robin also met, to the best of her computation, two more brothers and their families, and three sisters and theirs. More of the huge Lopez family were away in Mexicali, Tijuana and Tecate to the north, earning or being educated, Isabella Lopez announced with simple pride. The sisters teased Conception terribly – they were all younger than she was, yet were the matriachs of growing families in their own right, while she was still single. Had she not yet found a man good enough for her? they teased. Perhaps, sallied one, a little breathlessly, relying on her impenetrable Mexican Spanish, the pretty gringo boy who followed Conception like a puppy.

At this Conception drew herself up to her fullest and said, 'Señor Miguel Vargas of San Francisco, may I present Señora Conchita Rivera?'

'I greet Señora Rivera with much felicity and gusto,' answered Mickey in his suavest and most aristocratic Castillian Spanish accent.

Conchita retreated in stricken confusion.

'She is the family's most promising diplomat,' chuckled Conception, switching to English for an instant. But then she was back into Spanish again. The brothers and sisters were only the beginning; there were uncles and aunts and nephews and nieces enough to populate a region, let alone a village. When they got to the second cousins by marriage and third cousins once removed, some of whom had driven up from Cortez or down from Mexicali to be here, Robin called a laughing halt. Just about the only person in the whole *barrio* Conception did not seem to be related to was the portly, cheerful priest who kept this church as one of a circuit in the area. 'I should not be here until the Sunday after next,' he confided in quiet, confident, heavily accented English, 'but when I heard Conception was coming back to see us, I came over especially. I should not have favourites, I know, but she was always a favourite of mine. I helped get her a place at the college in Mexicali, you know, before the army took her and made her the Major of Engineering you see before you now.'

'You did a good job, Father,' said Robin.

'I will have done my job well when I marry her and christen the first of her children up there in my old church,' he said. And such was the simple, timeless belief behind the words, Robin could not find it in herself to be impatient with the priest, though she had little time for anyone who expected able women to put childbearing before careers nowadays.

'Has Father Felipe been telling you of his ambitions for me?' asked Conception, laughing. 'He cannot forgive himself for his momentary weakness in putting me among all those boys at the college. Don't worry, Father. I have not strayed too far, and I will come back to you the instant I find the man I wish to settle down with.'

'Make it soon, my child,' said the old man. 'You are no longer a plump little chicken, ripe for the plucking.'

'Did he mean that in the way I think?' asked Robin, on the verge of being shocked.

'He's a priest!' laughed Conception. 'How could he have?'

Somehow Robin was not quite convinced.

In a moment of relative quiet, Robin looked around for the others and found most of them with Kramer sitting contentedly in the cool of the village meeting hall, sipping tecate and chewing on burritos. 'Everybody happy?' she asked, and was rewarded with the sort of collective grin which made her fear for the village's tequila supply.

In the late afternoon, the bell in the old church tower chimed twice and everyone rushed to the south end of the village. There, riding in a line up the side of the dry river and onto the rocky spur like the heroes from a cowboy film, came Conception's father and the other rangers. With a whoop of joy Conception was off. Leaping like a tomboy she cleared the end of the road, jumped like a gazelle across the rocks and arrived at her father's side in a great flurry of red sand. With one easy, graceful movement, he leaned down from the back of his horse and heaved her up into the saddle behind him. Then the line moved forward again and soon everyone was back in the *zocalo,* or main square outside the church. Here Robin was introduced to the tall, lean lordly man who was Conception's beloved father. Rarely had Robin seen such an easy but clearly deep relationship between father and daughter. Her own relationship with her father was very close – or she would hardly have come halfway round the world to do an errand for him otherwise – but the cheerful depth of affection between this whip-tough, lean old man and the dazzling woman who was his daughter was extraordinary. 'May I present my father to you?' asked Conception formally.

'Father, this is Captain Robin Mariner from England. Robin, this is Señor Ignacio Lopez, my father.'

A little ridiculously, Robin felt like curtseying. Instead she shook his hand and looked up into wise, dark, laughing eyes. But then the laughter in them died, and a frown gathered between the sweeping brows above the sharp Roman nose.

'This is Major Miguel Vargas, from San Francisco, Father,' said Conception, her voice suddenly hesitant, as though she realised she had blundered innocently into a mistake she did not quite understand.

'Major Vargas is known to me,' said Ignacio Lopez. 'Though it is so many years since I have seen him that he will not recognise me. How is the Captain your father, Major?'

'I have not seen him or heard from him in many years, señor.'

'And your mother?'

'She is well.' Mickey looked around Los Muertos and almost shivered. 'She would be a great deal less than happy if she knew I was here, however.'

'Still,' said Lopez quietly, 'now that you are here, and she knows nothing of it, perhaps you should take another step into the past. What do you think?'

'Well, I—'

'Conception will guide you if you cannot remember the way. Captain Mariner, can you ride?'

'Well, yes,' said Robin, thoroughly confused by now. 'But where to?'

'To his family home,' answered Ignacio gently. 'To the ranch-house west of here. To *La Casa Grande*.'

It was apt that they should come up to *La Casa Grande* on horseback. They could have taken any of the brothers' or cousins' trucks or four-by-fours. But they were going back in time in all sorts of ways, and the horses put them in the right frame of mind for it. They were all confident riders and the horses were as patient and well-behaved as the burros which had carried Robin down the sides of the Grand Canyon at the beginning of this. They rode three abreast, cantering easily across the arid red flank of the hillside overlooking the dead river valley, going up towards the Laguna Salada over what once had been a great landholding. As they rode, with little more noise around them than the wind, the thudding of hooves, the creaking of saddle leather, and the tinkle of the tack, they were able to talk. Or at least Mickey and Conception were. Robin concentrated on staying in the saddle and trying to keep up with the story that was unfolding.

The place had been founded in the early 1860s by Mickey Vargas's grandfather's grandfather. Against the shifting, violent background of the Civil War, the family fought to keep hold of as much of it as they could, passing *La Casa Grande* from increasingly weary father to increasingly resentful son. Mickey's grandfather Jesus Porfirio had tried to interest his son, Mickey's father, Jesus Miguel, in taking up the near ruin of the place 110 years after its foundation, in the heady days after the 1968 Olympics, but the stiff-necked Jesus Miguel had entertained other ideas, preferring to find his career as far away from the dying land as he possibly could. He had walked out on the old man, and had seen him only once, in the last year of the recession which ruined them all, when he brought his Mexican-American wife and son to show the staff of *La Casa Grande* and the people of Los Muertos.

Two years later, the old man had been in Mexico City, trying to get clearance to sell the whole place off when he had been caught and killed in the earthquake.

Jesus Miguel and his wife had split up. Mickey's mother had taken him back to San Francisco with her, and raised him indulgently and expensively, gleefully screwing every *peso* out of the distant, near-bankrupt father, as she oversaw Mickey's medical studies right to the bitter end. But Mickey himself had split away from her as well. She had never forgiven him for following in his father's footsteps and joining the services.

So here they were: the son of the man who owned most of the mountain and yet who never came near it, and the daughter of the man who ran the village, set up to service a house no longer occupied by anything other than ghosts and the memories of bitter disputes, destroyed hopes and sudden death, riding into the past with a stranger from another land altogether.

La Casa Grande nestled in a fold of the hillside, high above a bend in the dry river. It was easy to see how, a century and a half ago, this would have been a sheltered, verdant spot, green and well-wooded, overlooking almost an inland sea where the Colorado ran. The house itself was in the colonial style, with wide, south-facing verandas where Mickey's grandfather's grandfather must have sat at ease watching the rich flow of the river irrigating the mountain he had bought and stocked with steer. Now, the hot wind gusted over the wide scar of the dry valley, and blew red dust over the dry grass which just about held the desert slope in place. A pathway swept round to the steps at the front of the house.

Here they reined up, dismounted and tethered their horses. Robin especially could hardly bring herself to believe that any of this was real. The house, the setting, the situation was so firmly rooted in fantasies of cinema and romantic fiction that even pinching herself in the time-honoured fashion could not really convince her she was fully awake. Following the other two, she walked slowly towards the magnificent edifice of the empty, ruined *hacienda*. There appeared to be a solid roof of red tiles on the place, and the door sagged to reveal an inner shell, but that was all, it seemed. The place looked as though it had been deserted for a hundred years, and yet it had been occupied less than twenty years ago, when Mickey was little more than ten years old and had been brought here to be shown to his grandfather.

'Take care,' said Conception automatically as Mickey, entranced, took the first step up to the veranda. 'The wood is solid, but it has not been treated against termites since nineteen eighty-five. Walk light.'

Mickey went first, following her advice. Then Conception, also in the grip of some powerful memories. Then Robin, eyes wide and mind reeling.

No. The impression that the place was a shell was wrong, an illusion brought on by the sheer scale of the reception hall, rising more than two storeys to a shattered skylight. Inside the sag of the front door across the worm-riddled floor, a great staircase swept upwards to a galleried landing so deep that Robin had to remind herself she was not trapped in *Gone With the Wind*. But many of the steps of the beautiful stairway were gone and anyone foolish enough to test the galleried landing would be lucky to survive, for it was possible to see through great gaps in the flooring to the broken, sagging doorways of the bedrooms above.

Under the sweep of the staircase stood more doors which opened into several great reception rooms, before falling back into the shaded, modest reaches of the servants' quarters. Here they found a dining room, stripped of table, chairs, cutlery, crockery and glassware, its great decorative display cabinets gaping and mahogany drawers yawning. They found a library, its walls lined with shelves between sagging floor and drooping ceiling, all of them as empty as the frames on the walls which had once contained pictures or mirrors. They discovered a magnificent drawing room, most eerily empty of all, which opened out onto a continuation of the veranda overlooking a withered, sand-filled desert.

125

'Who did all this?' asked Robin, overcome by the relentless manner in which the place seemed to have been stripped of every item of worth. 'Robbers? Burglars?'

'Worse,' said Mickey Vargas with a strange laugh. 'Lawyers.'

'What?'

'That's right,' said Conception, softly. 'I saw them when they came. Gringo lawyers from the north.'

'From San Francisco, to be precise. From my mother.'

'Did your father ever see this?' asked Robin. 'I mean I know he never wanted to live here – if I've got the story right. But even so. Did he ever see what they did to this place? His home?'

'I don't know,' said Mickey. 'Why don't we ask him when we see him? It'll give us something interesting to talk about.'

'When we *see* him?' said Robin, wondering whether she should pinch herself again. 'When on earth will we ever see your father?'

'Tomorrow. Or the day after that, I guess,' said Mickey. He looked down at Robin and saw the expression on her face. 'It's old history,' he said, glancing across at Conception. 'Everybody knows it now. Everybody in Los Muertos, anyway. When my mother took me away to the north with her, she had my name changed to her maiden name, Vargas. But that's not the name on my birth certificate.' Mickey bowed, as though introducing himself for the first time, to both Robin and Conception. 'I am Miguel Ignacio de Hidalgo y Vega. My father is the captain of the *Colorado*.'

Chapter Thirteen

Captain Jesus Miguel de Hidalgo y Vega sat at his desk in the day room on the bridge of the *Colorado* and thoughts of his son could hardly have been further from his mind, though thoughts of Miguel Ignacio and his mother had been brooding in Jesus Vega's mind more regularly of late as he was forced to consider how much he had given up in order to follow the profession he loved – and how much he had lost now that that profession was finished with him. But even *La Casa Grande* lay far at the back of Vega's mind now as he looked across the desk at Hernan Gutierrez with something akin to blank astonishment.

The young lieutenant had entered the sanctum only a few minutes before bearing a sheet of paper containing urgent orders from Fleet Headquarters up in Ensenada. A running gun battle had developed between a large pleasure boat suspected of smuggling drugs and one of the smaller coastal patrol vessels, just to the south of *Colorado*'s current position. Captain Vega was hereby ordered to proceed with all despatch to the support of the patrol boat, now well to the north and in trouble. Vega should assume command of the situation if circumstances warranted it – the commander of the patrol boat would follow his orders without question.

'They take our guns, our tracking equipment, our long-range radio equipment and nearly eighty per cent of our complement, disregard our concerns and our complaints, and then they order us into action? Is this a joke, Lieutenant? A coastal patrol vessel would be far better armed and manned than we are at the moment. Surely this has to be a joke.'

'If it is, Captain, then it is not of my making. And it is too bizarre to have been dreamed up by our friends at Ensenada or even our masters at the ministry. No. It is something much more basic than that, I believe. It is, what do the gringos call it? Murphy's Law.'

The captain looked at the young lieutenant, his face set like stone.

'Murphy's Law states, I believe, that whatever can go wrong

will go wrong. It is inevitable, therefore, that once you render a warship incapable of fighting, you must order her into action. It is a fundamental law of the universe. Like gravity—'

'What are you babbling about, Lieutenant? No matter. Warn El Jefe. We will want full speed ahead as soon as he can deliver it. When the engines are ready, we will raise anchor. In the meantime, take over bridge watch and confirm with fleet command at Ensenada, *Colorado* ready for sea and action.'

Hernan Gutierrez left, and Jesus Vega leaned forward to study the orders more closely. Without thinking, he moved a book of music to one side and opened a drawer, revealing the silver gleam of a flute lying on a black velvet case. He slipped the music in beside it. The drawer was deep and capacious. As the music slid into the depths beside the lovingly maintained instrument, it moved another lovingly maintained, shiny object. This was an ancient but perfectly functional English Webley .455 calibre service revolver complete with handle clip and shoulder lanyard. Against the thin board of the drawer's bottom, it scraped as it moved with a sound like distant thunder.

A few moments later, Vega walked onto the bridge and crossed to the chart table. Here, under a great sheet of yellowing Perspex, lay the only chart the ship had used in more than ten years. Vega laid the sheet of paper giving his orders beside the black lines denoting their last course and current position, then he picked up the rulers and dividers he needed to plot their next one now that all the differential shiphandling equipment had gone. Really, he thought, with an unaccustomed spurt of frustration, he would be reduced to using his sextant if this sort of thing kept up.

But then, Jesus Vega thought, this sort of thing could not keep up for long. The decommissioning ceremony was due to take place the day after tomorrow. Then the ship would run up to the scrapyards at the new city of Cortez at the new mouth of the new River Colorado. He found his eyes were looking at the places on the chart, except that it was an old chart and they did not exist on it. But the meander of the old, exhausted river did, with notes about shallows, inconsistencies of flow and such. He himself would follow the river north and return to what little was left of the house an earthquake had kept safe for him through the simple expedient of killing his father while the old man was on his way to, rather than from, his lawyer's office. He would invest what was left of his pension in keeping the roof sound and his belly full; then he would sit on the veranda and he would play his flute in the evenings and he would grow old, go mad and die.

A shadow fell across his calculations and he looked up.

'El Jefe says everything is ready, Captain,' reported Hernan.

Jesus nodded once and straightened. 'Weigh anchor then,' he said and crossed to the helmsman's side. Away to starboard across the water the rising glimmer of the silvery heat haze above Los Mochis marked the lower sky. Immediately to port crouched the Isla Carmen in whose shallows they had anchored and under whose bulk they had been lying as they did their best to repair the wounds inflicted in Topolobampo. Down the deck to the main anchor winch ran the depleted deck watch, careful to stay clear of the dead grey canvas patches over the great holes fore and aft where the guns had been. The winch coughed into life and as the sound of the chain clattering into the forward lockers came up on the heavy breeze, Jesus Vega rang down for slow ahead.

'Due north,' he ordered quietly.

Punta Lobos began to slide purposefully down behind their port quarter. Jesus rang down for more speed.

By the time Isla Coronados was behind and Punta San Antonio promised on the left of the horizon up ahead, *Colorado* was at full ahead, plunging north at thirty knots, cutting across the water like the old ocean greyhound she still was at heart. Five minutes after that, they made their first direct radio contact with the commander of the coastal protection vessel.

As Punta San Antonio fell astern, Jesus Vega held his council of war. He used the bridge day room with the desk pushed hard against the wall. Lieutenant Banderas held the watch, with the most experienced helmsman watching him. They were running north under a dead calm, through an empty sea over a trench twelve hundred metres deep. Jesus Vega wanted to test young Banderas a little, for it was the captain's intention to leave the boy in command and to lead a two-pronged attack himself.

'The cruiser *Tiburon* has run here, to the Isla Cornuda here,' Jesus told his men. 'The coastal protection vessel *Alvaro Obregon* is standing by but the people aboard *Tiburon* have made a serious fight of it and the commander is in no position to follow them ashore, apparently. Especially as he believes them to be heavily armed with modern weaponry up to light machine-gun status. Several of his men have been picked off and wounded, indicating that the opposition have rifles, perhaps sniper rifles. The *Alvaro Obregon* has been raked with automatic gunfire and the commander has seen several explosions close to which he believes are either grenades or mortar rounds.

129

'The commander reckons that the opposition have sustained several casualties themselves and may be awaiting relief or reinforcements on the island. On the other hand they may just be dropping something off or picking something up before making a break for open water again. If they move in that direction, *Alvaro Obregon* will be hard put to stop them, as things stand. Speed is of the essence, therefore. We will remain in contact with the commander who will, at the very least, act as an observer for us.

'Subject to a change in the status on the island, I propose to do the following. On still afternoons such as this one, we can expect a haze to come down which should allow us to get close to the island unobserved. I propose that Lieutenant Gutierrez and myself should take a well-armed six-man team each ashore. For those of you who are not familiar with the island, it gets its name, Hammerhead, from its curving shape which, as you can see, makes it look like the head of a hammerhead shark.' Vega's hand moved over the chart and indicated an island shaped like a blunt crescent moon with its hollow facing south and its bow facing north.

How long his fingers are, thought Hernan Gutierrez. He had never noticed before how artistic the Captain's hands were.

'The island's volcanic origins make it higher than is usual for islands here and although it is less than two kilometres long and uninhabited, it is nevertheless quite high. *Tiburon* is in the south-facing bay here, with *Alvaro Obregon* between her and the open sea. I propose to come ashore on the north-facing beach here, cross the high ground, and launch a surprise attack from behind. Immediately before our attack – or earlier than that if we believe them to be suspicious – *Colorado* will join *Alvaro Obregon* and some distracting fire will be laid down. Lieutenant Gutierrez and I will both have two-way radios tuned to each other and to the commander of the *Alvaro Obregon*. He will be in contact with *Colorado* and will co-ordinate the action under my direction. Gentlemen, I think that is all unless there are any questions. None? Not even from you, Fernando? Very well. Teams will be as usual. Team two, please sign out your weapons from the armoury with Lieutenant Gutierrez and zero them in the usual way. Frederico, that means without killing any boobies or frigate birds. Do you understand? My team will pick up their guns and zero them with me in half an hour. A pity we have allowed target practice to slip during the last couple of weeks. Though I know the birds and the fish have been relieved.'

'He's calling us by our first names and making jokes, Lieutenant,' said Fernando warily as Gutierrez led his team down to the armoury. 'What do you think that means?'

Frederico looked down at his dynamic, ever-questioning, impatient little friend. He shook his round head hard enough to make his jowls and his chins wobble lugubriously. 'It means we're doomed,' he said. 'Good as dead, all of us.'

Tall, slim Raphael, a natural leader among the men, almost but not quite a petty officer, said, 'Don't be silly, Frederico. This is a little fire fight to say farewell to the old *Colorado*. No one will get hurt. Except a few trigger-happy gringo druggies. Don't worry.'

'Easy for you to say,' protested Frederico. 'You make only a quarter of the target I make.'

'Yes,' said Gutierrez, re-establishing his authority with easy camaraderie, 'but you bleed pure tequila, Frederico. Your wounds will be self-treating. And even if they weren't, you've got Velula to fall back on.'

That produced howls of laughter from everyone except Velula, the team's medic. He was the worst medic aboard, or so everyone said. There was much debate between the teams as to whether Gutierrez's men stayed so relatively untouched during actions because they were better trained, fitter and faster or because they were all terrified of what Velula would do to them if they had to rely on his ministrations.

Half an hour later, the captain's team got their guns and replaced Gutierrez's men at the after rail. There was no badinage between the men, or between them and their officer, but they were not a sullen team. They prided themselves on being the most professional and efficient men aboard. They viewed their captain with respect and awe and, though he would have been surprised to know it, a great deal of affection. He never gave it a second thought, but he led unvaryingly from the front and they respected that. If he always took them where the most danger was and made more work for their team medic Ociel, then that was his way, his macho, and they respected him for it. The captain did not believe in doing things by guesswork or in littering the seas he was paid to guard, so they towed targets at measured distances behind the boat and they all stood in a line at the poop rail and they fired sparingly and with care, adjusting their sights carefully. Although each man had a weapon of his own and was in charge of zeroing it for himself, each man also had a buddy and they swapped weapons in case they had to use each other's. The captain, as always, stood like an old-fashioned duellist – there was a rumour, which Ramon the bearded chief petty officer believed absolutely, that the captain had killed a man in a duel over a lady's honour in a dark, mysterious affair late in the wild seventies. He stood erect, sideways on. He extended his right arm level with his shoulder and kept both his eyes open. And where he aimed the ancient Webley, the huge bullet went, even more accurately than Ramon's red-dot sight allowed. After firing his own gun, the captain always took and fired each of the others' guns. Not to check on the zeroing, he said, but just in case he had to take one and use it himself. They believed what he said about the zeroing because they trusted him as they trusted themselves and they had never known him to lie, but they had never seen him use anything other than his ancient English revolver.

After he had checked all the guns and logged the rounds fired so far as well as those issued for later use, Vega took the little two-way radios and sought out Gutierrez to check the band settings and reception. Then he vanished into his quarters, and after a while there came the gentle music of a flute being played softly.

Just as Jesus Vega said it would, the haze came down at two. By four, it was impossible to see for more than a kilometre or so, but such was the quality of the light that that kilometre looked infinitely far. They had no radar any more, nor even a GPS navigator, but the commander of the *Alvaro Obregon* could see them and guide them with pinpoint accuracy. Right at the outer reach of his equipment, however, they changed course and ran out eastwards to gain the northern beach unsuspected and, they hoped, unobserved until the volcanic rocks of Hammerhead Island hid them from any equipment the smugglers might have aboard. They were in position by four, having cut speed and engine revs – as close as they could come to silent running.

Fifteen minutes later they were on the beach.

Although there were two teams, they went in one boat, and they rowed. They ran up on the sand and climbed out quickly and quietly, signalling to each other and maintaining strict silence. Jesus Vega gestured to Gutierrez to keep his radio switched off as agreed for a further fifteen minutes until they were well up into the shallow but precipitate hills which ran from side to side of the island in front of them. The sand of the beach gave way swiftly to rock and the folds of the rock gathered guano from the nesting birds nearby in sufficient thickness to support a scrubby kind of grass. The folds of rock soon flattened into rolling micro-uplands behind a high tide line, nestling under the shoulders of steeper heights. Here the grass

132

was thick, and thick with the nests of the birds which made this place their home. No matter how warily they walked, they disturbed some of the inhabitants, and each team could trace the progress of the other by the clouds of angry birds above their heads until they both entered the barren, rock-faced uplands. The whole configuration could have been the great plains gathering into the rugged peaks of the Rockies, but contained in a kilometre, not a continent.

Pulling himself up into a natural pulpit on the highest peak nearby, Jesus Vega looked down into the southern bay. There lay the *Tiburon*, moored almost at the surf line; a big, flat-bottomed gin palace of a boat with three or four sun decks and enough candystriped awning to decorate a fiesta. Her sleek sides were pocked and blackened, however. The awning was torn, singed and spotted with bullet holes. A line led back into the clear water, tied to what looked like a crumpled manta ray lying restlessly on the bottom – the ship's inflatable no longer inflated.

Jesus checked his watch and flipped the switch on his radio receiver. As he lifted it to his ear, his eyes stayed fixed on what was going on below. The people from the *Tiburon* were unloading boxes onto the beach and clearing an area beside them. An area, calculated Jesus, about the right size for a helicopter to land on. His eyes narrowed, quartering the sky, but you couldn't see much further up there than you could down here, and the screaming of the birds made it impossible to hear whether a helicopter might be approaching. He caught Ramon's eye and glanced meaningfully upwards. The bearded face nodded once and Ramon was on aircraft watch.

The radio buzzed, almost silently. 'In place,' whispered Gutierrez, and Jesus Vega felt a stirring of affection for the cheerfully indefatigable young officer.

'*Colorado* approaching,' reported the commander of the patrol boat out on the horizon. Jesus could have worked that out easily enough for himself because suddenly there was a new and almost frantic urgency to the activity below.

Jesus hesitated briefly, calculating. Would the smugglers just leave their contraband for the helicopter to pick up and cut and run now? Or would they brave it out? From the increasingly hectic activity, it looked as though they were getting ready for a quick exit. He trusted young Banderas to get the ship here and hold her beside the *Alvaro Obregon*, but he did not think he would be quick-thinking enough to run the *Tiburon* aground or to use the enormous power of the Westinghouse turbines to overtake and board her. So, calculated Jesus, if he wished to detain whoever was down there and charge them with whatever they were up to, then Gutierrez and he would have to lead their teams down there at once.

'Hernan,' he said into his radio. 'We go.'

He gestured to Ramon, who took his eyes off the sky and nodded with a blood-curdling grin. Ricardo, Paco and Ociel followed in his footsteps, moving swiftly and surely down the precipitous slopes just as the razor-sharp cut of *Colorado*'s bow chopped in out of the haze.

Nobody on the beach was looking up into the hills, they were all watching the ships and the sky. So it was that Jesus Vega and Hernan Gutierrez were able to pick their way through the sea-washed jetsam high on the hill slope and lead their teams almost onto the beach before anyone noticed them. They arrived on the sand at exactly the same time, one team at each end. Whatever was being off-loaded was piled in crates on the middle of the beach and a dozen or so strapping young men were crowded around it, most of them dressed in dark vests and fatigue trousers. Many had bandannas tied tightly across their heads, though one or two wore baseball caps.

The minute the first man saw the uniforms charging up the beach at him, he yelled to the others and dived into the middle of the pile of crates. Jesus's lips narrowed in frustration. The pile of crates made an effective barricade and if the smugglers had their arsenal in the middle with them, they could put up a strong defence. As the thought formed in his head, a man popped up from behind the crates, holding some kind of automatic weapon. Jesus Vega did not hesitate, but he felt Ramon slow at his shoulder. 'Wide!' yelled the petty officer and Jesus sprinted right as a withering burst from Ramon's automatic carbine chewed splinters off the tops of the crates. The man with the rifle disappeared.

Diving right was the best thing to do, reasoned Jesus. The barricade had to be open down there, for the smugglers had been coming and going from the tide line and the *Tiburon*. Then something black flew past him and out into the water. He hurled himself to his left, holding his pistol high, clear of the sand. The sea erupted in a white column which showered him with water, sand and minced sea life. He rolled erect again, aware that his cap was gone, and ran forward. The opening in the barricade was before him now and he was in a position to take a shot. The grenade had not actually been aimed at him, he realised, because no one within the three-sided barricade was paying him any attention. He stiffened into his preferred shooting stance, choosing his target. Something whispered past him, jerking his sleeve like an impatient child. He saw a hand come up, an arm swing back to throw. He drew a bead on it once and gently squeezed the trigger. The big gun boomed. He soaked up the recoil, still watching his target which slammed forward against the crates. Something small and black flew up out of the man's hand and fell back into the redoubt. The occupants were suddenly boiling out, like ants from a nest. Jesus felt another tug at his sleeve, higher this time, and a red-hot poker tip seemed to pass across the flat expanse of his belly.

Jesus's focus wavered then as he realised he was being shot at from the *Tiburon*. He swung round to look at the boat, taking his gun with him, looking for a target. And he shouted with surprise. That young madman Banderas had not stopped *Colorado* beside the patrol boat at all. The huge bows were towering over the *Tiburon* like the blade of a guillotine. And no one aboard appeared to have noticed – all were focused on the fire fight on the beach. Jesus seemed to lock eyes with the figure in the after deck holding a nasty-looking rifle with a red-dot sight a split second before *Colorado* ran the cabin-cruiser down. *Tiburon* slammed back until she caught on the sand, then she reared up and rolled over, coming to pieces in a spectacular display, like fireworks with no fire.

Jesus dragged his eyes away from what was being done to the bows of his command and swung back. An age seemed to have passed since he turned away, but it could only have been a second or two. The centre of the barricade erupted as the dropped grenade went off. Figures which had just thrown themselves out of it and were picking themselves up were thrown down again as *Colorado* slammed into the island.

Jesus Vega, expecting the impact, was only thrown to his knees, but then a great surf, born of the collision between the two boats and the sandy beach, washed over him and he was lucky to keep his powder dry. He fought erect out of the surge and the suck of it to find the fight was all but over. Gutierrez's men were sweeping in from his right and his own men, in file to Ramon's left shoulder, were sweeping in from the other direction. The smugglers between were throwing down their guns and putting up their hands.

With that situation sorted in his mind, Jesus swung back to check on the disposition of his command. It was one of the wisest and most fortunate things he did in the whole of his long life. For there, immediately behind him, perhaps fifteen metres away, the sniper from the deck of the *Tiburon* was coming erect in the water, his rifle held firmly across his chest. They seemed to see each other at exactly the same moment. Up came the rifle, the red-dot sight still wickedly agleam. Down came the Webley into the perfect firing position, bead drawn on the sniper's heart. But there, beneath the shoulder supporting the rifle's stock, lay a full, round bosom, covered by a skimpy bikini top. Automatically, before he could stop himself, Jesus Vega snapped his arm back until the ancient weapon, as out of date as his sense of honour, was pointing at the sky. For the most fleeting of instants they stood, the woman shining the red-dot sight in his eyes and the steel-haired captain pointing his pistol at the circling frigate birds. Then there were three shots in quick succession.

Ramon's came first. It was a single shot snatched desperately over his captain's shoulder and it hit the sniper in the left breast, smashing her ribs even as she pulled her trigger. The impact of Ramon's bullet was enough to turn the dying woman so that her shot missed Jesus by a hair and hit the chest of Hernan Gutierrez standing at the tide line behind, just as he drew a bead on her, also watching his captain's back. Hernan's aim was not unduly thrown off and his bullet completed the destruction of the sniper's left upper torso, slamming her back into the water as though she had been hit by the blast from a grenade. Only then did Jesus seem to realise what he had done; he returned his gun to the firing position and kept it centred on the woman until he had retrieved her rifle. One glance at her wound made any check for vital signs redundant.

Jesus turned, slipping the Webley back into its holster but leaving the leather flap open. He flicked the switch on the rifle and killed the red-dot sight. Then he slopped back towards the beach. On the way he found his cap, floating. He picked it up, beat it against his leg to clear it of sand and water and placed it on his head, before continuing through the surf to the beach.

Beside their battered crates the smugglers stood in a disconsolate group with their hands on their heads under the guns of Ramon, Raphael and the rest. Only Velula and Ociel were missing. They were kneeling on either side of the prostrate Gutierrez, working with silent concentration on his chest.

Refusing to speculate until he could see exactly what was going on, Jesus crossed to the little group, throwing the sniper rifle on the ground as he approached. 'How is it going, Hernan?' he asked quietly.

'Pretty bad, Captain,' wheezed Gutierrez. 'This clumsy *bastardo* Velula seems to think that even the slightest flesh wound must be probed, disinfected and cauterised a millimetre at a time.'

Only then did Jesus look down, surprised to discover that he had been looking away on purpose. He met Ociel's bright eyes above the

136

blood-spattered expanse of Hernan's gaping shirt. 'Velula is doing a good job, Captain,' said Ociel. 'Sit down please, sir, and let me check the wound on your chest. It looks worse than the one on the lieutenant's.'

Jesus sat down obediently, distantly surprised to note that his knees were all too willing to assist him in this, and then he looked out across the wreckage of *Tiburon* to the sleek cutwater of his own ship resting on the sand. He frowned suddenly, and Ociel, opening the front of his bloody uniform jacket, paused, thinking he might be hurting his captain. But no. 'There are a couple of boats inbound, Ramon,' called Jesus. 'Whoever's in charge of them reports to me the minute they touch the sand.'

The first was the commander of the *Alvaro Obregon*, almost inarticulate with thanks and praise for what *Colorado* and her people had done. Such leadership! Such bravery! He had seen it all from the battered foredeck of his command. It was no wonder that Captain Vega was a legend in the service. To have planned such an attack like the greatest of generals, to have given command of his own ship to that quick-thinking and resourceful young officer Lieutenant Banderas, to have led the attack with such skill and disregard for personal danger . . .

There was more, but Jesus Vega did not really register anything beyond the realisation that young Banderas had run *Colorado* onto the beach on purpose.

The final import of the commander's effusion was that he wished to go now, and he had orders to take the prisoners with him, living and dead. He also had orders to recover whatever was being smuggled but such was the state of his own command that he feared he could not run the risk of taking so much aboard. The younger man's worried eyes made clear his concern that with so many hale prisoners and so many wounded seamen guarding the contraband, the temptation to recover their loot might prove too much for all concerned. Jesus shrugged and winced, discovering for the first time just how bad the bullet wound across his belly was. He glanced down, surprised, to see Ociel busy with butterfly stitches in a couple of places along the bright purple welt. He looked up into the commander's worried face. 'Of course,' he said. 'Have you any idea what they were smuggling?'

The commander shrugged, 'Drugs?'

Jesus smiled tightly. It was as good a guess as any. Certainly the money being thrown at this one operation made it look like drugs at first glance. Boats, guns and personnel of this quality and number didn't come cheap. Suddenly, he felt a little more positive about the

137

fact that he had only a skeleton crew made up of his most trusted men left aboard his own command.

'Yes,' he said. 'You take the prisoners and we'll take the crates. But you'll have to get someone at Ensenada or Mexico City to make up their minds what to do with the crates within the next twenty-four hours, or it's all going up to Cortez for scrap.'

The commander of the second small boat was Lieutenant Banderas. Wide-eyed at what he saw all around him, and stuttering with shock at what he had himself done to his briefly held command, he came to report to his Captain.

'What is so important that it cannot wait until I get myself and my men back aboard, boy?' asked Jesus Vega, surprising himself with the gentle tone of the question.

'The tide, Captain. It is the tide which is so important, sir. The tide was at the very heart of my plan.'

Jesus Vega laughed aloud, and Hernan Gutierrez sat up, wincing. 'What is it, Captain?'

'Lieutenant Banderas here has out-thought the lot of us. Well done, young man. You have performed better service today than you realise, perhaps. And your plan was a good one – if you watched the rate of your approach with the utmost care!'

'I did, sir,' said the boy, owlish with awe. 'And the helmsman warned me, and El Jefe explained the revolutions . . .'

'I might have known. I might have known. Very well. You are now the senior officer left unwounded and it is your duty to get the contraband aboard. As you do, bear in mind the tide, if you please!'

'I will, sir. I will.'

Hernan Gutierrez and Jesus Vega walked side by side to the bullet-splintered and blast-scarred pile of boxes. 'He was able to take the chance of driving *Colorado* in onto the sandbank at the foot of the tide because he knew it was low ebb and he planned for it,' Jesus was explaining. 'It was a risk, but it destroyed *Tiburon* and probably saved my life. *Colorado* may be wedged tight now,' Jesus glanced at the tide line further up the slope, 'but there'll be six metres of water under her keel by moonrise tonight. She'll be safely afloat long before then.'

'Trust a kid straight out of college to remember that the tides across the bay can vary by seven metres and more,' said Gutierrez, amused.

'Eight up at Puerto Penasco, some days,' said Jesus Vega companionably.

'Eight-metre tides, that's fearsome,' said Gutierrez.

'Right, Ramon,' said Jesus, changing the subject. 'What's in these crates?'

'I haven't looked, Captain.'

'No. But you'll have thought. Unlike that inexperienced young commander. Do we really imagine drug runners are going to use several million dollars' worth of cocaine as a kind of Alamo? Even under these circumstances? Take the top off, Ramon. Banderas will be here to take it aboard in a moment and I want to know what we're dealing with before he gets here in case we have to keep it just between ourselves.'

'But, Captain,' said Gutierrez, 'what could be more difficult to deal with than drugs?'

'I hesitate to speculate. But I'd say this contraband has to be something which could stand a good deal of rough handling without losing too much of its value. Something which could take at least a bullet strike without leaking away. Let's have a look, shall we?'

Ramon loosened the splintered boarding on the topmost case and lifted it to reveal dry leaf and coir wadding. Gutierrez reached out his hand automatically, but Jesus stopped him with a gesture. 'Knife, Ramon?'

Ramon produced a panga such as coconut harvesters use, and Jesus slipped it in among the coir and stirred it gently about. At once a snake's head reared and struck with dazzling speed the fangs shattering against the sharp steel of the blade. Then it retreated into the rustling wedding in the box.

'Animals?' said Hernan, awed and fearful. 'Animals?'

'Insurance, I'd say,' said Jesus Vega quietly. 'But even so, we'll have to move this very carefully and lock it away in our most secure accommodation. Ah.'

With this satisfied little monosyllable the captain lifted the point of the panga and there, impaled upon it, its broad point through the gape of an eye socket, was a mask in the Mayan style. Clearly very ancient. Clearly very rare. Obviously made of pure, thick, gleaming gold.

Chapter Fourteen

No one had called him Joe Aloha for thirty years, but now that he was going back to say goodbye he couldn't get the old nickname out of his head. It was what they had called him in his company in Vietnam, and when he came round on the foredeck of the USS *Colorado* on that terrible day, he had told the field nurse with the white, worried face that this was his name: Joe Aloha.

Distantly, Joe heard them announce that his flight was boarding. He raised his hand to his family and hugged his wife. She was a woman of steel, he thought; a woman of the old sort, like his own mother. He had seen her, on the night after his eldest son was born, when her milk came on, he had seen her wade out into the bay below their home, as his own mother had, and suckle baby sharks on it. She risked her young life and gave freely of her goodness to the children of the great tigers so the gods of the big fish and the deep waters would watch over him. Only certain women of each generation would dare to do such a thing. He was proud to be the son of one and the husband of another.

They called Joe's flight again and he turned, leaning heavily on his cane to balance the weight of the flight bag, favouring the leg the sharks in the Mekong Delta had ripped to shreds before the *Colorado* came to his rescue, and limped to the departure gate.

Joe eased himself into his seat with difficulty. He was a huge man, great of height and girth, designed for the great ocean-going canoes of his people, not the restrictions of an airline seat. But at last he was comfortable, with his stiff leg out in the aisle but close enough to the seats in front for no one to trip over it. He introduced himself to a little old lady sitting immediately beside him, whose face and demeanour brought such unfamiliar expressions to his mind as 'chipper' and 'spry'. Beyond her was a lanky and uncommunicative youth listening to his personal CD.

Joe sat back and watched as the video, echoed by the hostess, went through the safety procedures. He listened only distantly to what was said, his mind a rage of memory and speculation. He had not expected to be so moved by exercising what had seemed a simple whim based on a news report about the decommissioning of a Mexican coastal protection vessel. But, as is the case after the intense trauma of coming so close to death, a surprising amount of hidden emotion lay buried in recesses he had never even suspected, thirty years on. And some of it was surfacing now that he was going to say farewell to the trusty old friend who had saved his life.

'Good afternoon, ladies and gentlemen, this is the captain. On behalf of Intercontinental I would like to welcome you aboard this non-stop flight from Hawaii to San Diego. I am sure you will have a comfortable flight, but I should warn you that we have been alerted to severe weather running to the north of our route. We will be taking a good swing south to avoid it but, in the meantime, for your comfort and safety, I will be leaving the seat belt signs switched on throughout the flight and I would ask that you move around the cabin as little as possible and keep your belts fastened at all times when you are sitting down.'

'Bad weather,' said the little old lady sitting beside him, her thin face creased with worry. 'Do you think that's anything to worry about?'

'No, ma'am,' he said easily, his deep voice rumbling over the English like a river over restless boulders. 'If there was any cause for worry, they'd surely hold the flight.'

Joe first experienced the storm as part of his dream. The increasingly restless movement of the big jetliner changed the nature of what he was dreaming and added snatches of memory so that when he jerked awake he was not certain *when* he was, though he knew where at once. The dip of the fuselage rolled the cabin slightly to the side so that Joe looked down, past the lady in the next seat, over the lolling form beyond and out at the storm ahead.

From childhood, Joe had known the look of stormy skies from below. Looking up from the shore across the vast expanses of the South Pacific, he could tell from the clouds and their reflection in the water what would happen in the air above his island and in the ocean around it for the next twenty-four hours and more. The navy, a secondment to naval intelligence, and television weather satellite pictures had taught him the look of storms from above. He had never seen such a storm from such an angle as this one, but his wise eyes understood what they saw well enough.

Looking through the window, with the sun above and behind him, Joe saw the swirling tail of the thing ahead, like the smoke of a restless

142

fire mountain. Below the smoky tail, lines of rain ran down into the distant, lava-grey water. Ahead of the tail coiled the huge black heart of the thing, towering up so high that the tops of the black slopes of cloud seemed to sweep the indigo floor of space itself.

To Joe's dazzled eyes, the enormous totality of the storm seemed to be contained in the frame of the Perspex window – impossibly, like a trick photograph. And yet that was how he remembered it, as the cabin rolled the other way then dropped in the turbulence of the storm's wake, and he slumped back into his seat with enough force to make it creak beneath him. The cabin's drop through the turbulence slowed. The jet slipped smoothly back into control. As though the whole manoeuvre had been a carefully prepared part of the flight plan, the jet swooped away on the southern track, and the storm coiled its way southwards, seeming to move almost as fast as the aircraft.

'I blame all those CFCs,' said the little old lady with the absolute certainty of age. 'The greenhouse effect. Global warming. They say El Niño is worse this year than ever before. I despair, I really do.'

'It's nothing we should worry about, ma'am. Our kids'll sort it all out, after we're all asleep and laid to rest, likely as not.'

'Well, I hope my sons will sort it out a good deal sooner than that,' said the old lady tartly. 'One lives in Los Angeles and the other in Las Vegas, and it looks as though that monster down there is going to hit the both of them, one after the other, harder than merry hell.'

The first storm warning came in over the radio just after Chester Shaw climbed into the car but he was taking a nip of bourbon to steady himself for the drive and so he missed it. Then, savouring the fire of the spirit in his belly, he leaned forward and switched over to the tape deck. The old Ford's sound system didn't have an interrupt facility for weather or traffic reports, so Chester drove off up the freeway in even more ignorance than usual.

As he turned onto the southernmost section of Highway 1A1 up the Florida Keys and set the car's broad, battered bonnet to the north, the weather seemed to threaten nothing other than burning, humid heat. Chester powered on for an hour or two, listening to his Meat Loaf tape and wondering when he dare take the next nip of bourbon. He was in a hurry, but also in two minds. It was six hours' hard drive to the airport; if he didn't hurry he would miss his flight. Perhaps he should have taken the local airline up from Key West to Orlando after all.

Chester had booked the ticket from Orlando to Yuma on an

impulse and was still in two minds whether or not to take his seat. The flight money had come in a letter from his brother-in-law, enclosing a newspaper cutting about the *Colorado*. In words that were his brother-in-law George's but with a sentiment that was pure big sister Martha, the letter suggested that a formal farewell might close the whole sorry chapter in Chester's life.

If you could call twenty years a chapter.

When Chester had bought the Ford, during his years bumming about in Sonora in the early nineties, there had been a dashboard ornament with a picture of the Virgin in a frame. The Virgin was still there, but now she was behind a picture of Chester, in full dress uniform, young, trim, confident, straight out of West Point. He had looked like that for about six months before everything went haywire for him when his whole command was wiped out at Grenada.

Round the picture he had hung his medals, still on their dress ribbons, so they chimed like St Christopers, keeping the old car safe. They were good metal, these medals, unlike the Virgin's frame which had tarnished in the salty humidity of the Keys. They were as bright now as the day he put them there, though the ribbons had faded almost to white. Usually when he looked at them, on the few little trips he took up and down the Keys these days – almost never as far as the mainland – they meant absolutely nothing to him, any more than the photograph did. But today, they kept catching his eye as he drove, and the effect was so disturbingly distracting that he pulled off the freeway and paused for a slug of bourbon sooner than he'd intended to.

Chester was burned out. Everyone was agreed on that. His army invalid pension – one of the chiming medals was a Purple Heart – kept his battered old boat running. Like most of the other burned-out cases down here, washed up on the smallest, least frequented Keys like jetsam washed up on the tide, he sponged off his folks too, when he could. And like their books, the book he had been writing since he got back from Sonora at the turn of 1995 was the book of his experiences, some kind of explanation, reason, excuse, for having wound up where he had wound up, as though he had had some control over things; as though he could at least make some kind of order, some kind of sense of it all.

It was in the mistaken belief that there was some kind of order or sense to any of it that Chester's brother-in-law George had sent him the money wrapped in the news report about the imminent destruction of an old Mexican coastal vessel. But Chester had been fooled into seeing some kind of a pattern there too, or he would never have wasted good drinking money on a plane ticket. He would never have dared look himself in the face over a bowl of tepid water and drawn a shaking razor over his chin, just in case one of the guys who pulled him – him alone of all his command, wounded to the heart and head and fervently wishing to die – out of the bloody water might be there, also saying goodbye.

Coming out of his reverie, Chester looked in his mirror and frowned. There was a black line on the horizon behind him, as though someone had taken a thick piece of charcoal and drawn it right across the bottom of the blue sky.

Meat Loaf clicked out of the tape deck, the way it sometimes did on the fourth or fifth replay. Chester pushed it back in before the babble of the radio made any sense to him. He looked in his rear-view again, but the hump of the empty freeway was hiding the sky and the gathering bulk of the next island made it impossible to see the sea. Even so, as he roared past some tall condos, Chester found himself wrestling with the Ford's big steering wheel as the first gust tried to chuck the big car up onto a fourth-storey balcony.

Chester wasn't much of a captain and no kind of a sailor at all. His boat *Waste of Space* was really just a kind of floating dosshouse. He relied on the local radio stations and short-wave for weather predictions on the rare occasions he took her out, and the Key West coastguards had never let him down. He never really needed to bother with reading the state of sea and sky around him. If the coastguard broadcast predicted bad weather, Chester was battened down hard with a two-litre bottle of bourbon and that was that. And he didn't come up for air until the coastguards told him it was over.

Had Chester been less preoccupied and more sober he would at least have registered how clear the road had become in spite of the fact that he was getting deeper into civilisation. But as driving conditions rapidly got more difficult, he just concentrated on staying in the road. By the time he lifted the old Ford onto the next causeway section, half the sky behind him was black. The wind was beginning to get really gusty and a combination of rain and spray was washing across his windscreen faster than the wipers could slosh it away. Undaunted, Chester put his headlights on and reached for the bourbon again.

This time when Meat Loaf came out of the stereo, Chester missed it and it fell onto the floor. Cursing and looking down, Chester drove onwards, failing to see the first POLICE STOP sign by the side of the road. A particularly strong wash of spray hit his windscreen, jerking his attention back to the road, but unfortunately breaking one of his wipers so that although he saw the second STOP sign, he could not quite make out what it said. When he saw the roadblock itself, he was too late to stop, and would not have done so in any case, that shock of surprise sobering him just enough to warn him how drunk he would seem to a traffic cop.

The roadblock was a public safety measure – no one in the Sheriff's Department or the Highway Patrol really thought anyone would actually try to run it – so Chester was able to swing round the tail of the car parked across one and a half of the carriageways and vanish into the stormy murk unchallenged. He had a plane to catch and no arrogant son of a bitch from Highway Patrol was going to stop Captain Chester Ulysses Shaw, US Marines, Ret'd.

Relieved at his lucky escape and reaching that level of drunkenness which looks like sobriety reborn, Chester took a swig at the bourbon and pressed his foot to the floor. Behind him, the might of the huge hurricane which was hurling itself out of the Caribbean seemed to hesitate, with its centre away to the south. Then, for reasons best known to itself, it decided to swing the whole great wheel of its system north and west.

With the simple luck sometimes afforded to the drunk and the hopeless – though almost never to the drunk behind a steering wheel – the storm allowed Chester to live a while longer yet. He made it in off the highway to the first motel forecourt he could see. He wrestled with himself, seeing the impossibility of proceeding and yet suddenly agonised to be missing the flight, the ceremony, the chance of rebirth. Then he got out of the Ford into the storm. He dropped his bourbon on the way into reception and watched it wash, terribly diluted, down the gutter. Then he stumbled into the brightness of the reception, his tears indistinguishable from the rain upon his face, and found the place welcoming, free, and full of travellers benighted like him, and refugees from the storm. He slept rolled up in a rug on the floor and awoke sober to an overcast morning.

In spite of the pointlessness of the exercise, Chester completed his drive north. Dazed with the novelty of near-sobriety, he made it to the airport and even to the check-in desk where a cheery flight attendant told him the flight to Yuma had been delayed because of the hurricane. But the big winds had gone west and north through Texas now so it would be leaving soon. His reservation stood and his seat was waiting for him. Naturally there was a bar service aboard, she said. And of course all the drinks would be free.

Peter Phelps had never captained the USS *Colorado* but he had been her last executive officer. After ten years in the Mexican service, the

Americans who had captained her were getting thin on the ground now. Only the last two were left. One was an admiral and the other was in a retirement home. The scuttlebutt was that the two men had got mixed up somewhere along the line – the wrong one was in Happy Acres and the wrong one was in the Pentagon.

'Peter,' called Betty, Phelps's wife. 'Will you stop looking at yourself in that uniform and get in here? We have to finish packing and then there are all these forms about Bobby's college loan.'

Retired now and running a little car dealership in Portland, Maine, Phelps was proud of the fact that he still fitted into his old uniform. Betty might tease and complain a little, but she was happy enough about it, especially when he took her to the functions he arranged as leader of the local Veterans Association. Last year, as local rep, he had taken her up to some of the big stuff in Washington DC. She had had the picture of him shaking hands with the President on the mantel until quite recently.

But now the other side of all that partying had come up. Neither of the ex-captains could go, but someone had to represent all the US Navy crews who had served aboard *Colorado* over the years. She had been a lucky ship, a popular posting; a step up for many. There had been a collection. He was to pick up a commemorative wreath on his way south. Though he had become commander and full captain himself before he called it a day, Peter Phelps recalled the old *Colorado* with more affection than any other ship he had served on or commanded. When they asked for a week of his time in such an undertaking, Peter had been glad to say yes, even though Bobby would be off to college in the fall and he still hadn't got round to filling in his personal or business IRS forms either.

'*Peter!*' said Betty, coming in through the bedroom door and seeing him standing there in full uniform.

'I'm coming, darling,' he said, turning away from the mirror. But instead of the expected impatience in her eyes, there was something else entirely. Something he knew came into his own eyes on the special occasions when she wore that black silk negligee he had bought her in Hong Kong. 'Hey now,' he said gently. 'And it isn't even Saturday night.'

'You won't be here Saturday,' said Betty, pulling the tails of her blouse impatiently out of the waist of her jeans. The movement emphasised perfectly how slim her waist was still, how full the chest above, how firm the hips below.

'Now you mention it, I won't,' he said, his square, capable fingers busy at the bright buttons of the dress jacket. 'And, I should

147

point out, you weren't here last Saturday either. At your sister's or some such.'

He unzipped his fly and dropped his pants exactly as she had dropped hers, onto the warm blue bedroom carpet.

'Hey!' she said, kicking her panties at his head. 'I spent an hour getting the creases in those pressed right. You hang them properly, sailor boy.'

He did as she directed and turned.

'Now,' she said throatily, kneeling astride on the bed, pushing herself forward like a hot and happy centrefold, 'talking of properly hung sailor boys . . .'

Aldo Cagliari also stood in front of the mirror in his bedroom at his house outside Waukegan overlooking Lake Michigan. Not his house – he never thought of it as his house. His parents' house. Still theirs, though they had both been dead for years. The house was empty, no one else lived within its cramped, ill-maintained walls; he hardly ever came here himself. He would have sold it to maintain his habit or to support his companies, but the realtors always sang the same song – the property was worthless till he spent some money on it. Only the bright, new, well-decorated properties were moving these days, they had said for twenty years.

Aldo, too, was wearing uniform. It was a naval lieutenant's uniform and he had worn it for five years' short commission, way back in his youth, as a way of getting out of this house and seeing the world; getting some training for anything other than the motor business or farming. It was far too tight now, but there was no one there to tell him that and it seemed to him that as long as the seat seam held across his ass and the buttons across his belly didn't burst when he sat down, then he would look OK. The way he looked was incidental in any case. It was all a charade. He only needed to look like a navy man again – resurrect his old serial number and forces ID – to convince some Mexican official that he had once served on the USS *Colorado*. To get aboard like Mr Alighieri had told him to, and keep an eye on Richard Mariner.

Aldo himself could not quite figure what Mariner was up to. The guy seemed straight as a die to him. So why Mr Alighieri thought he had the narcs in tow was well beyond his computation. But, he guessed, a law-abiding guy like Mariner might see it as his duty to do a bit of legwork for the authorities. Keep an eye out. Keep the old 'Special Relationship' alive and well, for what it was worth these

148

days. And, aboard *Colorado*, that could be as dangerous as trying to set up as the opposition.

Aldo, depressed, back on the bottom rung professionally and financially, was a little surprised to find himself still alive. All the way back up here from Vegas he had been pondering his existence – and who his real enemies were. Downstairs in the study, the phone began to produce that strange strangulated sound it gave when a fax was coming in. Aldo turned away from the mirror and his dark reflections. Still in uniform, given a bit of military bounce and swagger, he pounded down the stairs. In the dull light of the study he could not at first make out what was coming through the fax. But then he realised and sat down, shaking a little as the paper fed out into his hand.

Jody lay on a big bed. A hand towel rested demurely across her nipples and ended at her navel. Another, smaller, was draped over her tummy to protect her decency, just, in spite of the wide stretch of the legs facing the camera. At the bottom of the picture someone had scrawled, 'Jody says *Hi*.' The photo, especially in black and white, would hardly have turned heads anywhere, except that the message on the bottom, written between the ankles, drew attention to the fact that they, like the wrists, were handcuffed to the bedstead.

After the picture came a series of documents in English and Spanish granting Lieutenant Aldo Cagliari, USN Ret'd, permission to visit his old ship *Colorado* on the occasion of her decommissioning ceremony in two days' time. Below the faxes came the brief message: 'Top copies, visas etc. waiting with tickets at O'Hare. Pick up no later than midnight.'

Aldo looked at his watch. Plenty of time. If he really wanted to be bothered. The temptation swept over him, suddenly, to just sit down, sniff a line or two and let it all wash over him and away. What did he really care about some brainless bimbo GoGo dancer from Vegas? Let them keep her and play whatever sick games they wanted with her. Let Mr Alighieri marry her if he wanted – a worse fate then any other Aldo could think of.

But then the fax continued making its strangulated whirring and the companion to the first picture of Jody arrived. This time the towels were gone. Right at the top of her right thigh, where the flesh folded most softly, was written a big crude letter H. On the other thigh, an I. In fact, as the fax fed out, it was possible to see 'Hi' written on Jody's tummy, ribs, breasts; anywhere humiliating and embarrassing. And in big letters on the wall above the clown smile of her over-made-up face. Aldo hoped the letters had been written there with lipstick, he really did. The message was clear. Screw this up, Aldo, and the writing's on the wall for you. And, he reckoned, reaching for the phone, it definitely will not be written in lipstick.

'O'Hare flight inquiries?'

'I have a reservation on the two a.m. flight for Mexico City. I would like to confirm seat and departure, please. As he spoke, Aldo was absently tearing the pictures of Jody off the fax roll and folding them into his insurance envelope. It wasn't much insurance. On the front it said 'IN THE EVENT OF MY DEATH OR DISAPPEARANCE, PLEASE FORWARD TO THE LAS VEGAS POLICE DEPART-MENT.' His problem was that he didn't have anyone he knew or trusted well enough to give it to. But then, suddenly, overwhelmed by some self-destructive whim, he put this envelope into another one and wrote across the front of it the address of the FBI in Washington DC.

'Hello, Lieutenant Cagliari?' said the girl at O'Hare. 'We recommend all our passengers get in as early as possible this evening, sir. With the terrible storms in Wyoming, Utah and Colorado, our schedules are beginning to suffer. Especially on flights heading south . . .'

It was one of Richard Mariner's faults – and he admitted to many – that he could not simply leave things to underlings. He delegated – few delegated with more care and wisdom – but when the chips came down he liked to be there himself, acting as long-stop for his girls and boys. So it was that he found himself sitting on his bed at the Luxor, wrapped in his white towelling bathrobe, checking through the minutiae of the first set of contracts. He had a photocopy, and the margins were dotted with annotations in his decided handwriting in the bright green ink he used for contract work.

At the foot of Richard's bed the big wide-screen television was completing the international section of the news. The financial section, immediately before, had been relatively satisfactory. In spite of the fact that a lack of general information about his homeland in the section of the broadcast he had seen so far had left him slightly edgy, nothing important seemed to have happened in his absence, and that was the way he liked it. Dividing his attention between the screen and the work on his lap, he began to favour the contract again, but he left the TV on in the background, just in case.

Conway had done a first-rate job on this, Richard was thinking as he worked. She really deserved something for such excellent, unstinting work. The gold shaft of his favourite Shaeffer glinted as he marked another section to double-check with her in the morning, before breakfast.

'There are those I know who blame such things on global warming,' said the television gently in the background, just grazing Richard's consciousness. 'But it looks as though our area is going to be experiencing some pretty unusual weather conditions during the next day or two. Bobby-Jo? What does our weather girl say?'

'Well, Cal, it isn't just us. It's the states away to the north as far as Colorado and Wyoming too. I'm sure everyone remembers the ice-storm winters and the heat-wave summers with which the last millennium ended. This new millennium seems determined to get itself in the record books too, young though it is.'

'How's that, Bobby-Jo? We expecting snow?'

'No, Cal, not snow, but rain, I'm afraid, and lots of it. Turning to the weather map behind me here, we can see the problem. Or, should I say, the problems. Plural.'

Richard glanced up from the neat print of the page in front of him. Bobby-Jo turned out to be a demure young lady in a summery but formal green cotton suit. Cal seemed to be a blue-eyed, grey-haired faintly familiar face framed in the upper right corner of the screen. Behind Bobby-Jo was a map of the southern Rockies area, with Las Vegas at its centre, falling away east and south into Arizona, Texas and the Gulf; tumbling more steeply to the west into California and the Pacific. 'To the east of us, as I'm sure everybody knows,' Richard didn't – he had missed the US news, 'Hurricane Benedict has crossed the Texas coast east of Galveston and is driving straight up into Colorado, Utah and Wyoming. The western fringes of the storm are even now being pushed up by the strong rise of the eastern Rockies, and rain is beginning to fall very heavily there. We predict during the next couple of days that the major areas of severe flooding from Hurricane Benedict will move up here, over Texas, New Mexico and Arizona, before swinging west over Colorado and Wisconsin towards Salt Lake City, Utah.'

Richard watched the swirl of storm outline turn into rain clouds bucketing all the way up the eastern slopes of the Rockies, with more and more clouds jostling to get in there like shoppers at a Harrods sale.

Cal continued, sounding genuinely concerned. 'That looks pretty bad for the folks in the eastern section of our area, Bobby-Jo.'

'It surely does, Cal. But I'm afraid it's only half of the story. Over

151

here to the west, El Niño seems to have been up to its tricks again. We have a huge storm pushing in over Los Angeles.'

'I guess folks will remember our footage of the flooded orange groves.'

'I'm sure they will, Cal. And they'll be seeing a lot more footage like that, I'm afraid. Well, this storm is headed straight over our own heads and then it looks set to do a twist east of Salt Lake City too, before breaking up over the eastern Rockies. Here in the Wyoming and Colorado areas, though, as you can see, there might well be a mighty tussle with the dying hurricane which will be moving into the same air space at the same time.'

Behind Bobby-Jo, the swirl of the storm pattern over Los Angeles broke up into more threatening little cloud shapes, each one raining for all it was worth, the whole lot marching eastwards over the Rockies like Hannibal's armies over the Alps. Like Caesar's legions, the cloud diagrams of Hurricane Benedict came the other way. The great state of Wyoming looked as though it would be a battleground for a week or more. Images of Roman armies did not seem enough to Richard suddenly. The place would be like the Somme.

He looked at the diagram, as Bobby-Jo and Cal had a few final words of worried dialogue. There was something deeply disturbing in the pattern, but it did not immediately register. He looked down at the contract but could no longer concentrate on it. It was only when an announcer's voice came from the TV saying, 'Tonight's family film stars Meryl Streep in the adventure thriller *River Wild* . . .' that the penny dropped. He looked up, seeing not the pictures of the raging river or the intrepid woman fighting it, but Bobby-Jo and her weather map.

For there, sandwiched between the track of Hurricane Benedict and the spawn of El Niño as they converged into the sodden battlefield Wyoming was destined to become, there lay the headwaters, feeder streams and the watercourse of the mighty Colorado River.

Chapter Fifteen

Even after their unscheduled stay in the village of Los Muertos Sierra de Juarez, the team in the *Pequod* arrived in the brand new city of Cortez at the brand new mouth of the Colorado earlier than expected. The city itself looked largely like a building site. It was established on the western bank of the river's deepened, strengthened estuary, and was spreading across a newly constructed bridge onto the Isla Montague at the mouth of the river. To the east of Isla Montague lay another little island and, beyond that, the village of Golfo de Santa Clara. Because the estuary did not run exactly north-south, but swung several points to the east during its final kilometres, there was a surprising amount of vacant acreage on the east bank to the north-west of Golfo de Santa Clara. It was envisioned that in the near future this land would be subsumed into the burgeoning metropolis of Cortez, but at the moment it was what the west bank had been until less than a year ago – desert-backed swampland running from the sluggish, shallow, mangroves of the coast up over the highway and the railtrack into the Desierto de Altor. Surveying this desolation from the heights of the eastern levee's southernmost reach, the crew of the *Pequod* enjoyed a lively debate as to whether it should be called in the future the Left Bank or the Lower East Side.

And they were a crew now, thought Robin, surveying them with no little affection. Somewhere along the line, in the rapids or the irrigation ditches, under the mosquitoes or the fiesta *pinatas* which had looked like animals and cartoon characters at Los Muertos, raining sweets and presents for the children as they smashed them, this group of disparate people had become a unit; a crew. Which was a pity, really, because they were all just about to split up. After the reception in Cortez, Robin and Mickey would be heading south to San Felipe for tomorrow's ceremony. Conception was due to be returning to Mexico City, though not until early next week. Kramer and the others were due to be picked up by a visiting American destroyer down here on a goodwill tour and currently holding open day in Puerto Vallarta. Kramer reckoned that they would have time for a little boating in the Sea of Cortez before the navy stopped glad-handing the locals, and everyone else thought he was right.

They were sitting on the eastern levee. It gave the best view of the gulf – the western levee ran into the foot of the Isla Montague bridge whose high span blocked much of the southward view. It was also quiet, a good place for rest and reflection. On the west bank, above and below the bustling highway over the bridge, stood the new dock and ship maintenance facility, and even now the great foundries and engineering works there were gearing up for their first major project – the reduction of the *Colorado* to scrap. As the spur from the main rail line had not reached here yet, the massive weight of scrap iron the old ship represented would be carried north in great pantechnicons, and large numbers of these monsters seemed to be labouring through the shipyards, over the bridge and up Highway 5 already. The western levee was a noisy, dirty, depressing place. Even here, a good fifteen kilometres away across the island and the arms of the estuary embracing it, the sounds of the throbbing industry filled the air like distant thunder.

Robin looked down at the silent mangroves and thoughtfully slapped a mosquito on the back of her hand, thankful she had put up with the foul anti-malarial pills after all. Something big and slithery moved among the tangled roots down in the salt marshes below. There was a coughing grunt, a *snap* like the closing of a man-trap. Something gave a shriek such as she imagined a dying child might make.

Maybe civilisation wasn't such a bad thing after all, she thought.

Actually, when they got into the swing of it, civilisation Cortez style was pretty good. They were met in the gleaming port marina facility well upriver from the shipyards by the mayor and a representative group of city fathers. Leaving the battered *Pequod* tethered beside several million dollars' worth of ocean-going indulgence, they were whisked away to their suites at the Cadiz Camono Hotel, finest in the blossoming city. Here they unpacked what little baggage they had and did their best to make themselves presentable for a major corporate reception and publicity binge which was clearly designed to last far into the night as the Mexicans celebrated their achievement – unique in over a century – lavishing publicity on them with much more alacrity than the networks further north had done. They were due to assemble in the banquet centre in an hour for the beginning of the full formalities, they were informed. There would apparently be press and dignitaries from Mexicali, Mexico City, all over.

Robin sat wrapped in a soft towelling robe, steaming quietly in

154

the air conditioning after a lengthy, scalding shower, and looked at the pathetic display of battered clothing she had laid out on the huge, firm bed. Everything she owned was stained, soiled, creased or torn. It occurred to her that the smart and eminently photographable little Chanel suit she had brought from England for the *Colorado*'s decommissioning ceremony was still packed in her suitcase in the Luxor. She looked at her watch. That was another thing she needed to talk to Richard about; he must be sure to bring that with him and arrive aboard early enough tomorrow to allow her to change.

She crossed to the phone, obtained an outside line and called the Luxor. She stood, soaking up the coolness of the marble floor through the soles of her feet and gazing distractedly at the bright pink and purple designs on the white walls as connection clicked through. And, for a wonder, the bloody man was there.

'Mariner?' The rumble of his voice brought her out in goosebumps. Perhaps he wasn't quite so bloody after all.

'Hi, Mariner. Mariner here.'

'Hi, darling. What can I do for you? Just on my way into the final meeting of the day.'

'Final meeting period, I hope, Richard. You have to be on a plane at midnight at the latest or you'll never make the ceremony. Talking of which—'

'Can't guarantee it, I'm afraid, darling. The weather's shut down all the major airlines until after the weekend, by the look of things. Haven't you seen the news?'

'Well, you simply have to be here. I can't go to a full naval ceremony at midday tomorrow wearing nothing but T-shirt and jeans, for crying out loud!'

'That at least is easy to fix. I made arrangements when I realised about the card. Where's your nearest bank?'

'In the lobby.'

'I'll wire funds there as quickly as I can.'

'Immediately would be good. I have a full formal reception at one.'

'I'll do it before I go to the meeting. Keep the receipts.'

'As always. And you get yourself down here p.d.q., darling.'

'I will. And Robin?'

'Yes?'

'I'm so glad you're off the river.'

'What? Why?'

'Watch the news. 'Bye.'

Robin phoned the American Express bank in the lobby first, gave

155

them her room number and got their promise to alert her the instant funds arrived. Then she turned on the TV, found CNN and got their equivalent of the Cal and Bobby-Jo show. CNN's footage of the flooded soft-fruit farms in Los Angeles, the dangerously over-brimming LA Aqueduct and All American Canal, not to mention the already flooding headwaters of the San Joaquin River, made Richard's point pretty well, even before she saw the diagrams demonstrating how two of the biggest, wettest and most destructive storms in decades were going head to head above the states of Colorado and Wyoming. I have to tell Kramer about this, she thought, and was on her way out of the door to do so when the phone rang.

'Come in,' called Conception's voice and, obeying, Robin found the major buttoning a bedraggled battledress top over a less than effulgent white T-shirt. Her battledress trousers seemed, if anything, to have stretched. For the first time in their acquaintance, the dazzling Mexican looked dull, dowdy.

Conception glanced up at Robin, also in jeans and dirty T-shirt, then looked at her reflection in the mirror. Her long face, like her trousers, seemed to stretch. 'What?' she asked.

'This,' said Robin, holding up a piece of white paper.

'What is that?'

'This is a credit note for unlimited corporate funds. All we have to do is keep the receipts.'

'What receipts?'

'The receipts from the five fashion boutiques above and below the bank in the lobby downstairs.'

Realisation rose in Conception's eyes like a sunrise and a smile dawned on her face.

When Kramer saw the pair of them an hour later, the last thing on God's green earth he wanted to discuss was water flow through the upper Colorado basin. The American military engineer knew nothing at all about fashion houses and little enough about fabrics, cuts and styles. He just knew he had never seen anything quite like these two up close and actual. Robin was wearing a white halterneck cut low enough to give a demure glimpse of a lightly tanned cleavage only her bra manufacturer knew she possessed. The white dress didn't quite make it to her tanned knees and was trimmed in just enough navy to give it a nautical swagger. It was set off by a navy and white handbag and a pair of extravagant white and navy strappy high heels.

156

Kramer thought it was the impact of the dress but suddenly the face below the gold of her hair looked longer, the cheekbones higher, the lips more defined and the steady grey eyes deeper, darker lashed.

Nevertheless, Kramer gave Robin little more than a glance, for beside her stood the belle of the ball. Conception wore a blouse in burned orange and white, cut low enough to reveal a high, deep, unsupported cleavage and the upper line of a matching tube top. The blouse was tucked into a severe white belt which at first glance looked to be a little wider than the orange and white miniskirt beneath it. Then, after an eternity of Hershey's Milky legs, there came the most outrageous burned orange high heels he had ever seen. Conception's idea of make-up, like her idea of dress, lacked all the subtlety of Robin's and had all the impact of an armoured division. The sight of the pair of them, side by side, made him hesitate, agape, and Mickey Vargas slipped in like Flynn before him.

The first part of the reception was lengthy, but the food was of such high quality that nobody really seemed to mind. Robin and Conception, certainly, seemed to be in some kind of a contest to see who could pack away more, though Robin threw the towel in at the *dilce de crema batida de chocolate con naranja llameante in tequila*. The dessert of chocolate mousse and flaming orange slices, however, matched Conception's ensemble to such perfection that she indulged in a second helping.

The indefatigable Mexican rather regretted the second helping when the proud mayor announced that the next section of the festivities would involve a tour of the fair city of Cortez culminating at the civic opening of that jewel in the corporate crown, the aquarium. In a city less hot and humid, the tour would have been, perhaps, accomplished in an open-topped bus. In Cortez, the quick eyes of the city fathers had seen the tourist potential of trams and trolley cars. One or two simple adjustments had adapted these vehicles for use on ordinary streets and off they went, Mickey's head full of memories of the dizzying cable cars of his home town and Robin's a little more prosaically of the main promenade of Douglas in the Isle of Man.

Cortez was much of a muchness, laid out in the neat and logical American fashion, with straight wide streets intersecting at regular distances with straight wide avenues, breaking the building site up into regular blocks which mostly, as yet, seemed to be made of open-sided multistoreys partially walled with single layers of breeze blocks, floors supported on scaffolding, floor after floor. It seemed to Robin a little like Noddy's way of building his house – putting the roof on first and working from there. But there was no denying the industry. And, as they moved south into the older part of the city, the blocks rose majestically, completed and painted in magnolia and sand, with terracotta tiles and extravagant balconies trimmed in white. The 'old' parts of the city were to the river side as well, beautiful dwellings, many advertising time-share and condominiums, rising right up onto the levees themselves and overlooking the steady brown flow of the river, five metres and more below. At this point the river was slightly more than a kilometre wide and the estuary was a kilometre or two downstream. Robin thoughtfully leaned across to Kramer. 'Seen the news?'

'Nope. What? Good scandal brewing at the White House?'

'No. Big storms brewing in Wyoming at the headwaters of this thing.'

'No worry there. We designed this to take twice its top projected annual flow, about three times its current flow. I can show you the math.'

'And none of it relies on the dams and reservoirs upstream taking some of the load?'

'The way they did during the El Niño floods twenty years ago?' He shrugged a little uneasily. 'Like I said the night we met. They're all full anyway. We couldn't rely on them much. So we didn't.' There was a short silence as the full import of her words sank in and Kramer turned to her, his square face creased in a frown. 'Just how big are these storms in Wyoming?'

The city of Cortez was right to be proud of its aquarium. The building and the collection it housed went far beyond a standard aquarium. Robin had taken her children to the London Aquarium on many occasions and was prepared not to be all that impressed. But impressed she was. The collection was housed in three huge sections. The ocean section was several storeys deep and in this vertical slice of life in the Sea of Cortez, hammerheads cruised the upper waters, watching, with their strange beady eyes, the dolphins held in a separate sizeable tank. With the dolphins swam the turtles, which had a beach the size of a respectable bungalow to lay their eggs upon. Below the dolphins swam parrot fish and angel fish in wild profusion. Below the hammerheads cruised huge manta rays, sifting the sandy tank floor and keeping clear of coral caverns where huge moray eels watched them like crocodiles entombed. Among the corals of both tanks climbed the starfish and the huge sea urchins, the sea horses and the bright water snakes. In picture only sailed the lords of these waters, the great migrant humpback whales which came each

158

season to the head of the Sea to perform their courtship rituals and to mate. But beyond the photographs and the paintings stood a great room with a huge screen where they seemed to swim in life.

Next door, a long corridor half as wide as a football pitch housed the river and the creatures from its depths and from the salt and mangrove swamps nearby. Here were the great river fish of the estuary, migrating salmon, spiny sharks, what looked to Robin like pike and perch and bream writ large. Downriver, towards the mangroves, lurked the catfish, the flat fish and the suckers. The bright snakes sunned themselves contentedly on sandbars under lamps. On greater sandbars by far sat fat crocodiles – or alligators, Robin could never tell – while above them the mangrove roots moved, occasionally, revealing themselves to be huge, pendant constrictors.

In the final section, the desert behind the mangroves lay represented with everything from cacti to rattlesnakes, gila monsters and iguanas to scorpions and tarantulas.

Entranced, if slightly overpowered, the guests of honour came out into the stultifying indigo of evening and to their third set of speeches with photocall. At the end of which, with the time coming up to 8 p.m., the mayor announced that they would be proceeding directly to a state banquet in their honour at the *ayuntamiento*, or town hall.

The thought of another reception was too much for most of them, but only Otto Kramer was quick-witted enough to do anything about it. He looked across at Robin and decided that she wasn't the sort of companion he wanted for the adventures he had in mind. He personally did not trust Mickey Vargas and Mickey had his hands full with Conception by the look of things. But the acting captain of the *Pequod* needed company and cover. Kramer's eyes narrowed, sweeping the half-dozen members of his own team. Not many laughs among them either. But he'd feel better leaving the others to face the speeches and the press if he had at least one of his own in tow. He caught young Andy DeLillo smothering a yawn and went behind him as he snuck out of line and into the shadows. 'I'm off, DeLillo. Want to come exploring?'

'Heck, sir, I don't know if we should.'

'Course we shouldn't. But who's going to make anything out of it way down here? And make it Otto for this evening, shall we? You packing any greenbacks?'

'Well, yeah. As per assignment, ah, Otto.'

But Kramer hadn't waited for the rest of the reply. He had annexed the attention of the youngest photographer there and was exchanging dollars for addresses and directions.

159

Before Andy DeLillo's head stopped spinning, Kramer and he were in a taxi heading downtown. 'The best clubs don't start up properly till nearer midnight, but we can cruise a few if we're careful what we drink and we'll still be hot to trot when the class stuff hits the floor. What's your preference?'

'Preference in what?'

'Women. Young? Old? Fat? Thin? Blonde? Brunette? Black? White?'

'Well, I . . .'

'God, DeLillo, you're not gay, are you?'

'No, sir . . . I'm . . .'

'A virgin?'

'Sort of engaged. I have this girl back in Boisie, my home town, and we're sort of waiting for each other.'

'Come on, DeLillo. We'll find one that looks like your fiancée and screws like a fairground ride. This could be the night of your life, boy. But check the price up front and always keep your equipment wrapped.'

DeLillo had never seen Kramer like this, frenetic, irresistible. The boy stood no chance.

The taxi dropped them in Cortez's clubland. Like everything else about the burgeoning city, it was constructed, and staffed, on the confident assumption that discerning Americans would bring their much-wanted dollars here and would be best enticed to part with them by showing them what they wanted and charging them a good price for it. The pavements on the wide straight streets were packed already with a dazzling array of people. Locals, passing through to and from their work. Families with children down to toddlers and babes in arms, looking for a well-priced *taco* or *quesadilla* rather than cook for themselves. Mexican tourists here already from all over, looking in wonder at this new attraction where there had been only desert before, the fathers in conservative trousers, the mothers in modest skirts, in spite of the heat and humidity. Behind *padre y madre*, however, came their sloe-eyed daughters, pouting and dreaming, their dark gazes ever drifting into the fascinating, forbidden depths of the clubs and bars, their bosoms rising wistfully beneath their skin-tight little tops, the jewels in their navels blinking in the lights above the buckles of their belts and the short, soft falls of their tiny skirts. Kramer, whose taste ran strongly to such sights, was in heaven long before they hit the clubs themselves.

With Andy DeLillo drifting in and out of his area of concern, Kramer went through the list of places the young photographer

160

had recommended. Even the ones with decent cabarets ran to well-rounded showgirls in diamanté bikinis and feathers. It was in one of these that DeLillo disappeared and Kramer, who was well on his way through the first litre of tequila by this stage, thought a little woozily that if the lady who took the kid away *was* in fact anything like his fiancée, then things must be pretty desperate in Boisie, Idaho. With his cover story of a boys' night out now firmly in place, Kramer paid the one call he had come out here to make.

In a bar down by the docks, he met a man called Tomas Sagreras, a local businessman, ship-breaker and thug. Their meeting had been arranged long since and was brief.

'The river's no good,' said Kramer. 'There's stop-offs and caches up and down it but the Feds seem to know about most of them. You'll have to use the road.'

Sagreras thought for a moment, then nodded once, decisively. 'You are the expert,' he said thickly. 'I will tell Mr Alighieri what you advise. Mr Alighieri said to tell you payment will come in the usual way.' But the Mexican mafioso was talking to an empty chair.

Like the photographer said, the stars came out at midnight, and Kramer was out there at the witching hour with his telescope at the ready. He no longer had much idea of the name of the club he was in, but the cabaret was a female bodybuilder working out in a very complicated multigym wearing nothing but her support belt, which was at least unusual in Kramer's experience. His eyes wandered to the dance floor and there he saw what he wanted. His favourite look of all was 'Heroin chic' and this girl had it in spades. Her face was slim, fragile, porcelain-white under the blue light. Her hair was black and straight, falling over the hollows of her high forehead into the dark pools of her deep-set eyes. Her cheekbones and jawline were razor-sharp. Her neck was long, falling to skeletal shoulders and a black tube top with little more than a pectoral thickening within it. Closer to, he saw that her tummy sank inwards so that her skirt waist sat on hip bones and drooped a little. With the sort of woman DeLillo was entertaining, you looked down cleavage. With this kid you looked down between her belly and her belt.

She saw him staring so intently and came across to him. Her expression remained fixed. Her huge eyes blinked once, slowly. 'What do you want?' she asked in Spanish.

'You. What do you want?' he answered, also in perfect Spanish.

'I am expensive, in all sorts of ways,' she said dismissively.

'I will pay.'

161

She looked at him, some glimmer of speculation coming into the depths of those great, dark eyes. 'We will dance. I will think.'

His hand went out. She took it. He danced as fluently as he spoke, and she began to move with him, against him. In the mirrors around the place he could see the cabaret performer expanding her oiled pectorals, pumping powerfully in on the black leather pec deck, and, below her, he could see his girl communicating over his shoulder with a young guy in black.

As soon as the dance was over, Kramer crossed to the young man. Immediately above his head on the stage, the bodybuilder was doing ballet stretches on a bar before a mirror, preparing for some work on the big muscles below her waist. 'How much?' asked Kramer. 'What currency?'

'A lot,' answered the young pimp, weighing up Kramer's size, power, confidence, uniform. 'Dollars.'

'That's not what I meant,' said Kramer. He stopped for an instant before crossing the line. If this was some kind of honey-trap, he was in it now. 'Coke? Crack? Tabs? Chill? Breeze? What?'

The young man looked at him for two heartbeats. 'She likes coke.'

'You her supplier?'

'I know who is. I can fix her up if you can afford it.'

'I can. And get a little extra for me while you're at it.' He leaned forward and took the young pimp's hand gently in his own. He placed the palm of it softly against the inside of his right thigh where his ace-in-the-hole gun nestled out of sight behind his baggy fatigue trousers. 'I'm on the level,' he said quietly. 'But if you or the girl tries anything silly, I'll come after you so fast it'll make your head spin, and I'll bring my whole fucking regiment with me. *Capisco?*' It was the Italian question as much as the Spanish threats which swung things, telling the Mexican thug that the American was connected.

Half an hour later, Kramer and the girl were in a neat, tidy little room as functional and Spartan as her body. He was naked, sitting on a chair beside the bedside table. The only things he wore were the gun strapped to his right thigh and the leather sheath strapped to his left. She was naked, sitting on the bed. Her languid air in the club had given way to excitement. Her deep-set eyes were sparkling, the nipples on her slight bosom were erect, the whole of her back, over her corrugated ribs and pointed hips right down to her hollow buttocks, was erect with goosebumps. Kramer was cutting out the lines of coke across a little mirror on the table. He was using the black

162

blade of his big, non-reflective Special Forces sheath knife to do this – the knife which Robin Mariner had failed to see in the moonlight. Beside the mirror lay a little glass tube, which she obviously used to sniff the stuff.

Kramer had tested quality and strength by rubbing a grain or two across his tongue tip and then a tiny pinch around his gums. He was as certain as he could be that he wasn't being ripped off and this was good stuff properly cut; neither of them was likely to die of an overdose or of any kind of poisoning before the morning, though he was personally in the mood to try and arrange for at least one of them to get screwed to death. He tested a little more by wetting her eager nipples, sprinkling it on and licking it off.

He allowed her to spend a little time playing the same game on him.

He went back to work with the strange black blade of the knife on the glass while she gasped throatily for breath, her torso heaving like that of the bodybuilder in the cabaret. He smiled at the comparison.

'One line for you,' he said. 'Then one for me and we'll start playing some more serious games.'

She took her line at once.

'Lie back,' he ordered, when she opened her eyes again and put the glass tube down.

'Your line?' she inquired throatily, obeying nevertheless, all languid promise.

'Coming right up,' he said quietly, almost to himself.

Kramer took the mirror with a firm hand, holding it so hard the edges cut into his finger and thumb unnoticed. He brought it over to her belly and held it just a centimetre or two above the fragile, shaven dome of her pubic bone. With practised, expert fingers, he let the line of white crystals slide down onto her flesh from the highest point of her cleft, halfway up towards her navel. She lay in a kind of trembling stillness as though bound with invisible ropes. Gently, so gently, he neatened up the line with the black blade of his knife, scraping it across her skin with a gentle rasping, like a razor. When he had finished, he gave the knife to her and she took it like a lover accepting a flower. Then he put his left nostril to the hollow of her stomach, pinched his right nostril closed, and moved his head down her, slowly, taking one, long, perfectly controlled inward breath as he did so, burying his face in her lap as he finished.

'Now that,' he said, his voice muffled and perfectly content, 'is what I call a rush.'

*　　*　　*

163

When Kramer fell asleep with the skeletal prostitute curled, sated and content in the hollow of his belly two and a half hours later, the last thought on his mind was not her expertise, his fulfilment, or the perfection of the things that they had done and shared in his strange and twisted secret world. Nor was it about the deal he had made with the Mafia to finance his unusual hobbies and habits. It was about the projected flows of water through the many and varied watercourses feeding the upper Colorado.

Chapter Sixteen

Robin woke early, full of decision, energy, and anticipation though she had a sneaking suspicion that Richard was going to let her down and miss the ceremony. At least the outfit she had bought was suitable both for yesterday's ceremonies and, with a little adaptation, today's very different one. She folded it carefully off the hanger which had held it all night and slipped it into the bag she had carried it up from the shop in. Then she showered, pulled on fresh-washed, impeccably pressed jeans and T-shirt fresh from the hotel's cleaners, slid the slightly more battered but strong and practical river-proof footwear on her feet, dragged a comb through her hair, decided against make-up at this stage, and was ready for the off.

She arrived in the Camino's spacious lobby just after eight and found herself, apart from the night porter, alone. A little at a loss, she drifted through to the restaurant, following the fragrance of fresh-brewed coffee. She was not thinking of breakfast particularly – after two huge meals yesterday, food was not a high priority – but she wanted to sit and think. In the restaurant, she discovered that someone else had had the same idea.

Mickey Vargas sat in uniform trousers and open-necked shirt, staring out of the window at the hotel's decorative fountain and courtyard. Robin took a cup of coffee and went to sit beside him. His long face did not register her presence at first, but then, without looking away from his brooding reflection, he said, 'How are you going to get down?'

The gathering realisation that she was going to have to get herself to San Felipe under her own steam and without Richard had been occupying a corner of her mind as well.

'There's an Alamo rental office beside the bank in the lobby,' she said. 'They start at thirty-five dollars a day but I'd be going for the upper end. I go no further in this adventure without air conditioning.'

'It's only about sixty kliks down Highway 5,' he said. 'An hour, ninety minutes max. What time's the ceremony?'

'Four till six. Then a farewell party.'

'I guess they arranged that because there are a lot of folks coming to say goodbye to the old girl.'

'I suppose so. But I might skip it, I could well do without another party after yesterday.'

'This one will be low-key and dignified.'

'Oh yes,' she said with gentle irony. 'You know the guy who's throwing it.'

'No,' he answered, taking her words at face value. 'I don't know him at all really. That's one of the reasons I'm here.' He looked as though he wanted to say more but he stopped himself, eyebrows raised in gentle surprise that he had let slip more than he intended.

Robin changed the subject, briefly marvelling that she had failed to notice earlier how self-controlled he was. Always on the look-out; always on guard. 'You want some breakfast?' she said. 'Smells pretty good to me.'

After breakfasting on white flour tortillas stuffed with scrambled egg and smoked fish liberally seasoned with fresh parsley and sprinkled with Oaxa cheese, Robin found her energy redoubled and her patience more than halved. She popped up to her room one last time, called the Luxor and was informed that Captain Mariner and his party had all checked out. She asked for information as to where they had gone and for any messages which might have been left for her, and the receptionist began to give her details, but Robin found the conversation hard to follow because of background noise. 'Are you having some kind of party or convention there?' she asked at last, exasperated.

'No, Captain Mariner,' said the receptionist. 'That's just the weather this end.'

'The weather? It sounds like a riot in an earthquake with a good bit of World War Two thrown in.'

'I haven't heard it described quite in those terms, Captain Mariner, but that's exactly what it feels like to m—'

The line went dead at that moment and nothing the hotel could do was able to re-establish it.

Frustration boiling over, leavened with concern for Richard – and guilt that he was probably out in that Armageddon looking for a flight south no matter what the difficulty or danger because she had ordered it – Robin flung the rest of her stuff together and vacated her room.

In the hall she bumped into Conception. At the very least the Mexican had danced all night and she looked incredibly well on it.

'I'm off to San Felipe in a few minutes,' said Robin at once. 'Mickey's coming with me. We're sharing a hire car.'

'OK. It's an easy run. I'll stay with Kramer and the boys. They're off boating and it should be fun.' Conception caught the look on Robin's face and grinned. 'No. I mean it. Real fun. They're taking *Pequod* out into the bay. She's not really ocean-going, but if we're careful of the tides we should be OK. The currents shouldn't be too bad, even with the big river back on line. If we're lucky we might see a whale or two.'

'Then what?'

'Mexico City. Home. Back to my normal posting at the monastery and my dull, drab life.'

Robin let that one slide. Nothing about Conception would ever, she suspected, be either dull or drab. Least of all her life. 'You've got my card,' she said. 'It's got my e-mail and my contact numbers.'

'And you can always reach me,' said Conception. 'Major Conception Lopez, Ministry of the Interior, Mexico City. There's only one of me.'

'Major,' said Robin, sticking out her hand. 'That I can believe.'

When Robin got back to the reception, Mickey Vargas was waiting. Robin could see Kramer in the restaurant but he was deep in conversation with one of his men and it seemed better not to interrupt them. Instead, Robin crossed to the Alamo car hire desk. 'What can you give me,' she demanded, 'in the way of air-conditioned self-indulgence?'

Twenty minutes later, Robin was picking her way gingerly westwards through the bustling grid of the city's streets in a silver Lincoln Town Car. The air conditioning was turned up full and the radio was tuned to a local station whose diet of non-stop classical music had just reached the Moldau River section from Bedrich Smetana's *Ma Vlast*. The musical representation of the great river soothed Robin as effectively as the air conditioning cooled her, and Mickey, though still moodily withdrawn in the passenger seat, proved an excellent map-reader and explicator of signs and one-way systems.

'You can turn right at a red light here,' he said after ten minutes.

She did, and they were on Highway 5.

The highway ran south out of Cortez and down the east of Baja Norte as far as San Felipe which was in all sorts of ways the end of the line. In recent years it had been extended down as far as Catalina where it swung in from the west coast, joining Highway 1, and so together they reached right down the length of the Baja California to La Paz, Ensenada de Muertos and Cabo San Lucas.

The original section of the highway was a battered, dusty old road, running up along foothill slopes with the central mountains crouching behind, away to the west in the dusty haze. To the left, the downward slopes reached towards the Sea of Cortez itself, though the first thing Robin noticed looking in that direction was another of the glimmering inland seas which seemed to dot the lowest parts of the landscape. She asked Mickey what it was called but he just shrugged. Smetana had been replaced by Rachmaninov's brooding *Isle of the Dead*, so she hummed along, tapped the steering wheel and drove.

The mountains gathered like great waves on the right, then fell into a wide valley out of which snaked Highway 3, bound south and east from Ensenada. The confluence of roads seemed to bring extra traffic and the highway became quite busy. Robin started paying less attention to the music and more to the road. And this was lucky because soon after this junction they came across a man sitting in the shade of a broken-down Buick with his feet dangerously in the road. Every other face Robin had seen recently, other than those of *Pequod*'s crew, had been dark. Their hair had been black and very thick. Their figures, even those of the mayor and his wife, had been slight and slim. The face of the man by the broken-down Buick was pale. His hair was sandy, thinning and short. His figure was on the plump side of big. She slowed the Lincoln and had stopped just beside his battered shoes.

Robin opened her door and a stream of cold air washed down over the somnolent figure. He was wearing a battered blue suit and a grey-white shirt, open at the collar. He seemed to be asleep. The fumes of tequila reached Robin as she swung her feet out of the car. A pair of eyes, even bluer and more battered than the suit, opened. They squinted speculatively up at her. 'Angels I was not expecting,' said a slightly slurred drawl.

'You need help.'

'Lady, you said it.'

'Mickey, check the car, would you?'

'Waste of time, Mickey wherever you are. It was shot when I accepted it back in Yuma. It's shot to hell now.'

Mickey opened his door and the suction pulled more tequila fumes into Robin's face. 'Where are you bound?' she asked.

'San Felipe,' he said. 'Got an appointment with a boat.'

'Me too,' said Robin.

'This thing's a mess,' called Mickey. 'It's a miracle it got this far, but it ain't going no further.'

168

'Right,' said Robin. 'You got any stuff?'

'Got my uniform.'

'And his bottle,' said Mickey.

'Mickey,' said the stranger, getting up, 'that bottle's been deader than the motor since bright new beautiful Cortez. Still,' he added cheerfully, reaching into the Buick for his case, 'limousine like yours ought to have a bar tucked away somewhere in the back.'

'Climb on in and take a look for it,' said Robin. 'It'll give you something amusing to do on the run to San Felipe.'

'Don't mind if I do,' said the stranger, climbing into the back.

And that was how Robin and Mickey made the acquaintance of Chester Ulysses Shaw.

Robin pulled into San Felipe half an hour later, coming in past the shrine of the Virgin on its hill to the north. She did not need Mickey's translation or guidance to find her way around the little town. There were only three main streets and they all ran parallel to the bay, falling back in series from the shore. They were joined by little cross-streets whose simple one-way system was easily defined by the way the cars in each were facing. Battered old signs pointed the way down to the bay and the ancient harbour. Brand new ones guided the discerning visitor towards the marina with all its facilities, two kilometres to the south of town. Here there was berthing for hundreds of boats, hotel rooms and condominiums available for time-share.

From the moment they pulled off the highway onto the slope down to the bay, their final objective was in plain sight, anchored well out in the bay, sitting on the blue-black line denoting deep water at the top of a golden expanse of beach nearly a kilometre wide. Robin slowed to a stop on the deserted jetty and they all looked out at her.

'Long ways out,' observed Chester.

'The tides here make six metres,' said Mickey knowledgeably. 'She'll be right alongside shore in four hours. What's the time?'

'Noon,' said Robin.

'She'll be in at four then. Just in time for the ceremony. There is a brain at work here, it seems.'

'Or a guy with a set of tide tables,' said Chester.

'Four hours,' said Robin. 'Chester, are you booked in anywhere?'

'Nope. Hoping to bunk down aboard or sleep in the Buick. Just drop me here, why don't you?'

Robin and Mickey exchanged a look. Their guest had not found a bar hidden away in the luxurious fittings in the back of the Lincoln. He would find one five seconds after he got out of it.

169

'No, really,' he persisted, beginning to stir himself. 'I'll stumble into something. I usually do.'

'I'm sure you will,' said Robin in a chilly voice.

'Hey,' said Chester, struck. 'You sound just like my big sister Martha.'

Robin engaged DRIVE and began to roll slowly forward. 'Mickey?'

'I was going to ask my dad to find me a bunk.'

'Cool,' said Chester, subsiding. 'Ask him to find one for me too. If he's talking to you.'

Mickey frowned and for a moment Robin thought Chester had pushed things too far. The conversation since he had joined them had covered a lot of ground and should have established that the father-son relationship represented here was even more touchy than the husband-wife relationship.

'I'm booked into the Marina,' said Robin firmly. 'I have a big suite in case Richard shows up. They do water taxis there as well so we should have no trouble getting out to the *Colorado*. In the meantime, let's all go out there and freshen up, shall we?'

'Yes, Martha,' said Chester.

'Yes, Captain Mariner, we were expecting you,' said the receptionist at the new Marina Hotel. 'Your suite is ready and there is a message for you. Unfortunately it is incomplete and we have been unable to re-establish contact with the party sending it.'

Robin tore open the envelope and looked at the message. 'At McCarran,' it read. 'Coming south come hell or high—'

'Is that all?'

'I'm afraid it is. Do you know who it is from?'

'It's from my husband. When did it arrive?'

'You will see that the night clerk who took it timed the message at five a.m. today, Captain.'

'And there has been no word since then.'

It was so obviously a statement that the receptionist did not answer. She turned instead to the other two. 'Is either of you Lieutenant Cagliari?' she asked.

Robin was poring over Richard's message like a spiritual medium trying to soak up meaning from between the words, from within of the weave of the paper, so she did not hear the question, or the name.

They kept Chester with them as they went up to Robin's suite. She slipped her key-card into the door and opened it to reveal a palatial set of rooms. Robin saw a reception area, a distant bedroom and

170

the promise of a shower *en suite* beyond that. Mickey saw a wide-screen TV and a chance to catch up with some of what was going on in the world, a large window overlooking the marina, the bay beyond and his father's command sitting in the middle of it. Chester saw the bar fridge.

They went down for lunch almost immediately, before Robin touched the taps, Mickey the On switch or Chester the fridge door, and found the dining room almost empty. 'Thirteen hundred hours is time for siesta down here,' said an open-faced, blue-eyed stranger, rising from a large table which he occupied alone. 'Only gringos would dream of eating now, apparently. Captain Peter Phelps, USN retired.' He held out his hand. 'I was *Colorado*'s last executive officer when she was in the US Navy. Are you folks down for the ceremony?'

'Yes,' said Robin, and performed the introductions.

Chester caught the eye of a distant waiter who was clearly hoping not to get caught up in this unfashionably timed meal. 'Tequila,' he said, and that one word got the ball rolling, as it often does in Mexico.

Over lunch they discussed what they each expected from the afternoon's events. Peter Phelps had no more idea than the rest of them. 'I've never attended a ceremony like this before,' he said. 'I'm just going to turn up in what your people call number one whites, I believe, Robin. I have a wreath of remembrance to offer, purchased with money collected among the old crew members. I expect to be told what to do and when to do it, and to stand at attention and wait in the meantime.'

'Mickey? Any ideas?' asked Robin.

Mickey shook his head, his long face set and closed. Peter Phelps looked at Robin with frowning inquiry but she shook her head. Now was not the time to have *that* discussion again, she thought.

'Chester?'

'Well, I guess it'll be like a religious service. Kind of like a burial at sea, you know? I'm not a church-going man, and I'd be a Boston Baptist if I was, so I can't really guess what the Catholic service will be like. But one thing I did learn when I was bumming around in Sonora is that the Mexicans are a thoughtful and a religious people. A burial at sea in the Catholic style gets my bet, though I suspect there'll be a civil side to it too. The old girl is government property, after all. There's likely to be one hell of a lot of paper-signing somewhere along the way. 'I'm just going to stand to attention like the captain here but in the background and in the shade. I'm going to say a quiet

Baptist prayer for my men who went down on Grenada and I'm going to try not to breathe too deep or I'll bust every button and seam on the old dress uniform I brought. Hey, *muchaco*, can I have another tequila here, *por favor?*'

Chester was partway down his next tequila when he looked up suddenly. 'Hey, there's another gringo. Must be one of us.' He raised his hand, and Robin turned from her contemplation of the grey ship on the dark sea in time to see a pale shoulder vanish into the shadows outside the dining-room door.

'Must be that guy the *chiquita* at reception was asking about,' Chester continued. 'What was his name? Roma? Napoli? Capistrani?'

'Cagliari,' said Mickey. 'Hell, *Cagliari*!' He turned to Robin. 'You don't suppose it's the guy we met at the Luxor, do you? The one with Jo and Jody in tow?'

'The one trying to screw up Richard's business deal,' grated Robin. 'Well, I think I'd just better find out.'

But when she got out into reception, the strange gringo had vanished and no one knew where he had gone.

They all went back to Robin's suite to shower and change at two thirty and things really started to bustle at three. The tide was coming in across the sand at incredible speed and *Colorado* was sitting up and slipping inwards. Out of nowhere, apparently, a helicopter appeared and hopped from the jetty out to the destroyer several times, carrying little groups of official-looking people. The water taxis started speeding out from the marina and one or two fishing boats began to ease out of the old harbour too.

They met Peter Phelps down in reception at three thirty. There had been no contact from Richard or from *Colorado*. The mysterious stranger was nowhere to be seen. Their taxi was ready, the reception-ist informed them, requesting that they go down to the jetty now. Robin led the way out to the waiting water taxi. She wore the dress providentially purchased last night, and a low-heeled sensible pair of shoes in navy with white edging. Peter Phelps was next best dressed in dazzling whites, beautifully pressed and fitting as if they had just been tailored for him. Mickey's US Army major's outfit, all browns and camels, was smart but did not compare with the navy whites. But at least it fitted him better than Chester's lieutenant's uniform in the same colours but several sizes too small. Tight enough certainly to reveal a suspicious bulge in his right-hand pocket. A bulge which went *chink* when he sat in the water taxi.

Robin was watching Mickey. She knew little enough of the story

172

about the bitter separation and the enraged mother using the little boy as a weapon to hurt the distant, icy father. She was worried about how the little boy would react now that he was going aboard his father's ship. And, indeed, about how the monstrous father might react, confronted with the son brought up to hate, despise and destroy him. She was also extremely worried about where and how her errant husband was.

The water taxi came to a halt at the bottom of *Colorado*'s main companionway. Robin climbed out first, her hand held by a courteous petty officer in immaculate whites almost as brilliant as the teeth in his bearded smile. At the foot of the companionway stairs reaching up to the forecastle head high above she stopped to glance over her shoulder. Mickey was right behind her. Willing strength and certainty into her nervous young friend, she went on up.

At the top of the companionway there was a reception line. As she stepped onto the hot metal deck, a young lieutenant with a thick shock of dark hair and a ready smile stepped forward. 'I am Lieutenant Heman Gutierrez,' he smiled.

'Captain Robin Mariner, representing my father Sir William Heritage and my late godfather Sir Justin Bulwer-Lytton.'

She glanced around as she spoke. The captain was the tall, white-uniformed figure at the far end of the line. Between here and him were half a dozen smiling officials disturbingly reminiscent of the mayor of Cortez. Behind the captain's trim figure sat a helicopter, clearly designed for the comfortable transport of the great and the good. She heard her name repeated and looked into the smiling face of the first dignitary.

Behind her, she heard, 'I am Lieutenant Banderas. And you are?'

'Major Miguel Vargas, United States Corps of Engineers.'

She floated down the line, from one smiling face to the next, from one courteous hand-clasp and bow to the next. In her head the chant rang like a kind of mantra: *Captain Mariner, Captain Mariner, Captain Mariner; Major Vargas, Major Vargas, Major Vargas . . .*

And then, quite suddenly, she was in front of the captain. He turned towards her stiffly, having received some whispered message over his right shoulder, and her eyes widened. He was so similar to Mickey, but with an added power that was almost disturbing. He bowed, stiffly again. The long, deep-set eyes below the perfectly tilted cap met hers. His lips moved. She turned, took Mickey by the arm and pulled him towards her. 'Captain Vega, may I introduce—'

And all hell let loose. Sirens started blowing, the helicopter fired up, the captain turned away without even having glanced at his ashen son.

173

Heman Gutierrez was saying something urgent which she could not quite follow at once. 'I am sorry, Captain Mariner. You come below now. Ceremony maybe happen later. We have big emergency now. Boat sinking off Isla Montague near Cortez. Many people at risk. Very dangerous. We are nearest, we must go to rescue.'

'Boat?' said Robin, dazed by the speed of events. 'What sort of a boat?'

'Rubber boat,' said Heman Gutierrez. 'Inflatable boat. Has burst. Is sunk. The crew gonna die unless we get there pretty quick.'

Chapter Seventeen

The pilot's name was Patterson. If there was more to it, Richard never discovered what it was. Patterson was a big, square, no-nonsense individual whose bulk seemed ill-suited to his chosen profession. Richard found him at McCurran by the simple expedient of asking the apologetic girl on the charter flight desk where the pilots hung out when they were unoccupied. Still regretful at her inability to get him any kind of regular flight southwards in spite of his obvious concern and borderline distress – expressed in that courteous, quiet English way which she found irresistible – she was pleased to tell him about the semi-official club they had made for themselves in the back of one of the hangars out on the field.

Richard's cabbie knew the hangar and soon found the place. Richard walked into the little room, hesitated, holding the door as the wind tried to tear it off its hinges, and met every glance bent upon him as they all looked up to see who was letting the rain in. All the pilots in at the moment were men; women probably had more sense than to hang around here in a storm drinking coffee and waiting for fair weather.

'I need a pilot with his own plane ready and willing to fly me to Mexico now,' he said.

There was a silence disturbed only by the buffeted groaning of the door, held against the blast more steadily by his big right hand than by its rickety hinges.

'I'll pay what I have to,' said Richard, 'but I do want to get there in one piece.'

Most of the pilots turned away. Those nearest the door grumbled about draughts and spray. Those nearest the coffee machine demanded a refill. There was no alcohol and precious little nicotine around. Richard, heartened by these two facts, swept the room with his intense blue gaze and only one pair of eyes met his. A big man pulled himself erect. He was too bulky by the look of him to fit behind the controls of a 747, let alone anything smaller, but steady and confident in appearance. No pretension. No pilot's shades, epaulettes or wings. No hair, just thick, sand-grey stubble. He wore an open-necked olive shirt and combat pants that looked as if they had seen combat. *No bullshit* was written all over his square, grey-jowled face. 'Name's Patterson,' he said, in a gentle voice which seemed to carry across the room. 'I'll take you. Got a little Beechcraft all fuelled up and ready to go. Ain't doing anything else for a while by the looks of things.'

Richard got his grip and his suit-holder from the cab and was about to pay it off when Patterson arrived at his side and said, 'Hang on to this guy. We'll need a lift across to my hangar.'

The hangar was a small, solid affair, well-maintained and recently redecorated. Outside, a big bright sign said PATTERSON AIR: *SEE THE GRAND CANYON LIKE NEVER BEFORE.* Inside, it was neat and tidy. A Mexican-American engineer sat beside the fuselage of a turboprop monoplane reading the *National Enquirer.*

'*Hola*, Pepito,' said Patterson as they entered. '*Andale!* We have business here.'

Pepito looked up in frank astonishment. 'This guy wants to go to the Grand Canyon in *this*? And you're thinking of taking him? One of you's nuttso, Patterson.'

'Naw, Pepito. He wants to go to Mexico. You want to come along for the ride?'

'Of course. But you know they'd probably never let me back across the border.'

As the slight figure in pristine white overalls stood up, Richard saw that he had been sitting on a float. This was a seaplane. The unexpected nature of the craft almost made Richard think again, but then he realised that they would be following the Colorado for much of the way south so floats might prove useful insurance.

'OK,' called Patterson from the office behind the plane. 'I need a destination. I also need an idea of what you're carrying or we'll have to set down at Calexico or Yuma and let customs and immigration have a look at you.'

'I'm not carrying anything except clothing,' Richard called through, following the echoes of his voice towards the office. 'I'm just trying to get down to an important ceremony aboard a ship at San Felipe in six hours' time.'

'San Felipe's about three hundred kilometres south as the crow flies,' said Patterson. 'Shouldn't be too tough unless the weather intensifies.'

Richard reached the office and discovered Patterson busily typing. Unusually, Patterson typed standing up. There was no chair in evidence in the office at all and the big man's fingers flew across his keyboard with practised assurance. Richard looked at the screen in front of the pilot and realised he was filling in a flight plan ready to e-mail it to the tower and out to the relevant authorities. A fax machine stood beside the printer so that Patterson could print out and fax off anything that needed hard copy. Fast and efficient. At the bottom of the flight plan form Richard noticed a box labelled 'Readiness of Aircraft'. Patterson had already put in '100%'.

'Haul your stuff over to the aircraft,' said Patterson. 'I'll only be a moment here.'

He spoke too soon. As he pressed SEND, his phone started ringing. He answered on the first chirrup and then spent several moments in animated conversation.

Richard crossed to the plane and Pepito held the door in the side open for him. Richard slung the case and the suit-carrier up into the body of the little aircraft and climbed in behind them. There were half a dozen seats and he selected the one which offered most leg room.

Patterson shoved his head up into the cabin. 'We got a request, Captain Mariner,' he said.

Richard turned, crouching in the confines of the little cabin. 'Request?' he asked, unaccountably remembering Horatio Hornblower's orders from the British Admiralty in his favourite nautical novels of Napoleonic times, 'You are requested and required . . .'

'From the tower. They have two other people desperate to fly south. A hydro engineer wants to stop off at one of the dams down the Colorado. A TV reporter wants a ride. But it's your party. Your charter. What do you say?'

'If it's important, let them come. OK with you?'

'I guess. The engineer is pretty senior at the Bureau, apparently.'

Richard found himself wondering what an FBI agent would want down here – but then he realised that the Bureau Patterson must mean was the Bureau of Reclamation which looked after the Colorado.

And the reporter's just a reporter. But they're bad people to piss off and it's not much of a favour they're asking. We'll have to stop off and drop at least one of them en route, though. Probably both. Hopefully at the same place.'

'But you can come down almost anywhere in this thing, can't you?'

'Any flat land or quiet water,' acknowledged Patterson, with the slightest of edges to his voice.

Richard heard it. 'But where we're bound there isn't much of either,' he said.

'That's about the strength of it, I guess.'

'Oh well, what the hell. Let them come. How soon can they get here?'

'By the time we're ready for take-off. So they say.'

'Fine,' said Richard, sitting down and buckling in. 'We'll take them at their word. Let's go.'

The little monoplane was sweeping across the apron towards the main runway when a cab came screaming up alongside, shrugging off great clouds of rain and spray. Patterson slowed. 'Get the door, Captain, if you'd be so kind.'

Richard flung the side door back and the two vehicles came to a stop on the stormy, rain-swept tarmac. The back of the cab opened and two figures bundled out, unloading a pile of possessions and equipment.

Neither seemed any better dressed for the expedition than Richard was in his damp pinstripe business suit. The first figure wore a cotton blouson and a beautifully tailored linen skirt. The second wore jeans, hiking boots and a red plaid shirt. Though they were both slight and feminine, Richard would have bet that the second was the hydro engineer. He would have been wrong.

The first woman leaped upward and Richard swung her easily inwards, reaching for the second. 'Thanks,' yelled the first, with a powerful, carrying voice. 'Sue Hagan, Doctor of Hydrology.'

'Welcome aboard.'

'Great,' yelled the second, following close behind the doctor. 'Josie Mendez, CNN.'

'Richard Mariner,' said Richard as he jerked the door shut. 'And the pilot's name is Patterson.'

'Welcome aboard,' yelled Patterson. 'Sit down and buckle up quickly, please, folks. It's not like we're in a queue waiting for clearance here.' As he spoke, a gust of storm wind seemed to take the little plane and chuck it forward down the runway. The three passengers were glad enough to tuck themselves into the solid seats and buckle up tight. Patterson was chattering sixteen to the dozen into the radio and revving the sturdy little turboprop, keeping the aircraft under control easily, with a sure and practised hand.

'OK,' he yelled back. 'This is where your captain tells you not to use personal phones, laptops or any other electrical equipment and the senior flight attendant explains what to do if we crash. If we crash, pray. If you use any electrical stuff, we'll crash. Gottit?'

'That include my tape recorder?' called Josie.

'Small portable, limited field should be OK. Wait until we're in

178

level flight – or as close as I can manage – then give it a go. If I sing out, switch off quick.'

'Sure,' sang out Josie in reply.

They all sat quietly then, listening as Patterson got his final clearance from the tower and turned his lone turboprop onto the giant tarmac runway designed for 747s. All of them held their breath a little as the Beechcraft gathered way and began to hurl forward, the storm wind fitfully under her skirts. Rain squalls came from behind and went gusting past them at first. Then Richard realised they had overtaken the last couple and were pulling ahead of the wind. Abruptly, the ground tumbled away to their right in a depressing patchwork of sodden browns, greens and greys. Then they were over the steaming garishness of Las Vegas itself.

'Well,' announced Josie with a redundancy rarely allowed in a reporter, 'we're up.' Then she turned the full force of her attention onto Richard. 'So, Richard,' she said. 'You're a big Englishman in a big hurry. What's the big attraction south of the border?'

'My wife, and a ceremony I promised to attend with her.'

'Oh? Sounds intriguing. Tell me about it.'

Dr Hagan, with nothing else to do other than to look out of the window at the storm clouds and rain squalls enveloping them was soon drawn into the conversation.

'So,' she said, 'your wife's gone all the way down the watercourse with the Corps of Engineers?' There was a stirring of naked envy in her voice.

'From the foot of the Hoover Dam to the Sea of Cortez,' Richard confirmed.

'And she's waiting for you now in this San Felipe place?' asked Josie.

Richard checked his watch. 'She should be in the Marina Hotel there, wondering with diminishing patience where *that* is,' he said, gesturing to the suit-carrier with a rueful grin.

'What's in there?'

'My number one uniform whites and her best Chanel suit.'

'Let me guess which one she's worried about,' chuckled Josie. 'But why're folks like you going out to say farewell to an old Mexican coastguard vessel?'

Richard explained. It was a good story, but as soon as she had got her head round it, Josie's interest began to wane. Not all good stories make good TV news, he guessed. She turned her attention to Dr Hagan and allowed Richard to look out of the rain-streaked window at the scudding, storm-veiled countryside below. The Beechcraft was

179

riding low, Patterson preferring to keep below the clouds where he could, because the worst of the hurricane system – and it was still strong enough to register as a hurricane even this far north of its power sources on the Caribbean and the Gulf – was pushing in north of them now. The cubic kilometre or so of water it had dropped so far had exhausted the tail of the storm, and while the main front still had another couple of the same for Wyoming, it was drying out down here. They were just south of the Davis Dam now and heading towards the confluence of the Bill Williams River and the Colorado. The Colorado looked surprisingly close, and very angry. The water was running wide and red. Richard was surprised at how much water there was in the channel so close to the foot of a major water regulator. Without thinking, he called across to Dr Hagan, and was surprised to find his question fitted seamlessly into Josie Mendez's interrogation.

'The dams' sluices are all wide open at the moment,' the hydrologist explained, widening her answer to suit both interrogators. 'The storms have filled all spare capacity on their way upstream. There's no slack in the system at the moment. Every drop that falls upriver gets passed down the watercourse.'

'That looks like borderline flooding to me,' said Richard, his voice concerned. And, schooled in the antics of storm systems through all his years as a navigating officer at sea, he knew there would be a good deal more to follow it down in twelve to twenty-four hours' time. It occurred to him that now might be a good moment to get Robin on his personal phone and update her on his position.

'So,' said Josie, 'the river-control system's at capacity but holding.'

'Full capacity, yes.'

'Right the way down?'

'To the border? Yes.'

'To the Sea and the city of Cortez?'

There was an instant of silence. 'I was not on the design team or on the actual work teams, but I have been fully briefed. Yes. The whole river will be full to capacity all the way down to the sea when this water reaches that far – in another four or five hours. But there's nothing to worry about. The levees at Cortez have a simple design. The left levee on the Baja California side, where the city has been built, stands three metres higher than the right for the last ten kilometres of its length. The right levee, overlooking swamplands and the unpopulated Sonora side, is lower. So that, in the unlikely event of the water rising to danger levels down there, the flow at the river mouth will be guided away from the city itself.'

'That's all fine and dandy,' said Josie quietly, 'but what about further upstream? The river flows through country which is a good deal lower than sea level. Always assuming the Imperial holds and we don't get another Salton Sea, surely there's a risk further downriver where the dry valleys lead west through the Sierra de Juarez to the Laguna Salada. What happens if the system fails there?'

'We have no reason to expect it will fail anywhere,' said the hydrologist. 'You can see that the river is lively but well-contained . . .'

She chose a less than perfect moment to make this point, for they were now passing over the confluence of the Bill Williams and the Colorado. The headwaters of the Bill Williams were right under the track of the storm and the river was not in spate but in full flood. Its ochre water was forcing the red Colorado up high against its western bank and spreading in a yellow flood like restless vomit to the east.

'Now that's interesting,' purred Josie. Richard saw her hand move, even as his own hand slipped into his pocket for his phone. 'The system doesn't seem to be containing the Bill Williams too well. Looks like they'll be passing a flood downriver from Lake Havasu. I'll bet there's not room for an extra drop in the All American Canal, and if there's any spare capacity in the Central Arizona Project I'll be pretty surprised as well. You have any comment on that, Dr Hagan?'

'Of course not. But you'll see that Lake Havasu will soak up most of the Bill Williams floodwater. Very little will be passed on downstream from Parker Dam, I'm sure.'

'So this is just a courtesy visit to the Headgate or the Morelos or whatever? You aren't trouble-shooting? Preparing?'

'Preparing for what? You can see . . .' They were over the northernmost waters of Lake Havasu now, and it did indeed look as though the yellow flood from the Bill Williams River was losing itself in the dark, familiar red of the Colorado's flow as that, in turn, settled into the slate-grey mirror of the lake's apparently placid surface.

'I see a system at full stretch.'

'But holding, Ms Mendez.'

'For the moment, Dr Hagan. But what about the future?'

'The future?'

'The *immediate* future. My people at Meteorology say that both Hurricane Benedict and the Pacific weather system they've called Tropical Storm 004 are still water-laden. They say they expect maybe three cubic kilometres of rainwater to fall in Wyoming, Utah

181

and Colorado within the next twenty-four hours. Those three states contain the upper basin of the Colorado. They are its catchment area. The Fontenelle, the Flaming Gorge and the Navajo are all way past capacity already, the same as your reservoirs down here. What falls on them goes into the flow, every drop. And, as I'm sure you know, three cubic kilometres represents twenty-five per cent of the whole river's projected annual flow. And all that water will be coming down here in the next twenty-four to thirty-six hours. You can't contain what you've got coming down on you now. How in heaven's name do you think you'll be able to control an extra flow of that magnitude?'

Richard pulled his personal phone out, but before he could start dialling Robin's number, Patterson called back, 'Switch off the equipment.'

Richard put the phone away again and Josie Mendez stopped recording. Only then did Dr Hagan realise that her words were on tape. Her mouth went pinched, but then, oddly, she relaxed, as though something of a burden had been removed from her.

'I'll be down in the Sea of Cortez when this lot hits,' Richard said quietly. 'It sounds as though things might get very destructive down there.'

'The Sea of Cortez has been soaking up the vagaries of the Colorado since the Ice Age. This is the first flood that's likely to get right through to the ocean in a while, but it shouldn't raise more than an eyebrow or two down there.'

'I wouldn't bet on it,' said Richard. 'The tides up by the estuary are the most extreme in the world. What if the sea is up by eight metres on the top of a high one and then this lot comes down on top of that?'

Josie followed his thought through. 'And the new estuary is tidal in past Cortez, isn't it? That's why you have your funny levees with the eastern one lower. The coast's so flat there that there's a ten-kilometre inwash on an eight-metre tide.'

'Is there?' said Richard, swinging right round to look at the remarkably well-informed reporter. 'Well, that'll make things more of a challenge. If the river floods over the back of a flood tide . . .' He paused, his mind racing.

'What?' asked Josie, her knowledge wide but her vision of implications more limited.

'It could all back up,' said Sue Hagan quietly. 'It could create a high-water surge a couple of kilometres further upriver as the water coming down gets stopped by the tide flooding in. You see it happen

182

all the time at the seaside where a big wave comes in, breaks and washes out—'

'And the back-wash makes the next wave higher still,' completed Josie. 'Is that going to happen to the Colorado?'

'It's a possibility, that's all. The odds are heavily against it.' The scientist glanced down at Josie's tape recorder and her mouth went thin and tense again. 'And what I've said is strictly off the record,' she said formally. 'It is a personal view. It does not reflect the position of the government, the Corps of Engineers or the Bureau of Reclamation.'

'Coming down at the Palo Verde now, Dr Hagan,' sang out Patterson. The Beechcraft looped left and began to settle.

'Can I use my phone when we're down?' Richard asked Patterson. 'Sure.'

Josie Mendez had not finished with Sue Hagan. 'Why here?' she asked. 'I thought you were going to the Headgate Rock or the Morelos. This is a big system. Why are you here? Don't tell me you think the Palo Verde irrigation system's at risk!'

'No comment,' snapped Dr Hagan.

Patterson was bringing the Beechcraft straight down the steep-sided valley onto the water behind the dam. The lake looked flat, grey and calm. The whole procedure had such an air of calm routine about it that the suddenly angry and alienated woman snapped open her seat belt and rose, partly in preparation to disembark, partly to escape her interrogator. As she did so, a gust of storm wind came roaring down the valley behind them and flung the aeroplane forward. Sue Hagan hit the rear of the seat in front of her with her stomach and collapsed back into her own seat, clearly winded. Josie Mendez reached across her instinctively, holding her still and protecting her against any further sudden movement.

Patterson managed to pull the plane's nose up for an instant and the Beechcraft hopped over the top of the dam, scant metres above the water, and entered the still, lower air of the valley downstream. Richard saw what Robin had seen a few days earlier – the Palo Verde farmlands spread out like a bright green quilt. Lines of water glinted, like silver streets surrounding city blocks. Then the Beechcraft was pulling up and swinging round a Patterson tried an upriver approach. This worked better. Richard noticed again how little brickwork stood between the top of the dam and the surface of the water they were landing on. There was no spare capacity here – the same as everywhere else.

Patterson taxied over to a landing stage and leaped out into the gusty but dry afternoon. Sue Hagan went out after him and Josie Mendez followed. Richard climbed out onto the dock to find the two women in heated conversation. As he dialled the first of Robin's contact numbers he half listened to them.

'You can't just follow me into this situation! I have a job to do here and I'll be damned if—'

'Come on, Dr Hagan. There's a major public safety issue here. Anyway, only the dam's senior manager can stop me . . .' Josie paused, realising that the dam's senior manager was probably answerable to Dr Hagan or someone in her office in any case.

Sue Hagan was no fool. She saw Josie's point clearly enough, and was obviously weighing a balance of evils as she caught her breath and counted to ten. 'Right,' she said. 'But no more sneaky tricks. You record anything, you ask first.'

'Agreed. And I'll call for back-up, if I may. There'll be a local team with a camera . . .'

Before Sue Hagan could demur, Josie had her personal phone out. But, like Richard, she discovered that the high valley sides cut them off from access to the outside world. 'I need a land line,' said Josie. 'I'll call out when we get into the dam's management office . . .'

The two women made their way down the landing stage. At the end of it they turned and waved. 'Thanks . . .' came distantly on the gusty wind.

'Don't mention it,' said Richard, almost to himself. Then he turned to Patterson. 'Can I ride up front with you for the rest?'

'I guess. Don't touch anything unless I tell you.'

'And I'll want to use your radio to call out if I can't use my personal phone.'

'Sure. Be my guest. But we'll have to wait here for an hour or so while I do a thorough check on the airframe. She didn't like that steep dive and turn on our first attempt to land here. She's a solid little thing but she ain't no stunt plane.'

It was not until they were passing low over the Imperial Dam with Yuma glimmering in the hazy distance much later in the afternoon that Richard managed to get through to the reception at Robin's hotel, only to be told that she had left for the ceremony moments before in the company of several gentlemen.

Richard sat back, frustrated. 'I'm going to be late,' he said. 'But it'll be a long ceremony, I expect, and the party afterwards will probably last until midnight or so.'

184

'That we should make,' said Patterson. 'Maybe I should have brought a tux, huh?'

Richard opened his mouth to reply but the radio buzzed urgently and he passed it to Patterson who soon became embroiled in a complex discussion with customs and immigration.

Richard surveyed the lower section of the river as the conversation dragged on. The soggy greens and browns of further north were nowhere in evidence down here. The clouds appeared to lift at the border and everything south of Yuma seemed bathed in sunshine. The river, a blue ribbon contained in mathematical lines of leveed straightness, ran serenely into the rich sand colours of the distant southern deserts of Sonora and Baja California Norte. Immediately below, the border spawned towns and villages strung like bright rhinestones along the thread of Highway 2 joining Tijuana, Tecate and Mexicale to San Luis Rio Colorado. Away to the right, the irrigated farmlands around Meridia and Ciudad Morelos caught his eye.

Richard thought about what Josie Mendez had wormed out of Sue Hagan. The hydrologist had practically admitted that the Colorado was going to flood along its length but especially down here. Within the next few hours the waters he had seen spewing out of the Bill Williams would be here. And a day at most behind those, riding down on top of them, would come the other couple of cubic kilometres of water falling on Wyoming now.

Richard had done some river management on the River Mau in West Africa a few years back. He could imagine all too clearly what the volume of water the reporter had predicted would do if they came through here uncontrolled. His inclination was to get involved, to try and do something about it. But in reality, the best he could hope to do was to alert people – always assuming they didn't already realise what was happening – and then try and make sure he and Robin were well on their way back to London before the full force of the catastrophe came rolling down the river course below him.

He considered asking Patterson to set down in Cortez when the grey heat haze of that bustling, burgeoning city began to roll down from the horizon. He dismissed the idea at once. He had no contacts and no standing here. He would waste a lot of time trying to find out who to talk to, and then would probably be dismissed as a crank. And he had to get to the ceremony and party aboard *Colorado*. Obviously it was too late to deliver the Chanel suit, but he had fences to mend with Robin. He had let her down in a range of ways this time and he felt guilty about it. She was an extraordinary woman and he loved

185

her to distraction. His clear sense of duty and his all-consuming need to do the right thing too often kept them apart, but the situation had been going from bad to worse lately. The lack of contact between them during the last few days while she had been risking her life down the Colorado and he had been risking God knew what in Las Vegas was only a part of it. In the old days he would have kept her informed. There would have been no nasty surprises like her experience in Yuma. He had had time enough to reflect on his own shortcomings during the last week and he really felt he needed to save his marriage before he rushed off trying to save anything or anybody else.

But all these pious thoughts went straight out of his head when he saw the distress flare. Patterson was focused ahead, bringing them low over Montague Island, following the centre of the Colorado's flow and keeping clear of the turbulence above the bustling building site of the main city. They were low enough to see the faces of the drivers of the big lorries rolling relentlessly across the bridge from the levee on the western shore, but high enough to see the eastern shore and the water south of it. Richard saw the sudden flickering flash from the corner of his eye. It was diminished by the brightness of the afternoon, but he never doubted what it was. 'Patterson,' he called. 'Come left. I thought I saw a distress flare down there.'

Patterson had been as impressed with his passenger as Richard had been with his pilot and he did not hesitate. The Beechcraft swung left and began to lose height. While Richard looked dead ahead, scanning the hazy horizon, Patterson began to sweep the emergency frequencies on the radio. Even though Richard needed reading glasses these days, there was nothing the matter with his distance vision, and his eyes beat the ether. 'There!' he called after five minutes of steady flight.

Well out in the sweep of the river's tidal flow, there was a mess of wreckage. It was impossible to see precisely what it was or exactly what was going on at first, but there were people in the water and whatever vessel they had been sailing in looked damaged, upside down and sinking fast.

'To help most effectively, we'll have to land,' said Richard.

'That'll depend. I'll want it calm and safe. I don't want to run into whatever sank them.'

'And you won't want them all fighting to get aboard the instant you're down, either. How steady is this plane sitting on her floats?'

'Fairly steady. But there look to be ten or more in the water. That'd be plenty to pull her over if we're not careful.'

'Got an inflatable aboard?'

'Sure. Six-seater. Federal regs – we're a seaplane, after all.'

'Perfect. Land her upstream from them and I'll open the door in the side and slip out the inflatable. That'll give them a safety platform to climb into or hang onto, and it'll give us a safety buffer in case they're panicking.'

'Good plan. But look around them carefully. Something must have sunk them. Sandbar or such. If we run into it, we'll be swimming too.'

Richard quartered the red-brown wash of the water, but to his eyes it seemed to flow with innocent smoothness out of the ochre desert and away into the blue of the sea with hardly a ripple. No: that wasn't quite right. There was a great deal of disturbance where the people were in the water. And, some way beyond them, was another heaving frenzy. Richard focused on this second one, trying to assess whether there were any people down there too. But there was nothing to see on the surface except heaving ripples and flashes of movement. Whatever was happening there was happening under water.

Richard looked further south still, and caught his breath. He closed his eyes – literally, as he had in childhood when presented with an unexpected sight – and looked again. It was still there. 'Patterson,' he said. 'Do you see that? Away to the south about ten kilometres?'

And Patterson said, with quiet awe, 'Son of a gun . . .'

Powering out of the afternoon haze, kicking up a bow wave which told of speeds in excess of thirty knots, came the slim bows of an ancient Second World War destroyer.

Chapter Eighteen

Conception had been regretting her decision to come on *Pequod*'s last excursion for some time before disaster struck. She had been surprised to discover how much she had grown used to the company of Mickey and Robin. Only when she came aboard without them at the marina steps at Cortez did she suddenly feel their absence. Kramer was in a strange mood, and the rest all seemed sullen and deflated, as though this final adventure was one chore too many on the day after their civic reception, victory parade and assorted feasts.

It was Kramer, on some kind of frenetic high, who jollied them all along. The high point of yesterday for most of them had been the visit to the aquarium, and this was their one and only chance, he said, to see some of the wildlife displayed there in its natural habitat. But there would be something of interest to the physicists among the engineers as well as the zoologists, he promised. The inflatable had no draft. They could sail across the artificial estuary, examine the eastern – lower – levee and see how it was designed to work *in extremis*, then slip round its outer edge into the mangroves. If that was not enough, they could paddle further on out into the deeper reaches of the Sea of Cortez and look for some of the more exciting aquatic wildlife. This appeared to enthuse even DeLillo who seemed to be in a state of shock today.

It was an easy enough paddle across the calm water of the estuary opposite Cortez. The tide was full but slack. They had maybe ten metres of water under them and it wasn't going anywhere much as the incoming tide hesitated, considering whether to yield to the downward pressure of the Colorado's easy flow. The crossing was maybe five kilometres and it took a couple of hours' easy paddling to accomplish it. But it was not without incident. The river's water was red and thick, but the tidal surge from the Sea of Cortez was unusually clear, allowing those with zoological leanings an early treat or two. In the limpid stillness, it seemed possible for light and vision to plumb the depths and see among the shifting shadows there the vague shapes of giant manta rays flying low over banks of sand and silt in search of food.

Indeed, the arrival of a steady flow of rich provender from the heart of the North American subcontinent seemed to have rearranged the balance of life up here quite radically. As they were exclaiming over the balletic grace of mantas which reached fifteen metres from wingtip to wingtip, they were surprised by the arrival of a big old swamp alligator, exploring round the outer end of the levee and claiming new territory for the creatures of the mangroves. He flipped beneath the waves and resurfaced with a bright yellow-and-black-striped parrot fish held crossways in his jaws.

'I hope he doesn't take an interest in us,' said one of the men.

'Too right,' breathed DeLillo, who was now Conception's opposite number.

'No worries,' said Kramer. 'I could scare him off with this anytime.' He held up a flare pistol tethered to the strapping that held the radio securely in place and Conception gave a dry, unconvinced bark of laughter.

Kramer didn't have to try out his weapon, for the alligator, clearly wary in its new environment, gave them a wide berth, only to have his scaly length replaced in the glassy upper water by a squadron of turtles apparently flying in strict formation.

As they followed the turtles eastwards, the flood of the tide passed and the river began to reassert itself, washing the clear water, its denizens and the *Pequod* riding on its back southwards towards the open sea. The paddling became even easier, and soon they were able to relax and allow the increasing thrust of red water washing beneath their keel to take them surely and swiftly where they wanted to go.

The levee along the eastern shore swept down upon them and then rushed past them like the side of a long line of freight cars passing a level crossing. There were very occasional steps on the river side, with little concrete landing stages, but it was not until they ran past the third of these that Kramer decided to do anything about it.

After they had examined the construction of the levee and indulged in a detailed and obscure discussion about how closely it matched the plans laid for it, and how well these plans had fitted with the requirements of the environment, they piled back aboard and let the red surge carry them round the outer end of the levee into a still backwater where the renewed power of the river washed fresh water into the western end of what had been salt swamps for more than a century. Such was the calm of the day and the apparent safety of the expedition that they didn't even bother to strap in again.

Those of them for whom zoology was a hobby exclaimed over the manner in which the flora and fauna seemed to be adapting so readily – or re-adapting, as was closer to the case. But with the arrival of the cool red water of the Colorado, clarity departed and the bottom became impossible to see. The alligators pulled themselves out onto distant banks to raise their body temperatures in the sun. The only creatures the *Pequod*'s crew saw with any clarity were the quick green frogs which scuttled through the maze of snake-like roots, trunks and branches of the trees, and the massive crabs which came out to hunt them. The tree frogs and crabs were not the only swamp creatures the engineers encountered, however. As soon as they were within the confines of the swamp itself, clouds of large black mosquitoes appeared. Against these agile monsters, the worst the Colorado had offered them up to now seemed like midges. With deeply disconcerting suddenness they appeared and fell upon the crew of the inflatable. As though starved of good red blood for a salty century, the mosquitoes attacked their faces and hands, piercing earlobes and eyelids, lips and nasal passages with tongues like red-hot needles. They crawled into hair. They slipped down collars and slithered under T-shirts. They pushed the gaps between buttons wide and tested the security of trouser waists and belts.

'Kramer,' called Conception through narrowed lips, looking up through slitted, streaming eyes as another in a swiftly-forming army of mosquitoes took a fancy to her blood, 'I don't know about these lowland swamp mosquitoes, but the mountain variety round here carry malaria.'

They had all brought courses of foul anti-malaria tablets and many took them religiously, but that was no reason to test their effectiveness right now. They turned and paddled for the sea with the same concentred teamwork that had seen them safely over the last set of level V rapids on the Colorado. Blindly, on the edge of group panic, they powered *Pequod* due south at speeds they had never dreamed were possible, with the gathering rush of the river under their keel, the infested swamp at their backs, the open sea before their faces and the black mosquitoes ravening in their ears and eyes.

And that was what they were doing when they hit the whale.

The whale was an elderly humpback. He had lugged the fifty-odd tons of his body into the Sea of Cortez outside the usual season of whale visitation because he was virtually senile and had wandered away from the whale roads and their singing families to die alone in silence.

191

The water of the Sea of Cortez seemed different to him. It was a slight but significant difference and, although he knew well enough where he was and was nearly at the end of his last reserves of energy, he decided to explore the new water. So he swam further north than usual. In the north he surfaced unadvisedly near the idling hull of the sea-going cruiser *Tiburon* one night. The smugglers aboard the brightly lit boat spotted his wash and, strung out and jumpy, they opened fire. The massed weight of their weaponry was nowhere near enough to kill him, but they hit him several times in the head with a range of fire, much of it automatic. They half-blinded him and, more importantly, they lobbed a couple of grenades into his departing wake and deafened him as well. Since then, his life had been a battle against weakness, blood loss and the increasingly adventurous sharks which followed the rich streams spewing from his head, shoulders and sides.

In the end, a combination of shelving sea floor, disorientating, debris-filled water rushing at him in new currents, the relentless attacks of the sharks and simple shortness of breath had forced him to the surface. He was nearly twenty metres long and his hump rose a good solid metre above the surface to the stub of his fin. Had it not been for the mosquitoes gathered around their heads like the sharks gathering around his own, someone aboard *Pequod* would have seen him. But they did not. Had they been running with an outboard instead of paddling; had their sides been of anything other than inflated rubberised material, he would have heard them coming and turned aside, almost deaf though he was. But they were running silent as far as he was concerned. Even when they hit him, had he not been so near the end of his life and his tether, had he not been so badly wounded and fighting so desperately already, he would have turned aside and run. But all these things which had combined to start the incident combined to finish it as well.

The *Pequod* ran straight up onto the humpback's wounded, agonised head. It was more than he could stand and he reared his head and shoulders out of the water, sending the boat and its occupants flying through the air. The empty frame of the inflatable cartwheeled over the wounded hump, bounced off the bullet-riddled fin and slammed into the water immediately above the great whale's tail with enough sound to register in the wreckage of his aural system. The tail slammed up and down, bursting the inflated sections on *Paquod*'s left side like so many party balloons. The whale whirled, slashing at the water with its great encrusted forehead, bursting the right-hand sections. After that he thrashed from one side to the other

192

for a moment, but there seemed to be nothing more there. Panicked, confused, lost, out of energy and hope now, he powered away south, with the rush of the strange river water behind him and the jaws of the patient sharks ahead.

Conception hit the water with the back of her head and it felt like cement to her. She blacked out for an unknown period then came to. The whole of her chest and head felt as if it was on fire, in a murky half-light of wildly rushing water which apparently she was trying to breathe and which in turn seemed intent on washing her away. She could not swim against it for her legs were tangled round each other and her hands were fastened immovably round a couple of items attached to the clothing on her chest. For a moment of freezing panic she could not work out which way was up. The cold current was whirling her determinedly over and over. Then a boot hit her in the head and caused her to think two thoughts almost simultaneously. Where there were boots there was life – probably on the surface. And the surface could be attained by pulling the toggle clutched in her right palm, thus inflating the neck section of her lifebelt. An instant later she, too, was at the surface, choking and puking but, like the others, alive and kicking.

Conception had been under water the longest. She had been swept under all the others and was furthest out to sea. Nearest to her was Kramer. Just beyond them was the wreckage of the *Pequod*, held partially afloat by the last few remaining inflated sections. Side by side, they struck out towards her, both all too well aware that the currents unleashed by the falling tide and the Colorado's gathering outflow would wash them further out to sea in the whale's wake. Unless they were lucky enough to be spotted, then their only chance was to call for help and get out of the water before the ocean-going alligators came off their sandbanks to look for some dinner or the big sharks tired of whale meat and came back along the humpback's blood tracks looking for dessert.

The inflated sections of the *Pequod* lay on the water almost obscenely, like the guts of some long-dead leviathan bulging with putrefaction. Conception took hold of the bright orange safety rope which ran through steel rings all round what had been the waterline. It pulled loose at once. She hung in the water, wondering how to secure it so that they could take turns hanging on in relative safety. Kramer blundered past her, floundering unhandily forward as he fought to get out of his life jacket. 'Got to dive,' he gasped, tearing the bright

193

front wide and wrenching his arms free. 'Got to get the radio and the flare gun.'

'Good thinking.'

'Hold this.'

'Got it.'

He vanished under the water beside her and she felt him forcing his way past the pendant curtains of the wrecked inflatable. It occurred to her that if Kramer got lost under there then she would have to go down after him. Then DeLillo came alongside, with the others behind him. 'Where's Kramer?' he gasped.

'Gone fishing,' she gestured downwards. 'After the radio and the flare gun.'

As she spoke she began to loosen the straps of her own life jacket. Kramer had been gone a good two minutes and the agitation in the wrecked inflatable beside her legs was becoming wilder. One minute later, with no sign of Kramer, she handed two life jackets to DeLillo. 'Hold these a minute,' she said. 'And keep a firm grip on this too. Pay it out as I go but be ready to pull me in if I jerk it hard a couple of times in succession.' 'This' was the loose line from the *Pequod*'s side. Holding it firmly in one hand as though she was Theseus taking Ariadne's advice, she dived into the dark labyrinth of the floating wreckage, trailing the bright orange thread behind her.

The whole of the passenger well of the inflatable seemed to have exploded under the weight of the humpback's mighty tail. It hung now in deadly tangles and tatters. The gloom in there disorientated Conception. How in heaven's name Kramer had expected to get in, get the equipment and get out again she could not imagine. The current made the shreds flutter and dance like torn curtains in a horror movie, while feeding more silt-thick water into the situation, darkening things still further. Not that that made a heck of a lot of difference, she thought. Without goggles or face mask she was practically blind in any case.

Just at the end of her lung-full, stunned at how much of this pendant wreckage there seemed to be, Conception pulled aside a slimy wall of rubberised canvas and screamed aloud, losing most of her remaining air. Kramer was there, immediately in front of her, clutching the radio equipment, weirdly illuminated by the red-tinged beam of a torch he had also found, helplessly entangled and screaming into his death throes like a madman. The sight of her shocked him back to sanity and he hung there, still in the water, while she worried at the deadly web like a terrier. Then he was free and she was able to lead him back along the bright orange thread out of the underwater maze and up into the life-giving air of daylight.

They didn't waste time on conversation – thanks or otherwise. Using the floating side of *Pequod* and their life jackets to make a relatively dry and steady platform, they set up the radio and started broadcasting broad-band Mayday signals. Confident in the presence of so many others and the seemingly reliable floating wreckage, Conception hung on to the safety line left-handed and laboriously untied her boots, loosening them until she could kick them off. Then she loosened her trousers, peeled them inside out down her legs, and kicked until she had got rid of them too. Her shirt was next and last. The heavy material of her sport bra and support pants was better than bikini cotton, should she need to worry about her modesty. Then, using the line again and borrowing Kramer's torch, she went down, as lithe as a seal, to get the flare gun and anything else of use she could find.

Oddly, there was little sense of danger. The water was deep, but the wash of it warm and familiar after so many days of following the river down. She had seen the whale but had not really understood its actions – or the fact that it was being attacked by sharks. She had seen the alligators but did not consider it a serious possibility that they would bother to swim out as far as this. The giant manta rays were harmless and, in any case, one could have swum mere metres below the wreckage she was exploring and she would have been none the wiser. Following the torch beam, lulled into a thoroughly false sense of security, Conception followed the keel downwards, went under the sunken side of the inflatable and rose up what was left of the passenger well. It seemed to her that the floating section must be part of the stern, and that was where the flare gun was likely to be. And so it proved.

Conception came to the surface behind the last inflated pieces and called to the others. She got no reply, even though she was certain they were just on the other side of the low black wall floating in front of her. She tucked the pistol and the flare gun and the torch securely down the front of her panties and beat on the fat side as though it was a drum, calling at the top of her lungs as she did so. There was not a whisper of reply.

Conception found this extremely disturbing. As far as she could figure, all the other survivors were a couple of metres away, on the other side of the black bubble. The inflated sections were too high for her to see over, and they were too long to allow her to see round. If she wanted to look on the other side she would either have to go down

195

again and follow her orange thread back through the wreckage, or she would have to let go of the thread and strike out across the surface – and she was suddenly extremely reluctant to do either of these things.

Conception put the fat black bulge to her back and looked south, all too well aware that this was the direction in which the relentless thrust of the river's outwash was pushing them. She could see little. Even in the relative calm, at the top of a tall tide with the river coming up from under her, she could see only as far as the crest of the next wave. She waited for the arrival of that wave and strained to see ahead from its crest, she saw only as far as to the crest of the next wave as it came advancing out of the haze. She wished she had not come to this side of the wreck alone. She wished she still had her life jacket on. She wished most poignantly she had never seen *Jaws* – though it was a good twenty years since she had done so.

Conception turned, gasped a breath or two, settled the gun securely in her underwear, scraping her belly painfully with the barrel, pulled the torch free and tightened her grip on it, still holding her breath. Finally, she let her breath out, draining her lungs so that she would sink swiftly and return efficiently without having to fight her natural buoyancy all the way. She slipped under the water and pulled the bright safety line, watching it as it snaked ahead, almost luminescent in the torch's beam, leading the way to safety. She went deep, and had to arch her back fiercely in order to get back up from the deepest part of the sunken inflatable. As soon as she did so, she felt the flare gun begin to slip. Wildly, she grabbed at it, dropping the line without thinking. Grabbed and missed. She felt it slipping out of her pantie waistband altogether. She grabbed again, using both hands – in spite of the risk to the torch. She caught it this time and jabbed it home so fiercely, she winded herself – or would have done had there been any wind left in her.

Just beginning to register how deep she was in trouble, Conception flashed the torch beam upwards, and there was the bright line, above her head, tangled in some tatters of rubberised canvas hull. She reached up for it with her right hand, still shining the torch with her left, and as she reached it, a moray eel thrust its face out of the tangle beside it, into the light.

Had Conception not been holding onto the line so tightly, she would have died then, for she screamed so forcefully that she emptied her lungs even of residual air, and sank like a stone. The eel disentangled itself from the black rubberised curtains with arrogant, sinuous grace. It was nearly two metres long and as thick

196

as her thigh. The torch beam glittered off the white of its belly, the deepening green of its flanks, the massive underhang of its jaw. Frozen by simple disgust, she hung there as her heart thundered, and the edges of her vision began to throb to its beat, failing as her brain became starved of oxygen. At last she could wait no longer. She jerked her hand downwards with terrible desperation, pulling her long body relentlessly upwards towards the moray's even longer body. But the instant she moved, it was gone, flicking away out of the torch beam and into the darkness, as though her movement had frightened it.

Conception exploded out of the water into the life-giving air in little better case than Kramer had been, but alive, at least, and still possessed of the flare gun. 'You bastards!' she spat at them, as soon as she could breathe. 'Why didn't you answer when I called?'

DeLillo was nearest and he shrugged, his boyish face folded into a look of innocent confusion. 'We never heard you, Conception. Are you sure you called out real loud?'

Rather than trade insults with him, Conception simply ordered, 'Give me a hand up.'

Obligingly – a little too obligingly given her current attire – DeLillo took her at her word and placed a broad hand where a bicycle seat might go while she pulled herself up over the top of the inflated section for a moment. A moment was all it took to understand the mystery. *Pequod* had not lost all her inflated sections. By the look of things she had lost them amidships left and right. This was not the stern, as Conception had believed, it was the bow. The stern, where she and Kramer had gone to get the equipment, was also afloat, nearly ten metres away.

But as fate would have it, what had so nearly killed two of them held all of them safe for a little longer, for the moray eel had not vanished into darkness because it was scared of Conception or her flashlight but because it had sensed the first shark returning from the movable feast that was the dead humpback. And the shark, the first of many, cruised up to that empty, south-facing stern section of the wreckage and then swam away, disappointed, its supper held safe for the moment by the distance between the two floating sections of the inflatable and the thickness of the wreckage hanging in between.

The next thing that happened was that Kramer got an answer to his distress signal. He spoke no Spanish, but the coastguard service here was used to dealing with American tourists and had multilingual emergency operators.

'They're sending help,' Kramer exulted.

'Great,' snapped Conception, her mood darkened by her feelings of loneliness and risk, by the fright the eel had given her and by the fact that she couldn't think of a way of getting back at DeLillo for taking advantage of her need for a hand up. 'So give me back my life jacket.'

As Conception forced her body back into the jacket, she caught DeLillo looking at her chest.

'Give a lady a break here, DeLillo,' she said icily. 'What's got you in a lather all of a sudden?'

'I . . .' he gulped and turned away.

'Hey,' called one of his friends. 'DeLillo's been looking at NNO's tits! What's the matter, little man, didn't you get your bell-rope pulled when you were out with Kramer last ni—'

And that's when the shark took him. Right there, in the middle of the word 'night', out of the centre of a line of men all hanging side by side along the length of the inflated bow, each within a metre of the next. DeLillo's friend jerked under the water, life jacket and all, and vanished.

It was so clean, so surgical, so unexpected, that they all just gaped at the swirling water where he had been. DeLillo actually laughed aloud with shock and surprise. There had been no warning – no threatening dorsals, no mysterious washes of water, no cold currents, no psychic intimations, nothing. The man just jerked under the water and vanished in a flash of drowned colour and a heave of surface. The people either side of him, fully dressed, didn't even feel the movement of the water against their skin.

Then DeLillo's friend exploded into the air again, ten metres away. He made no sound. He simply looked down with apparent horror into the water below him, his head hanging and rolling as though his neck had been broken. Then, toppled by the weight of the head, the body rolled forward and it was briefly clear that he had been chopped in half.

As the torso hit the water another heave of water overcame it. There was a whirlpool in the already red ocean and a small volcano of bubbles. Then the corpse was gone. Perhaps there was a flicker of fin above the surface but none of the men was looking too closely then. They were all bunched up into foetal positions, thighs gathered to their chests, offering the smallest targets possible. Conception dragged the flare gun out of the waist of her panties and shot it straight up into the air before she, too, curled herself into a ball.

Conception was torn by three conflicting emotions. Primarily and most poignantly, she was angry at herself for firing the flare without

198

ensuring there was someone out there to see it. That flare was likely to be their final hope if their rescuers were slow or short-sighted. Then she was angry with herself for having put herself at risk by fucking around with the flare gun at all – she should simply have folded herself into a ball, pulled herself up onto the slick black surface beside her and looked after number one. But finally she was angry with herself because she could not remember the name of the man the sharks had just eaten. She had spent more than a week in his company and talked to him on several occasions, yet she could not bring to mind his name. And that made her very angry indeed.

Whether it was because of the anger or because of shock, time started playing tricks on Conception about then, for it seemed that she had only been hanging, balled up and pressed tightly against the side of *Pequod*'s floating bow for a moment or two before she heard the droning of an aeroplane. Child of the seventies, woman of the eighties and nineties that she was, she had really only heard the sound of an aeroplane like this in films about the Second World War. She looked up, but could see nothing in the glare of the afternoon sky. Time slowed down then and it seemed that she spent an age splitting her search between the sky and the heaving sea.

When DeLillo spoke, it was in a hoarse, braying bellow. 'I can't keep my legs up. It's tearing my belly muscles to hell and gone.'

'You got to, kid,' called Kramer. 'You lower your legs, you ring the dinner gong.'

And just then, as though to emphasise his words, a tall sand-grey dorsal fin cut the red water one wave away and began to circle the wreckage. They all watched it, with fascination that went beyond fear. 'Shouldn't we be splashing and yelling?' called Conception. 'Trying to drive it away?'

'Let's not rush into that,' answered Kramer. 'I reckon that'd call more of them over for a look-see before it frightened this one off. Let's stay quiet and wait for the guy in the little turboprop to direct the rescuers to us.'

'You don't think he'll be able to help us himself?' quavered DeLillo.

'Only if he can drop shark repellent and a new inflatable,' answered Kramer.

'Or if he's a seaplane,' called Conception. And it wasn't feminine intuition or Mexican-hispanic psychic ability. She saw the little Beechcraft come skimming out of the haze, the blessed length of its bright yellow floats glinting in the sun.

They all watched Patterson's careful landing almost as though he was hypnotising them. Only Conception, who was furthest from the plane as it taxied carefully closer, directed her wide-eyed gaze at the red heave of the impenetrable water, feeling now the almost uncontrollable urge to drop her legs and ease the burning of the muscles in her stomach. She was suddenly overwhelmed by the need to pee and caught herself wondering if the warmth and scent of her urine would attract the sharks like blood.

The Beechcraft stopped and swung side on, bobbing and rocking on the chop as the southward pressure of the river steepened the north-running swells of the sea. The side door halfway along the fuselage opened and a smooth yellow bundle like a big gelatine-covered painkiller flew out into the water. No sooner had it landed than it exploded, expanding out into a six-seater open-topped life raft. A huge figure loomed in the doorway. Conception had not seen much of Mickey's rescue so she had no idea who this was. She was struck by his size and the volume of his English accented voice, as he bellowed, 'Climb aboard. We can take six in here and six in the life raft. You'll be safe until the rescue ship arrives. But hurry!'

Perhaps it was a mistake to tell them to hurry but Richard had not seen the shark attack and did not know how near to all-out panic these people really were.

They needed little urging to hurry. As soon as the outer side of the inflatable was firm, those nearest to it threw themselves forward, floundering through the water until they could get the yellow rubber side under their armpits. Here they paused, their bodies too numb to allow them to swing nimbly and swiftly upwards. As they hung there, hesitant, some of them realised that their legs were dangling dangerously again and bunched up once more, slowing themselves down further. Their hesitation made things worse because more survivors from *Pequod* were floundering towards the escape route which was now blocked by the sluggish bodies of their colleagues. Instead of retreating, they hung on to the tired bodies clinging to the life raft, pulling some of them free of it. 'Kramer!' bellowed Conception. 'Organise them! Get a system going! All this splashing around'll bring the sharks back!'

'DeLillo,' ordered Kramer. 'Come across with me. We'll boost the tired ones up into the life raft.'

They splashed across and ruthlessly pushed their way through the ranks of exhausted survivors. It was brutal. It was little short of bullying. But it worked. The two men singled out the choke point of the blockage – a plump, balding man well past the end of his tether. They pushed and pulled, and punched where necessary,

200

until those who had been clutching onto him all fell back and he was hanging there alone. Then they reached down and together heaved him upward. He flopped forward like a broken doll and rolled into the passenger well. Then he lay there, choking. Kramer hauled himself up and struck at him. 'Move, you son of a bitch!' he yelled.

'It's all right,' boomed a deep English voice. 'I can take it from here.'

Conception looked up again. The big shadow from the cabin had become a tall, powerful-looking man dressed in a charcoal pinstripe business suit and the shiniest shoes she had ever seen. The shoes were standing on the nearest of the plane's bright floats and the big man was holding on to a line which reached out of the door and gave him enough freedom of movement to stoop, catch the first survivor and heave him up into the plane like a sack of corncobs. There was a brutal thump as he landed on the cabin floor and a scurry of movement as the pilot slung him up into a seat. The whole plane rocked. Kramer and DeLillo heaved again. The next broken doll slumped up into the life raft's bilge. The big Englishman stooped and heaved. Conception's thoughts lightened. They had a good rhythm going here. Only fifteen or so left to go. There had been a round two dozen with Robin and Mickey aboard. It looked as though she was destined to be the last, though, apart from DeLillo and Kramer.

Conception had spent a lifetime fighting for equal rights in a male-orientated macho society. She wasn't about to start demanding special treatment now. She was lighter, fitter, better equipped to survive, and stripped for action. By her reckoning, DeLillo probably had a better claim to a place in the life raft if space grew tight and someone had to hang in the water and wait. She never doubted that Kramer would wait until last. That was what leadership was all about.

'All the seats full,' bellowed the pilot from inside the Beechcraft. 'That includes yours and mine, Richard. We can lie three more in the gangways.'

'My shoes have just filled with water,' called back the Englishman. 'That means the floats are sitting very low. And it'll upset Mr Lobb,' he added, half under his breath. 'Let's hope we can preserve the turn-ups for Mr Gieves.'

Conception calculated, half listening to this impenetrable monologue. There were still ten left, apart from Kramer, DeLillo and herself. Two in the aisles. Six, maybe seven on the raft. The rest of them hanging. She stopped looking at the plane she would never enter and started looking around for dorsal fins again. She saw with a shock

201

which came near to winding her that there were several clearly visible now, surprisingly close, made inquisitive by the noise and disturbance of the rescue. Without even thinking, she curled herself up into the tightest ball, the whole of her skin super-sensitised to any stirring in the water nearby. 'Kramer!' she called. 'They're back!'

As soon as Conception called the warning, a ripple of terror went through the last of the survivors. Kramer and DeLillo were heaving the first of those destined to occupy the life raft into place. The big Englishman was hanging on to his strap and watching with eagle eyes. He had a big pistol in his hand and had clearly stopped worrying about Mr Lobb and Mr Gieves for he was under water to the ankles and soaking to the knees. He saw her looking and gave a thin, tense smile, crow's feet crinkling charmingly beneath raised eyebrows. 'For emergencies only,' he told her. 'But shouldn't you be in the life raft?'

'No. I'm fine here,' she croaked. 'Better than most of them.'

He nodded and grinned grimly once again. 'It's your call,' he said. 'I'll nominate you for the Medal of Honour later.' She wasn't sure how serious he was, but somehow the words which might have been cutting irony managed to carry no real offence. Quite the reverse, in fact.

A big heave of water came in from behind her, making the life raft lift and the Beechcraft bob worse than ever. 'Won't be long now,' he said, though Conception wasn't sure what he was talking about.

The shark took DeLillo then. The young engineer was in the middle of heaving the next survivor aboard the life raft when his head jerked under the surface. The survivor, half over the bright yellow side, began to slide back, bleating. Someone aboard caught him and pulled. His legs flipped up out of the water and they were both all there. 'Quickly,' yelled Conception to Kramer. 'Get the rest in.'

But Kramer had thrown his hands up and was being dragged aboard himself. Conception looked along the bloated black side and there were two men hanging at the far end, their eyes wide and dark in dead-white faces. The last one by the yellow raft went aboard beside Kramer, heavy enough to allow some water over the bilge and into the bottom.

A tall sand-coloured fin cut the restless water between the black wreckage and the bright life raft. Conception's knees actually broke the surface, pressing her breasts up into a considerable cleavage. Her shoulders and arms tensed and her grip on the orange safety rope lifted her body half out of the water. Over the unbridgeable reach of shark alley, her eyes met the sky-blue gaze of the Englishman. He was frowning.

DeLillo exploded out of the water immediately beside Conception then. He threw his arms up and gripped the swollen side of the *Pequod*. Conception put her left arm protectively round the boy's shoulders, sliding back into the water beside him. The water was warm, full of hot little currents which pulsed vividly against her chilled, heat-sensitive skin. 'Conception!' he said, his voice little more than a broken whisper. He frowned. 'I'm sorry. I'm sorry. Tell Mickey . . .' Something jerked him. Something which brushed like sandpaper brutally across the outer curve of her bottom and thigh, actually pushing her up out of the water as though she was riding on it. His fingernails dragged down the surface of the rubberised cloth, scraping across the weave with a sound like a zip unzipping, leaving lines of white, then red as the nails shredded away. 'Watch Kramer,' he said, then he repeated, 'Watch . . .' but the word became a scream which mingled with her own and was choked off as he was jerked down again, while her own went on and on.

'Kill him!' she shouted at the Englishman standing apparently hesitant, the gun in his hand. And the Englishman acted, seemingly prompted by her words, firing a steady stream of bullets at the diminshing heave of water which had claimed DeLillo. Close beside her, the black inflatable section exploded and began to sink with unnerving rapidity. In a blinding flash of insight, she realised why the Englishman had waited – so his bullet would not make things worse for her.

They could get no worse now, Conception thought grimly. Her support was gone. Her head was just above the water and the rest of her was probably sending out a range of signals to the sharks all of which meant 'Lunch'. The last two engineers left in the water with her, also robbed of *Pequod*'s support, began to splash their way across to the yellow side of the Beechcraft's life raft, which was low and shipping water. As her hands had no further function holding the sunken lifeline, she wrapped them round her knees and made herself as small as possible. Then, with the water lapping past her chin, she waited, exercising all her enormous self-control in the simple act of refusing to panic or scream. She was certain now that she was going to die here and she simply would not go down weeping and screaming.

One of the swimmers she had seen heading for the life raft exploded out of the water terrifyingly close at hand, his body held crosswise across the face of a shark, his side gripped in its metre-wide jaw.

The shark and its prey slammed down into the water immediately in front of her, and in that instant before the bloody, foaming spray swept over her, Conception found herself looking straight into the cold, strange eye of a hammerhead.

That it should be a hammerhead made things worse for the terrified woman. She had purposely not been imagining what the creatures feasting on her friends and working their way along to her were like. But that they should be the most alien and terrifying of the shark family was too much for her to bear. She screamed at the top of her lungs and emptied her bladder without realising it. She unclenched her hands and beat at the water right in the alien's face, striking the shrieking engineer in the back and legs as the shark bit home, shaking its head in a welter of blood and bubble from ruptured lungs. She actually punched the shark full in the eye just at the moment its head swung towards her, and the shock of the impact hurled her back and under.

Amazingly, more shockingly than anything that had happened so far, that movement threw Conception into the arms of another swimmer. Up beside her, holding her surely and securely, there came a broad-shouldered, white-haired man whose brown face and eyes marked him as a Hawaiian islander. 'Stay still,' he ordered, gently. 'Help is at hand. They are just going round the inflatable. I swam ahead to help . . .'

'Who on earth . . .' Conception choked.

'Call me Joe Aloha,' he said gently, the depth of his voice and the certainty of his tone giving her strength just when she needed it most. 'The sharks are my brothers,' he told her – and she believed him.

Or she did for an instant. No sooner had Joe spoken than another hammerhead came charging in at them. Because Joe was there, she had no fear. She lashed out as though her arm was made of steel and punched it right in the face, hard. Hard enough to turn its head, at least. Its stalk-borne eye brushed past her. Its right pectoral chopped into her, winding her, spinning her out of Joe's firm grip and bursting the inflated neck section of her life jacket. Its side brushed against her like the asphalt on a road she remembered from a bicycle crash in her childhood. Its tall tail smacked her brutally from hip to shoulder as it turned to renew its attack.

Conception's head burst out of the water and she shook the spray from her eyes, watching as the hammerhead turned and came back for her. It was right on the surface, its wide, weird face planing through the red chop of wavelets caught between the Beechcraft and the sunken *Pequod*. The Englishman was coolly emptying the full load of his gun into the hillock of cartilage skull behind the strangely configured eyes, but this was having no effect. She could feel Joe striking out towards it in another extraordinary feat of bravery, but she knew nothing was going to do her any good at all.

Conception's final conscious thought was, 'I hope this isn't going to hurt . . .' But she knew very well it was.

The shark's whole face lifted out of the water and she saw the white underside of the cruciform eye stalks running past the tooth-lined maw down onto its belly. But what filled her vision was its mouth. And its teeth.

Her lips moved silently in a prayer precious from childhood.

The eye stalk on her right exploded. A gun report, loud enough to shock her, slapped into her right eardrum. The shark hurled its head away to the left, its gaping mouth missing her by mere centimetres. She saw into the massive wound which had been its eye. The gills immediately behind the wound burst open and another report stunned her. A sure, strong hand grasped the wreckage of her life jacket and she was lifted like a weightless thing out of the water and into the broad bow of a lifeboat.

Gently, Conception was placed on the warm wood of the top of the forward locker, and she looked up, dazed, to see a tall man with long grey hair unsnap a smoking pistol from a lanyard attached to his epaulette and strip off the pristine perfection of his captain's uniform jacket to reveal a vest marked, like a robin's breast on an American Christmas card, with dried blood. Then, equally gently, infinitely courteously, he wrapped the warmth of the jacket round her and laid her back on the locker to rest, his long eyes glinting with gentle concern, his long hair blowing in the wind. And she allowed the darkness of relief to wash over her as, distantly, someone pulled Joe Aloha safely out of the water too.

And so it was that Major Conception Lopez made the acquaintance of Captain Jesus Miguel de Hidalgo y Vega.

Chapter Nineteen

Richard came aboard *Colorado* with the last of the survivors. He stood tall and steady in the stern sheets as the lifeboat was winched smoothly aboard. Patterson lifted the Beechcraft into the air and winged off to Cortez's little airstrip in search of some aviation fuel. Richard raised his hand and Patterson waggled his wings, then the Beechcraft disappeared into the haze and the lifeboat swung inwards onto the deck.

Richard stepped out onto the grey metal and hefted his grip and suit-carrier out, off the stern locker top where they had sat beside him on the short journey across. He paused on the deck, looking around, seeking some familiar face or senior uniform among the quiet bustle all around him. He saw a solid-looking young man wearing the badges of a first lieutenant and crossed to him. 'My name is Richard Mariner,' he said quietly. 'I believe my wife is aboard.'

'Hernan Gutierrez,' said the lieutenant, sticking out his hand. 'That was good work, Captain. There would have been many more dead had it not been for you.'

'I need to talk to your captain too, when he has a moment. It's quite important. But my wife first, I think.'

'Of course. Raphael, take the *Señor Capitan* to the *Señora Capitan*, *por favor*.'

A tall young man swept Richard good-humouredly into his wake as he strode across the deck and then ran up the companionway outside the bridgehouse and in through a door into the B deck corridor. 'The *Señora Capitan* Mariner is not happy with us or with our *Capitan* Vega,' he confided cheerfully as they went. 'She wished to take part in the rescue, but *Capitan* Vega, he is a traditional man. Even though the *señora* may be well qualified and widely experienced, he would not allow her to place herself in any risk. That is what *we* are paid for, after all. Even now.'

Thus warned, Richard was ushered through a door into what was obviously the officers' wardroom. Raphael looked around the bright area with a wry smile and left, closing the door with theatrical softness. Richard hefted his baggage to the nearest table top and straightened. 'Hello, dear,' he said quietly across the room to Robin, who stood framed by a long window, frowning slightly. 'Have we got a cabin? I'd like to change. My shoes and trousers are sopping wet.' His gaze swept round the room as Robin came across towards him. There was one other person in there with her, a square, American-looking man with a thick blond crewcut. 'That's Chester Shaw. Army man,' said Robin. The afterthought was unnecessary – Chester was still in uniform.

Richard began to introduce himself as Robin reached his side, but Chester let go of a bourbon glass to hold up a broad hand with a quiet laugh. 'Robin here told us all about you while we watched you at work in the Beechcraft, before Joe went out with the boat. It's an honour to make your acquaintance, sir.'

'Yes,' said Robin quietly at his side, hugging his arm gently. 'We have a cabin. Come on.' She raised her voice. 'Excuse us, please, Chester.'

In the corridor outside, Robin fell silent again.

'Are you all right?' Richard asked gently. 'It must have been horrible to see people you had sailed down the river with get torn up like that. The seaman who showed me up said Captain Vega wouldn't let you join in the rescue. That must have been hard.'

'It was too hectic to make much of a scene,' she said. 'As soon as the emergency call came in, he had us all shepherded off. I got maybe two words with him and that was all. He put us in the library and the others in the officers' wardroom. He didn't really register anything about us except that we were in the way and he wanted us safely out of it. God alone knows how Joe Aloha got aboard, but from what I saw I'm glad he did. I just wish Captain Vega had let the rest of us help too.'

'It was quite reasonable to keep you safe, though, darling,' said Richard.

'And, apparently, typical. But it's left a couple of things to clear up.'

'What sort of things?' Richard did not like the tone of Robin's voice. There was something really worrying her here and it was not like her to beat around the bush.

'The emergency call came in just as I was about to introduce him to Mickey Vargas.'

'Mickey's aboard? Good. We'll see him later. I may need his backing when I—'

'It's important they get introduced carefully and sensitively, I

208

think. Because Mickey is, apparently, Captain Vega's estranged son and heir.'

'Well, I'll be damned. That's quite a coincidence.'

'No it's not. At least I don't think it is.' They had reached a cabin door now and Robin opened it. She ushered Richard into a cramped little junior officers' cabin with a pair of bunks on one side, a wardrobe on the other and a worktop covering a washbasin below a brass-ringed porthole on the wall opposite the door. 'And if it is, it's not the only one.'

'What do you mean?' asked Richard, frowning now in turn.

'Did you know Aldo Cagliari was in the navy?'

'No, but I'm not surprised. Why?'

'Because apparently he had something obscure but important to do with the *Colorado* somewhere along the line. He's aboard now, up in the officers' bar. I haven't seen him or talked to him, but he's there all right.'

'Now that *is* a coincidence,' said Richard, his frown deepening. There came an instant of silence. Then he said. 'On the other hand, of course, it might be nothing of the sort . . .'

'That's what I think, Richard,' said Robin, her frown matching his. 'I haven't managed to come up with any reason why those two being aboard here isn't coincidental but I just don't believe in coincidences as outrageous as that. There's something simply not right about it all. What on earth is going on here?'

'Whatever it is, it may have to take second place,' said Richard, beginning to strip off his jacket. 'There's quite a surge coming down the Colorado valley now. It'll be here in a couple of hours. And within the day there'll be a full-blown grade A disaster coming flooding down on top of it. We have to warn the captain at once, and he'll have to alert the authorities and prepare to take any further action that he can.'

Jesus Vega was sitting in his personal cabin writing out his report of the incident so far. It was only a preliminary outline, from *Colorado*'s point of view, but it was important that he got the facts relating to his command clearly and concisely down now. Later he would get a statement from the importunate Hawaiian guest and, from the man called Kramer, the names of the dead, as well as his report on what caused the disaster in the first place. And finally he would get details from the extraordinary man in the Beechcraft who had kept so many of them safe for the vital moments before *Colorado*'s lifeboats had reached the scene. As the nib of his gold pen scratched gently across his report, Jesus allowed himself a glance towards his bunk.

On his bunk, wrapped in pristine sheets, lay the sleeping form of the woman he had saved from the very jaws of the hammerhead. Her damp black hair lay across his pillow like a nest of serpents and the dampness of her body moulded the cool starched linen to her lower form like a second skin. Above the waist, she was wrapped in his jacket still, precisely as he had laid her here after carrying her fainting form aboard.

In a while, when Jesus had finished this first draft and was forced by duty to go out and ask some follow-up questions, Captain Mrs Mariner would be invited in to lend a little of the support she had been so insistent in offering earlier. As the only other female aboard, only she could possibly tend to the wounded woman, take the captain's uniform jacket from her, remove her wet clothing, dry her body and tend her wounds. Like many another ship's captain, Jesus had qualifications in first aid and could perform the basic requirements well enough himself. But to do so with this woman was something which threatened to take him beyond the boundaries of his iron self-control.

There was a sharp rapping at his door. He rose, his mind too deeply occupied to register the pulling of his bloodstained vest across his lower chest. He crossed to the door and opened it. Bright blue eyes met him on a level with his own. A feeling of dynamic energy and impatience washed into the room. It was the Englishman from the plane, in full dress whites, as pristine as Jesus's usually were – though obviously lighter in weight, and of a more modern design. Behind the Englishman stood Captain Mrs Mariner, also exuding that feeling of decisive, desperate haste.

'Please come in,' said Jesus in the flawless English he had schooled himself to acquire years ago when he had hopes that such an accomplishment might prove useful to him.

With both of the dynamic Britons in the cabin, it suddenly felt crowded and small.

'Captain Vega, I have an important warning for you,' began the man, only to be interrupted by his wife.

'Conception!' she gasped, her eyes on the bunk.

She crossed to the sleeping Conception with no further word and began to check her wellbeing silently, efficiently, but with little observance of the proprieties, given that there were two men in here as well. Jesus strove to listen to what was being said to him by the

Englishman but was finding it very hard to focus on anything other than what was happening to Conception.

Richard took a deep breath and did his best to capture Jesus's gaze with the burning intensity of his own. 'My name is Richard Mariner. I should have been aboard long ago with Robin, my wife. Circumstances delayed me. I was aboard the Beechcraft aeroplane as you may have noticed because I had just flown down here directly from Las Vegas.'

'Indeed . . .' said Jesus courteously but vaguely. The sheet was folded back to the tops of her thighs. The jacket had fallen open and a path lay revealed up her belly from her navel to her cleavage. The skin on her legs was brown and that on her torso pale. The contrast, separated by the straining material of her underwear, was simply delicious. Jesus turned away and fixed Richard Mariner's gaze determinedly with his own.

'There is high water coming down the watercourse very fast indeed. The river will be full in a couple of hours. There is a possibility of flooding in the mangrove swamps, but at this moment, with the falling tide, I believe Cortez will be safe.'

'That is good. We are going to Cortez. We will dock at the commercial end of the marina. There is a berth reserved for us. Unless my orders have been changed yet again, this ship is due to be broken up tomorrow.'

Conception gave the softest of throaty groans and a rustle of fabric made it obvious that the jacket at least was coming off. It took all of Jesus Vega's iron will to keep his eyes on Richard Mariner's. But then, something about the look in those bright eyes really did catch his attention. This was a man to be taken seriously, and he had an important point to make.

'You don't understand,' said Richard with all the force of his character and concern. 'This is only the beginning. There will be another flood coming down on the back of this one within the day. Possibly as much as three cubic kilometres of water. Your city and perhaps your country are at considerable risk here!'

Richard was about to give more detailed explanation now that he had Captain Vega's undivided attention when the door flew open. There was no knock this time, merely the arrival of a slim young man in a US Army major's uniform. He strode across the cabin, paying no attention to Jesus or to Richard. 'Robin!' he said. 'Is she all right? I've been searching all over the ship since the lifeboats came aboard.'

'She's fine,' said Robin, straightening and pulling the sheet up

211

again. The captain's jacket was hanging on the back of a bedside chair, and the sheet as it settled clung intimately to damp skin. 'But I think I'll either have to move her or ask you all to leave. She wouldn't thank me for doing anything more in front of an audience.'

Then, unaccountably, Robin seemed to freeze. Her attention left Conception and swept from Mickey to Jesus. 'Look, Mickey,' she said, in a very different tone. 'There's never going to be a right time to do this. So now is as good a time as any. Do you want to do it or shall I?'

The cabin became tiny, stultifying, all of a sudden. Something deep below the surface stirred in Jesus Vega, something long buried, unsuspected and as unlooked-for as his sudden infatuation with the beautiful woman called Conception. Mickey swung round, full face, inches from Jesus. They looked each other straight in the eyes and, apart from the difference in age, they each could have been looking in a mirror. '*Hola, padre*,' said Major Miguel de Hidalgo y Vega to his father.

It was inevitable that either Richard or Robin would be disappointed with Jesus Vega's reaction. There was no way that the captain could deal with the impending crisis and the unexpected arrival of his son at the same moment. In the event it was Robin who was shocked. The older man looked the younger coolly in the face and turned away. Thoughtlessly, he caught up the jacket and shrugged it on. 'The city is at risk, you say. Please explain to me how this is so.' He opened the door and ushered Richard out.

'Can you give me some charts – anything up-to-date you have showing the estuary and the river mouth. I'll explain what's due to happen.'

'Come to the bridge. I will show you what we have. There is nothing official showing the new waterways, however. It was not thought worthwhile to supply anything new to a ship so soon to be decommissioned and broken up.'

'That might be a problem for me, and will certainly be a problem for you. You'll need to get a pilot aboard to get you into Cortez if you haven't got any charts.'

'No. Things are not quite as desperate as that. Only a couple of days ago we were able to salvage some very up-to-date charts from a cruiser smuggling Mayan artefacts up and down the coast.'

This conversation served to take the two men up onto the bridge where the young officer who had impressed Richard was on watch.

'Good afternoon, Hernan,' said the captain amiably. 'Captain Mariner and I have come to consult the new charts.'

'They are all laid out on the chart table, Captain. I have marked our course, headings and estimated timings already. We should have no trouble with the depths as registered at this state of tide. Lieutenant Banderas's exercise with beaching and re-floating *Colorado* has given us very precise measures of her current draft. Three point six metres gives us ample room.'

'But that's less than twelve feet,' said Richard. 'I thought destroyers like this needed fifteen feet – five metres or more.'

'We are stripped to the bone,' said Jesus briefly. 'With a little more effort I believe we could get her to clear three and a half. If we wanted or needed to.'

Hernan waited an instant and then continued, 'We are in contact with the harbourmaster and are due to dock within the hour. Everything seems fine.'

'The harbourmaster and coastguards haven't warned you about a serious surge coming down the river?' asked Richard, concerned. He was beginning to feel that slight disorientation which comes when a disaster looms and no one else has any inkling about it. 'Somebody must be aware of what is happening,' he said. 'Who is responsible for the river management down here?'

'That would be the Department of Agriculture in Mexico City, I suppose,' supplied Hernan thoughtfully. 'Not an authority we would normally contact before taking up anchorage.'

'How would you contact them in an emergency?'

'It would have to be by phone. Our radio equipment will not reach Mexico City any more,' said Jesus more bitterly.

'But we cannot use the phone until we run a land line ashore and connect to TelMex,' added Hernan, frowning.

Richard reached into his pocket. 'I can, if I can get a signal,' he said, producing his mobile phone. 'Or rather, Hernan, perhaps you could. I don't think my Spanish is up to the job.'

As the first lieutenant tried to discover the number for the Ministry of Agriculture, Jesus led Richard through to the chartroom. Here a large, very new, rather damp and stained chart was laid out under a thick, yellowing Perspex sheet decorated with Hernan's calculations neatly written in Chinagraph pencil. The chart covered in some detail the coastal area from San Felipe to the twin bridges carrying the railway and Route 5 over the Colorado. Major areas of water inland were also marked. There was no attempt to mark dry rivers, small tributaries or inland towns. Richard did not know – though

213

Jesus did, and it struck him now more forcefully than ever – that the town of Los Muertos Sierra de Juarez and the derelict estate of *La Casa Grande* sat side by side in the desert-yellow blankness of Baja California Norte, close to the west of the river's course, though too far inland to be of any concern of the chart-makers.

Richard was crouching over the bright blue representation of the wide tidal estuary, with its mathematical levees and its carefully calculated tidal high- and low-water marks. The annotations, of which there were many, were in English, for the chart was American. 'Look,' said Richard urgently. 'The tide is falling. According to this you will be entering the harbour near the ebb, with the water level at this mark and the current as described down here. Have you an American *Pilot* to go with this?'

'It is being updated, I believe. A supplement is due out soon.'

'OK. Look, what you'll need to do, by the look of things, is proceed as though the tide is going to turn in an instant. Somewhere during your approach and berthing, the water in the harbour will effectively go from low ebb to full flood. It may go higher still.'

'No,' came a decisive voice from the doorway. The two men straightened and turned. Mickey and Kramer stood there. It was Mickey who had spoken. 'No,' he repeated. 'Even if what you are saying about the flood is accurate, the water should not rise above the high-water marks in Cortez harbour because of the levee to the east.'

The two engineers came in uninvited and Mickey explained about the design of the levees. 'The mangrove will be at risk of a bit of flooding,' he concluded. 'But Cortez should be safe enough.'

'Even so,' persisted Richard, 'you will have to take the sudden rise in water level into account. And, by the look of things, you'll have to talk to the harbourmaster about flows and currents within the harbour basin itself. You'll need to tie up very carefully – you won't want *Colorado* to be tossed up against the harbour wall.'

'It wouldn't matter all that much,' said Mickey quietly. 'Not if she's going for scrap in a day or two anyway.'

Jesus swung round, stung, and looked properly at his son for the first time since his entry into the chartroom. 'She goes for scrap when I say so, boy,' he grated. 'And I won't give her up while the city's at risk and there's important work for her to do.'

'What could there be for this battered old relic to do, father?' asked Mickey almost gently. 'You're just hoping for a few more hours, like a prisoner putting off his execution for a few more moments of life.'

Jesus looked at Mickey, his face like rock; like ice. Then he looked over to Richard. 'Tell him what is coming next,' he said, his voice almost cold enough to cool the room.

'Maybe as much as three full cubic kilometres of water.'

Mickey laughed in his face, a short disbelieving bark. 'Not possible,' he said. 'Not even in your worst nightmares. Who told you this bullshit?'

'A woman called Hagan. Dr Sue Hagan. Senior hydrologist with the Bureau of Reclamation.'

Mickey stood, with his mouth open, his eyes almost invisible, as though he had suddenly become Chinese.

'Sue Hagan's the woman who'd know, Mickey,' said Kramer uneasily. 'Where'd you have this heart-to-heart, bud?'

Richard began to explain about the plane ride and Josie Mendez but was interrupted by the arrival of Hernan Gutierrez. 'I have talked to the ministry,' he said shortly. 'There is a red alert out now for the whole river system from the border to the sea. There has been some water damage to both the Imperial and the Morelos Dams. They have been unable to contain the extra flow.'

'We will dock with care and prepare—'

'I beg your pardon, Captain, but that is only the beginning. The ministry is warning of the possibility of major damage within the next twenty-four hours, as Captain Mariner has said. There are people dead, apparently at somewhere called Headgate. We should watch the news, they say.'

'How can we watch the news?' snapped Jesus with a bitter mixture of anger and frustration. 'They removed both the aerials and the televisions at Topolobampo.'

'If you've got a transformer, I believe I can help you there,' said Richard. 'Until the battery in my phone runs out, at least . . .'

Colorado came stealing up the coast under a deceptive calm, with still winds and flat water as far as the eye could see. On her port quarter, the coast of Baja California Norte changed with unsettling abruptness from the timeless desert, speckled with mysterious towers of rock, distant mountains simmering in the afternoon glare, to the busy outskirts of a burgeoning city. She eased past the furnaces of the breaker's yard, as though all too well aware that all she really represented was just so much scrap for the smelting, and up into the tidal basin at the mouth of the levees. The evening sky could have been painted by Turner, all gold and haze. At the mouth of the marina she hesitated, as though fearing that the ebb of the tide had closed the harbour bar to her. But as Hernan had said, her clearance was three point six metres now, and the ridge of the bar sat solidly at four. So in she slipped, with the harbourmaster's launch fussing in front of her, busily important, leading her to her place at the lower end of the commercial docks.

On the bridge, Hernan and Banderas stood watch and conned her safely home. Jesus stood with Richard, Mickey and Kramer, watching the news service broadcast from the Internet coming in from the ether via the phone and an infrared link to the laptop.

As *Colorado* entered the stillness of the marina, Robin arrived. The silence warned her that all was not well – and the graphic on the laptop screen told her what was wrong.

Jesus strode over to the bridge door. 'Ask the harbourmaster if he has warned all the owners and masters.'

'I hope he has,' said Banderas *sotto voce*, 'there's millions upon millions of pesos' worth of stuff out there.'

'This sort of stuff they price in dollars,' said Hernan. 'But you're right, there's still millions and millions' worth.'

As soon as the destroyer had tied up at the big berth designed for the cruise-liner trade in the hopeful future, Jesus, Richard and Robin crossed to the port bridge wing, the after section of which overlooked the marina basin's mouth. It was stultifying on the bridge wing. The sun was setting due west and dead ahead, its full power was on their shoulders and the backs of their heads. The air was still and the humidity high. Teams of men stood by the winches fore and aft where the captain had stationed them against the moment they would have to shorten the lines and keep the ship from throwing herself too powerfully against the fenders. Another team of sailors stood along the length of the shoreward side, each of them in charge of one of the heavy fenders designed to keep the ship safely and snugly against the wall, no matter what was happening on the seaward side. The wall of the dock rose perhaps five metres above the deck, level with the bridge wings. It came as no surprise to any of them that there was thunder in the air. A long, low rumbling seemed to wrap itself round them.

'It's up over the mountains,' said Jesus. 'The thunder came almost every night when I was a boy. Between six and eight. You could set your watch by it.'

'It's early tonight then,' said Robin, looking down at her watch automatically.

And Richard said, 'Actually, I don't think that is thunder at all . . .'

The thundering sound seemed to swing suddenly right round

216

the ship, from the west to the east. From the land side to the river side.

Richard moved out to the furthest reach of the bridge wing, looking across the calm water of the anchorage towards the harbour mouth. The water five metres below him was behaving strangely, as though the whole of the marina's concrete bottom was a glass on a juddering table. Ripples perhaps half a metre high were running in from the edges of the marina, crossing each other, turning into a restless chop in the centre. Over the top of the contained restlessness within the manmade lake of the marina came a broadening band of ripples, almost waves, spreading into semi-circular patterns from the entrance. *Colorado* began to stir, like a restless horse pawing the ground and eager to be at the gallop.

Jesus ran through the bridge itself to the rear of the starboard wing, where he could look down on the men at the winches and the fenders. 'Watch out,' he called. 'I think it's—'

The bridge wing door burst open behind him. Mickey and Kramer came running out. 'They've just broadcast a red alert for Cortez,' said Mickey breathlessly. 'Maybe there will be work for *Colorado* after all.' He crossed to the after rail at his father's straining side, looking down past the crewmen to the handiwork against which *Colorado* was due to be hurled. Kramer, also more interested in the civil engineering aspect of the looming crisis, stood at his shoulder, looking in towards the levees and marina walls.

Richard and Robin joined the little crowd silently, then stood looking out towards the river. So it was they who saw it first. A great heave of water swept down past the opening towards the Sea of Cortez, and as it did so, a branch of water split off the main trunk of the flood, rolling over the harbour bar, unleashing a maelstrom into the heart of the marina.

The flood of river water boiled in through the opening like a tidal wave, pushing into the south of the almost circular bowl of the marina and it kept on piling in and in and in. Soon the deeper water to the south swirled round to the north, lifting all the anchored boats and ships as it went – lifting *Colorado* almost last of all, so that the men at the winches and the fenders had ample warning. But as the height of the water in the seething river course outside made plain, the warning was of a process, not of a single incident. The swirl of water, having gone full circle, was swept into the next wave pouring in through the opening, so that a whirlpool began to form in the centre of the marina. It was a whirlpool of considerable depth and power, for the river's surge was a solid eight metres higher than the water level which had been sitting so contentedly awaiting the turn of the tide.

As though full tide had arrived in eight minutes instead of eight hours, the water level in the marina soared. *Colorado* rose up the wall of her berth at unprecedented speed. The whole ship heaved and shook wildly as the winches fought to keep some kind of control over her ropes and the team along the starboard side fought to keep the rumbling, grumbling fenders from ripping themselves free or tearing themselves to pieces. For the officers on the bridge and on the bridge wing, there was nothing to do but watch. The eight minutes of the incident passed so swiftly that none of them could have done anything much in any case.

Around them, millions of dollars' worth of far more prized, and totally unprepared, craft were smashed to pieces. Many were on long lines, sitting low in the water and expecting a sedate ride upward during the night. They were swept down the watery slope of the whirlpool to jerk against their ropes, tilting and filling and drowning. Those to the south were pushed north by the fierce gyre of the current, smashing into the sterns of those before them. It was a miracle that those boats which caught fire burned out quickly without exploding.

Colorado survived with a scraped and slightly twisted starboard bridge wing, a scorched port quarter, two wrecked starboard fenders and a seized winch – which El Jefe cheerfully said he would fix in the morning. By sunset, the battered old destroyer was riding serenely, almost alone of all the vessels in the Armageddon of the anchorage. Her bridge wings were now a good eight metres above the grey concrete plateau of the dock. Her mooring ropes were tight. Her riding lights were bright and most of her crew were helping the harbourmaster clear up the wreckage.

Cortez had survived, apart from some downtown sections flooded by drains designed to empty just below the high waterline instead of just above it. The mayor and his good lady wife were able to attend a civic function in celebration of the city's first official birthday with no worries about the immediate future. The system so cleverly designed by Mexican and American engineers had worked perfectly. Here the streets were largely dry. No one in the civic limousines got their feet wet tonight. Almost nobody in the ubiquitous Volkswagen Beetles made in their millions in La Paz did either.

In the mangrove swamps on the Sonora side, it was a different matter. A Niagara nearly ten kilometres wide had thundered over the edge of the lower levee, tearing trees loose, destroying habitats, spreading ocean irresistibly where saltmarsh had been before, washing a range of creatures out of their natural habitats. Washing them out but by no means away.

And, as the flow persisted during the next eight hours without diminishing in the slightest, the physics of the moon and the spin of the earth began to work. While the crew of *Colorado*, their officers, and a good number of their guests came wearily back from their voluntary emergency duties around the marina and clambered thankfully into their bunks, the water continued to work. Even under the onslaught of the overflowing river, the tide began to gather and to climb. Although the river toppled over the upper rim of the Sonora levee, the tide began to push irresistibly into the concrete jaws of the manmade estuary. The wash of the rushing river rose on the back of the salt tongue of the tide. And the tide was high tonight – the first of a series of spring tides gathering to eight metres and more. The crest of the high water rolled back and back, so that the top of the restless downward surge slipped upriver, eventually even beyond the lower section of the eastern levee.

At last, when the moon was setting and the tide was full, and everyone involved was sound asleep, the high crest of the downward surge steadied and seemed to sit, like the static rapid far upstream in the Grand Canyon where all of this had begun. It steadied, it sat and it overflowed, into a dry river valley which the Colorado had explored hundreds and thousands of years before. With relentless certitude, as though the river had a will and this was it, it overflowed just below the bridges carrying Highway 5 and the railway across its levee-contained breadth.

The first waves of the floodwater washed away across the desert under the last of the waning moon until it reached the lower end of the main street of Los Muertos Sierra de Juarez and the dry, dead pastures below the worm-eaten veranda of *La Casa Grande*.

Chapter Twenty

Saturday was a day of confrontations. There were many reasons why this was so, but perhaps most important among them was the fact that *Colorado* was like a ghost ship; like the Flying Dutchman's legendary vessel. She should have been dead; at least she should have been a hulk at the breaker's dock waiting to be smashed up and smelted down, yet here she was, battered but grimly alive. She should have been decommissioned, silent, her crew disbanded and her story all told, but she still felt full of loose ends, unresolved situations and unfinished conversations which refused to be cut short; she still felt full of life, as though she had one last vital job to do.

All around the quiet ship, the water sat high, dark and subtly restless. The marina had become riverine, and the water within it answered to dictates more immediate even than those of the sea. The water seemed to heave all the time in the corner of one's eye, as though the harbour contained a collection of huge serpents with slick, red, muscular sides which writhed around the ships and the wreckage with powerful and sinister intent.

The flow of the river had not abated and the tide which had risen with the waning moon was falling now under the rising sun but, oddly, that seemed to make no difference to the water level in the marina or the harbour as a whole. According to the marks on the charts laid out on the room behind sleepy Lieutenant Banderas, the officer of the watch, the tide stood at the flood. And stood, and stood without variation. In fact, the young officer now knew, looking a little apprehensively away across the anchorage, the water level had only stopped there because the wild river was hurling its excess over the top of the lower levee, away on the Sonora side. Banderas was young, willing and able. He was not imaginative. He did not have any inkling of what the overflow of millions and millions of tons of water was doing down there. And, because he had no natural sympathy, or empathy, with the creatures caught up in the catastrophe, he did not think to wonder at the stirring of the water around the seaward side of the vessel, where a group of dispossessed alligators had come to hunt among the rich pickings after the disaster of the night.

The day itself had an expectant air, not unlike the battered old ship at its heart. Richard's laptop was closed now and his telephone switched off, the batteries for both recharging. Hernan Gutierrez had tried to get his land line aboard, only to be informed that his ship no longer existed and that TelMex were not about to charge the naval standing account for services in the name of a vessel which was lingering in that twilight between decommissioning and break-up. Not even the full weight of the captain's authority had been able to move the phlegmatic representative. And, although *Colorado*'s old-fashioned equipment now reached Fleet Headquarters in Ensenada, by the time they called for authority, there was no one there competent to give it. That was a further confrontation the captain and his senior officers were saving for later in the day.

As the light gathered, Jesus Vega sat in his day room automatically filling in yet another report sheet, his mind preoccupied with the future. His gold pen flew surely and with practised ease across the paper detailing last night's disasters – how *Colorado* had survived, what damage she had sustained and how. The breakers, no doubt, would want explanations for any damage to the ship they were just about to rip apart. The Fleet authorities up at Ensenada certainly would. It was of the Fleet authorities that he was thinking. They had been quick enough to order him hither and yon, in spite of the state of his command, but they were disquietingly silent now. Last night had shown that *Colorado* might still be useful if the crisis worsened. He should check with Fleet at Ensenada before letting the vultures in the scrapyard have her.

Jesus flipped over the page to the section about personnel and paused. He would detail how all aboard had volunteered and how much they had done to help around the marina and the commercial end of the harbour. But the fact that he was writing about his people made him pause. He put his thoughts about Fleet to one side. He pulled the ancient chrome microphone towards him and placed its Bakelite base on the blank page. He depressed the button and the tones denoting 'now hear this' sang out through the quiet ship. 'This is the captain. Will Major Miguel de Hidalgo y Vega report to my day room at once, please. I say again . . .'

Mickey knocked a moment later, and entered on the curt invitation. He was dressed in full uniform, every bit as spruce and tightly buttoned as his father. Jesus was standing over by his porthole looking out in apparent absorption at a series of five-metre logs

222

drifting aimlessly across the anchorage. He did not turn until he heard the door close. Father and son eyed each other over the width of the room – and a good deal else besides. 'Why are you here?' asked Jesus.

'I was assigned.'

'You could not have refused?'

'Perhaps. I did not choose to. I was a natural choice. As far as the US Army is concerned, this is good personnel management, something of a diplomatic coup.'

'You did not explain their mistake?'

'I did not choose to. I wanted the representative to be me. I wanted to be here.'

'Why? To see my final humiliation?'

'No.'

'To check for your mother and the vultures she employs whether I had anything more worth taking?'

'No.' Mickey's voice remained controlled. Level. A tight line above his perfectly trimmed moustache showed the effort it was costing him. 'I had other reasons.'

'I see. And what were they?' Jesus was also speaking with icy control, but it was costing him something too. Neither took even one step into the vacancy which separated them.

'They are my reasons and they are private. I will discuss them with you if I feel you need to know.'

'I could insist.'

'A threat, *padre*?'

'No, *hijo*. But I do not like secrets aboard my ship. It may be that if you do not tell me why you are here then I will simply put you ashore. I will be putting the rest of your raft mates ashore today, I have no doubt, though I will keep the other guests aboard until they have made arrangements to return home, or I hear further about the interrupted ceremony or the ship gets taken out from under me.'

'For a man who does not like secrets, sir, you have a ship full of them here. More secrets than guests, I would think. Let us hope some of them are put ashore or taken out from under you along with your command.'

'Secrets, Major? What are you talking about?'

Mickey took a step forward, like a robot, tom out of his stasis by feelings he could hide but no longer quite control. 'Do you not know? My God, if I—'

There came a sharp rap at the door.

223

'Go away!' snarled Jesus, looking, almost with hatred, past his son at the mahogany door panels.

Mickey thought his father was looking at him, talking to him. He turned and, before Jesus could speak another word, he opened the door. Hernan Gutierrez entered, exchanging places with him.

'I cannot go away, I'm afraid, Captain,' the lieutenant announced brightly as the door closed behind him and Mickey's footsteps echoed hollowly down the corridor. 'There still has been no contact from the authorities in Ensenada, but I have waiting in a lengthening queue outside the harbourmaster, a representative of the city mayor, a professor from the Department of Antiquities who has with her a senior official from the customs service, and the owner of the breaker's yard where we should currently be berthed. Each of them must see you at once. Which one would you like to see first?'

'What are you doing here?' Richard's question echoed Jesus Vega's a deck or two down.

'I got every right to be here,' said Aldo Cagliari, on the defensive. 'At least I served aboard. I got a better right than some fairy story about your father or father-in-law or whatever.'

'Robin's father. And it's not a fairy story. But I don't believe you're here just for old time's sake, Aldo. You were up to no good in Vegas and I think you're up to no good now. Everything I said on the car ride back from Lake Mead the day we tested the AC2 still goes. If you're staying aboard, then you'd better stay out of my way.'

'Or what? If that's a threat, you'd better have something to back it up with.'

'I'll back it up when the time comes, Aldo. With all the legal force at my command, don't you worry. And think on this in the meantime. I'm a legitimate businessman going about my legitimate business, in the place I am supposed to be, for good, legal provable reasons. If that brings us into conflict, it can only be because the same does not apply to you. There's nothing to find out about me. There's no chink in my armour. But we can't say that about you, can we? You've got more chinks than armour, I'll bet. And I have people an e-mail away who will be happy to do some more digging for me. So you can't hurt me, no matter what you do, but I can't fail to hurt you once the gloves come off. So like I said, stay out of my way and hope I forget you're aboard.'

Aldo Cagliari watched Richard walk away down the corridor, his eyes narrow – but more with frustration than hatred. Mariner was probably right, he thought, but the limey bastard simply did not

224

know what level this little confrontation was moving onto. His nosy friends up in Vegas or New York were likely to find out more than they bargained for, especially if they came across Mr Alighieri or any of his soldiers. And those that survived would be spending the rest of their time looking into the mysterious deaths of their ex-employer and his wife, as likely as not.

But the Mariners still looked straight to Aldo. If there were drugs aboard as well as the fortune in smuggled Mayan artefacts he had heard so many whispers about, then either they knew nothing about it or they were way out of the league he thought they were in.

Only time would tell. Time and further, increasingly sinister deviation from the schedule Mr Alighieri had described to him. In the meanwhile, perhaps he should go and have a glance at the treasure trove below before the authorities came in and took it away. And looking through boxes like the ones he had heard described would be a task best undertaken holding the powerful sixteen-shot Beretta 92 he had smuggled aboard with him. Come to think of it, maybe he should be carrying that the next time he talked to Richard Mariner as well.

'We put them in the magazine,' Hernan explained to the customs man, his eyes on the professor of antiquities who walked slightly in front. She could examine his antiquities any time she wanted, thought Hernan. Of all the women he had seen recently, only Conception Lopez ran her close – and the captain was keeping her close in his cabin. But now he had the professor, whose bottom under the lieutenant's limpid gaze seemed to fill the rear of her severely cut cotton trousers like sand dunes under silk.

'Why there?' inquired the customs man.

'I beg your pardon?'

'Why the magazine?'

'Because it is the most secure place we have aboard.'

'Is that all?' asked the professor, flinging the question over her shoulder with a toss of glinting auburn hair. 'You must have many more convenient secure areas aboard.'

'No, professor. Security was not the only reason. We also have the capacity to flood the room with inert gas. It is a fire-fighting system, but we used it in this case for our own safety. We filled the room with carbon dioxide on two occasions, just to be sure. The boxes, you see, had been packed with poisonous spiders, scorpions and snakes to protect the merchandise.'

The professor stopped suddenly. Hernan bumped into her. The

experience was delicious; she was so soft, so pneumatic, so fragrant. 'Sorry,' he lied cheerfully.

'You are certain that the inert gas will have disposed of them?'

'We believe so.'

But the professor was no longer happy to take the lead and Hernan's view returned to the usual tedium of the forward engineering deck corridor with the number one gun magazine squarely at its end.

'There was an armed guard on the door at all times,' he said over his shoulder. 'At least there was until last night. Then things became a little hectic.'

It was possible to switch on the lights in the magazine from outside the door and Hernan did this, before unlocking the padlocks and easing the big security latches wide. 'You're sure you want your first examination aboard?' he asked. 'I mean we can get a team of men down here in no time and put this lot on a lorry for you. Then you can take it all up to the museum or the university. Or to the bonded warehouses where customs can keep it all under lock and key.'

'The professor and I will make the initial inventory here,' said the customs man with icy formality. 'A hoard such as this one needs carefully recording and equally careful security preparations. We cannot just put it somewhere and leave it.'

'Well, you'll have to move it soon,' said Hernan, loosening the door and listening for the telltale hiss and sniffing. The inert gas was odourless, but the system delivering it had a distinctive metallic odour which the ventilation eventually dispersed. Hernan's nose had proved a good deal more reliable than the gas-sensitive equipment they had had aboard – until Topolobampo, at any rate.

He swung the door open confidently, glancing back at the professor's chest, confirming with some pleasure that her upper works matched the perfection of her poop. The upper works in question attained a marked cleavage in the vee of her tightly buttoned blouse as she gasped. Hernan looked at her face and swung round, frowning. The boxes lay in a jumble of wreckage in the middle of the floor surrounded by the empty racks of the shell storage and delivery systems. At least they should have been empty. But they, like the floor, were alive with the living contents of the boxes. Hernan stood stunned in the doorway, his eyes darting feverishly. Clearly the fire-fighting system was no longer delivering inert gas. And, Hernan noted in the moment before he slammed the door, the air vents were open and a good many spiders and snakes were scuttling and slithering into them, disturbed by the professor's scream.

226

The sweating lieutenant leaned his back against the closed door, checking nothing unpleasant had climbed out over the raised rim into the passageway at his feet. The ducts leading from those air vents ended in gaping holes on the upper decks where the air conditioners had been removed.

'Someone has to go in there and take care of those things,' said the customs man, his voice shaking with loathing and disgust.

'That sounds like a job for the customs service,' said Hernan shortly. 'I'm afraid I'll be too busy crawling around the ducting and bilge systems below making sure nothing too nasty comes dropping out of the air vents onto our guests or onto us. The men at the breaker's yard will just have to watch out for themselves,' he concluded with a good deal of grim satisfaction.

Jesus had dealt with the harbourmaster and the mayor's representative with courtesy and equanimity, but he took an instant, abiding dislike to the owner of the breaker's yard. Tomas Sagreras was a beefy, blustering man, all sweat, slime and self-importance. He purported to be a man of standing and respect, a responsible businessman with reasonable deadlines to meet and a need to get on with what he had contracted to do; what he had cleared his books and his yard to do, starting today – starting now, in fact. His yard was currently full of pantechnicons waiting to carry the first of the scrap, equipment and so forth north. And yet this man, thought Jesus fastidiously, this upstanding businessman had presented himself in a grey-green vest with hair sprouting at armpit, pectoral, red neck and chin. He looked like a greasy ape and he bellowed like a bandit. His case was simple: *Colorado*'s continued existence was personally and financially inconvenient to him. The captain should surrender her at once or the hirsute Neanderthal would make it his personal mission to render the captain's life as uncomfortable as his own was becoming at the yard. So what was the captain going to do about it?

The captain knew he should acquiesce. Those were his orders, after all. But Sagreras was so offensive, he showed him the door instead. Then he tried once more to speak to someone senior at Fleet Headquarters, and this time he succeeded.

'Admiral Tortuga,' he began, 'my standing orders state that I should surrender my command on the ship-breaker's demand—'

'Well, then—'

'But only after the decommissioning ceremony has been conducted, which it has not, and after the paperwork has been duly completed, which it has not.'

'Indeed, then—'

'Moreover, the ship has performed two major humanitarian services in the last twelve hours alone. We are the only vessel left undamaged in the whole harbour at Cortez and I am reliably informed that a major flood may be imminent.'

'In that case, Captain—'

'But not only do I have this ship-breaker named Sagreras beating on my door, I have TelMex refusing to run a line aboard and I find I have no credit to get in any supplies for my crew and our guests. On top of which I am still guarding a fortune in smuggled Mayan artefacts.'

'Your guests must please themselves, of course,' said Admiral Tortuga distantly. 'The Mayan gold is important too. I see your point about power, communications and supplies, but you are right, it is the paperwork which is crucial. Your position will have to be referred to the committee.'

'I see, sir. And how soon will the committee meet?'

'Tomorrow, perhaps, or the day after. It is difficult to say.'

Jesus ground his teeth in frustration. 'But I need guidance now, sir, as I've explained.'

'Well, if you could complete the paperwork—'

'Admiral, unless we get some supplies, my men will be using the paper in their ablutions.'

'Captain Vega, there is no need—'

'Unless you issue a direct order to me right now, to turn my ship over to Sagreras I propose to disregard my previous orders altogether and hold my command ready to help anyone in Cortez, out in the bay or even up the Colorado River who needs us during the next twenty-four hours. Is that quite clear, Admiral Tortuga? Admiral? Are you still there? Hello? Hello?'

It was as well, thought Jesus grimly as he hung up, that the harbourmaster and the mayor's man had already come with heartfelt thanks for *Colorado*'s aid during the crisis last night, and with offers of reciprocal help. With their assistance, Jesus reckoned on getting most of the supplies he needed. Like a kid with his father's credit card, he would run up whatever bills were necessary to keep his ship's company safe, comfortable and content in spite of the fact that his command and her place in Ensenada's accounting system no longer existed. The committee could sort that out when they next met.

Jesus left the radio room and looked round the bridge. Banderas was staring at the high water in the harbour. Richard Mariner, striving with limited success to be unobtrusive, was busy with his laptop. His wife was with him.

Hernan arrived, with a pale professor and a green-hued customs officer in tow. He had some story about insects escaping into the air conditioning.

'Go down to El Jefe,' said Jesus, paying only scant attention. 'At the very least he can advise on sealing up the open outlets.'

Hernan fixed his captain with an unusually speaking stare. 'So it is an engineering problem,' he said.

'If it is to do with the ducting and the missing air conditioning, then certainly it is an engineering problem,' said Jesus.

'But what about us?' wailed the professor and her pale minder.

'You can wait aboard until the insects have been dealt with, or you may go ashore. But then you may well find yourself at the breaker's yard whistling for your artefacts,' said Jesus. Oddly enough – and clearly to Hernan's disappointment – that seemed preferable to them, in spite of the obvious dangers to the Mayan treasure trove.

Although Sagreras had been given his marching orders, he did not leave *Colorado* at once. There was enough confusion aboard to allow the Mexican mafioso to renew an old acquaintance.

Kramer had been keeping an eye on the comings and goings. He was not privy to Alighieri's timetable or exact plans, but he was fairly certain that things were going awry here for his secret employers. His task had been primarily to scout the river as a possible conduit for drug smuggling and to keep the nosy Mickey Vargas away from anything that looked important or potentially useful. When Kramer saw Sagreras storm out of his meeting with Captain Vega, he contrived to appear at Sagreras's side and, together, they sidled down to the cabin Kramer had been using.

As soon as the cabin door closed, Sagreras let loose a torrent of the foulest Spanish invective. Kramer waited for him to let off some steam, then, in his best American-accented Castillian, he asked what the trouble was and offered his help even before Sagreras began to explain.

Fifteen minutes later, Kramer was up to date. Sagreras and Alighieri were close; brothers, almost. The Mexican was able to give Kramer details of the current plan, of the threat posed by the Englishman and his wife whether or not they were innocent bystanders, and the problems being caused by the intransigent Captain Vega.

'Richard Mariner seems to have Captain Vega pretty much in the palm of his hand,' said Kramer thoughtfully.

Aldo Cagliari should have taken care of the Englishman at the first sign of trouble Sagreras complained bitterly, but he remained suspiciously inactive.

Kramer gave a lean grin. He was pretty certain Mickey Vargas worked for the Narcs, he said. Perhaps he had turned Cagliari somehow. If so, what did Sagreras want him to do about it?

'I will go back to my yard now,' said Sagreras. 'I will contact Señor Alighieri and see what he advises. In the meantime I will get my men ready. You should lie low. Find out what you can, maybe do a little damage if you can. But take care. You will only be of use to Señor Alighieri and myself if you are a free agent.'

'That's cool,' said Kramer easily. 'But Mr Sagreras . . .'

'*Si?*'

'Remind Mr Alighieri I am a mercenary, not a Samaritan. You catch my meaning here?'

'*Si*, Señor Kramer. I understand.'

Under the aegis of the mayor's office, a team from TelMex arrived with a land line and a range of kit including a modem which allowed Richard's laptop immediate access to the Internet via their local provider CoCom, thus freeing up his personal phone. The harbourmaster's assistant then arrived with untraceable salvage from lost boats at the bottom of the harbour. These included another computer, a printer and a couple of powerful little portable TVs. Kramer went onto the mayor's computer first, e-mailing his report of the loss of the *Pequod* and four of the team aboard, then asking permission for the survivors to stay aboard *Colorado* for a while. Like Jesus Vega, he took silence as assent when there was no immediate reply, and went off to check on his fellow engineers.

Conception, by this time, was up and about again. She had been disorientated, mentally and emotionally, and uncharacteristically hesitant since awakening to find Robin tending her and to discover she was lying in the captain's bunk. Her mind was a whirl of relief; thankfulness bordering on hero worship for her ,dashing rescuer; shock to discover he was Mickey's father and the owner of *La Casa Grande*; uncertainty about what DeLillo's last words had meant and what to do about them. He had seemed to be warning her about Kramer. And he had asked her to say sorry to Mickey – or that's what it had sounded like. Sorry for what? Her previously boundless self-confidence had taken a severe knock. It would be a while before she unthinkingly saw herself as the unassailable centre of her own fundamentally benign universe, and thus rejoined the majority of well-balanced humanity again. She should have talked to Mickey but he was withdrawn, remote, strange. She would have talked to her saviour Captain Vega, but he was busy, distant, as remote as his son. She talked to Joe Aloha, talked to him at length, but she hesitated to involve him in any of her growing suspicions. She fell back into increasingly lonely watchfulness, therefore, turning Andy DeLillo's words over in her mind and keeping an eye on Otto Kramer from a distance. When he announced that he was staying aboard for the duration, however, Conception felt that she had to act. So she went to talk to the only other friend she had aboard. She went to Robin.

Ten minutes after Conception went to Robin, there was a rap at Jesus Vega's door and the pair of them entered to find him sitting at his desk looking at a large-scale tourist map of Baja California Norte. The track of the river had been widened to its new proportions with carefully drawn lines and was marked with annotations in his neat, punctilious handwriting, to which he was adding. When he saw who he had invited to enter, he put down his golden pen, rose courteously, and almost bowed. Conception, arch defender of women's equality, scorner of the old-fashioned and patronising chauvinist, felt her heart stir unaccountably.

'We have something to talk over with you,' announced Robin.

'Please sit down,' he answered her, but he had eyes only for Conception.

El Jefe and his men had begun to tape up the air-conditioning outlets with more than usual alacrity – for reasons not yet known among the guests – but they had not yet reached the captain's quarters. The air aboard was hot as the morning mounted towards noon. Conception and Robin were dressed as though for a party in the only light clothes they currently possessed. The effect upon the captain of Conception's tube top and short, tight orange skirt was considerable, but he was an urbane man and sat back easily, also putting the women at their ease.

Robin soon caught Jesus Vega's attention, however, by sketching in the background of her ride down the Colorado aboard the ill-fated *Pequod* with Conception and Mickey. She described the apparently accidental incident in the Grand Canyon. She emphasised quietly but firmly her belief that Mickey's and Captain Allday's safety lines had been cut; that Mickey himself might be up to more than met the eye here, and that someone else was trying to stop him.

Conception took up the story then. If Mickey and Allday had been working together, she told Jesus, they may both have been working with young DeLillo. DeLillo had said Mickey's name

231

before the shark finally took him, and he had warned her to watch Kramer. Though whether that was to do with Mickey and the big picture or with whatever DeLillo and Kramer had got up to the night the pair of them left the mayor's welcome party, she could not say with any certainty. But since Kramer intended to stay aboard with his team, perhaps the captain had better keep an eye on him too.

'We must talk to Miguel,' Jesus said at once. 'If there is more to this situation than he has told me, then he must tell me more, explain what is going on and what he is up to.' He pulled the chrome and Bakelite microphone over and stood it on the map.

Mickey did not answer his father's summons. In fact it soon transpired that he could not be found aboard at all. Banderas, still holding the watch as Hernan worked with El Jefe, was certain he was aboard, for no one had left the ship other than the visitors shown aboard earlier and the workmen who had come and gone in the interim. He sent out Ramon, his most reliable man, reasoning obscurely that the only two men aboard with beards should find each other easily, but there was no sign of the captain's son at all.

Ramon looked everywhere he could think of. He looked in the vacant crew area astern, vacated at Topolobampo and adopted by Kramer and his people. He found the officers and men from the Corps of Engineers in a quiet huddle, recovering from the exertions of the previous night and discussing the probability of further work tonight if the river rose again before the man from the breaker's yard returned with more authority, or more men. He checked in the officers' wardroom and found it empty, so he went on up to the officers' bar and there he found three of the guests in shirtsleeves, deep in reminiscence. Joe Aloha, Peter Phelps and the bleary-eyed Chester Shaw all shook their heads when he asked them if they'd see Mickey.

Ramon even checked with Hernan and El Jefe who were preparing to enter the air ducting with flashlights, improvised body armour as thick as the space would allow, and a range of scary-looking weapons, but there was no sign of him down there either. Short of knocking on every door in the whole ship and bringing Mickey to his father by force if he answered, there was no way of getting him to the captain's cabin if he chose to ignore the loudhailer. Ramon reported the fact to young Banderas on the bridge, who passed the information down to the captain in his day room. Ramon was not asked to report on the whereabouts of any of the others, so he did not. He did not mention that Aldo Cagliari was nowhere to be seen either.

Flooding at the Fontenelle, deaths at Flaming Gorge, the Navajo Reservoir overflowing, two settlements washed away: the headlines on the Internet news services spoke vividly to Richard, sending him a message that no one else seemed to understand at present. Only when things began to get hairy on Lake Powell and the Glen Canyon Dam had to open its floodgates and pass everything down into Lake Mead with dire warnings of a lot more to come in the very near future was there official comment from the Bureau of Reclamation. An unnamed spokesperson warned that for the next few days at least, visitors to their waterways would not be allowed to indulge in any water sports.

The pile-up of water at each dam was being presented by the Americans as a series of separate incidents. And, even after the experience of last night, it seemed that there was little cross-border monitoring of the newly reconstructed waterway. The news services offered no hint that the Mexican authorities had any idea that a major flood was swiftly heading their way. South of the border there seemed to be no plan for evacuating low-lying areas or controlling the flow into irrigation systems that were at risk. While the mayor's office in Cortez was grateful for last night's efforts, there was no sense that they were seriously expecting ten times more water to hit their fair city tonight. And if it did, explained the charming young man Richard pressed his concerns upon over his personal phone as lunchtime neared, had not last night proved how effective the city's flood defences were? The excess would run off over the Sonora mangrove swamps and away into the Sea of Cortez.

But someone had brought the late-morning edition of the local paper aboard. Richard's Spanish was limited, but on the third page, above a report which he understood only in the most sketchy way, a series of photographs showed the mangrove swamps. It was hard to tell whether they were in colour or not, for everything in them was sepia-grey. Forms were hard to distinguish. Trees lay hither and yon, branches and roots impenetrably tangled. The habitat of snake, alligator, tarantula, scorpion, sand crab and tree frog was all destroyed. Sandbanks, pools, rivulets, everything had been washed away; turned into a swampy disaster area. There were no animals – no creatures of any sort, living or dead – to be seen. Except, said the report, for the millions of ravening mosquitoes.

Richard switched off his phone, sat back and shivered, in spite of

233

the gathering heat of late morning. A news flash came up on his Internet screen. There was big trouble, apparently, at the Hoover and Davis Dams; Parker and Headgate were all on red alert. That was bloody quick, he thought. Automatically he checked his watch. If last night's experience was any kind of guide, that would mean there would be big trouble here at about midnight.

'Lieutenant,' he called to Banderas. 'Do you have the tide tables there?'

Chapter Twenty-one

Aldo Cagliari's years in the navy had been served on an old Spruance-class destroyer and even though it was a good thirty years younger than the ancient D60, the general layout was similar. Certainly, it was similar enough to allow the bored, restless, resentful man a pretty good guess as to the most likely stowing places for the Mayan contraband he'd heard about. Richard Mariner was having no obvious effect on events, or on *Colorado*'s place in them. It had been the captain, unprompted, who had apparently seen off the owner of the breaker's yard who, Aldo assumed, had to be the linchpin in this part of the smugglers' plan. The ape-like ship-breaker had not looked happy as he had left the ship and Aldo was certain he would be back soon. It did not occur to Aldo that Sagreras might have a contact aboard – or that his own actions might now be under scrutiny. He stepped into the shadow of the bridgehouse and apparently casually raised a corner of some heavy canvas that covered part of the decking. He had been carefully loosening it at every opportunity he had had since he came aboard.

Under it, Aldo had discovered a hole three decks deep. This could take him straight down unobserved into the very guts of the vessel and a cornucopia of hiding places for all sorts of things. The workmen at Topolobampo had left a ladder securely attached to the weather deck at the top and the deck above the magazine at the bottom. Apart from the fortune in Mayan gold said to be aboard the ship, there was Mr Alighieri's fortune in smuggled cocaine. Unobserved, Aldo slipped safely onto the first rungs of the ladder. Security aboard this ancient tub was a joke. He had walked aboard carrying anything he liked, including the big Beretta currently wedged in his belt, so he reckoned he could walk off with anything he wanted as well.

Now where in hell has Aldo got to? wondered Mickey an instant later when he stepped out of his own hiding place to discover the man he had been following all morning had suddenly disappeared.

Sagreras from the breaker's yard came back before noon. He did not come alone. At his side was a slim, Armani-suited young fellow with 'lawyer' written all over him. Banderas at least was impressed as he signed them aboard: to have called out an *abogado* at this time on a Saturday suggested hitherto unsuspected power. The ship-breaker himself was now dressed for business rather than work, and his suit fitted him unexpectedly well even though his shirt collar strained noticeably, tested to its limit by the absence of any actual neck. Banderas showed the pair of them down to the captain's day room, and stopped. Issuing from behind the door were the quiet strains of a flute accompanied by a well-tuned classical guitar. Banderas hesitated. He had heard the captain play many times, usually during brief respites in periods of intense stress. But he had never heard him play accompanied before and the only man aboard with a guitar was Hernan. If both superior officers were in there making music together, then Banderas was not about to disturb them. 'This is the door,' he said briefly and ran for the bridge. The ship-breaker grunted with ill-concealed derision at the back of the fleeing boy and gripped the door handle in a fist the size of a ham.

It was a spider which began it. During the intense, almost embarrassed wait in Jesus's day room as it became clear that Mickey was not about to answer his father's command, the spider began to unfold itself out of a hole in the wall. There had been a bright brass fitting there until Topolobampo, but Jesus had hardly noticed that it had gone missing, along with so much else. He noticed soon enough when the huge spider, banded in russet and black, with a body the size of a dinner plate, began to ease its way into the room. With a scarcely stifled exclamation, Jesus jerked open his desk drawer and snatched out his venerable Webley. Both women leaped up and Jesus thought they must have been frightened by the monster. He drew a bead on it but Robin called, 'No! Captain, don't shoot!' She took a deep breath, remembering the revulsion she had felt when the poisonous tarantula had fallen on her face-mask during Mickey's rescue. 'It's a bird-eating spider,' she explained. 'It's harmless to humans. My daughter Mary has an identical one as a pet, and I've trained myself to handle it in emergencies. Mary's is a most striking creature, but this one is even more lovely. Aren't you, my precious . . .' As she spoke, she crossed to the spider and put out her cupped hands. They hardly trembled at all. With slow, easy inquisitiveness, the spider tested her with a multiplicity of eyes, sensory hairs, olfactory senses. Then it lifted its forelegs and climbed easily into her hands. 'I need somewhere to put it, somewhere with sides too high to climb,' said Robin.

'Take it to the galley,' suggested Jesus. 'Cook is the only person aboard likely to have a container that size.'

He opened the door for Robin and she and the spider departed.

Jesus turned to put the gun back in its drawer, only to find Conception had lifted his flute out of its black velvet bed. 'Something of a contrast, this drawer,' she said softly. 'Do you play this often?'

'When the opportunity presents itself,' he answered, placing the Webley carefully in its box. 'The sea air can play havoc with her even though she is made of metal, not wood. But I have it easier than Hernan Gutierrez. He has a guitar which comes in and out of tune depending on the wind and the tide.'

'Have you music or do you improvise?'

'I have music,' he answered. He lifted the gun box out altogether and propped it against the opening in the wall, wedging it in place with a chair. Then he sat on the chair and looked up at Conception as she ran her hands gently over the silvery length of the instrument.

'Where is it?' she asked.

'Here.' He reached down to the locker under his bunk without moving from the chair and pulled out a pile of sheet music. She put the flute down and took them. 'These are mostly guitar arrangements,' she said, frowning slightly.

'I have them because I love the composers' work,' he admitted. 'The Spanish tradition . . .'

'Tarrega, Granados and Falla,' she said with quickening approval. 'Lauro, Rodrigo. These are some of my favourites too. Where does Hernan keep his guitar?'

'In his cabin.'

'Would he mind if I borrowed it?'

'I don't think so. You may have to tune it though.'

'That will be no problem,' she said with a smile. 'I was born with perfect pitch.'

Fifteen minutes later, Robin returned to report on the safe bestowal of the spider, but on hearing the gentle intertwining of flute and guitar in Tarrega's *Recuerdos de la Alhambra*, she went away again. Half an hour later, the musicians were just coming to the climax of Rodrigo's *Fantasia Para un Gentilhombre* when the door burst open and the ship-breaker and his *abogado* pushed their way in.

Calmly, unhurriedly, Jesus put his flute away. He would clean it later. Following his lead as she had followed him through the sensual beauties of the music, Conception stilled the guitar strings with an open hand and rose lazily. 'I will take this back to Hernan's cabin,' she said, her voice husky from a combination of passion and restraint

237

– she was used to humming along with music of this intensity while her fingers worked on fret and string, but she had found she could not do so without disturbing Jesus so close beside her.

Conception eased past the burly man from the breaker's yard. As the door closed behind her, the lawyer went into the attack.

'This paper,' he said, opening his briefcase, 'is a contract between Señor Sagreras here and the relevant authorities in Ensenada and Mexico City. According to the detail in this paragraph, initialled as you see by all parties, this vessel has been his property since six p.m. yesterday evening. He wishes you to deliver it to his yard before six p.m. this evening or he will deem you to be in breach of contract and he will invoke the penalty clauses, here and here, against the signatories there, there and there. You will see that these are the names of admirals and government officials in the Ministry of Defence and the Department of Naval Affairs and at Fleet Headquarters. Your senior officers and ministers, sir. If those clauses are invoked, I suggest you will have little to look forward to but summary court-martial and dismissal from the service.'

'Since six p.m. yesterday evening,' said Jesus quietly, 'I have not been a serving officer at all. My commission ended with my ship's. Nothing you can do will hurt me. I will consider your request, however, for I do have officers and men aboard whose careers I would not wish to damage. And no doubt if we have not handed over the ship by six, Señor Sagreras will return with his thugs to take it by force.'

Jesus held up his hand as the sharp young lawyer opened his mouth to protest. 'But the decision is not mine alone,' he warned. 'Here is the name of another admiral in Ensenada who has asked me to wait until the next sitting of the decommissioning committee. And here is the name of a senior customs official who is seeking secure accommodation for the contraband we have aboard.'

Sagreras lurched forward as though struck sharply between his massive shoulders. 'Contraband?' he snarled, spraying spittle past prominent yellow teeth and thick lips. 'What contraband?'

Jesus's eyebrows rose. 'Mayan artefacts recovered from smugglers further south,' he answered.

Sagreras sat back, apparently content.

'I will contact these men,' said the lawyer smoothly. 'You will hear from us again by four. And we will expect you to anchor at the breaker's yard by six and to vacate the ship immediately afterwards.'

Jesus thought of the creatures in the ducting. 'Perhaps,' he said. 'If you obtain the relevant authorisations. But there is still the

238

matter of the river and an impending flood. If danger threatens, you will have to wait.' He stood, the action calculatedly unexpected and threatening. Sagreras leaped up too, as if to ward off attack. 'In the meantime,' Jesus continued, blandly staring the bellicose ship-breaker down, 'I will warn my people and check further with the authorities myself. Good afternoon, gentlemen.'

The instant the two of them left the day room, Jesus reached for the tannoy microphone 'Lieutenant Gutierrez, report to the captain at once,' he ordered, then he crossed to his porthole and looked out, unconsciously humming a flute melody from Tarrega as he reviewed his performance and calculated what Sagreras' reaction to it had revealed.

Hernan was there five minutes later, still wrapped in his anti-venom armour, carrying a stained baseball bat and a huge torch. 'Captain?'

'Good, Hernan. I see you are dressed for the job. I want you to tear this vessel apart. Use who you need and go where you like. There is something hidden aboard. Something important to Sagreras the ship-breaker. Probably drugs. I want it found and I want it on deck under armed guard by six o'clock tonight. And bring up the Mayan gold while you're at it. That may persuade your attractive young professor of antiquities to return to your side. What do you say?'

Hernan said, '*Si, Capitan!*' with rather more enthusiasm than he felt.

Aldo found Cuzco just before four, and the noise made by the living man when confronted by the dead one was enough to bring Mickey into the situation too.

Aldo had no sense of it, but he was unusually lucky during the early part of that afternoon. His exploration of the hole left by the gun turret led him surely downwards into areas not far from those being sanitised by Hernan, El Jefe and their team. Aldo had examined the lower deck area at the bottom of the hole and noted the new work there. It might have been something necessitated by the removal of the equipment, but all the rest of the work seemed sloppy in comparison. The welding on this particular area was carefully, expertly done. He slipped out of the gaping hole into the nearest corridor, stole a torch left unattended by one of Hernan's men and, keeping a plan of the forecastle head in his mind, he began to explore the pathways that Cuzco took by accident during the fire.

Aldo heard the sailors as an increasingly distant stirring as he eased himself into tighter and tighter places, driven on by a gathering

239

certainty that he was onto something here. The certainty was born of the fact that in one or two corners – more and more as he went down towards the chain lockers – he found crystals of white powder like sugar, and his expert tongue had no trouble in identifying what it was. These crystals were protecting him, although he did not know it, from the creatures released when the Mayan boxes fell. Every spider, snake and scorpion that had tasted the powder was curled up somewhere dark and secret, dead or dying.

Cuzco had died almost on top of the pile of drugs, but the movements of the ship during the last few days had moved him. Much of the bilge area the corpse shared with the cocaine was partially flooded. The adventure with the *Tiburon* and Banderas's beaching of *Colorado* had knocked his stiff body off the plastic-coated pile and down into the restless water. As wetness and heat combined, Cuzco became swollen with the passage of time, so he floated, sitting high like the ship herself. Last night's pitching and heaving in the flood had sent him back along the bilges until he had beached. Then the rigorous pumping which follows any such stress to the hull had drained the bilge almost completely, leaving him high and dry, face up, half standing against a slope of the ship's side, still pointing his gun as he had been at the moment of death.

But Cuzco was no longer alone. To Aldo, in time, he would represent something fearful. Even to Mickey he would prove an unsettling shock. But, to a significant number of the creatures released from the boxes in the magazine, Cuzco represented food. The dead workman was the only food available, in fact, apart from each other. He was, therefore, festooned with a range of ravenous creatures, making meals in various ways of his softer bits. But these creatures, like the ones up in the cocaine-sprinkled ducting just above, were poisoned and dying, for the corpse, too, was covered in the deadly stuff.

At last Aldo came to a maintenance hatch which led directly into the bilge. Certain now that he must be close to his goal, he eased it open and flashed his torch in. The stench was overpowering, but the ex-sailor remembered how sickening the smell of stagnant bilge could become and so he was content to fold his handkerchief over his nose and mouth before proceeding. He went down a short ladder and found himself standing on a slippery slope. A flash of torch beam at his feet showed green slime on the metal. A lengthier examination of the way ahead showed a long low corridor ending in some kind of sloping turning, clearly at the bottom of the hull itself. He went on.

240

As Aldo did so, Mickey arrived at the open hatchway and looked down into the dark. A breath of wind, just enough to lift the corner of the loosened canvas, had put Mickey on Aldo's trail again, but he was hesitant about following him down here. It was not fear, it was a dividing of focus. Mickey saw Kramer as his prime area of interest. Aldo was almost a sideline. And, he suddenly realised, it must be getting late in the day – a glance at his watch confirmed sixteen hundred hours – and he had left Kramer alone since that painful talk with his father this morning. He was actually considering simply going away again, when Aldo started making choking, screaming noises. Mickey went down into the bilge without further thought.

He followed his torch beam along the slippery, sloping passageway that Aldo had followed, and like his quarry he plunged the torch beam through a clinging, fetid darkness. He found Aldo on his knees, in a tangle. He had dropped his torch and his handkerchief and was fighting to pull a big, square automatic out of the back of his waistband, but the gun had become tangled and stuck. 'Aldo,' called Mickey softly, and the big man jumped and flinched, looking up into the light, seeming to see it for the first time. Then, with apparently no thought, he hurled himself at Mickey. Mickey should have realised that this was a possibility, but the man had seemed in such distress he had come closer than he would normally have done. Aldo hit him in an illegal football tackle, shoulder low in the guts. Mickey went over backwards and his torch flew away. Like Aldo's, it remained alight and, when it landed, it rolled down the slope where the wall became the floor and shone with unrelenting brightness on Cuzco who stood like a referee over the gasping tangle of their brief, brutal fight. Heads, elbows, knees and fists slammed into each other and into the metal all around. Voices gave animal grunts, smothered by each other's bodies and by the darkness. In the distance, the banging sounds made by Hernan's and El Jefe's teams seemed to crescendo and die. It was possible, for a little while, actually to hear their voices, though no words could be distinguished. The fight went on, almost silent but nonetheless fearsome for that, until at last, more by luck than judgement, Mickey drove his forehead down into Aldo's face with enough force to slam his head back against the steel below, and the big man grew suddenly still. Breathless, shaken, Mickey pulled himself erect, retrieved his torch and went back to the hatchway by which he had entered. His plan was simple now. They needed to restrain, perhaps arrest Aldo, find out who the dead man was, and examine this part of the ship with a fine-tooth comb.

But when Mickey reached the hatch, he found it was closed and locked tight. He began to hammer on it and shout at the top of his voice but to no avail. Outside, deaf to his entreaties, Kramer lingered for only the briefest moment, pleased with the ease with which he had killed two birds with one stone – a feat he had not managed since cutting Mickey's and Allday's lines at the rapids. Then, with a smile of quiet satisfaction on his lean face, he turned and went on his way. It hadn't taken much to make him take the first step – just a word from Sagreras as he followed his smart young lawyer down onto the dock.

If Hernan looked with favour on the professor of antiquities upon her return, she certainly did not look on him with anything other than mild disgust. Summoned from his work between the bilges and the chain lockers by his captain, he had reported at once, still wearing his ridiculous outfit, still clutching his bloodstained club and stinking of effluent. Jesus hid the fact that he wanted his first lieutenant out of his day room as quickly as possible before he stank the place out.

'The professor and her associates are ready to take the Mayan artefacts now, Lieutenant,' he said placidly. 'Have you closed down operations below?'

'*Si, Capitan.*'

'And cleared the magazine of the creatures in there?'

'As many as we could find.'

'Good. Then we need the artefacts on the dockside as soon as possible, please. I believe the professor here has two trucks waiting.'

Only a team with the combined abilities and dedication of Ramon's men working hand in glove with Fernando's could have moved the Mayan treasure so swiftly and efficiently. And if they kept their gloves and protective clothing on in spite of the blazing heat of the afternoon, then that was simply because they were jumping to obey the orders of their officers and the arrogant demands of the customs official who, had he been allowed his way, would have searched each body and every orifice amongst them in case anything had been misappropriated.

But the work was done by five. The gold in its wrecked boxes was loaded into two ancient trucks and driven off towards the new university campus up in the north of the city.

'Look at that,' said Ramon regretfully, scratching his chin through the stubble of his beard with the thumb of his massive glove. 'They didn't even say *gracias* or *adios.*'

'The lieutenant was hoping for *hasta la vista* from the professor,' teased Raphael cheerfully.

242

'That's true,' admitted Hernan wistfully as he led his men back aboard. 'What a body. I hope she makes good use of her assets outside the university. She's the only woman I've seen recently to equal the captain's lady love. Just thinking about a woman like that wasting her time with stuff that has been dead or buried for five hundred years makes my blood run cold.'

Conception Lopez was standing on the bridge listening to the telephone on the end of the land line just at that moment, and her blood was running cold. On the other end of the connection, so distant that she had to strain to hear him, her father was speaking to her. 'It has taken me all day to find you, *chiquita*. I have been wishing to talk with you since first light, but you have been difficult to trace. I believe we need you here, Conception. You and any of your river engineers that you can bring. We have reported the situation to the authorities but they do not seem to see it in the same light as we do here. There is no immediate danger, true, but we have reason to be fearful for tonight. We are certain there is a great flood coming.'

Conception glanced across the bridge at Richard Mariner who was focused on the Internet news on his computer. It was a relief to know her father was not alone in his fears. But it was worrying to know from her conversations with Richard – and with Robin standing there behind him – that her father's fears were right.

'We agree here, *padre*,' she said. 'But the danger is to the whole river. And you are well clear, surely.'

'No, child. Apparently we are not, and that is why I have called and called until I reached you, for I can think of no one else who can help or advise us so well.'

Conception's heart swelled with pride at this. How many men would turn so unhesitatingly to their offspring in a crisis? How many would have offspring so well qualified to offer help? But then her blood chilled again. If they needed the sort of help and advice she was best qualified to offer, then they were in trouble indeed.

Conception fought to keep her voice calm and level. 'What is the problem, Father? What exactly is it that you need my help and advice with?'

'It is the river. The river has been reborn. It flows past Los Muertos and away past *La Casa Grande* down towards Laguna Salada.'

'The flood water of last night must have crested on the tide well back from the estuary. Some water was bound to come over the top of the levee, though I am surprised that there was enough to flood the dry valley as far from the Colorado as you say. If such a thing happened last night, it may happen again tonight but the levees are particularly high there beside the two bridges. I am sure you have little or nothing to worry about.'

'Thank you for your words of comfort, my child. But I fear it is more complicated than you suppose. We have been out and checked the levees. As you say, there are the marks where the river overflowed. They are clear, and the top of the levee is dry again now, for it has been fearsomely hot this afternoon. But there is more to it than that. There must be some damage, some undermining or weakening of the walls. It is this which makes us worried because although the water level in the Colorado has settled and the tops of the levees are dry, the river past Los Muertos is as deep as it was this morning and it is *still flowing.*'

'That's it,' said Richard, rising. 'We have to do something at once. We've had enough shilly-shallying. Time for action now.'

Conception and Robin looked at him. Perhaps it was a man/woman thing. Pale with worry, Conception had brought her father's concerns to Robin and the two of them had been discussing alternatives. The discussion was intelligent, focused and meaningful – but it was discussion.

Richard fitted the news into the pattern of building danger he had been tracing all day and without more ado he was ready to act.

'We have to go to the captain first,' he said decisively, turning the laptop round so that Hernan, newly arrived on watch, could see it if he needed to. 'Then it sounds as though we'd better get up to your village as quickly as possible, Conception. If the river came by last night and is still flowing now then I agree with your father there must be a flaw in the Colorado's containment system. God alone knows what will happen tonight when the big flood hits the top of the spring tide at midnight, but it is quite possible the whole dry valley will flood between the Colorado and the Laguna Salada.'

'If that happened,' said Conception, 'the whole village could get washed away. They would all die.'

'But how will we get up there?' asked Robin, fitting in beside Richard, automatically forming their old team, tempering his sometimes unthinking decisiveness with her intelligence, empathy and ability to see further through mazes of implication than he could.

'Call up that professor at the university for a start, see if we can borrow the trucks when she'd got the Mayan artefacts out of them.'

'A couple of trucks will be of limited use if things go pear-shaped,'

244

said Robin. 'Even if they are packed to the gills with experts. We need a solid base. A communications platform. Somewhere with hospital facilities if the village hits bad trouble. Somewhere we can rely on. Co-ordinate things from. Land choppers if we have to.'

'Precisely,' said Richard. 'That's why we need to talk to Captain Vega.' But Conception had already gone – and they had to run to catch up with her.

The captain was not in his day room, however. They had to search the bridgehouse for a good five minutes before Hernan, hurrying down from the bridge himself, told them where Jesus Vega was and what he was doing. As they rushed down through the bridgehouse at Hernan's side, Richard, Robin and Conception described what they were doing, and why. Hernan's face, already folded in a worried frown, became at once darker in expression and paler in colour as he listened.

Jesus was on the foredeck of his command enjoying what looked like the final moments of his power. He was standing stiffly at the head of the forward gangplank looking down at the dock. Behind him stood two teams of seamen, fronted by CPO Ramon, back ramrod straight and black beard thrust out. Fernando, Raphael and the rest were all fully armed, standing at parade-ground attention across the pathway where the gangplank issued onto the weather deck, their guns not on their shoulders but across their chests. The line looked threatening, as it was intended to do. At the foot of the gangplank, also looking threatening, stood Sagreras, his lawyer – his suit cast aside in favour of overalls – and a sizeable number of breaker's men bearing clubs.

The air between the two armed camps crackled with tension which only the captain could defuse. And he could only do that by surrendering his command. Rarely, if ever, had Jesus Vega hesitated as he was doing now. There had been no word from Ensenada, so Jesus's last word to Admiral Tortuga stood as the last word on the subject. But were conditions really serious enough to warrant *Colorado* acting as a free agent? Mickey's words returned – perhaps he was just clutching at straws here, lengthening the last moments of command, like a condemned man loitering on the gallows steps. He drew in breath to tell his men to lower their arms and invite the breakers aboard.

'Captain Vega,' came a commanding voice at little less than full bellow.

Jesus turned, his eyebrows raised in surprise, to see the big English-man hurrying across the deck with Hernan a little in front of him and

245

the two women immediately behind him. 'Captain, we have urgent news,' Richard called.

Jesus turned back from the brink and crossed the deck towards the little group. 'What news?' he asked, stilling the shiver of concern he felt in case something had happened to Mickey.

Hernan walked past his captain and replaced him at the head of the gangplank, looking down with warlike eyes.

Jesus Vega found himself surrounded by three importunate people. Although his eyes rested most often on Conception, she was too breathless and overcome to make much sense, so it was Richard he listened to, and his clear statement of the case and the dangers made the difference in the end. That, and the Englishman's inspired plan to check the integrity of the levee, protect Los Muertos Sierra de Juarez preserve *La Casa Grande* which stood so close behind it, and lengthen the life of *Colorado* by a little.

When Jesus Vega turned, he felt the power of Richard's presence at one shoulder and of Conception and Robin standing at the other. Fleetingly, he wished his son could have been here also, to share the moment. 'Lieutenant Gutierrez,' he ordered loudly, his voice ringing across the marina, full of vigour and decision. 'Drop the plank, cut the lines and prepare to depart at once. We have one last vital mission to complete.'

Chapter Twenty-two

When *Colorado* was running at flank speed with El Jefe bellowing, sweating and swearing down in his engine room, her four big Babcock and Wilcox boilers drove her Westinghouse turbines to deliver nearly 60,000 horsepower to her twin shafts, spinning the pitched blades of her two screws with sufficient force to drive her slim hull along at 35 knots. She was running at flank speed now – El Jefe swore her system had never run so hard for so long – but she made only slow progress against the relentless counter-current of the flooding river. Ramon stood at the wheel with Jesus at one shoulder and Richard at the other, while Peter Phelps hovered solicitously in the background.

If the chief petty officer was overawed by the presence of so much seniority and experience so close behind him, he did not show it. All his attention was focused on the job in hand, for, although the river was effectively contained with mathematical symmetry in parallel banks and ran over a bottom dredged to theoretical flatness some seven metres below, the water came at them like a live thing.

Deep within the thrust of it, currents whipped about like colossal fire hoses out of control. The relentless pressure of the river carried debris which it had collected since it escaped the control of the Morelos Dam. Some of the heavier, deeper hazards tumbling seaward had been borne down from even further up the watercourse than that, let past through wide-open floodgates or down emergency sluices like the one Richard and Aldo had explored on the AC2. The laws of physics dictated that the greatest mass of this dangerous debris was carried in the central currents, so *Colorado* was running as close to the Baja bank as possible, but even there, a bewildering array of dangers lurked.

Every minute or so, it seemed, the great old vessel's head would swing suddenly off line. On more than one occasion, the whole juddering length of her ground along the inner slope of the levee, her port bridge wing actually overhanging the right-hand carriageway of the road running along its top, allowing Robin and Conception, holding tight to the outer rail, to watch the traffic fleeing the northern suburbs of Cortez as the first flood alerts came in.

Immediately on giving his orders, Jesus had run up to the bridge with the others close behind him. He had stood beside the helm, watching the gangplanks fall and the lines slide into the water like headless snakes, while Sagreras and his men, taken by surprise, could only stand on the dock and bellow threats.

Once they were out of the harbour, Banderas took the helm – for the first time since he had rammed the cruiser *Tiburon* on Hammerhead Island – and Jesus turned and opened the bridge extension of the ship's address system. In the calm, measured tones which he reserved for the deepest crises, he informed all aboard of his decision and his proposed actions.

'My officers and crew, I know, will stand by me and by *Colorado*. There are some others aboard, honoured guests, who have promised their help as well. There are yet others aboard from whom I have no right to expect help. Whether or not they remain aboard is for them to decide. Anyone who wishes to leave may use the captain's launch to do so. To those of you who wish to stay, I can promise nothing but danger, hard work, and a close acquaintance with disaster, for we are bound upriver into the very teeth of the impending flood. Even now, the levees are failing and there is no saying what will happen when the high water hits at midnight. But we have engineers aboard who can fix the levees or advise us how to control the flood. We also have medical facilities, should they be required.' He did not add that his own *casa* was at risk, that Conception's village and family could die if *Colorado* took no action.

Soon, the men to whom he had offered the launch presented themselves – all except Aldo Cagliari and Mickey. Otto Kramer spoke for the Corps of Engineers. They all owed *Colorado* a favour, he said. Many of them owed her their lives. They would stand by her now, in memory of those who had not made it aboard at the very least. Then he retired below, to plan with his engineers how best to repair the reported damage to the levee. Little enough had been salvaged from the wreck of the *Pequod*, but there was a battered, soaking river chart which his team would pore over, looking for the weak point in the artificial watercourse.

Peter Phelps, spruce, businesslike and at full attention, offered his services in any capacity and was posted on the bridge, with Richard. Joe Aloha and Chester Shaw followed close behind the punctilious officer, Joe exuding a confident calm and Chester reaching that state

248

where alcohol gave him razor sharpness. Both were familiar with the old ship's medical facilities and promised to make a careful inventory of all the first aid aboard, and ready anything that might prove useful in an emergency. Robin, trained like Richard to accident and emergency standard, offered to help them. Conception went with them, hoping the simple activity of making an inventory would calm her down a little.

Then, with all aboard tasked, focused and facilitated, his mind hardly dwelling at all upon the whereabouts of his son and the other missing guest, Jesus ordered Ramon to the bridge and then opened a line to the engine room and spoke to El Jefe.

It took three tries to escape the marina. On the first attempted exit, reversing away from the dockside still filled with extremely irate breaker's men, *Colorado*'s whole poop nearly tore off when the current coming over the harbour bar hit her like a boot in the behind. Jesus immediately ordered full ahead which threw the ship into the safer central waters of the marina where she turned and tried again. This time the same unrelenting force of water hit her forecastle head like a roundhouse punch and nearly knocked her out.

On the third attempt, the brain child of all three captains on the bridge, she steamed round the perimeter of the ruined marina to get up speed, then threw her sleek bows straight into the inward rush of the water and squeaked out through the opening at an angle, before swinging hard to port into the full force of the river, with her slim grey hull already running at flank speed.

The cars on the north-bound carriageway beneath the spectacular sunset hooted their horns and flashed their lights at Conception and Robin up on the port bridge wing, as *Colorado* proceeded at a snail's pace alongside the river road. Only the big blood-foaming bone between *Colorado*'s teeth told of a ship running at almost 35 knots – nearly 65 kph – relative to the water. Against the cars, she seemed to make hardly any progress at all. But before the sinking sun was lost behind the tallest tower blocks of the suburbs, the labouring destroyer caught up with the hooting drivers trapped in the total gridlock at the first roundabout on Route 5, where, unknown to those aboard *Colorado*, the two trucks from the university had crashed into each other and scattered Mayan gold all across the freeway. No one was seriously hurt, but one of the drivers had suffered a scorpion sting.

Choking on the fumes, Robin and Conception came in off the bridge wing and crossed to the chart table where Jesus's adapted tourist map of Baja California Norte and Sonora was spread like a pressed flower beneath the Perspex. Above it, Richard's laptop was open and its split-screen facility was tuned to the CNN website on one side and the Mexican News Service on the other. Since they cut the TelMex shoreline, Richard's laptop was the only computer still with Internet access and his personal phone was back in service maintaining the connection.

With *Colorado* settled onto her upstream passage, Richard was keeping an eagle eye on the worsening situation. Kramer joined him, looking over his shoulder, then more generally around the bridge.

'What are the plans?' he asked.

'Run hard north to where the trouble is,' answered Robin and turned away, focusing with Richard on CNN's concern about whether the complex of waterways issuing from the Imperial Dam was likely to suffer the same devastation as the Palo Verde irrigation system. The governor of Arizona had just followed his colleagues in the state capitals of Colorado, Utah, Nevada and New Mexico by announcing a state of emergency and summoning the National Guard. The residents of Yuma had been warned to head for high ground and Imperial Valley was braced for the worst, all the way down to the shores of the Salton Sea.

'High water will be here in four hours tops,' called Richard, watching the little clock at the top of the screen and checking against the timetable of alert and disaster upstream that he had earlier stuck to the screen with a Post-it note. 'We've still got twenty kilometres to go and at this speed that'll be cutting things fine.'

'We can't go any faster, Richard,' said Jesus shortly.

'And we can't bring the bridges any closer,' said Robin, slipping her hand onto Richard's hunched shoulder. 'But we'll be fine. We're making seven knots relative to the road markings and signposts over there.'

'Better confirm that,' said Peter Phelps, crossing to the bridge wing. 'We lose the road in a few minutes' time, from what I recall of the inward journey. There's a roundabout, then it goes off into the desert. At least that's how I remember it when I did the grand tour down to San Felipe yesterday or whenever the hell it was . . .'

'Yes,' said Robin. 'That's the way I remember it from when Mickey and I drove down.'

Conception looked up, suddenly struck. She had been living in Mickey's pocket for more than a week and now suddenly it was as though he had ceased to exist for her. She was by no means fickle and she saw now that her feelings for the young officer had been born of loneliness, circumstances and appreciation of his bravery. But her

250

feelings for Mickey were as nothing – less than nothing – compared with what she was beginning to feel for his dashing, romantic father. She had gone more than twelve hours without seeing Mickey and she hadn't even noticed the fact. Her sense of humanity and natural justice piqued, she went off to look for him, once again glad to find something to do which eased her sense of impending disaster.

Jesus Vega was struck by his son's absence too. He looked around the bridge. Hernan was with his team clearing up below, keeping an eye on Chester and Joe Aloha in the medical facility, helping Cook prepare for any refugees, fit and wounded a like, and making sure that the banded bird-eating spider was the only visitor from the Mayan crates around the areas they would need to use. He had his own team led by Fernando and the depleted team Ramon normally led to help him. El Jefe had every other man who could be spared down in the engine room with him, keeping the beautifully maintained but technically antique engines running well above specification.

'Mr Kramer,' said Jesus, 'I am concerned about Major Vargas's whereabouts. Please form a team of men from your command and go and find him and bring him to me.'

'Yes, sir,' said Kramer crisply and without batting an eyelid, and departed.

As the night began to gather and the brightness of the northern city suburbs began to fall away behind her, Jesus ordered *Colorado*'s running lights full on, and called for darkness in the bridgehouse so that he could see through the murk ahead. Providentially untouched in Topolobampo, the two great searchlights mounted on the bridge wings were also available to him, and soon Rephael and Fernando were called up from Hernan's command to man these. Little by little, through the dense, sweltering dark, with the first of the night's thunderstorms glittering dangerously over the Sierra de Juarez, the intrepid old destroyer followed the tunnel of light up the gathering flood of the river for which she had been named more than fifty-five years earlier, at about the same time as the man behind the helmsman's shoulder had himself been christened in the tall adobe church in the village of Los Muertos below the slopes of his father's estate.

There were so few light bulbs left on board the ship, Conception would have been forced to give up had she not bumped into Hernan and accepted the big broad-beamed flashlight he earnestly pressed upon her. She also accepted his advice. Hernan and his men, and also Joe Aloha and Chester, had been in most of the easily accessible places in the bridgehouse. El Jefe and his engineers had done the same below. Hernan, El Jefe and their teams had earlier looked in many a deep, distant and unpleasant place below. All with no sign of Mickey or Aldo Cagliari. It was logical, therefore, that she should search in deeper, darker places still, if she was serious about finding the missing men. And she should take one of the precious little walkie-talkies with which the teams kept in touch with each other and the bridge. She tested the torch and demonstrated command of the two-way radio and off she went.

No sooner had she done so than Kramer and a tight little team of four appeared, all on the same mission. Hernan had not taken much of a liking to Kramer and he offered a good deal less advice, a smaller torch and no two-way. As soon as they left – to search the bridgehouse literally from top to bottom – Hernan called Conception and warned her of the competition.

Lingering in the stuffy darkness immediately outside the door, Kramer eavesdropped on Hernan's curt words of warning. Then he vanished silently into the darkness behind his men, his mind a whirl of rapid calculation.

As Jesus conned *Colorado* up the river, with Peter Phelps at his shoulder and Richard growling information from the chart table further back, far below their feet a game of cat-and-mouse began to develop. While Kramer's men looked for any sign of Mickey or Aldo Cagliari, Kramer himself was equally interested in the whereabouts of Conception Lopez. The relationship Kramer had watched develop between these two as *Pequod* came down the river had disturbed him and he didn't want Conception finding Mickey first, especially as Mickey was with Cagliari. He eased the big gun which lay snugly against his thigh, but if it came to killing, the big black-bladed knife against the other thigh was likely to be the weapon of choice – unless the confrontation took place down in the foundations of the forecastle where the relentless battering of the wild water was already making enough noise to cover a small war.

There was, in fact, a small war going on in the secret compartment in the bows. It was a war against the gathering darkness of failing flashlight batteries and the creeping, slithering death which approached in those shadows. Two men were fighting that war side by side, everything else put behind them as they stood against an enemy which both of them found almost overwhelmingly horrible. In spite of the temptation to blaze away with the weapons they had at their command, they soon found themselves considering other stratagems.

252

Once their peace had been made – a swift compact when they realised the full horror of their situation – they had used the combined brightness of their torches to survey their position as fully as they could. So they had found the cocaine at last. It was difficult for them to assess the full size of the consignment because the plastic-covered bales of the stuff were alive with spiders, snakes and scorpions seeking refuge from the bilge water. In the foul slop at the base of the contraband hill lay the convulsed corpses of those that had dared to taste the gleaming temptation of the section Cuzco had blasted open. But the creatures on the illicit cargo were by no means the only creatures there. Between the safety of the high-piled packages and the food source represented by Cuzco, a long line of desperate insects scurried up and down the sloping, slimy floor. So intent were they on feeding, at first, that they hardly seemed to register the lights or the two who carried them. But this was a situation which could not last long.

'We have to find some way to signal,' growled Mickey, his voice made ragged by disgust and the fetid atmosphere.

'Only the hatchway,' choked Aldo.

'Yeah. We have to set up a defensive position there, in case we run out of light before anyone hears us. We don't went to end up as dessert.' He flashed his torch beam back towards crawling Cuzco. Aldo didn't look: he had seen more than enough already. During the next half-hour, however, he looked almost everywhere else in the little area they shared with the illegal cargo and its grim guardians. There were no exits – clearly the stuff had been sealed in here and was designed to be cut free during the breaking of the hull. The unwelcome guests obviously found ways in and out but there was nothing man-sized on offer. Nor were there any power lines, fire systems or any other circuits which could be broken to alert the people on the bridge. The only thing they could find of that sort was a heavily protected light beside the hatch. It was thick glass, screwed tight shut behind a cage of heavy-duty wire. There was something written on it but there were no wires running to it and it was not lit up. Neither Aldo nor Mickey had brought any kind of communication device. They each had the clothes they stood up in – damp, dirty and smelly – a torch and a gun. Escape was impossible. So they eventually came full circle to Mickey's first suggestion of making a defensive redoubt near the hatch where they could fight off the swarming enemy until the last moment and stand the best chance of communicating with the outside world.

At first, the plan seemed easy enough. There were a couple of steps up to the hatch where they could sit and try to call or tap some kind of communication with the outside world. These were well away from Cuzco and he represented the main focus of interest for the non-human occupants of the place. But when the two men switched off their torches, they were surprised how swiftly things came closer, exploring. The first few shots squeezed off in revolted reaction to this realisation went ricocheting dangerously: the reports in the enclosed space hurt their ears – their whole heads – and the bullets seemed to do no damage to the enemy at all.

So during the first few hours of their incarceration they would switch off their torches, call out for help until their voices went raw, then tap on the nearest piece of metal with anything that would make it ring, pausing between calls and beats to listen. They would wait until the rustling of inquisitive life came too close for comfort then switch on the beams and dance around kicking and stamping, slaughtering anything that had come within the danger zone. It worked well enough with spiders and scorpions on the floor. They were lucky that the snakes did not consort with their eight-legged brethren and that the walls were too slick and slimy to climb.

And, as they sat in the dark, tapping in rusty Morse code and waiting while life and death worked out their strange race to see which would reach them first, they called out less and less. Instead, they talked. Mickey began it, apparently casually, telling of his own childhood and the convoluted pathways which had brought him here. He spoke with absolute candour, and soon Aldo found himself reciprocating.

Both men found it increasingly difficult to keep control of this process, for they were in a strange atmosphere, with adrenaline and a range of other natural drugs awash in their bloodstreams, and the effect of these was being deepened by the micro-particles of cocaine hanging in the thick air, left over from Cuzco's explosive death. Aldo had most to hide, and his immediate memories and dreams were the most disorientating. There in the suffocating darkness in front of him, Jody seemed to come and go, suffering a range of indignities which all too rapidly became an inquisition full of agonising tortures in the guilty man's fevered imagination. He knew what he was seeing could not be real. He understood that the woman was not there, and nor were her shadowy torturers. Something sinking rapidly ever deeper into the lower fathoms of his understanding told him that she could not suffer such torture without succumbing, over and over again. And yet she hung there, like a side of beef in a butcher's shop, more real than his flashlight, more real than his gun, far more real than the guy beside him with the quiet, probing voice, and she looked at him with such wild, mad accusation that he found it very hard to bear. Things came to such a pass, indeed, that even when the torches were on and the enemy spies being slaughtered, Aldo could still see her so clearly that he was forced to walk round her.

Mickey was in little better state, but he was still clear enough in his mind to see that the big man at his side was coming apart. Whatever invisible horror Aldo was trying to avoid – and Mickey would have wagered it was the dead man round the corner, from the look on Aldo's face – it was obviously getting more and more real; more and more dangerous.

The next escalation in the horror of their situation was inevitable. Aldo's torch failed to light when they went out on their next hunt. After that, with Mickey's growing dimmer and dimmer, they stayed in darkness for longer and longer. And still they talked. Aldo was making less sense now, but all his reserves of self-control and cunning were so focused on concealing from Mickey what he could see – and why he could see it – that all his other little secrets seemed like nothing in comparison.

Both men were lapsing into dangerous semi-consciousness now – they had been in the poisonous place for more than eight hours. A hungry spider had just scuttled up to Aldo's twitching right boot and tried a nibble of his lace when the bow swung smoothly sideways, with a good deal of rattling and thumping. Both men started awake. Mickey automatically switched on his torch and the last candle-power of light showed him the massed ranks of his crawling enemy. He leaped forward, kicking and stamping, with Aldo like St Vitus beside him. Over the noise of their wild dance, the engines grumbled into life and the ship began to move with more purpose. Abruptly, there came a lurch, as though she had backed into a brick wall. The two men staggered forward. Providentially the creatures ahead of them fell back. The ship lurched forward and the men staggered some more, then they stumbled back to the temporary safety of their steps as *Colorado* came to speed and swung round. Luckily both of them were seated for the second attempt to exit the marina, for the shock of it threw Cuzco across the chamber and brought the high-piled bales tumbling down. In the almost total darkness of the dying torch battery's last glimmer, the two men climbed to the top step and curled up almost as tightly as Conception had done, surrounded by hammerhead sharks.

The battering, thumping thunder of water hitting the cutwater, hard debris rumbling along her bottom and occasionally hard levees grinding along her side swept over the two of them then. It was stunning, incapacitating; almost as agonising as the gun-reports had been. It would have hidden the whooping of a charge of the Mongol horde, let alone the quiet scurry of eight little scorpion claws. For Aldo it almost drowned out the sounds his phantom woman was making. The sound, as effective as a white-noise torture device, went on and on relentlessly until Mickey seriously thought of using the last shells in his gun to shoot himself. But then, as *Colorado* settled into the flooded river's flow, north of the jammed roundabout on Route 5, the sound began to quieten and, the greatest miracle of all, the light above their heads blazed into high-wattage life.

EXIT, it said, brightly. And, shockingly, the yellow light containing the bright red word reflected across a skim of heaving water which looked to be deepening by the instant.

While Aldo and Mickey sat staring up at the mocking sign and marvelling how many assorted horrors its light had now revealed struggling towards them in the deepening flood in the bilge, and while Conception, driven by her sense of what was right, looked for Mickey, and Kramer, in the grip of much darker emotions, secretly followed her, Richard walked across the bridge, apparently casually, and looked down towards the bows.

'She's taking a hell of a battering down there,' he said quietly. 'Running at flank speed into a flood is going to put a lot more stress on the forecastle than running at flank even into pretty high seas. She's designed to pitch and ride rather than to twist from one side to the other like she's doing now. And there have been several hard strikes against debris borne by the river too.' He paused. Jesus and Peter Phelps both drifted over to his side.

Robin glanced up from her calculations on the tourist map and the computer screen and smiled a little grimly. Richard was in his element and, even in these frighteningly unfamiliar waters, she felt perfectly content and safe in his hands. The thought was errant, sudden, and, like the flood, ran counter to much of her recent thinking. But it was true and the smile widened.

'Perhaps we should call El Jefe up and see what his thoughts are on the added strain of putting the hull through this with bloody great holes where the gun mechanisms ought to be,' said Richard. He raised his voice. 'How long have we got until we get to the bridges, Robin?'

'Three hours thirty at the most.'

'If these conditions continue for that length of time, things will get a great deal worse,' Richard continued thoughtfully. 'We don't want her coming to pieces at a critical moment, like this levee up ahead looks as though it's doing.'

'The least we can do is check the bows and the chain lockers,' suggested Peter.

'Sounding the bilge should be enough,' countered Jesus, thoughtfully. 'I don't want to call El Jefe away from the engines unless I absolutely have to.'

'Has he got a two-way nearby?' asked Richard. 'We could have a conference without getting him all the way up here.'

El Jefe's two-way was in the engine control room – any nearer the massive boilers or the screaming turbines and it would have been useless. The three above went out onto the port bridge wing and overlooked the velvety blackness through which the thunderstorms above the Sierras were drawing ever closer. 'To check the bilge is a good idea,' said El Jefe distantly. 'But I also agree with Captain Mariner. We should look at the fabric of the bows as well. If the bilges start to fill suddenly then that could be a sign that we are already too late. *Madre de Dios*, I wish I could get my hands on the motherless eunuch who ordered the removal of those guns. Their absence will be causing the hull to flex more acutely than it is supposed to do! We can only hope that the fact she is riding so high will keep stress to a minimum. *Hijo de puta!* You cannot do that! Here, let me, you dickless excuse for a fornicating—' Contact with the engine control room was severed abruptly as El Jefe became involved with an entirely different form of stress.

'Well,' said Peter Phelps, as quietly as the thunder of their passage northwards would allow, 'there are only three ways to check on the bows: from above, from below and from within.'

'To look from below is clearly out of the question,' said Jesus.

'So it's from the forecastle head above, and from the chain lockers within – or the cutwater bilges if you have any,' completed Richard.

Peter's teeth glinted white in the darkness as he grinned. 'Toss you for the duties,' he said, and Richard gave a bark of laughter.

'You're on!'

For once, the lucky limey lost – perhaps because the canny Yankee flipped with a big old silver dollar. A moment or two later they were all back on the bridge. Jesus, in command, stood back behind Ramon's solid, straining shoulder and looked ahead narrow-eyed down the converging pathways of light at the relentless wilderness of water hurling down on him. Peter went down the internal companionways, heading for the A deck corridor leading out onto the weather deck. Richard paused beside Robin, his bright gaze scanning the map and the laptop screen. 'I'm going below,' he said.

'I'll come. I can leave this.'

'I don't think you'll enjoy it. I have to check the chain lockers and the cutwater bilges.'

'I thought you would,' she said. 'Especially when I saw that big silver dollar glinting in the air. It's not a one-man job. You know that. Even under these conditions you'd be quicker and safer with a partner.'

'A captain's mate,' he joked, weakly enough. 'I'd thought to pick up one of Hernan's boys. He's still got some pretty able seamen down there with him even if we do have the cream up here.'

'It'd be quicker and safer if I came. And no one's likely to need me for a while. What can I tell them that they can't see well enough for themselves?' She gestured at the bright overlay on the Perspex above the captain's additions and annotations on the tourist map. 'If it's rising twenty-one hundred, then we must be there,' she pointed to a clear mark annotated in her own neat, forthright hand. A line led up the centre of the river, with timings beside it, to a clearly marked anchorage where the two bridges crossed the flood. A double line led down towards the same point, with timings in brackets to show that they were much more approximate. 'The guys in the Yuma lock-up should be getting pretty wet just about now,' she said quietly, with not a trace of regret in her voice.

They both looked up at the computer screen, but nothing changed. No new news came in. After an instant Richard said, 'Right. Let's go.'

As the lift hissed away into the lower depths, the CNN screen lit up: FLOODS HIT YUMA – *Latest Pictures Exclusive* . . .

Peter Phelps stepped out onto the deck, surprised by how much louder and more frightening the water noise was down here. It had seemed bad enough up on the bridge wing, but down here the overwhelming turbulence seemed to be amplified as well as contained by the walls of the levees on either hand. The effect was oddly claustrophobic, as though the far bank were as near as the one rushing by on his left. But Sonora was a couple of kilometres east to starboard. Such was the thunder of the overflow there, however, that it seemed much closer, although they had left the lower section of the levee well astern with the northern suburbs of Cortez which it was designed to protect.

258

Feeling oddly as though he should be wearing oilskins and a well-secured safety harness, Peter began to walk along the length of the deck. The forecastle head was a mere forty metres away, but the walk was surprisingly difficult. In a way by no means apparent up on the command bridge or the wings spreading out on either side of it, the main frame of the hull was vibrating and beginning to writhe as it was crushed between the forward thrusting of the massive engines and the backward pressure of the flood. *Colorado* was designed to ride over such stress, to toss her head and porpoise through green waters. Peter remembered her doing that very thing times without number in all the oceans of the world. But this was different. This was something the designers who had fathered her in the dark days of the last world war had never dreamed for her. And she did not like it.

Peter felt her head yaw in towards the shore. Far above, Ramon swung the wheel and spun her out towards the middle of the channel; Peter could feel every twitch of the manoeuvre in each fibre of his body, but no sooner had she eased out into relative safety than a thunderous roar told of invisible, half-submerged debris running down her starboard flank, and she twisted in towards the shore once more. He hurried forward, suddenly worried, suddenly sensible of every rivet in her skin straining to pop free. Briefly he regretted the boyish elation and bravado after winning the bet which had sent him down here so thoughtlessly alone. But at least he had the big flashlight and the walkie-talkie. 'Phelps here,' he said into the open channel to the bridge. 'Proceeding to the forecastle head, out.'

Oddly, Peter found he needed the torch more and more as he crossed the forty metres towards the knife-point of the forecastle head. The searchlights overhead seemed to give everything below their lightning-white beams an odd impenetrability, as though their dazzling brightness sucked light from all around and made darkness gather unnaturally down here. It was a disturbing fancy, even though Peter knew well enough that it was simply the light playing tricks with his eyes, forcing pupils which needed to be wide and receptive into defensive pinpoints every time he looked too far forward into the incandescence where the beams converged. His flashlight served him well, however, guiding him past traps like the loose cover over the gun pit, until at last he was aware of the forecastle rail gathering in claustrophobically on either hand. His last command had been a Spruance-class destroyer and he couldn't remember her forecastle ever feeling as threatening as this. Nor, indeed, did he remember ever feeling so exposed and at risk in all his years aboard *Colorado* herself.

Right at the forepeak, the Mexicans had added a little sort of jackstaff he couldn't remember having been there while he was aboard. From this there hung a small flag whose dogged immobility seemed weirdly at odds with the noise going on all around. From the feel of the ship, from the roar of the water down here, the flag should have been streaming back in a 60 kph headwind at the very least. But the rag drooped, stirring fitfully, for in spite of all the sound and fury, there was a dead calm in the air.

Peter steadied himself, put the two-way in his pocket, took the flagpole in his right hand and held the torch firmly in his left. He took a deep breath to steady himself, and leaned forward, shining the broad beam downwards. Immediately a geyser of warm foam spewed up into his face. The ship dipped and heaved. He swung back in, gasping and spitting. He shook his head to clear his eyes and leaned out once again.

The cutwater plunged like a knife blade straight into the foaming heart of the river. Peter watched it as it sawed up and down with a slight but relentless motion. It was strange to see the water come plunging down at it like this. The writhing of the surface made it seem as though she was cutting through a strange, low surf, parallel to a deeply plunging coast. But the surf seemed not to be rolling in and out, as waves do on a real shore. It seemed to be running straight down on them, as though completely alien physics were at work. And just as Peter strove to imagine how water could possibly behave like this, so the ship herself strove to cope with it. Suddenly one of the parallel waves along which they were surfing whipped out of line, some tiny flaw in the forces holding everything in straining stasis for a nanosecond. Peter saw the wave strike in towards *Colorado*'s stem like the head of an anaconda a couple of kilometres long. He felt the ship slam sideways and shudder as it hit. Felt the weirdest, floating sensation as, in spite of Ramon's best efforts, she slammed up alongside the levee again. He saw, though his eyes could scarcely credit it, the hard line of the cutwater seem to waver. It did not buckle or bend; he was certain of that. It simply wavered as though it was dissolving, ready to run away altogether, as though grey steel had been changed by the alchemy of the wild forces around it into liquid mercury.

Then the foot of the forecastle head, three and a half metres below the wild, writhing surface, hit what was left of a waterlogged tree trunk which had been washed down all the way from Wyoming. *Colorado*, still in the grip of the forces Peter was striving to comprehend, gave a kick like a startled horse. The whole of the jackstaff came away and Peter found himself in flight. He let go of the treacherous pole and reached for the two-way in his pocket, still thinking clearly, unaware how close to death he was. Like an Olympic diver, he spun in the air, falling outward from the point of the forecastle head. Down three short metres he plunged, in a parabola which took him out ahead of the racing ship, beyond even the raging foam of her bow wave.

The instant he hit the water he was jerked under and in towards her with a speed and force far beyond anything he could ever have comprehended. She leaped down upon him like the family pet gone wild and the shock of the impact when she killed him was masked only by the second strike as the after section bounced over the submerged tree trunk, rearing her whole poop out of the water altogether and miraculously preserving her propellers for another hour or two yet. Jesus saw him fall. Only the desperate nature of their plight prevented him from stopping his engines. He ran out onto the starboard bridge wing and looked down. For the briefest of instants he saw the heroic American's white uniform and above its collar, a shapeless mess whose colour matched the wild red water perfectly. Slowly he returned to his post and pressed the 'All hail'.

The first impact, which killed Peter Phelps, came near to doing the same to Conception, for it threw her down the lowest companionway onto the fourth and bottom engineering deck. She landed well, but bashed her head as she rolled along the corridor towards the narrowing access to the foremost sections of the forecastle. She rolled sideways and lay there while the ship settled briefly. The second, vicious, bump – which saved the propellers – lifted her off the floor and turned her over like a doll tossed carelessly aside. When the ship steadied once again, she was lying flat on her back, her tube top long past performing its original function and her bright skirt inside out across her tummy.

This was the sight which met Kramer as he came down the companionway onto the least frequented passageway aboard, which was, of course, already familiar to him. He stopped at once. He glanced furtively over his shoulder, and ran forward silently on thick soles amid the all-consuming thunder all around. As the captain's voice made some distant announcement about Peter Phelps, Kramer slithered to a stop and knelt at her side, his tongue flicking over his lips like the tongue of one of the snakes creeping up on the prisoners in the cutwater bilge a metre or two further on. She had a pulse in her throat but she did not stir when he called her name, when he slapped

261

her face and rolled her head over to reveal a sluggish ooze of blood by her right ear. Nor did she react when he cupped her right breast and squeezed it until the nipple bulged out between his fingers. Nor, indeed, when he reached very much lower and squeezed a good deal harder. He licked his lips again, his face suddenly pale and a little drawn. He unzipped the fly of his combat trousers and reached in. With practised expertise he pulled out the black-bladed knife and then hesitated, looking down at the feast spread out so defencelessly before him, calculating where to begin. He reached for the high-cut leg of the panties and slid his knife in beside the point of her hip, tensing to cut the material away.

'Is everybody all right down there?' came Robin Mariner's voice, close enough to make him jump. The knife tip jabbed down. Conception stirred.

'Hello?' called Robin, from closer at hand.

Kramer pulled his knife away from Conception and sheathed it. He rose silently to his feet, looking up and down the corridor, too preoccupied to see the bright trickle of blood from the little cut at her hip. The hatch into the cutwater bilge stood a little way ahead on his left. It was closed by big wheel-powered bolts which could be locked or opened only by turning the wheel on this side of the cover. But the chain locker on his right had a proper door, albeit of metal, which looked as though it could open or shut from either side. He opened it and stepped in, not quite closing it so that he could keep an eye on the corridor. His blood was so inflamed by Conception and the thought of what he had almost done that he was calculating whether he could find some way of arranging a double-header if the English bitch was all alone. What did they say? Might as well be hung for a sheep as a lamb . . .

Robin came down the companionway at a run, calling, 'Conception! My God . . .' She threw herself down onto her knees by her friend's side, her hands busy restoring her decency, but in the middle of this process, Conception sat up straight, her hand drawn back to slap Robin's face. Robin lurched away, with a slight cry of surprise. 'Conception?'

Conception halted the blow and sat frozen as her eyes and mind began to clear. 'Someone has been touching me,' she grated. 'While I was out, there was someone . . .'

She went up onto her knees, staring suspiciously around as she pulled her tube top down. Her fingers went under the hem of her skirt to her hip. They came away red. 'I've been cut,' she said, her voice dripping outrage. 'I'll bet it was Kramer. That creep . . .'

Kramer tensed then, ready to burst out of the chain locker and kill the pair of them. He was within a breath of doing so when Richard arrived on the scene. 'Are you two all right?' he asked, looking up and down the corridor as suspiciously as Conception had. 'You've blood on your face, Conception. What's been going on here, for heaven's sake?'

'That's what I'd like to know myself,' spat Conception, pulling herself erect.

'Conception was knocked out when the ship lurched,' said Robin. 'She was interfered with while she was unconscious.'

'If she was, then the culprit's still down here,' said Richard. 'There was no way out except past us.'

'Right!' said both women at once, swinging round to look at the two doors immediately ahead of them.

What the fuck, thought Kramer, reaching for his gun. I guess I'll have to kill them all.

But as the thought formed in his mind, a fusillade of gunshots rang out from behind the bilge hatch on their left.

The water seeping in past the scattered bales of cocaine ran back along the length of the bilge, gathering depth, sweeping up snakes, spiders and scorpions alike towards Mickey and Aldo trapped on the top step under the mocking light. Because of the wild gyrations of the forecastle head – indeed, of the whole hull – during the last few minutes, most of the living creatures had done their best to scuttle for cover, so most of what that foul wave contained was a flotsam of dead bodies. The wash of water was considerable. While it was not quite enough to splash over the two living men crouched by the hatch at the far end, it was enough to rouse Cuzco. He fell forward into the deepest part of it, then as the ship settled back onto an even keel he heaved and bobbed, as though he was being worked from inside by the creatures which had infested him.

Neither Aldo nor Mickey had any idea there were people within a metre or two of them, just outside the hatch. They had given up calling out and tapping hours ago, overcome by stupor and torpor.

But when the dead Cuzco washed up to Aldo, rearing up out of the water on the crest of a little wave, with a choking sound Aldo steadied his back against the hatchway and emptied his pistol straight into the corpse's head. The effect of the bullets was striking, but as nothing compared to the effect of the gunshots. The hatchway behind them slammed open and both men tumbled backwards, sprawling out into the corridor at the feet of the astonished Mariners.

263

Aldo's gun slipped out of his numbed fingers and skittered away across the corridor to Conception's feet. She stooped and picked it up in one fluid, automatic movement. Then she turned, thin-mouthed, to test the door into the chain locker, but it seemed to be securely locked. Before she could check any further, Richard's voice, hoarse with shock, called, 'Let's get this hatch sealed again and help these two up to the sickbay. It looks as though someone has one hell of a report to make to Captain Vega, not least that he's got a serious leak in his bows.'

Chapter Twenty-three

'Miguel. *Hijo mio . . .*'

Mickey had forgotten how gentle his father's voice could be. He opened his eyes and found Jesus sitting beside him.

'How are you feeling, my boy?' Jesus asked, in tones Mickey remembered from half-forgotten childhood accidents.

'I am well, *padre*,' he answered, and was surprised to find his voice was ragged and his throat sore. This was made worse by the fact that he had almost to shout over the thunderous rumble of *Colorado*'s progress, the thrashing of her engines and the relentless rhythms of her pumps. He reached to massage his aching larynx and found his father had been holding his hand. He tried to sit up and Jesus helped him. He was in the sickbay. Aldo Cagliari was lying on the next bed, still unconscious. Through the door in a bright little dispensary Conception was talking to Robin Mariner and the huge Hawaiian man with white hair.

Only then did everything fall into place.

Mickey looked back at the set face beside him. It was time for the truth, he decided.

In fact father and son were of one mind, but it was the father who spoke. 'We are coming alongside the bridges. We can go no further and must secure our position here. The floods will be upon us within half an hour, according to Captain Mariner. One of our number is dead and there are more likely to join him. The time for secrets is past, *hijo*. Secrets will be more dangerous than weakened bows now.'

'You're right,' said Mickey wearily. 'It is time for the truth.'

He opened his mouth to accuse his father of ensuring comfort in his retirement by smuggling tens of millions of dollars' worth of cocaine during his last voyage aboard *Colorado* when Robin and Conception abruptly came through into the little room. And Mickey found he simply couldn't bring himself to say the words – to shame the old man in front of them.

'It's like this, *padre*,' he said instead. 'I'm not exactly what I seem to be.' His eyes sought Conception's dark, smouldering gaze and tried to hold it – with no success. He found himself staring instead into the calm depths of Robin's intelligent grey gaze.

'I'm a major in the Corps of Engineers like it says on my papers,' he began. 'But I'm also working undercover for the Drug Enforcement Administration. Mexico isn't the source of hard drugs it used to be but the opening of the Colorado seemed to the administration to be offering the drug barons and their contacts down here just too good an opportunity. There were names being bandied around at pretty senior levels and rumours of a massive shipment coming north.

'I came down the Colorado with the guys on *Pequod*. I was the natural selection. Some of my work for the Corps of Engineers had been on the Colorado project. I've done a little white-water work – though they gave me Allday as a baby-minder in case the going got too tough for me. I'd a better reason than most to come aboard here when I'd looked along the lower river course to see whether or not there might be stashes – or places where stashes could be put.'

'Like the bat cave,' said Robin, the pieces of the puzzle falling rapidly into place.

Mickey nodded. 'Like the bat cave. My job, in short, was to check whether the river could be used as a conduit for drug transportation. And it can.'

'But someone found out about you. About you and Captain Allday,' said Robin.

'I guess we were careless at some time or another. She wasn't DEA. She was just a white-water expert they recruited to watch my back. She must have let something slip. That's all I can think.' He glanced across at his father. 'Someone cut our safety lines . . .'

'Kramer,' said Robin. 'I think he was going to have another go at eliminating you when you went off to explore bat caves that night, but I woke up and spoilt his plans.'

'Of course!' said Conception. 'Andy DeLillo warned me against Kramer with his dying breath.'

'And Killigan, my FBI contact in Vegas, didn't trust him either,' said Mickey.

'Killigan was worried about us coming down to this ship, wasn't he?' said Robin, after a brief silence during which another section of the puzzle fell into place.

'How did you work that out?'

'Reverse logic. *Colorado*'s cutwater bilge is full of drugs. Richard's seen them. He told me and your father while you were out cold. Full report. You must have come aboard because of that. But they arranged for you to come aboard weeks ago – so they must have known the shipment was supposed to come on *Colorado* back then. Aldo's involvement with Richard and our plans to be here when *Colorado* was broken up must have looked very strange to Killigan.'

'It did,' said Mickey. He looked across at Aldo asleep on the next bed. 'And Aldo was hooked up to Alighieri. That closed the circle for us, because it was Alighieri who was fingered as the man due to dispense the drugs when they came north over the border.'

'He must be a very irritated man, then,' said Robin, 'because it looks to Richard and me as though the drugs in the bilge should have been run northwards with the first of the scrap on Friday. It seems to us that that's probably why Sagreras the ship-breaker in Cortez got so desperate today.'

Conception leaned forward suddenly, her eyes like melting chocolate. 'He could not have known, you know. Your father can have had nothing to do with this. If he had been a part of this mobster Alighieri's plans, how could he have dreamed of bringing the *Colorado* north into such danger as he is doing now? Only an innocent man would do such a thing. An innocent man and a brave one.'

Mickey slumped back against his pillow then as he understood the truth of Conception's words. He had seen his father through his mother's eyes. A different man to the one he thought he knew so well sat quietly beside him.

'We must find Kramer,' said Jesus Vega urgently. 'And we must lock him away with this scum here.'

As he spoke, the whole ship seemed to hurl itself sideways and run, shuddering, hard aground. Jesus jumped to his feet and was gone at a flat run. Mickey, Robin and Conception followed hard on his heels.

On the bridge, Jesus found Richard standing at Ramon's shoulder scanning the river ahead as he exchanged information in broken English with El Jefe.

'What was that?' demanded Jesus, striding forward, his own eyes busy.

'We don't know what it was,' said Richard shortly. 'But we know what it did.' El Jefe's voice amplified Richard's terse information in terms which came close to making Robin's cheeks burn. 'The bottom of this motherless fornicating river shoals like the ass of a raddled whore. It is covered with debris like pox. It has twisted my propellers and turned my port drive shaft into a corkscrew. I can let the starboard engine run for perhaps twenty minutes to try and hold us here, then all the gears come off the turbine and we are shafted, screwed, buggered and roundly fucked.'

267

Richard glanced at his watch. 'That's a bad position to be in just as the big waves hit,' he said. 'But we're more or less where we want to be now. If we can find some way of securing the ship . . .'

The two captains hurried out onto the port bridge wing and looked down at the levee. It stood close under the port bridge wing, seemingly almost close enough to jump down upon. Immediately ahead, apparently arching over the forepeek in the converging blaze of the searchlight beams, stood the solid span of the road bridge, with the higher arch of the rail bridge just beyond, striding across the night like a shadow. Already, under the lumpy, uneven rhythm of the damaged drive, the long hull was beginning to grind backwards, centimetre by centimetre. The solid spans of the bridges, so hard won, were sliding away upstream out of the cone of the searchlights. The two men exchanged glances as Robin, Conception and Mickey joined them. 'We have no steerage way against the river,' said Richard. 'If we don't secure her head, the next flick of current will take her out into the main stream. She'll turn and be pushed back down to Cortez.'

'She'll be washed over the lower levee into the swamps on the Sonora side,' said Conception with a shudder. She had found swimming with hammerheads bad enough. But there were alligators down there – and they really did scare her.

'Not likely,' said Robin. 'She's got so little draft that if she turns sideways onto the stream, she'll roll over altogether. Especially if the high water hits us then.'

'We have to secure her to the levee,' said Jesus and Richard, their words overlapping, both voicing exactly the same thought at the same time.

Jesus turned to his son. 'Could we do that, Miguel?' Conception's eyes misted. The simple faith the father could place in the expertise of his offspring reminded her poignantly of her own father, and how he had started this desperate adventure by asking her for help.

'Certainly,' said Mickey decisively. 'After all, the top of the levee is strong enough to bear an eight-lane highway further south.'

'Good,' said Richard, then he carried on speaking, extending the thought into a plan of action. 'If we secure *Colorado*'s head to the levee, we can attach the anchor lines to the capstan winches. If we're careful and if we're quick, we'll be able to pull her into position with a series of securely anchored lines.'

Jesus Vega was in action even before Richard had finished speaking. He pulled out his little two-way. 'Hernan, come to the port bridge wing at once. Banderas, tell Hernan's team and mine to prepare for some shore work. If need be,' he continued, breaking contact and crossing to the outer rail, craning over to look down, 'we can send them ashore from here. Secure a line, send one man down to anchor it for the others.'

'No!' said Conception excitedly. 'We won't need to do that. Look!'

They followed the gesture of her pointing arm and there, on the road bridge ahead, stood half a dozen figures waving wildly. 'It's my father,' said Conception. 'Some men from the village. Oh, thank God . . .' The tallest of them was holding something in his hand and gesturing to it. The searchlight's last beam, falling away as the ship ground back another thirty centimetres, caught it, making it glitter.

'Of course!' exclaimed Richard and was through into the bridge at a run. He snapped off the computer – he no longer needed much in the way of warnings – and switched his personal phone to *Receive*. Immediately it started ringing.

Having men ashore speeded things up. A line from the bridge wing was caught and held by a dozen eager hands. Hernan swung down nimbly across a narrow stretch of water and a drop of four metres at most. As he did this, Jesus and Richard used the internal two-way radio to warn El Jefe of their plans and he sent up his best man to oversee the deployment of the port anchor winch.

One of *Pequod*'s battered crew appeared suddenly, looking for Kramer, with a team of four at his back, full of questions for the men ashore about the state of the levee wall. Jesus made the instant decision that he wanted all the engineers ashore in any case, so off they went. In Kramer's absence, Mickey went with them. Richard also came to a decision. 'You'll need a good deck man down there ashore. A master mariner. You can't just drop the anchor and hope it will hold.'

'I agree. But I need a good man down at the capstan winch as well.'

'Robin is the best deck officer I've ever served with,' said Richard. 'Send Robin to the forecastle and I'll go down onto the levee.'

'Done!' said Jesus. But then, aware how security aboard was slipping in the face of the mounting emergency ashore, he radioed Hernan and ordered a well-armed team to secure Aldo Cagliari and to find and secure Kramer too.

A couple of moments later, Jesus and Conception were alone on the bridge wing, he with his two-way walkie-talkie and she with Richard's phone. Between them they had contact with every section of the teams working so feverishly to preserve *Colorado* from the coming catastrophe, so that she in turn could be used to preserve all those others at risk.

'*Donde esta Miguel?*' asked Jesus suddenly, looking around the bridge, a little bewildered. He had not noticed Mickey depart with the engineers.

Conception gestured down into the dangerous dark. 'He's down there,' she said softly.

Richard strode across the broad top of the levee, with Mickey at his side. The spring in the young officer's stride – even under these extreme conditions – told of a stupendous lightening of the spirit. In a few bellowed phrases, Mickey brought Richard up-to-date with the conversation he had just had with his father and Robin. Soon they were joined by Conception's father.

Up the inland edge of the great flat-topped wall they pounded, Richard, Mickey and Ignacio Lopez, shining the biggest torches they had down the earth-covered slope. They noted with gathering concern that it was wet.

'It's leaking badly enough to have filled the dry valley here, just as you say, Señor Lopez,' said Richard.

'It's bad,' commented Mickey.

'With worse coming soon,' said Richard. He turned to Ignacio. 'Where are the villagers?'

'Most of them are in the church. It is the highest building in the village, the furthest up the valley slope. It will be the last one the water will reach.'

'Once we are securely anchored, we will be in a position to make plans,' said Richard. 'If we're going to help them, we can only do so if *Colorado* herself is safe. First rule of first aid.'

The other two nodded grimly and the little group ran back.

There was a line coming ashore from the anchor already and everyone else on the levee was straining on it like a tug-of-war team as Robin and El Jefe's man let out the anchor chain as carefully – and quickly – as they could.

Richard threw his strength onto the rope right at the front so that he could look up at the movement of the great iron double-fluked anchor. It was easy enough to see, even though there was little light down here, for it was surprisingly close at hand. The destroyer's flat forecastle head was only a couple of metres above him and the anchor was very nearly level with his head already. But through the rope, he could feel the way the ship was slipping back downstream. 'Heave!' he yelled, setting up a rhythm designed to swing the weight of the anchor forward and out, like a pendulum. In his rush upstream with Mickey and Ignacio, he had seen a perfect anchorage point, and, indeed, another one a couple of hundred metres north of that. Their only problem would be moving the anchors to the correct positions.

Richard swung round to Ignacio who was straining at his shoulder. 'How did you and your people get over here?' he asked.

'In my son's old Ford flat-bed truck. It's up on the bridge.'

'Could he get it down here?'

'Of course.'

'We need it as soon as possible!'

'Manuel!' called the old man, summoning a square, solid-looking chap in a Planet Hollywood T-shirt.

The port anchor hit the levee then, and the team playing tug-of-war with it heaved it millimetre by millimetre over to the point Richard had chosen for it. Half of them were away down the inland slope of the levee – two or three actually overlooking the restless river winding away to Los Muertos – when Richard settled it securely and called them back up to start work on the starboard anchor which would have to come right round the forecastle head and be carried a great deal further up the bank to the second securing point. That is, if the increasingly restless river gave them time to finish their task.

Up at the sharp end, in more ways than one, Robin was becoming worried. Richard had obviously become so engrossed in his immediate task that he was letting the time slip dangerously away from him. According to her watch, the flood should be virtually upon them. Leaning anxiously against the point of the rail where the treacherous little flagstaff had been, she looked ahead into the restless, rumbling darkness, trying to gauge when the deluge would come. But she had little time for speculation. El Jefe's finest had engaged the gears on the main port capstan and on Richard's signal he began to tighten the anchor chain, pulling *Colorado*'s head more snugly into the bank. At once, much of the wildness went out of the long ship's movement. Robin looked back up to the bright slit of the command bridge, pausing to exchange a wave with Conception's silhouette. Then, calling to the Mexican engineering officer, 'Be prepared to give out line very quickly when the big surge comes,' she crossed to the team working on the starboard anchor. Already the long line secured to the great ring at the anchor's top was curving across to the team on the levee. How small, frail and vulnerable they looked. How far away. Headlight beams cut the darkness above them just as a sheet of lightning lit up the mountainous horizon behind Los

271

Muertos Sierra de Juarez. An old truck heaved itself off the bridge and down onto the broad flat top of the bank behind them. Robin turned and took over the port anchor capstan. It was a tricky job to let the anchor chain out at the right speed and she soon became engrossed in paying out the links in rhythm with the swinging of the anchor, one of her team down on the point of the forecastle head calling back progress reports. At last he called, 'It's in the truck!'

Robin's link with the machinery became almost mystical then as she kept enough of a brake on the chain to stop it tumbling straight down into the water under its own weight, yet allowing it just enough freedom for the truck to grind forward without getting the anchor jerked out of the flat-bed on the back every couple of seconds. And so Robin, like Richard, lost track of time, just at the crucial moment. And it was probably as well that they did so, for this meant they worked at full stretch up to the very last moment, in a process where any slowing, any hesitation at all might well have proved fatal.

Otto Kramer also had little idea of the time. But he knew that what time he had was running out fast. In the moments of confusion after he found Conception unconscious and uncovered just outside the forward chain locker, and slipped so nearly out of control, he had retrieved not only her torch but her radio. On that priceless little piece of equipment he heard Jesus Vega order his crew to find and secure him, and learned that all his own engineers had been sent ashore. He also heard the Mexican sailors coming after him, reporting in to Hernan Gutierrez and occasionally to the captain himself. And so Kramer began to retreat. But he did not know the ship as well as even Aldo Cagliari had done and he decided to retrace his steps to the one place that had served him best – the starboard chain locker.

In this claustrophobic little room, fathom after fathom of anchor chain lay piled, all green and slimy. The place stank of rust but at least the only opening into and out of it apart from the door was the port through which the chain ran over the winches and out to the anchor. This at least meant that there was nothing in here which scuttled, crawled or slithered – except for the measured stirring of the anchor chain itself, as Robin fed the second hook across to Richard on the levee. Kramer was an engineer, not a sailor. Even had he known what danger he faced hiding among anchor chains while the anchors were being deployed, he would probably still have come here. But he was unaware of the danger. While the chain fed out link by link under the careful control of the officer on the deck above him, he had ample time to avoid its serpentine stirring. But when disaster struck, he had no chance at all to avoid its leaping coils. With even less warning than Peter Phelps had got, Kramer suddenly found himself wrapped in the coils of a steel constrictor, and all his madness, murderousness and machinations blinked out like a tiny light.

Richard was in the flat-bed of the truck carrying the starboard anchor. Mickey was beside him. Conception's brother Manuel was driving, with the rear window of the driver's cabin open. 'OK, slow ahead,' Richard called, his hand resting on the cool, gently vibrating metal beside him on the flat-bed, his eyes following the inverted parabola of the chain up to the point of the forecastle head. 'Come right,' he called. 'Stay as close to the river edge as you can.' Manuel obeyed, allowing Richard to see the chain reaching unhindered back to the starboard hawsehole – and also allowing the men running wildly along the top of the levee inland from them plenty of room as they streamed past, heading for the high point of the bridge, the closest approach to a safe place available to them.

Richard suddenly realised that the trembling of the anchor under his hand now held just the faintest echo of a far greater juddering going on under the wheels of the whole truck. Manuel swore as the shuddering wheels began to lose their grip on the shaking levee and the truck was pulled towards the river by the weight of the chain. 'Go for it!' bellowed Richard, and Mickey immediately translated the obscure command into limpid Spanish. Mercifully, Manuel needed no second bidding. Richard saw the juddering chain fall loose as Robin let the brake off, and the Ford leaped forward towards the inland curve of the levee above the leaking section, where the top transformed into a track swinging up onto the bridge.

The little two-way in Richard's pocket chirruped urgently, but he needed no warning of the rapidly gathering crisis. He looked back along the rattling length of the chain, just in time to see it jerk as close to taut as that weight and length of chain could come. Away at the very maw of the starboard hawsehole, some debris caught up in the last few metres of the chain – a length hardly ever used – was spat out into the wild water and for a moment the tumbling mess of it looked almost like a body. But then it fell apart into so much scattered rubbish and Richard dismissed it from his mind. 'Mickey!' he bellowed. He threw himself sideways and hit the wooden wall of the flat-bed and saw Mickey hit the other as the anchor was jerked bodily out of the truck like a rotten tooth tied to a slamming door. The pale grey anchor caught the light, turning surprisingly high in the air, then it slammed down in the truck's wake, its flukes chopping into the top of the levee like the talons of a hawk in the side of a mouse.

And as it landed, it blasted a great spray of water up into the air.

Richard was thrown against the right side of the truck then, on his knees, holding onto the splintery wood like grim death. The anchor, hooked into the top of the levee, suddenly looked as if it was under glass. 'Now what in heaven's name is going on here?' gasped Mickey breathlessly beside him.

A bright, gelatinous veneer streamed over the anchor, as clear as crystal. It was floodwater webbed with quick foam. Overflowing water reached out of the river and lapped at the wheels beneath Richard and he was thrown back as the rear of the truck swung out of control, the front tyres shrieking – a whisper among thunder – on the dry slope up to the bridge's side. It's here, thought Richard. Three cubic kilometres of floodwater; it's here. Now! Richard saw *Colorado* rising, borne up on the first slope of the deluge, thrown forward by the last of the engine's power no doubt, but held captured by the anchors. Richard saw – something he had never expected to see in all his life – two full-linked anchor chains stretched to almost straight tautness, the power of the wild water seeming to overcome the laws of mathematics, physics, everything.

The truck made it up onto the span of the road bridge and stopped. Battered, bruised – probably bloody – Richard leaped to his feet up like an active teenager, caught up in the awful power of the scene. Holding on to the rack on the truck's cab roof, he stood looking upstream over the heads of Ignacio Lopez, his men and Kramer's engineers. So, with the possible exception of the three on *Colorado*'s bridge above him and Mickey standing shuddering beside him, he got the best view of all.

Had it not been for the rail bridge they would all have died there and then, ashore and aboard alike, swept away and battered to pieces. But the rail bridge took the brunt and, like a soldier dying to preserve his mates, it gave up its own life for theirs. The flood hit the rail bridge so hard that it exploded up over the central span like a breaker rolling over a sandcastle. But the rail bridge was a solid construct, massive and strong. It cost the first wave of the roaring deluge a great deal to destroy it, so that, although it exploded against the solid side of the road bridge next, much of its wild destructive force was spent.

Such was the construction of the huge road bridge, too, that the debris from the rail bridge – and all the other debris held in the first great foaming fist of water – was channelled out under the central span, away from the downstream bank of the levee where *Colorado*'s stout sides were already flexing under the sheer weight of the water.

For all the debris it carried, bridge and all, it was a surprisingly clean flood here. The mud-filled walls of water which had come roaring down the Rocky Mountain slopes into the heaving streams of the upper and middle valleys had been filtered by the dams it had passed and the lakes behind them. There was mud enough, no doubt, among the wreckage of Gadse and Tabasco, Hermosillo and Chapultepec, but the riverside townships like San Luis Rio Colorado found that the Morelos and the Yuma dams had taken much of the mud out of the main flow, a good deal of it deposited in the American city just north of the border. But at least some of the submerged rubble rumbling down towards Cortez had once been the bridge at San Luis.

The road bridge, like its mighty brother way upstream, flexed when the flood hit it but, protected by the railway bridge, it held. Hard water, as heavy as the rubble from the San Luis bridge, thundered down on the men standing there, knocking them about like ninepins. Only Richard, spared the worst of it by simple luck, stood firm; Mickey was washed away from his side in an instant and the truck itself was swept back across the roadway until the southern balustrade held it safe.

Things went hard for Robin, too. The foam which leaped over the road bridge rose over the destroyer's bow as well. It was the kind of green-water assault *Colorado* had been designed for and so she dipped and pitched almost ecstatically and it was only by a miracle that both the anchors and their chains held firm as the wall of water washed back to explode across the foot of the bridgehouse. Robin and many of the men working with her were swept back also, to find themselves sprawling like battered, breathless flotsam at the foot of the grey steel wall when the water had passed. But the canvas covering the gun holes in the deck could not possibly withstand an assault like that, and metric tonne after metric tonne of water tumbled three decks down into the bottom of the gaping holes the gun mountings had left. The wild flood washed away into the bilges, sweeping the rest of the unwanted guests from South America with it. The bilge behind the cutwater in particular filled with water and drowning creatures for a good few minutes as *Colorado* fought to get her head back up, like a prize-fighter after a knock-down blow. Had he not been dead already, Cuzco would have perished along with all the others then

275

before the pumps began to regain a little control. And the mess which was all that was left of Otto Kramer was washed clean out of the chain locker.

Robin, picking herself up and seeing the hole in the deck before her, reached for the battered but still-functioning two-way radio. 'Captain,' she gasped. 'We have nothing else to do for the moment. Should we re-cover the hole in your foredeck with something solid enough to take the weight of a helicopter?'

Jesus Vega, impressed beyond words by her cool-headedness, said, 'Yes, Captain Mariner. If you can achieve such a thing . . .'

And Conception at his shoulder growled, 'If she can't then no one can.'

Everything Richard could see upstream in the wild dance of the converging beams of light from the heaving *Colorado* was a barely contained wilderness of rapids charging down towards him, spilling away at their crests to wash down the landward slopes of the overwhelmed levees. The pattern of waves dissolved mercifully into a self-defeating welter of foam around the ruined pilings of the railway bridge, but at the northern face of the road bridge they built up again to thunder over – through – the fractured levee and down the foaming river washing towards Los Muertos.

Richard hurled himself round to look back at *Colorado*. Only her draft was keeping her in the main stream now – that and the fact that she was well down by the head. She was leaning dangerously to port, held by the anchor chains. All around her, water was foaming straight over the levee wall down into the rapidly filling valley and it seemed to Richard that the only thing stopping her following the wild high water for the moment was the three and a half short metres of hull sitting uneasily under the surface; just enough to catch against the lip of the levee – for as long as the artificial bank held firm.

But at last it looked as though the chances of *Colorado* staying safe were beginning to improve. The headwaters of the flood were past. The mass of water behind them began to calm, running relentlessly at, but no longer over, the very lip of the levee. The battered old destroyer settled and the chains securing her began to sag a little.

Richard walked across the back of the truck and climbed stiffly down onto the roadway, hardly noticing that he was up to his ankles in water. He slopped across to Ignacio Lopez and helped him to his feet, then the pair of them began to look for Mickey. Clearly the engineer had some thinking to do at the very least, for between *Colorado* and the bridge itself, the levee was still pouring

276

water like a colander down into the raging river heading towards Los Muertos.

'If this keeps up for any length of time,' said Ignacio, yelling over the thunder of the water into Richard's half-deafened ear, 'we'll have to change the name of the town from Los Muertos Sierra de Juarez to Los Muertos Rio Colorado.'

Before the tug-of-war team went back to other duties, the battered, breathless Mickey looped their rope securely round his waist and got them to lower him down the streaming side into the muddy torrent so that he could make some sort of assessment about the damage to the levee. He was already so wet and filthy that a few more moments in the mud-slides down there would hardly make any difference. Ten minutes after they lowered him over, he was jerking on the line and they dragged him up looking much as he had looked before they lowered him down: like a drowned rat recently pulled from a flooded sewer. It took him a moment to catch his breath, leaning one-handed on the steady form of Richard, stooping, coughing and choking as the big Englishman talked quietly to his father over the little walkie-talkie.

Richard was not the only one with a call going through. Ignacio was in contact with his tall, elegant wife and Father Felipe who stood beside her at the door of the adobe church in Los Muertos looking down through a thunderous downpour. The lightning, only a series of blinding blue-neon flickers from here, interfered with the line, but less so than the combined roar of the falling rain and the rising river. 'Things are looking bad here,' Isabella Lopez was saying. 'The force of the river is fearsome. The whole hillside feels as though it will slide down into the flood. It is like an earthquake here.'

Ignacio looked up to the outline of his tall daughter's slim form moving restlessly across the brightness of the bridgehouse clearview. 'Put Father Felipe on,' he said, then listened grimly as the wise priest's assessment of the situation matched his wife's almost word for word. As soon as he broke the connection, he crossed to Richard's side, unusually hesitant. Richard was in his element here, confident, seeming to know what to do for the best – and he was talking to the captain of the ship which offered the best hope of refuge, if she remained where she was and they could work out a way to get the villagers across more than five kilometres of flooded, river-side road before the flood hurling past the village tore this to atoms too.

But it was Mickey who spoke first. 'Tell him I think there is a severe lateral crack about three metres below the rim of the levee,' he gasped. 'It's difficult to be certain but that's where the damage

277

starts on this side. I cannot estimate how long the crack is – the damage looks to be over one hundred metres long. The water is coming out with such force, it is tearing the levee itself to pieces.' Richard relayed the message but, as he did so, his eyes narrowed and he was clearly making some kind of calculation. Partway through the relay, he simply handed the handset to Mickey and ran down the river side of the levee until he was on the very edge, his blue gaze following the beam of the torch down to the maze of eddies swirling around the destroyer's still restless bow. Ignacio followed him and spoke earnestly as the tall Englishman crouched, deep in his calculations.

It would not have surprised Ignacio at all to find at the end of his explanation that Richard had heard nothing. But the opposite was the case. No sooner had he finished voicing his concern than he found the bright blue gaze locked with his own. 'Give us another half an hour,' said Richard. 'There's something I went to try which might make things easier for us all. For the time being at any rate.' He looked at his watch, then stood up. 'We need to get your people up here, onto the ship if we have to – we've been preparing for that – but right across the bridge if we can. There are no reports of any flooding north of the mangroves in Sonora, so the eastern bank at least is safe. But if we are going to move your people out of danger then we have to stem the flow of the river escaping down there at least while we transport them, or the rescuers will end up in as much danger as anyone else, with no way out either. There'll be a limited window of opportunity even if we can bring it off, so everybody must be ready to move the instant we arrive. And you do realise that things will get much worse in another hour's time, when the tide comes to the flood?'

'But this part of the river has never been tidal,' said Ignacio, surprised.

'Precisely,' said Richard and was off, calling ahead, 'Mickey, if you've finished with the walkie-talkie, I need it. What are your engineers going to do now?'

'Measure the crack. Look for ways to control the flow,' answered Mickey, handing over the little two-way radio.

'What if I could maybe block it a bit? Like the Dutch kid with his finger in the dyke?'

'It'd have to be a hell of a big finger, Richard. That's a massive crack. I doubt even you have access to a finger one hundred metres long.'

'No, I don't,' answered Richard briskly. 'But I know a man who does. Could I maybe send some of your men out with Manuel in the Ford to check the roads along the side of the new river? No chance of repairs, I know; but they might be able to advise on a new route if there are any sections closed. Señor Lopez, are there any bridges between here and Los Muertos which might be damaged by the flood?'

'None.' Ignacio's answer was sure and clear. 'It is a clean run from here to the village.' But of course he had taken no account of the battering the road bridge just behind them had received. Neither had Mickey nor Richard. They assumed that because it was still standing, it had survived the first impact unscathed and would offer a safe passage across to the Sonora side when they needed it. They were wrong, but they would not find that out for some time yet.

'That's lucky,' said Richard, unconsciously prophetic. 'Bridges simply cannot take this kind of punishment for any length of time. Mickey, are any of your people medically trained?'

'No, but Joe Aloha and Chester Shaw seem pretty competent.'

'Good thinking. I'll get them up and out in a moment when we saddle up and get ready to ride out.' Connection clicked onto the little two-way. 'Robin?' he continued without even pausing for breath. 'Are you still up there on the forecastle? Are you? That's amazing. I'd never have thought of that. Strong enough to land helicopters on? Good. But listen, darling, I'll clear it with Jesus in a minute, but if I gave the word, could you put your deck repairs aside for a moment and winch in the starboard anchor? How far? Let's see . . .' He was back at the inner lip of the levee, crouching, calculating. 'Twenty metres, maybe twenty-five. Yes, that'll pull her well forward. Yes, you should be able to tighten the port hook as well – but you should feel the benefit of it all along the hull too. OK? Good. Out.'

He pushed another switch and took a deep breath as he did so. 'If I get the go-ahead here, Señor Lopez, then you and your people should gear up for a quick dash to Los Muertos and back. Captain, I don't know if you have ever heard the story of the little Dutch boy who found a leak in the dyke near his home and was able to save the whole of his village by stopping the hole with his finger . . .'

Chapter Twenty-four

Father Felipe Rojas had never prayed so hard in his life. The little church was full of his parishioners and normally he would have been happy to see such numbers – usually reserved for Christmas or the Day of the Dead – but not tonight. Tonight he knew too well that every soul in here was as fearful, as awestruck and as helpless in the face of disaster as he was himself. Or as he would have been without his faith. He just wished that the bountiful and ultimately merciful deity to whom he addressed himself so fervently was a little more consistent in the unfortunately worldly matters of answering supplications as and when required, or at least in affording His protection of the good and the guiltless.

All day long Father Felipe, with Conception's parents Ignacio and Isabella Lopez, had stood in the tower of the old adobe church watching the resurrected river deepen, spread and gather strength as it flowed from the Colorado down to the Laguna Salada. How swiftly its relentless power had mounted the lower slopes of the dry valley, tearing away first the south-bound main street, then the houses on either side of it. There had been no reaction from the authorities to their warnings or their pleas for help. Only at the end of that sweltering, threatening afternoon had Ignacio at last managed to contact Conception; only as the first thunderhead mounted over the Sierra like another mountain created in the sky had the old man been able to go with his son and a few hand-picked helpers in search of his daughter and the friends who would help her help them.

But it looked to Father Felipe as though that help would arrive too late now. Only in his contemplations of the Revelation of St John the Divine and that section of Genesis telling of Noah had Father Felipe ever imagined a storm like the one which had unleashed its fury on Los Muertos immediately after Ignacio and the others left. Hour after hour the rains had poured down. The rumbling of the thunder was continuous but even that took second place to the titanic pounding of the downpour. Down off the mountain slopes above and behind the little township, floodwaters had come thundering in a deadly

281

rush of run-off, sweeping anything left unsecured – and much that had been carefully secured – straight down into the ravening flood of the rising river.

It seemed to the exhausted priest that much of the town had gone now, swept away and gulped down. It was difficult to distinguish between the gun-barrage rumble of the fearsome thunderstorm and the earthquake rumble of the rising river. And that was apt enough, for the two were clearly destined to be one. The deluge above and the deadly tide below were destined to close together like the gates of Hell itself – and all, it seemed, that stood between, a tiny wedge of light and life waiting to be crushed into the darkness of icy ocean depths, was the little adobe church with every soul left alive in Los Muertos in steadfast prayer inside it.

Just when it seemed that things could get no worse, Father Felipe was put very forcefully in mind of the Book of Job. Looking for a silver lining a little desperately, he thanked God that he had called his watchers down from the tower half an hour earlier – when, actually, he had given up hope of any rescue. The lightning so far had been sheet lightning, seemingly contained within the lowering clouds. The first real branch of forked lightning struck down at the little church's tower with the force of the last trump. It may well have been that graves were opening up behind the trembling building. It was certainly the case that the violent impact of the lightning strike felled the tower like a tree beneath a woodsman's axe. The whole tall construct toppled across the little square, tearing the entire south side of the church away as it fell. With a sound strong enough to drown the thunder and the deluge alike, it slammed onto the slabs of the village square, exploding into rubble as it hit, and the old bell, which had hung there for longer than the history of the place could tell, rolled clanging like a funeral peal down into the echoing flood.

The central beam of the roof sagged, but the strength of the side beams and buttresses held it up so that its clay tiles cascaded down into the square above the wreck of the stricken tower like the fall of a house of cards. Riven by the shock and the enormity of destruction, no one in the congregation even screamed until the weight of the rain fell upon them like a plague, then all hell was let loose. The congregation scattered and, in spite of the fact that even half a shelter was better than none, they boiled out of the gaping wound in the old church like its very life-blood. And, calling on them to return to safety and to prayer, Felipe and Isabella ran out after them.

Ignacio Lopez, driving the lead truck with Richard at his shoulder, swore and swerved as the headlight beams chopped down onto a

282

rubble-filled square full of fleeing, screaming people. Richard's hand slammed down on his shoulder and Ignacio jammed his foot on the brake at its mute direction. The truck skidded, sliding sideways into the outwash of the destruction, coming to an uneasy, lumpy stop with a mess of masonry beneath its stout tyres. Richard was out into the deluge at once, leaping across the devastation with sure-footed, indefatigable energy. Ignacio looked back and was relieved to see Manuel bring the second truck swinging to a slightly more sedate stop beside him. Then Ignacio was out in the wet himself, looking for his daughters, his wife and his priest alike.

It took only one glance at the ant's nest of fleeing villagers for Richard to know that they needed more transport. On the way over here from the *Colorado* and her namesake, he had agreed that Ignacio would check the situation, helping Joe Aloha and Chester Shaw aid the wounded, while he himself would look for transport. His Spanish was clumsy but serviceable enough for that, especially as Ignacio had described the most likely parking areas. All he needed really was someone who looked as though they knew the relevant facts to stand still and answer a few simple questions. By the greatest of good fortune, this was the moment he met Conception's mother. He was certain enough of the resemblance to call, 'Señora Lopez!' and she stopped at once, turning to him. 'My name is Richard Mariner . . .'

But, as he had known her at a glance, so she knew him. 'What can I do, Captain?' she asked.

'We need more transport. Where can I find any trucks? Anything?'

Isabella looked around the running ruin of the square, dashing an impatient hand across her flooding eyes. 'There!' she called, gesturing to the church hall standing mercifully preserved. It was in her mind to explain to the captain that he would find transport trucks and a good deal of tequila there from Conception's fiesta of a couple of days earlier, which his lovely wife had also attended, but the time for such pleasantries was long past. He was off in any case, sprinting through the storm towards the building. Isabella turned, looking for Father Felipe and a focus for her actions. She saw the priest helping Ignacio to load the terrified children into one of the flat-beds. Close behind, though half hidden by great sheets of rain, she saw Conception helping Manuel do the same with the elderly. Her heart swelled to see that her family still stood as foundation to this place. Disregarding the rain by a great effort of will, she ran across the flooded, rubble-strewn square to help them. As she did so, the wind buffeted her, almost lifted her off her feet, then it dropped to a dead calm. And in that calm, under the relentless hammer blows of the rain, she heard the rumble of the river quieten all of a sudden, as though God Himself had turned off a tap up by the Colorado River. So strong was this impression, emphasised by the sudden calm, that when she reached Ignacio's truck she found Father Felipe on his knees. 'Up you get and lend a hand, Father,' she said, not unkindly. 'There will be time to thank the Almighty when we have finished doing His work.'

Richard stood at the rear of the church hall. Far behind his back the small entry in the big double doors stood open to the mayhem of the town square. Immediately behind each of Richard's shoulders stood a flat-bed truck – perfect to replace the two from the university they had hoped for but never got hold of. On either hand stood a pile of crates as tall as he was, each crate full of twelve litres of finest tequila, by the look of things. In front of him, where the southernmost section of the building had stood, there was an opening like that at the rear of the stricken church. Below the tumbled ruin of the hall sloped a slippery slide of semi-liquid mud. At the foot of that swirled a pool, a flaw in the new-born river's bank. As Richard watched, the flow of the river continued to ease rapidly and the swirling in the pool settled sufficiently to show that it had become a resting place for several of the biggest alligators dispossessed by the floods in the mangrove swamps. Richard's attention was only scantily upon the great beasts below, for his whole soul was with Robin, five kilometres east of here. Only she could have switched off the river like that. Only she could have positioned *Colorado* in the manner he had described and so exactly in the place he had planned, so that the one hundred and twenty metres of her hull sat precisely over the one hundred metres of the crack in the flawed levee. The length of the ship would have stopped the floodwater from turning westwards into the old dry valley running past the village here and turned the main flow back southwards towards Cortez and the sea. And, he knew, knowing her as well as he knew himself, she would have paused for a heartbeat, hardly more, to watch the diminution of the flow escaping westwards through the wounded dyke before she turned to her next project, and swept El Jefe and his engineers, unemployed now that they had no engines to attend, into the strengthening of the torn decks so that life-saving helicopters could land fore or aft on the holes where the guns had been – if and when the authorities caught on to the enormity of the disaster they were facing here.

In the meantime, Richard and the rest now had to get these people out of the village and up to *Colorado* If before the tide came to the flood and the flood swept down here once more with renewed – redoubled – force. He looked at his watch, frowning in the near blackout, to see the ancient steel face. High tide in ninety minutes. The flood would be reborn well this side of then. He calculated that the full force of the conflict between the flooding river and the incoming ocean would last for an hour at least and there would be no controlling the floods then.

As Richard turned, the right main door of the church hall rattled open along its long runner. Conception staggered in with Chester Shaw beside her. '*Hola!*' she bellowed.

'It's only me,' Richard answered, as Joe Aloha loomed behind her.

'We're looking for hurt and wounded,' shouted Chester.

'I'm looking for my flat-bed,' shouted Conception.

'No wounded, Chester,' called Richard. 'The trucks are here, though, Conception. We'll take one each. You got the keys?'

'They'll be in the ignition,' called Conception. 'This is Los Muertos not Las Vegas.'

Chester and Joe slid the second big double door open as Richard and Conception fired up the trucks. Then they backed them carefully out into the main square while the townsfolk in the skittering shadows behind them worked to clear a pathway for each vehicle through the wreckage of the tower, largely by hand. Neither driver saw the children darting out from their safe refuges beneath the big trucks. But Joe saw.

The two girls, not quite teenagers, elfin and fleet of foot, darted straight ahead, made thoughtless, if not blind, by fear. But the end of the hall was no longer there. Where their sandalled feet should have discovered flooring leading back into the sanctuary of rudimentary kitchens, they found only the slippery slide of mud. No sooner were they there than they were gone. Calling wildly to Chester, Joe Aloha threw himself forward. He did not pause to calculate what danger might lie at the bottom of the path the girls had followed, he threw himself down the slope after them.

Chester came stumbling in from the door, half sober and groggy. He was working quite quickly given the circumstances but he felt he was moving slowly, as though his body was made of balloons. The first thing he did was to trip over an end of tow rope and fall flat on his face. Picking himself up, more dazed than drunk, he became entangled in the rope which was hanging from a hook on the wall and caught himself on a shelf above it, sending a kerosene lamp spinning.

He paused, catching his breath and steadying himself. He wiped the warm rain out of his eyes, never suspecting it was blood from a head wound. He stepped out of the coils of the rope and walked forward, squinting through the monochrome dazzle of the storm. At the edge of the slope he paused. Below him, the water in the little pool thrashed as the two terrified children tried to use Joe as a stepping-off point onto a climbable section of bank. But the bank was as slippery as oil. They would have been better trying to get back up the slope; it didn't look all that bad, thought Chester. He whirled and ran back for the rope which had tripped him. It was the work of only a moment to uncoil it and throw it down. He worked swiftly and well but he felt the alcohol fumes fuddle his mind and slow his fingers in the crisis. It was almost angrily, therefore, that he hurled the line down to the first girl. '*Grab it!*' he bellowed in the colloquial Spanish he had picked up in Sonora but never bothered to use. 'Grab it and climb! I'll be here to help. Don't worry, *chiquita*.'

Obediently, the first girl was onto the line and up it like a squirrel. With Joe's great hand behind her, the second followed swiftly. Chester had the rope looped round his waist now and was standing with rock-like solidity as though his soles were rooted to the floor. As the girls came to the top of the rope, he leaned down and grabbed their hands, swinging them up and past him like oiled seals. As he did this, his eyes were on the pool of water and his voice was bellowing down at Joe. 'Grab the line, Joe. I've got you safe. Grab a hold and pull yourself up now. It's not so hard, I promise you . . .'

The big man did exactly as Chester advised, grabbing the rope and heaving. Chester staggered forward and back as Joe's weight came onto the line. He had a sensation of himself as being almost out of focus, head and shoulders swinging out and back, dragging drunken images of themselves through the stormy air. Then he staggered forward for real as Joe gave a strangled shout of pain. Teetering on the very edge of the mud slope, Chester looked down. Horrified, he saw Joe, completely out of the water except for his one, thin leg – the one which had been savaged in the Mekong Delta. He saw that this leg had become snagged somehow in a great log of flotsam sent down here on the flood.

'Let go the rope,' called Joe.

'Hang on, I'll pull you free,' answered Chester, still unaware of exactly what was going on. 'It's only a—'

The alligator reared, opening a mouth the better part of ten metres square and shockingly, vividly red. Chester staggered back, still feeling that he was performing slowly and clumsily because of the drink. He was working as swiftly as humanly possible but it was still too slow. The alligator's massive jaws snapped shut across the small of Joe's back. 'Let go the rope,' he called desperately. 'Chester . . .'

Chester heard the words and understood their full import. He heard the sound of the monster's jaws closing, crushing Joe's ribs like so many dry twigs. He felt himself torn forward by the naked power of the thing in the pit below. Like a puppet whose strings have been jerked, he skittered towards the brink, collapsing as he went, so that when he reached the edge he was flat on his face. Wildly, as though in the grip of a fit, he writhed, letting the jerking rope snake free.

When his convulsion was over he lay looking down at the heaving water, helpless, blameless, immeasurably guilty, the same man who had lost his command in Grenada, twenty years ago, in the ruthless grip of some pattern after all; seeing some strange meaning in it all as Martha had prayed he would. Two good men had died tonight and only the worthless one was left alive. But up after him, climbing the slope with terrifying ease on their long clawed feet, came half a dozen enormous alligators, one after another, grinning as they came.

Smeared alike with mud and guilt but washed clean at last of sloth and self-pity, Chester stood, reborn. With hardly a thought he reached across and toppled the tower of tequila crates down into the pit. The tower on his right and then the tower on his left, like Samson. He watched them fall and shatter on the slope, hard glass exploding against itself and spewing liquor and splinters over the monsters and down into the alligator hole. Now it was their turn to hesitate, giving him time to turn and stride back to the shelf with the kerosene lamps. In an instant he had one brightly alight and he smashed it on the lip of the precipice. It spewed its fire down and set the whole swirl of oil and tequila alight. The burning alligators twisted and slithered back down into the cool swirling depths below the flaming mud and the blazing surface of the pool. Had Joe been a Viking rather than an islander, this would have been the funeral for him. But still, it would do for a man born to swim with sharks who swam with alligators at the last.

This thought stood grimly and soberly in Chester's mind as he turned and ran back out into the square. With Richard Mariner driving, he was the best qualified first-aider they had left, even if that wasn't saying much. Those two kids Joe had given his life to rescue needed a check over at the very least – and from the look of things that would only be the barest beginning. He had a big job to do. A job that only he could do, now.

Tomas Segeras arrived at the bridge which had carried Route 5 over a dry river valley for as long as he could remember, and stopped, hardly able to believe his eyes. The ship-breaker's position in the driver's seat of the big pantechnicon gave him a clear view of the tossing expanse of the new-born river. Spray was breaking over the right-hand parapet as though the bridge had become a sea wall suddenly, and a half-sunken one at that. Behind him in the cavernous trailer a well-armed army of thugs waited to do his bidding. The obvious thing was to send them across on foot and so lighten the load before he drove the rig across himself. Even if he lost a couple, he had plenty to spare. But then an unexpected movement in the corner of his eye made him look back. The water was dropping. With magical suddenness, as though someone had simply switched it off somewhere upstream, the restless flow began to dwindle and the central span of the bridge reared out of the water fully, like the back of a sea monster. Sagreras smiled a wolfish smile. Luck was with him after all: she always favoured the decisive, the ruthless.

The ship-breaker was not the kind of man who would let a fortune be snatched away by the whim of a stiff-necked anachronism like Captain Vega. If the useless little self-abuser of a lawyer could not get *Colorado* into his yard by exercise of the law, then Sagreras was happy to take that law firmly into his own hands. It had taken him a little longer to load his men onto his biggest pantechnicon and head north than it might have, because they had stopped at the yard's armoury. Sagreras's yard was by no means average in possessing a fully equipped gun store, but neither was it unique. The night watchmen all went armed with more than their attack-trained Doberman dogs. There was occasional warfare among the powers along the waterfont, even in such a forward-looking city as Cortez. And, of course, it was well-known among certain closed but dangerous circles that Sagreras's yard was often the repository of goods well worth stealing, whose theft would almost certainly go unreported to the authorities. And if, like the sister yard at Topolobampo, the Cortez breakers were technically under the protection of their larger and more powerful northern associate, the Alighieri scrap and shipping empire, not even the Vegas Mafia had an arm long enough to strangle healthy competition all the way down here. The men in the back were no longer armed with clubs. Sagreras had handed out an assortment of weapons, including automatic handguns and semi-automatic assault rifles, plus the odd light machine gun and even a quartet of ancient Russian RPG-18 shoulder-launched guided missiles thrown in for luck.

The traffic jams had slowed Sagreras, but not as much as might be expected, for he was ruthlessly single-minded in his pursuit of the fortune the ship represented to him. Even had the money not been such an irresistible temptation, the knife-edge balance of his position if he lost the ship would have driven him to extremes. He was the linchpin of the whole operation. Putting the stuff aboard at his sister yard in Topolobampo had been his idea, for he had foreseen no difficulty in getting it up the carefully policed Sea of Cortez, off at Cortez city and spiriting it north along with the legitimate scrap of a coastguard and customs vessel bought by one of Alighieri's subsidiaries. All Alighieri's men had had to do was make a fuss about using the River Colorado as a smuggling route when questions about the *Colorado* had been asked in inconvenient places, get Kramer to check along the river just as a little extra insurance, and then sit back and await delivery of the scrap as the DEA ran around checking the river instead of the ship, let alone the scrap she was destined to become.

As things stood now, Sagreras reckoned all he had to do was get the stuff out of the destroyer, no matter what it took, load it onto the truck, then run it north with the tidal wave of refugees he knew was all too close behind him across what was left of the inundated, unprotected US border. If he pulled off such an audacious coup under the nose of Señor Alighieri, he was a made man, a brother in power as well as in title. If he failed in such a public arena he would go down like the *Titanic*.

Sagreras had driven willy-nilly through the scattered hoard of Mayan gold which he counted in any case as only so much small change. He had run his powerful tyres without a second thought across several wrecked vehicles blocking Route 5 and, indeed, over several helpless people. But he was ahead of the pack now, and his quarry was virtually in sight. It had to be. He had snatched fleeting but regular glances at the river and he had seen no sign of *Colorado* coming south again. The road running east from the northern end of this span would take him to the great bridge which crossed the Colorado from Baja California into Sonora, and the ship could never have sailed under that. With this grim calculation like a rosy glow in front of him, he engaged the lowest of his forward gears and ground the pantechnicon down onto the streaming bridge.

Five minutes later, as Sagreras pulled his great truck onto the shoulder of the northern bank, the first of the fleeing army of cars from Cortez breasted the rise behind him, its headlight beams cutting up into the stormy downpour like searchlights. He saw it in his rear-view and pulled to a stop on the eastbound roadway which crested the northern rise. He swung out of the rig and pounded back along the road to the tailgate where a flurry of hammerblows got an immediate answer. 'Paco!' he yelled into the great square cavern, and his call was answered at once by one of his lieutenants carrying an RPG-18 missile. Sagreras jerked a broad thumb over his shoulder at the set of headlights maybe one hundred and fifty metres away, running carefully down the southern bank towards the bridge. 'That car's too close,' he said. 'Take it out on the far side of the bridge and make it messy. But be careful. I want the rest of them behind it slowed down, not stopped altogether. *Comprende?*'

'*Si, Capo,*' said Paco cheerfully, in a weird mixture of Spanish and Mafia-Italian. He jumped down, walked clear of the vehicle, his hands busy with the familiar routine of readying the weapon, his eyes never once bothering with the cartoon-instructions painted on the side. He lowered himself to one knee in the downpour, steadied himself against the buffeting of the wind and, with a great deal more accuracy than might have been expected from either the conditions or the weapon, he turned the long black vehicle behind the oncoming headlights from the mayor of Cortez's official limousine into a very effective flaming barricade.

'I want to see you do that to the bridge of that fucking ship with the pompous prick of a Captain Vega broiling at her helm!' ordered Sagreras viciously.

'*Si, Capo,*' said Paco happily, and the thugs in the trailer cheered. 'If *Colorado* is anywhere near the main bridge across to Sonora, all you need to do is park up there and let me out. I can set up a firing platform on the parapet and blow the shit out of anything within several hundred metres with one of these *muchachas*. And we know better than anyone else that all *Colorado*'s teeth were pulled out in Topolobampo! They are finished, I promise you. They are – what do the gringos say? Ah yes: they are *toast!*'

'Are those vehicle lights ahead?' asked Ignacio Lopez's co-driver. He and Ignacio strained to see through the downpour, trying to work out whether they could see the ship's lights far earlier than anticipated or whether something had, unaccountably, turned onto the eastbound road ahead of them. So it was that they missed the distant, guttering pyre which was all that was left of the mayor's car. Manuel and Conception, further back in the convoy from the village, did not stop for fear of endangering their passangers, many of whom were badly hurt.

Richard, with Father Felipe at his side, did turn south and grind down the slope of the northern bank to the rickety little bridge across the still-gushing flood, calling out to Chester in the back that he might have more business in a minute. Richard climbed out of the truck into the deluge and squinted through the rain at what remained of the official limousine. As he did so, the flicker of approaching headlights became visible beyond the black rise of the southern shore, reflecting off the clouds like lightning.

'There's some kind of help on the way, for what it'll be worth,' he called to Father Felipe. 'Looks like we're too late to be of any use anyway.' Richard returned to the truck and swung it back up onto the highway at the crest of the rise. Approaching it this way, from the south, Richard and Father Felipe were looking northward from the crossroads down the next slope, along the Mexicali-bound Route 5. So they saw that the road to the north was closed now. Where the broad ribbon of the multi-lane highway had pushed purposefully across the desolation towards the irrigated havens along the border, there now lay a sullen lake of floodwater. Whether it had come from the river or from the sky made little practical difference. The multitudes fleeing from the devastation along Route 5 would be stopped cold here, in the worst possible place, right in the middle of nowhere.

But then, thought Richard, swinging hard right and pushing his foot down firmly onto the accelerator, no they wouldn't. No one in his right mind would stop out here at all. They would all swing east in Richard's vanishing tyre tracks and come down on *Colorado* like a horde of terrified locusts. Their only hope of keeping control of the situation was to accept only the most serious cases, and send those who could go on, across the road bridge into the relative safety of the Sonora side where there was no deluge, no crack in the levee and where the routes north, as far as he knew, were all still open.

'They're sending help into Sonora,' called Robin across the bridge to Jesus, who seemed strained and withdrawn. She had come onto the bridge to confirm that she and El Jefe had dealt with the hole aft of the bridge and there was a good landing area there now, and that they had nearly finished with the foredeck as well, just to be sure. It looked pretty ugly but it was strong. More scrapyard style than Bristol fashion, she joked, but shipshape enough to do the job.

Then Robin discovered the radio officer had managed to catch a commercial station on the FM wavelengths of his radio equipment at last and the restful stream of classical music, interspersed with jazz, was now also passing civil defence bulletins to the public, along with all its sister stations. 'There's emergency relief coming in through Puerto Peñasco from the south and along the railway from Hermosillo,' she relayed. 'The stuff on the railway is from Mexico City and all points east. It may take some time to arrive. In the meantime, relief teams are coming over the mountains by chopper.'

'The *Norte Americanos* are sending what they can spare of manpower and equipment south from Tucson and through Nogales,' added the radio officer, then he stopped. The captain was looking at him with eyebrows elevated: it was the first time in Jesus's experience that, given the chance, Sparks had failed to use the word gringos.

'If the whole focus is going to be on the other bank, to the east of the river, maybe we should be there,' said Sparks.

'I don't think so,' said Robin. 'Our job has to be to get people safely across from the west to the east where the main aid will be. We should wait here and guide the refugees over into Sonora. They'll have to stop the trains from Hermosillo just over there in any case, won't they? They can't come across the rail-bridge any more because it's no longer there.'

Robin's grim words made the three of them look up at the bridge just ahead of the tethered ship, and so they saw the lights of the big pantechnicon as it ground to a stop up there.

'Is that our people?' wondered Jesus Vega hopefully, suddenly aware that he had more ashore that he cared about than he had aboard his ship – for the first time in his life, or so it seemed.

'Doubt it,' called Robin, running off the bridge onto the shore-side bridge wing, 'unless someone in Los Muertos has gone into the road haulage business.' She turned onto the forward companionway which ran down the outside of the bridgehouse to the weather deck below.

The companionway faced aft on the down-slope between the bridge wing and C deck, so she never saw the streak of fire which was the track of Paco's missile speeding between his solid platform on the parapet of the bridge beside Sagreras's pantechnicon and the clearview of the command bridge window. All she knew about its impact was the great hand of force which took her and lifted her almost gently off the twisting iron stairway.

Jesus Vega was hurled sideways by the blast, which destroyed the helm and immolated Sparks in his radio room. Shaken, Jesus rolled

292

erect and leaped into action. He leaped, literally, for there was no deck left in the metre or so between his feet and the bridge corridor. He never for an instant doubted *Colorado* was under attack. He never thought twice about the necessity of fighting back. He and his crew were battle-hardened, and he could probably rely on Mickey and the men down on the levee, for they were fully trained soldiers as well as engineers.

All they needed, therefore, was some arms.

Jesus ran into his day room, leaving the door swinging. He reached into his desk drawer without looking, brushing the soft velvet of the flute case impatiently aside as he grabbed the Webley. With his other hand he reached for the armoury keys. Hernan arrived at the door, mouth open, gulping for breath. Jesus tossed him the keys and turned, ready to clip the lanyard to his epaulette. His gaze fell on his gun hand and he paused. What he had thought was the velvet of the flute case was the flank of an enormous spider which now hung from his sleeve. He smiled tightly and, thinking briefly of Robin and her arachnophile daughter, he shooed the thing gently down onto the desk. It was the last gentle thing he did for some time. He stabbed the button of the loudhailer so brutally that the Bakelite scored the desk top. 'All crew report to the ship's armoury, at once,' he bellowed.

As Jesus arrived at the armoury door, he felt the second missile thump into the bridgehouse and, distantly, over the all-encompassing noises of the river and storm, he heard the rattle of machine-gun fire.

'What's the biggest we've got left?' asked Hernan.

'The pair of Sig 710 machine guns,' answered Jesus. 'Set them up on the starboard bridge wing if it's still there or on the top weather deck at the foot of the radio mast if it's not. You need a field of fire across the bridge at once. If they've got many more of those missiles we can start planning our surrender now.'

The first men there were Hernan's own squad and he grabbed the heavy gun boxes with Fernando and fat Frederico, who was big enough in all ways to carry one by himself. The matching ammunition containers fell to Raphael and the lugubrious Velula. They set off upwards into the sinister, smoky air.

Ramon was next, with Ricardo, Paco and Ociel in tow. Jesus gestured at the next set of boxes, which contained the CETME Model L assault rifles bought in from Spain. These at least should need little zeroing – they had last been used on Hammerhead Island to recover the Mayan gold. 'Get a box down to Major Vargas on the levee first,' he ordered, 'then take up defensive positions and prepare to repel boarders.'

'A box to Major Vega, *si, Capitan*,' said Ramon, giving Mickey his father's name as a sign of new-found respect.

El Jefe was next, and he was more than ready to grab any of the weapons left and blow the crap out of the motherless sons of bastards on the road-bridge, he said, having seen his men hosed with machine gun fire on the foredeck. 'And no warning. No warning at all except for the sight of the command bridge blowing open like a fucking firework,' he snarled.

But his captain had less bellicose work for him. 'I need you to do a damage assessment,' Jesus said quietly. 'Take a radio and your best men and see what the damage is. It looks as though we'll have no option but to stand and fight until the river rises again and washes us all away. But if there's an alternative, I'd like to know what it is. Off you go now. I'll be with Hernan, either on the bridge wing or on the weather deck above it.'

Banderas arrived then, wide-eyed and white as a sheet, and Jesus put him in command of the rest of the engineers. Their orders were simple enough. Take the last of the guns and repel boarders at all costs.

It was the second of the missile hits that woke Aldo Cagliari. It woke him by the simple expedient of blowing him out of his bed in the ship's little medical facility and out of the drugged slumber he had enjoyed since his semi-formal detention. It released him from more than slumber, too, for the force of it tore the door off its hinges and the big American was able to roll erect, grab his clothing from the shattered gape of the wardrobe behind the door and hop out into the reeking corridor, pulling his trousers up over his pyjamas as he went. The medical facility was in A deck, the lowest bridgehouse deck, and the nearest door, at the end of a lateral corridor, opened out onto the foredeck. Aldo pushed this wide gingerly and looked along a wilderness of overlapping, bullet-scarred steel. The last time he had seen the foredeck it had been decorously covered with grey canvas. This war zone was so different that Aldo wondered for an instant whether he had been transported in his sleep to some other place, some other time. A low ceiling of tracer bullets from a machine gun firing out of the command bridge begat a fusillade of reply from the black span dead ahead, and he ducked back inside, disorientated and terrified.

From the A deck corridor there were only two ways to go. At least

294

there were people up above him, the tracer fire told him that, so he began to climb the stairway. He was the only person aboard to do this, because everyone else knew that it led to the gaping wound where the first missile had struck. Aldo soon realised something of what they knew, however, because the walls ahead became blackened with blast, like darkness itself painted over the white. The stairs began to come at odd angles. The light died. Then the wall simply burst out, bending away into the pelting night in sharp-edged curves. And there, in the centre of the steel-framed picture, hung the woman of his nightmares. Blackened, half stripped by the blast, dangling precariously from a steel tube banister. Sooty hair plastered to a fine skull seemed to run in streams down neck and shoulders onto mottled expanses of flesh painted with the same strange darkness as the walls below. But in the midst of the strange picture, dominating it, were wide, cool, calm grey eyes.

'Thank God you've come, Aldo,' said the nightmare apparition in a gentle English voice. 'I don't think I could have hung on for very much longer.'

Ignacio Lopez drove the Ford over a slight rise at a good speed. It was impossible to see what was happening up ahead but the glittering light and firework pyrotechnics worried him. As he roared onto the scene, he actually shouted with surprise, finding a blocked road on one hand, a burning ship on the other and a full-scale battle raging between them. He wrenched the wheel to the right and ran the truck off the road altogether, down onto the top of the levee. Here the fire fight was attaining almost First World War dimensions with lines of Sagreras's men facing ranks of Mickey's engineers across a field of running mud. Ignacio's arrival altered the balance of the battle radically. The truck came down on the breaker's men like an artillery barrage. They broke and ran. Those that lingered were swept away by Manuel following his father, then Conception arrived and that was that.

Up on the road bridge, Sagreras was screaming at Paco, who was taking careful aim with the last RPG-18 at the machine-gun nest in the starboard bridge wing. At Sagreras's order, however, he swung his aim at the trucks, intending to clear the way for the next set of hopeful boarders to run down the levee and get onto the ship. But his accuracy faltered here and the missile missed its target, thumping into the wide bank well behind the trucks. It hit something hard enough to trigger it – the metal crossbar of one of *Colorado*'s anchors. Its explosion, far less spectacular than the other three, did more damage. As soon as the anchor-chain sprang free, the great ship began to swing sideways out across the stream, her bow moored to the levee by only one of her anchor-chains.

Her movements were almost inevitable. Her head was anchored but only at the one point now, not two. Her stern was free – Mickey and his men had been fighting to secure this when Sagreras's first missile put an end to their work. The pressure of the flood trying to escape through the crack in the levee was more than balanced now by the force of the rising tide which was driving a tongue of sea water twenty kilometres long and ten metres deep up the river, like a dagger to its heart. The river immediately downstream of the great old ship was rising rapidly in the terrifying standing wave Richard had feared all evening. Less than a hundred metres to the south of *Colorado*, apparently against all the dictates of logic, sense or science, there was rising a hill of water ten metres deep. The stern of the destroyer was being lifted higher than the tethered head and it began to slide down the north slope of the hill of Colorado water and swing out across the rushing stream.

This was the situation when Richard arrived on the scene. He jammed on his brakes and skidded to a halt. The rain eased and the wind faltered, as it sometimes does at the top of the tide. He saw at a glance the ants' nest of armed men around the pantechnicon, the damage to the disturbingly restless destroyer, the skid marks down onto the levee and the black rose of the explosion where one of the anchors had been. The truck's lights, the lights along the side of the big rig on the bridge, the headlights of the other three Fords, the ship's lights and the one remaining searchlight gave him more than enough brightness to see the whole scene and draw his battle plan. Jamming his hand on the horn, he stamped on the accelerator and roared across the levee straight onto the bridge, scattering the men around the rear of the pantechnicon. Skidding to a halt against the outward swing of its rear door, he slammed into reverse down the empty road behind him. As he did this, the machine guns, given a better field of fire as *Colorado* swung out across the river and in towards the road bridge, stitched a nasty set of smoking holes along the lower part of the pantechnicon's side. Screams, smoke, and the first few flames belched from the inside as the incendiaries did their work.

It wasn't much, but it was enough for Tomas Sagreras. 'Come on!' he yelled at his men and he sprinted back to the cab. The machine guns raked the rig again as he fired up and rolled forward, his army running after him in disarray, doing their best to scramble aboard. Seeing them in his rear-view, moved, perhaps, by uncharacteristic humanity, he slowed. And that was his fatal error. The final burst of machine-gun fire raked the whole vehicle from one end to the other and the rear section exploded into flame. Those who had been scrambling aboard now jumped out again, running mindlessly for any kind of cover, and when Sagreras put his foot on the floor, the pantechnicon simply went out of control. It moved forward less than fifty metres in all before it swung hard right and slammed into the parapet. The whole lot exploded then, becoming on the instant a great shape of pure fire, as long a a freight car. And, as Richard sat, frozen, the section of the road bridge already damaged by debris from the rail bridge immediately upriver gave way and tumbled into the heaving river below, cutting off all access to the Sonora shore, and any hope of help. Behind Richard came the evacuation from Cortez like Napoleon's army retreating from Moscow. Ahead of him, the mass of masonry and flaming pantechnicon settled into the wildly foaming water which was tossing the swinging destroyer up the slope of the wall of water. And as Richard watched, the wall of water topped the broken levee and swept the uppermost three metres of it straight down into the flooded valley like the aftermath of a Dambusters raid.

Chapter Twenty-five

Richard ran down to the edge of the bridge, slowing only where the tarmac covering began to sag and slip from the stones of the arch. He did not fear the wave of traffic rushing up behind him for he was framed in the headlights of the truck, but the light all around him made the contrast with the rushing gloom below all the more confusing. He knelt, looking across the hundred-metre gap to the next firm span. He looked out at *Colorado*, swinging sluggishly across the stream as the great standing wave gathered under her port beam and swung her starboard against the current. The anchor she had lost was the starboard one, so she was swinging on the port hook, with the whole width of her hull sitting upstream of the line of tension. Logic seemed to dictate that if they waited, the increasing power of the downriver surge would swing her up here under the bridge. And from the look of things, thought Richard, she would fit quite well. Then, if they could position her properly, and hold her still for a while . . .

Richard ran back to Father Felipe who was sitting in the truck, looking with increasing nervousness into the rear-view mirror. 'We'll have to get them to leave their cars of course,' he said, climbing in and bursting into his plan halfway through, much to the priest's quiet confusion. 'But that'll be all right if we can park them somewhere safe. I expect a good number of people will prefer to stay with their stuff in any case. Rescue will be here in the morning, I expect. In the meantime, anyone who really needs to get to the Sonora side can use *Colorado* as a bridge. If we get some choppers in it'll help, but some kind of transport over on the next span of the bridge would be best of all.'

As he finished speaking, Richard swung the big old truck across the middle of the road and parked. The tailgate slammed down and Chester started unloading his charges with the help of the others from down the levee. Richard jumped down and Father Fellpe tensed to follow him. 'Not you, Father,' called Richard. 'I want you up here standing in front of the Ford and telling those people from Cortez to

299

stop right here. Tell them the bridge is down and this is the end of the road – at least until we get some pretty nifty shiphandling done. Now where has Robin gone?'

Had Robin not looked the way she did, Aldo would have left her to her fate without a second thought. But because she looked exactly like the Jody of his nightmares, he simply could not do so. After his experiences in the bilge, drug-enhanced though they may have been, there was a part of his mind which he felt was dangerously close to madness. And that part was where the figure of Jody dangled, always on the point of dying, never quite dead. His one hope of redemption, it seemed to Aldo, was to save her – as he would so much have liked to save the real Jody. Gingerly, he put his head and shoulders out through the sharp-edged hole. Between him and the hanging woman, just out of her reach but just within his, was a solid-looking section of companionway. He pulled himself back in, then, like a circus performer stepping through a hoop of fire, he arched his body into an exaggerated hook, turned sideways, and stepped out.

Once Aldo had put his weight on the outside step and found it would hold him, the rescue proceeded a little more quickly – and that was lucky, for only the promise of his arm round her waist gave Robin the strength to hang on, especially as the fire fight between the pantechnicon and the starboard bridge wing continued unabated, sending the occasional bullet like an angry wasp too close for comfort. Although any attempt at glancing over her shoulder would have been fatal, Robin was also aware that there was a nasty little re-enactment of the Battle of the Somme going on across the levee behind and below her.

No sooner was Aldo out on the step than he too became aware of just how exposed this position was. With a good deal of alacrity he reached across and slid his arm round Robin's trim waist. 'Have you got me?' she demanded.

'Got you,' he said, in the strangest voice.

'Are you braced?'

'Braced?'

'Yes, Aldo. Are you braced and steady? I don't want us both to fall off here the instant I let go of the rail.'

Aldo spread his feet to the outer edges of the little platform and swung his other arm round her, hugging her scorched tummy into his face and lifting as she opened her hands, as though he was unhooking her. His face scraped up until her breasts slid past his unshaven cheeks, then her toes touched the solid metal between his and she

300

slowly steadied. Like dancers in some underwater ballet, they turned, chests crushed together, until they were sideways on to the hole. It was obvious they weren't going to be able to get through it together. From this side, with all the serrated sabres of the blast-twisted steel pointing out at them, they would be lucky to get in at all. Robin sucked in a great breath, trying to steady herself, trying to get the stiffness out of her back and shoulders without knocking her strange rescuer off the little platform. 'You go first,' she said. 'It'll take me a while before I can bend my back at all.'

But suddenly Aldo's hands were on her body again. All the air she had sucked into her lungs escaped in a gasp – a sort of silent scream. The tail end of it formed five words 'Aldo! What are you doing?'

Aldo swung her up over his shoulder like a mannequin and fed her stiff body in through the centre of the hole in the wall as though she was an ill-wrapped, scorched and sooty letter, and he was posting her. No sooner did her feet touch the weirdly angled deck inside the hole than her body went from one extreme to the other – from rigid stiffness to abject flaccidness. She sat down hard and slumped forward, the coldness of the floor against her bottom warning her how much clothing the blast had torn away. Her knees were shaking. She felt sick and she wanted to visit the bathroom. In short, she needed to be away from here for a range of pressing reasons. And yet she could not move. And she could not leave Aldo either.

Robin looked out through the hole, just in time to see Aldo framed in utter black against the flash of an exploding missile. At once the ship jerked into motion, the bridgehouse rocking metronomically from side to side. All weakness cast away, Robin threw her head and shoulders out through the vicious hole, reaching for her rescuer. Her fingers actually brushed against him as he faltered there, fighting to keep his balance. But the stern of the destroyer reared up against the shoulder of the standing wave and the shore fell away, turning what had been a precarious foothold into a vertiginous toehold. Wind battered in from the east and rain flurried with unexpected force. From far away, came a strange blaring sound as though someone was speeding nearer with their hand hard on a car horn. Robin caught again and her fingers clutched Aldo's trousers, which felt oddly bulky over the pyjamas. Clutched, and slipped off the damp coarse broadcloth of the old uniform.

'Hold on,' she yelled; but there was nothing for him to hold on to except the razor edges of the blast-hole and the mocking swing of the handrail he had just rescued her from. Three bursts of machine-gun fire ripped the night like an old black sheet as he danced and wavered, then there came a *WHUMPH* of something powerful exploding into flame, followed immediately by a thunderous grating roar. The whole of *Colorado*'s long hull went wild and Robin threw herself back, visions of her breasts getting tangled in that forest of razor-pronged steel mixing sickeningly with the memory of a madly bucking, biting, runaway horse from her youth.

When she was able to drag herself back to the hole in the bridgehouse wall, Aldo was gone, as she had known he would be. So there was nothing for her to do but pick herself up, dust herself down and go and find Jesus Vega to see if a senior deck officer in her questionable state of repair had anything to offer that he might need.

When Richard came over on the captain's two-way, fizzing with energy, with news of a slight flesh wound to the heroic Mickey and a range of messages and orders, neither of the men on the connection had any idea how close they had come to losing someone precious. Richard watched as Chester bound a head wound which had come close to exposing Mickey's brain while Conception cradled the impatient young soldier. Jesus stood watching Robin slipping her battered, still-scorched body into one of his old uniforms, vaguely wishing he had Conception here with him as a kind of chaperone. Within minutes, blissfully unaware just how close he had come to the sad estate of widower, Richard was in detailed technical conference with Robin.

Ten minutes after that, Robin, with El Jefe at her side, and his best team behind them, was down on the foredeck, tightening the chain to the port anchor so that *Colorado*'s long hull would swing under the broken archway, to supply the missing span of the bridge. On the poop, Hernan and Banderas were with their teams, slinging lines up at the eastern arch, trying to secure the stern so that the length of the ship would make a roadway east, and the fleeing multitudes could still cross to the safety of Sonora. If there had been any way of moving the bridgehouse and the deckhouse behind it out of the way, they could have driven across.

The moment *Colorado*'s forecastle head ground in under the hanging edge of the broken bridge, Richard jumped down and ran across to embrace his wife. 'Not too hard,' she warned as he hugged her. 'I'm stiff and sore all over.'

'It's your age, dear,' he informed her. 'Have a nice Radox bath later on and you'll be right as rain.'

If only you knew, she thought, grimly humorous. But now was not the time to distract him with details. He was gone again anyway, up to the prow, where Conception and her parents were helping Chester to shepherd the hurt and wounded down onto the deck. Of Mickey there was no sign.

'Where's Mickey?' asked Richard as he lent a hand.

'Gone up to help Father Felipe,' came Isabella Lopez's answer. 'Ignacio here'll be off up there as well when we've settled the villagers. There's a lot of work to be done organising the refugees. But at least there won't be any more for us to worry about after the ones that are up there now. They say the bridge over the new river's been swept away.'

Colorado was under the span now, as though wedged tight between the bottom of the masonry and the top of the water. This position gave her a perfect view of the standing wave which looked literally like a muddy hill half as high as the bridgehouse, less than thirty metres south of them now. All conversation had to be carried on at full bellow, for, although the wind and the rain had eased, the top right section of the amazing water display beside them was falling over the side of the ruined levee like a slightly smaller version of the Niagara Falls, into the brimming valley of the ancient watercourse.

When Richard had seen the first refugees to the least damaged section of the bridgehouse and Chester had led them through to the medical facility whose contents were a good deal less damaged than its door, he grabbed Robin and they were off up to the stern to see what sort of a job Hernan was making of anchoring the poop. Just like the bow, it was wedged firmly under the jut of masonry, no more than an easy scramble below the road to Sonora. And, as if to prove the point, as they arrived young Benderas hopped easily down with Ramon and Ricardo behind him. 'That's both lines secure to the balustrade above the next footing,' the young officer reported, failing to notice Ramon's curt, approving nod of confirmation. 'The cables aren't quite as strong as the anchor chain at the bow, but they'll hold her here until we cut them.'

'Well done,' said Hernan.

'Right,' said Richard approvingly. 'Let's see who wants to go east, and shoot them on through before our neat little miracle here starts coming apart at the seams.'

'What do you mean exactly?' asked Robin as they hurried back along the one hundred metres of open deck.

'We are only going to stay here while the standing wave stays there,' said Richard. 'The minute it begins to disintegrate, we'll have to cut and run. That was why I wanted to check Hernan's rope work back there. When that happens, we're going to have to run back down to Cortez. It's our only hope. We'll have to slip the anchor chain, let her swing into the current and cut Hernan's ropes before we pull the bridge over. It's the only way out of this I can see.'

As the crew and the engineers helped Mickey and Father Felipe guide the weary stream of refugees across the deck from one side of the bridge to the other, the Mariners pounded up onto the bridge to pass Richard's thoughts and plans on to the captain.

'I agree,' said Jesus, who seemed to have gained in stature, power and decisiveness during their absence. Richard opened his mouth to add his next thought when Conception came out of the gutted wreck of the radio room.

'That's all useless,' she said grimly. 'God, I wish we could alert the authorities.'

'Good thinking,' said Richard, reaching for his little personal phone. 'Will this help?'

'Of course!' said Jesus, taking it and flipping it open. 'They'll all be in their offices in Ensenada on a night like tonight!' He started punching in the number from memory, glancing up as he did so with a wolfish grin. 'When I tell them what we've found in the cutwater bilge, I bet they could even get the committee together to decide what to do with us.'

The two-way buzzed just as connection was made and Conception picked it up. Jesus walked over to the less badly damaged starboard, suddenly speaking an impenetrable jumble of extensions, identity numbers and naval jargon. Conception handed the two-way to Richard. 'It's Mickey,' she said.

'Mickey?'

'I got good news and I got bad.'

'Let's have it.'

'We've got most of these folks sorted out now. No one seems too badly hurt. These are the fit and the quick-moving, first in the rush.'

'Stands to reason.'

'Good number want to stay with their vehicles so we've sent them on up the road as far as we can. The rest will be down with you in ten minutes.'

'Big numbers?'

'Not too many. Couple of hundred.'

'Then we're fine. Couple of hundred people over a hundred metres. Even taking it slow and careful, they'll be on the Sonora side in half an hour. What's the rest of it?'

'You may not have half an hour. The force of the overflow into the valley is so powerful that this entire sector of the levee is at risk. It looks to me as though the whole section and maybe the western footing of the road bridge will all get washed away within the next fifteen, twenty minutes.'

'Washed away,' said Richard numbly.

'That's right. And Richard, I haven't got to the bad news yet.'

'Well, let's not hang around here.'

'The whole damaged section of the levee has now lost the top four metres. And you know what that will mean?'

'Oh yes,' said Richard, numbly. 'I know what that will mean.'

Jesus burst back onto the main bridge then. 'That's it,' he exulted. 'The choppers will be here in half an hour.' Then he saw Richard's face and stopped. 'What?' he said.

'Now hear this,' said the chimes urgently, above the roar of the flooding river and the standing wave, above the shuffling mutter of a couple of hundred people being escorted down onto the deck. After the chimes, Jesus Vega's voice was cool, clear and so utterly calm that Ramon's beard bristled, standing up like the hair on his head, and the whites showed all the way round his staring eyes.

'We have ten minutes to show our guests to a safe, secure berth and batten down as tight as possible,' said the captain. 'We must secure every hatch we can. Close every door. Put away safely anything heavy, sharp or breakable. Major Varg— Major Vega's men will assist the *Colorado*'s crew. We must prepare for extreme conditions. Engineers stand with El Jefe in your teams as he disposes you and prepare to slip or cut the lines on my command. Senior officers and team leaders know what they have to do. Major Vega and Chief Petty Officer Ramon report to the bridge at your earliest convenience, please. The rest of you, do your duty. We have nine minutes.'

Jesus and Richard both got it wrong, which was fortunate. It took ten minutes to clear the deck and a further three to get everything, and everyone, safely stowed below. At the end of fifteen minutes, nothing had happened. The ship stood rigged and ready for her worst experience in the sixty years since her commissioning and the whole night seemed to freeze into stasis around her, as though she was trapped at the edge of a black hole, where time itself had stopped.

Ramon stood at the emergency helm four decks beneath the wreck on the command bridge; Richard and Jesus stood looking out through

305

the shattered clearview. Miguel Vega stood beside his father and it was as though Mickey Vargas had never existed. Conception stood a little behind them, looking over their shoulders at the still, expectant night.

Robin stood by Richard and, for the first time she could recall on a command bridge, his right arm was holding her instead of being clutched behind his back. Suddenly aware of the terrible frailty they all shared, and the danger they all stood in, she snuggled into his side and the grip of his arm became firmer.

Jesus's two-way chirruped and he slammed it to his mouth with such force that he split his lip.

It was El Jefe by the anchor chain on the forepeak. 'Can you hear it?' he demanded. 'Bugger me if it doesn't sound like an express train coming down from Mexicali. Jesus, Mary and Joseph!' Connection was cut.

Jesus lowered the radio and licked the blood from his lip. All of them were straining to hear the sound of the express train over the roaring of the wild water all around them. They never did. Instead there came a crackling as though the bridge had been struck by dark lightning. The whole ship lurched forward and the long hull wavered, screaming. Literally screaming, she hung between Hernan's line secured behind and the anchor chain falling away before, with every iron plate in her hull straining against the heads and shaft of every rivet in her.

'Now!' bellowed Jesus Vega, feeling her begin to come apart beneath him. '*Jefe!* Now!'

The whole ship reared back as El Jefe slipped the anchor chain. The five on the bridge staggered back, then rushed forwards, Richard and Robin running right up to the broken clearview with Mickey beside them, while Jesus stood his ground, calculating with icy precision, and Conception stood like a statue at his side.

What Richard and the others saw was this. The whole western footing of the bridge was rearing up and falling away and the road which sat on its back was unpeeling and rising like a six-lane rattlesnake getting ready to strike at them. The levee beside the bridge's foundation was sliding relentlessly westward too, what had been solid river wall becoming river itself, as though the levee had never existed. There was a jumble of rubble ahead of them for an instant and then there was nothing but white water. 'This is how it all started!' yelled Mickey to Robin, wild with exultation. All she could do was look down the slope of wild water into the seething abyss below and nod. She hugged Richard's strong

306

right arm round her as though it was a thick scarf on a cold day.

Richard's eyes were as wide as Robin's but his attention was on the soles of his feet. *Colorado* was stirring with a kind of life she had never known she possessed. The suction of the water seemed to stretch her as the pull of the chain had done before El Jefe slipped the anchor. She throbbed, like a greyhound against a leash, like a Derby winner at the off. She must go now, or die.

Jesus felt it too and, like Richard, he knew it was time. It was do or die for all of them. 'Hernan,' he shouted into his two-way. 'Cut the lines.'

They felt her change at once. She did not hesitate. She did not wait for the current to take her – she was right at its heart already. Instead she leaped forward like the thoroughbred she was. Her draft was three and a half metres, she cleared the ruined levee with half a metre to spare, more like a Grand National runner than a Derby winner now. Over the top of the beheaded levee she leaped with a wild kind of joyousness, seeming to rise and to fall, like the water she had become a part of; seeming to flow. Such was the liquid rhythm of her movement that those on the bridge were hardly thrown around at all. They stood, swaying slightly and staggering a little once in a while as the incredible panorama threw itself at them through the shattered clearview, the noise of it alone enough to stun them, the sound enough to scrub their minds as clean as the white foam they were part of. Like a twig in a millrace, *Colorado* swooped down the outer flank of the western levee, straight into the centre of the new-born river.

The right bank threw her inwards, tried to flip her over on her port side, but that was where the standing wave sent its crest down like a big surf and the white wall righted her again, though it ripped off the bridge wing as tribute. She bottomed then, smashing the foot of her cutwater hard against the bed of the new river; hard enough to find a flaw in her construction like the one which had killed Peter Phelps. Stunned, she reeled and the bridge party staggered for the first time as though as groggy as she. But the wings of the broken road bridge beneath the shell of the mayor's car steadied her, reaching in to scrape along her flanks, literally holding her upright until she found her way again. As she scraped through the shattered masonry, settling onto an even keel again, the bilge behind the cutwater began to fill, its forward seals all broken, the long sharp edge of her bow smashed open by the impact.

Water swirled into her, washing Cuzco and the creatures that had

307

fed on him out into the river where larger creatures waited to finish off what was left of him. And, little by little, the piles of drugs were torn open and washed out as well. The power of the water was enough to rip even the strongest plastic wrapping like tissue, and the wild swirl of the current gulped down the white crystals like hot tea taking sugar. The foaming tide flooded back through her, filling bilge after bilge along her bottom.

But that, too, steadied her, as her draft began to deepen to four metres, then towards five. The river rushed her along the valley, sitting so high that Robin was able to see the roadway to Los Muertos running along beside them under a sudden moon. She realised, then, and saw from her sudden stirring that Conception realised too, that that was where they were bound for. That was where this wild ride would end. In Los Muertos, or nearby.

Jesus seemed to realise it as well, for he suddenly began to give a series of orders over the radio to Ramon at the helm below. They had no real steerage way against the river for it was bearing them along at its heart. But even a fish may flick its tail, and that was all *Colorado* had to do.

Jesus brought her to shore beneath Los Muertos, but the rain had made the bank there slick and slippery. She glanced off and ran on, past the black-banked hole where Chester had set fire to the tequila after Joe Aloha died, and round, beneath a lazily westering moon, to a reach of riverine beach on the inner slope of a lazy meander. She came to rest there almost gently, running aground in five metres of water, and catching on the mud of the river bank and staying. The water rushed on past, down to the Laguna Salada but *Colorado* had had enough. She was at rest. She was at peace.

The first helicopter found her there almost at once, running low along the river she had just sailed, the great beam of its searchlight seeking her with its almost accusing finger. But the instant the white beam found her, the chopper seemed to skim up and away, shining its puny searchlight at the moon. The noise of its clatter on the air stirred the entranced quintet in the wreck of the command bridge. Wordlessly, Jesus, Mickey and Conception folded themselves into a tight, silent hug, master, heir and new mistress of the great house on the hill. Richard and Robin embraced too, but she could see over his shoulder, up the flank of the river bank, white as the flank of a sleeping lion under the moon, to where the searchlight on the chopper briefly blazed across the magnificent dereliction of *La Casa Grande*.

'Welcome home, Captain Vega and family,' she said, and was

308

surprised to discover she was crying. When Richard felt her tears, he gently, lovingly, began to kiss them all away.

Spurred by Robin's words and Richard's action, Jesus Vega released his son and swept Conception into his full embrace, kissing her with decorous gentility as she crushed him to her. Distantly, from below, as though the others aboard saw and approved, a wave of cheering echoed against the hillside, louder even than the bellow of the new-born river.

And so it was that the only one of them who made it back along the Colorado's main channel to Cortez was Aldo Cagliari. Miraculously preserved from alligators, he swept, face down and spread like a white crucifix, into the marina two days later. Corpses were so common then that it was a good while before anyone in the stunned city got around to doing anything about him. The harbourmaster had resigned. The chief of police had vanished with the Mayan gold recovered from Highway 5, and the burned-out remains of the mayor's car were still up by the wrecked bridge over the new river. And he and his wife were still in it, though it was difficult to tell.

So Aldo swirled into the centre of the marina where there was still a sluggish whirlpool full of all sorts of rubbish from all the way up the river to Wyoming. But, as fate would have it, the piece of jetsam which slid across his long-dead shoulders was from Las Vegas, his adopted home. It was the front page of a newspaper. The title was gone. All that was left was the newsprint and some pictures, so that when it settled on the white uniform across his shoulders and down his back, it seemed as though it had been written on the dead man himself. 'ALIGHIERI EMPIRE COLLAPSES' said the banner headline. 'The Don Is Dead' added a sub-heading just below it. 'FBI agent Jennifer McCall, posing as call girl Jody Jones, spent five days held against her will by vice and drugs baron Vergil Alighieri,' said the story. 'She was discovered and released by colleagues after an anonymous tip-off. At the same time, Mr Alighieri himself has succumbed to a heart attack. "We were, you know, making love," said the new woman in his life, pop sensation Fu Q. So he died with a smile on his face.

'Agent McCall used her time as a prisoner in Alighieri's house and garage to collect details about the Alighieri empire and its personnel. "They roughed me up a little," she said, "but it was nothing I couldn't handle. I'll be back in the office on Monday, then heads will begin to roll. A lot of evil guys out there had better start watching their backs . . ."'

Acknowledgements

For once I have no long list of authorities and research texts. Even Kelvin Hughes could not help me by supplying pilots or charts for this project because the River Colorado has not been restored; it does not currently exist in the way I have described it – certainly not south of the Mexican border. The city of Cortez does not exist at all, except in my imagination.

Instead, I have only one real authority – Mexico itself. *High Water* is the result of one year's planning and one month's research and writing in Puerto Vallarta on the Pacific coast. It is this lively and beautiful resort which forms the basis of Cortez City – except of course for the strip clubs, drug dealing and Mafia sections which come entirely from my own imagination, as do the equivalent sections in Las Vegas and Yuma, naturally.

But there are people I have to thank. First of all, I have to thank my brother Simon Tonkin and his partner Clive Marks for putting my family and myself up in their beautiful guest house Bugambilia Blanca in Vallarta, for giving me the freedom of the Internet on their computer for the bits of research I still needed to complete, and for introducing us to anyone in Vallarta they thought could be any help at all in completing the book. Next, I must thank Tom Barrington of the Computer Store, Vallarta, for his advice, help and support after my Brother Desktop Publisher, for once, let me down. Suzanne Hebert, manager of the lovely Boana Torre Malibu, also helped – it is upon a small section of her huge map of Mexico that my own is based. Bill Hindman gave freely of his time, expertise and of his Guides to Mexico. Finally, a great vote of thanks must go to all the people we met in Puerto Vallarta, every single one of whom was keen to help in any way they could.

In England it was the geographers of the Wildernesse School and the Bradbourne School who helped and advised. The climactic sections of the flood rising up on the back of the tide arose from many a lengthy talk with Paul Clark and Catherine St Ville, to both of whom, as always, much thanks. Warm thanks also to Tracy Wicks who found on the Internet and printed for me a range of priceless information on the Colorado.

In the end, as ever, I was only able to get the work done because Cham (and, in Mexico, my mother also) kept Guy and Mark cheerfully busy for the greater part of each of my 'writing' days. I simply could not work in the way I do without her, and the books are all hers as much as mine, dedicated to her and to my boys with all my love.

Peter Tonkin, Sevenoaks and Puerto Vallarta, summer 1999.